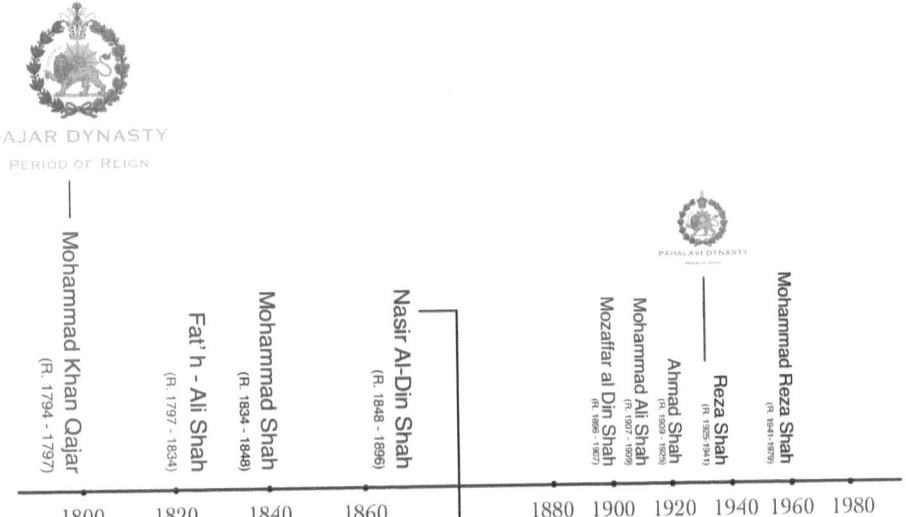

Mohammad Khan Qajar
(R. 1794 - 1797)

Fat'h - Ali Shah
(R. 1797 - 1834)

Mohammad Shah
(R. 1834 - 1848)

Nasir Al-Din Shah
(R. 1848 - 1896)

PAHALAVI DYNASTY

Mozaffar al Din Din Shah
(R. 1896 - 1907)

Mohammad Ali Shah
(R. 1907 - 1909)

Ahmad Shah
(R. 1909 - 1925)

Reza Shah
(R. 1925-1941)

Mohammad Reza Shah
(R. 1941-1979)

1800   1820   1840   1860   1880 1900 1920 1940 1960 1980

POONAKI GENEALOGY

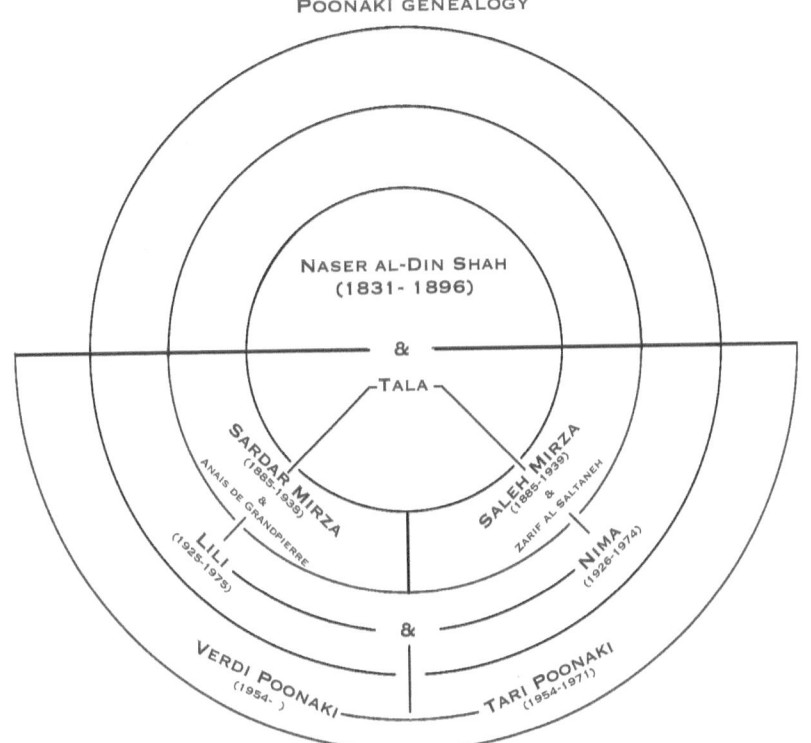

NASER AL-DIN SHAH
(1831- 1896)

&

TALA

SARDAR MIRZA
(1865-1939)
&
ANAIS DE GRANDPIERRE

SALEH MIRZA
(1865-1939)
&
ZARIF AL SALTANEH

LILI
(1925-1975)

NIMA
(1926-1974)

&

VERDI POONAKI
(1954-)

TARI POONAKI
(1954-1971)

1001
A DREAM OF NINE NIGHTS

ISBN (paperback): 978-1-963271-95-9
ISBN (ebook): 978-1-963271-96-6

Armin Lear Press, Inc.
215 W Riverside Drive, #4362
Estes Park, CO 80517

1001

A DREAM OF NINE NIGHTS

Yahya Gharagozlou

ARMINLEAR

CONTENTS

THE FIRST NIGHT: 0001

THE WRITER'S RESPONSIBILITY

"Gently to hear, kindly to judge, our play"

Henry V—Shakespeare

Titling a book *1001* comes with responsibilities. I don't defend the improbability of the number. An ancient tome tucked away lingers in our minds, an echo of childhood—*One Thousand and One Nights*, that ancient collection of tales. Yet, how many do we honestly remember? *Aladdin, Ali Baba and the Forty Thieves, The Seven Voyages of Sinbad the Sailor*—these endure. But for *The Tale of Fisherman and the Jiini* and *The Lovers of Bassorah*, you'd have needed a well-connected storyteller, perhaps a dayeh, a wet nurse, who carried the whispers of old voices. I had one.

Did you know *One Thousand and One Nights* happened over nine hundred and eighty-one nights? Scheherazade took twenty nights off to give birth to the King's twins. The math betrays the myth. Yet calling it *A Thousand and One Nights* rather than rounding it off to a thousand was a stroke of genius, a marketing triumph. We allow for poetic license. There will be times in this accurate historical monograph when I plead for poetic license; this is not merely a recounting of history but a journey through layers of storytelling.

The *1001* structure mirrors modern oral history, a genre revived in the twentieth century—multiple voices recounting, say, World War II. Truth, after all, is a mosaic. My early readers fed back to me and warned me that numerous narrators confuse naive readers. "Not us, of course, but the non-reader reader." I will eat the feed. I will check back with you after each night.

But you are not confused, are you?

I, the writer—a name on a cover, a whisper of ink—will be your guide. Step with me into this world where history and imagination intertwine, where stories peel back the thin skin of reality. Together let us build.

A kingdom for a stage, princes to act
And monarchs to behold the swelling scene!

Henry V – William Shakespeare

THE STORY OF THE STORYTELLER

"Lord of heaven and earth, thank you for hiding these things from those who think themselves wise and clever and for revealing them to the childlike."

Psalms 8:2

"Bismillah-e-Rahman-e-Rahim, in the name of God the merciful and the compassionate. If He deems me worthy of one more breath, then I, your true servant, Abol-Hassan Hekaiatchi, will recount for you, honored ladies and gentlemen, the trials and tribulations of Rostam and Esfandiar. Yes, you know the story; you have read it. But forgive my impertinence for you do not truly know the mighty Rostam's adventures until you have heard them from my own lips. "A telling story is in the telling of the story."

That was how my Baba began every tale, each one neatly pigeonholed in his mind. A whisper from him would catch the untrained ear, a wink of his wrinkled eye shared a secret; a raise of his bushy brow invited curiosity. Then—bang!—his silver-laden stick struck the ground, dragging his listeners from their opium-clouded dreams. A puff of his cheeks, and they felt the fear of the Almighty Himself. Deep and commanding, his voice wrapped around the room, leaving his audience murmuring, trembling, unsure of where the story ended and the truth began. My Baba was a master storyteller.

But that was then. Now, my Baba has returned. I cannot vouch for ghosts, nor for the nature of dreams. But ever since he chose to haunt my nights, whispering in my left ear, I wake each morning with a strange grainy residue; no amount of washing is enough to rid me of it. His presence clings to me like a shadow at midday prayer, distorting the warm, loving memories I once had of him.

In my dreams, his voice buzzes like a fly trapped in a fist, ceaseless in its admonishments—scolding me, my mother, his second wife, and the entire living world. He blames me for his massive coronary, which killed him in twenty minutes flat fifteen years ago. He blames me for his ghostly half-life in my subconscious, as if my choices in the past five or six years have tethered him to me. Carrying this restless spirit has made my waking life a misery.

These days, even the dead are misinformed. What does my father know of our times? He sees only my nightmares, and God knows they pale in comparison to my waking hours. He remembers only Friday prayers, the scent of kebabs sizzling in butter-drenched pilaf, the gurgle of waterpipes in the tearoom, the clinking glasses of vinaceous tea. He knows nothing of the collapse of respect.

Do you hear me, my darling Baba? We live in different times. And yet, you persist. I, alive and ruined; you, awake from eternal sleep, living vicariously through my dreams, hammering into me the same warnings you drilled into my head when you were flesh and blood. The storyteller who dies with an untold tale destroys a universe. He commits genocide, He must answer for it on the Day of Judgement.

Fine. I will repay my debt. I will tell my story. But not as you taught me. A story you, my darling Baba, have half followed in my dreams (mixed with celery, yogurt and skin softness). Nine nights of storytelling are riveting enough to overwhelm a man's dreams.

I know our origins with the Almighty and His special favor for us yarn spinners. When the All-Knowing breathed life into yarn-spinner's clay, he gave us the freedom of imagination and made us responsible for our creations. Still, the compassionate, in his infinite mercy, took pity on our plight and commanded Gabriel, the angel of death, thus:

"I have cursed man, the storyteller, with excessive imagination. In his final moment, *you* shall bear witness to the untold stories of his mind. I shall claim these as my own. But for those he takes with him to the grave, he shall answer."

Tariq-e-Saber, the fifteenth-century soothsayer, known as Black-Eyes, describes the fate of the talented storyteller Rumi (not to be confused with the eighth-century mystic poet): For seven consecutive years, with Gabriel at his deathbed, Rumi recounted tale after tale as he emptied his crammed imagination. In all that time, Gabriel, trapped and transfixed, couldn't recover a single life on Earth. The world suffered terribly: Old women with tumors the size of ripe figs writhed in pain, unable to die. On the fields, war-mutilated bodies twitched in search of their missing limbs. At the bottom of the ocean, drowned sailors, bloated like the throats of bullfrogs, gaped hopelessly for nonexistent air. Organic matter refused to decompose. Food became scarce. Firewood couldn't be used despite the cold winters, for the cut trees remained green as cucumbers.

Before emptying his store of stories, Rumi, at heart a compassionate man, pitied the undying world. Unfinished, he uttered a premature final "Amen." As punishment, the Almighty transformed him into a parakeet to wander the world, uttering nonsense until the end of time. From that day, the parakeet became the symbol of all storytellers—not a symbol of repetition, as many assume, but a sign of warning and responsibility.

I was trained from the age of three to be the greatest storyteller this benighted country has ever known. And yet, here I sit, scratching graphite on pulp in a tiny, stinking room above Mammad-Ali's grocery store. It is an improvement over my last quarters. Baba, do you remember Mammad-Ali, the cross-eyed grocer from two blocks down? We boys used to torment him, pointing at shelves to watch him scramble. Well, he has shown me the kindness of a mother—not a father—since I walked out of prison. Oh, yes, Baba. Prison.

Mammad-Ali has become something of a benefactor. I live surrounded by the scents of saffron, fenugreek, sumac, turmeric, cumin and dill weed. Morning to night, I hear the sharp voices of neighborhood wives barking orders at him. From my grease-covered window, I can see our old tearoom. Every morning, I have strong tea, with *lavash* and feta. Zahra, cross-eyed like her father, brings me rice and khoresht for lunch. At night, they send up leftovers. He gives me a roof over my head, and I thank him daily for his kindness. He, in turn, sends thanks to you for past favors.

But hear me, Baba: should you stumble upon a dream littered with written words, forgive my cowardice. The written word is memory, a catacomb; its treasures demand the trembling voice, the twist of a tongue. I hear your buzzing soul: "Where are the grimaces of the written word? Where is the cadence of a well-chanted poem? The war cry's rise and fall?"

Until the wind shifts, and our tongues are unshackled, this must suffice, Writing, for now, is my down payment. The Caspian tiger is all but extinct, and so too are men who can wager their tongues. I know I have failed you, Baba. If I am not careful, I may yet find myself transformed into a gibbering parakeet.

Let me set down how I came to possess this tale and the promises I made to a madman.

Thirteen years have passed since the glorious Islamic Revolution. The war brought misery to us all. Only a few months ago, I sat in our old tearoom—your tearoom passed on to me when you passed on—and cursed my fate. Ignorant of the limitless fall of a man, I cursed my luck. Forty generations of storytellers precede me; I could count five of them as I sat in the decrepit tearoom. Yet I, Salman Hekaiatchi, a direct descendant of the mighty Ferdowsi, son of Hassan, grandson of Karim, the incomparable storyteller of the court of Qajar, was reduced to serving tea in my establishment. I, who spent his childhood dandled on the knees of the aristocracy, took orders from Hamid—the self-righteous, gutter-born city pirate who calls himself my business partner. He calls my tearoom a "sanctuary," a place where "an honest man can obtain, without daily harassment, his narcotic."

My tearoom, once a jewel of the Grand Bazar, now stinks of urine. Built by the great Karim, the Golden Tearoom was famous for its mosque-like gold cupola, A throne among the city's gathering places, princes, cabinet members and wealthy merchants once held court here. Now it belongs to dealers, murderers, Afghanis, Palestinians, addicts—every form of lowlife imaginable. From where I sit, I can see the dome, stripped of its gold.

As a child, I ran through the rotunda, weaving between benches covered in Kerman carpets where the most respected men listened to my father's declamations. Servers moved like dancers, swirling charcoal in perilously wide arcs to make it glow before setting each ember with precision atop the well-packed, precisely moist tobacco in the waterpipes. At the center of the room, an octagonal stone piscina, tiled in lapis lazuli, spilled clear water from a lazy fountain into a cobalt-blue majolica gutter. My father used the fountain as a prop in his performances—now an endless sea, now a crushing waterfall—as he paced, retracing his steps for theatrical effect.

Today, the piscina is a chipped pool of stagnant, brackish water covering grimy, cracked tiles. Hamid and his jackals use it for their ritual ablutions before kneeling in prayer, murmuring their Nyyat in the tearoom corridors. They finish, then turn over their left shoulders—not for the recording angel, but to check how many customers are waiting for their fix.

I want to dream of Hamid's ruin. I want to dream for you, Baba, to show you what your generosity has wrought: Hamid, the boy you bought from a peasant family to work for you, now a rabid dog, shredding the hand that fed him. But instead, I dream of indulgences—meat-filled *piroshki*, fat figs split open in indecent ruptures, cream puffs so light they could levitate—and, women. They pass through my dreams, clothed, half-clothed, naked, all untouched. Yet the moment my arousal stirs, you appear in a rage, dragging me back into waking grief for bygone days.

If I could control my dreams for your benefit, I'd show you how Hamid has claimed to be your son. He denounced his father as a cuckold and his mother as a whore. Tell me it's not true, my darling Baba. Tell me he is not your bastard. But he has claimed half my inheritance, half of my tearoom. And who's to deny the claim of a revolutionary guard?

The day after I received the revolutionary court order, Hamid and his cronies moved in. At first, I welcomed the crowd. Business had been fading. He played at friendship, feigned conciliation.

He asked me to tell a story. But my kings and princes had to be replaced with revolutionary heroes. He took Keyumars, the first Shah of the world, and gave him the Imam's name. Zāl, the legendary albino warrior, became some white-haired Ayatollah.

"Now, my friends," Hamid said, sweeping the room with his hand, the other resting heavy on my shoulder. "We are in for a treat. A story from our portly storyteller, my brother, my partner. Come forth, Salman. Don't be shy. Let me show you off."

I set my tray down, the silver tea service clinking. I stepped toward Hamid, my eyes on the floor.

"Our storyteller," Hamid announced, "tells stories as well as he eats, and you can see he is magnificent at eating." He pinched my belly where it sagged over my sash. Laugher rang out.

"Portly, my ass," someone jeered. "The man is as wide as he is tall."

Another chimed in, "I hope his words flow as well as his food flowed in."

The room filled with laughter, thick as the tobacco smoke. From outside came the high-pitched whine of a key-making grindstone.

"Friends, shame on you for mocking our storyteller," Hamid said. He paused for effect and then added, "That job is entirely mine."

The guests roared. He squeezed the back of my neck, making my skin bulge between his fingers

"And, you, Aboli, a man of wealth and influence, have you no regard for our friend's feelings?" He wagged a finger. "This man's words will transport us to distant lands."

Like sewage, the scum of the world found my tearoom the perfect place to fester. Dealers trafficked openly, their wares spread across tables, underbidding each other in loud voices. Opium had once been the quiet indulgence of bazaar men sequestered in private rooms. Now Afghan gun traders sold Kalashnikovs for a few grams of hashish.

The taunts escalated to small acts of violence. They ordered me around like a servant. I decided to appeal to my partner and brother.

I stepped into my former office, three steps up in the corner of the main hall. I spoke carefully, reminding him of the tearoom's history, the men who once sat here. I pointed out the illegal trade happening before his eyes. He nodded gravely, rubbing his chin as though considering my words.

"This is shocking," he said. "You mean to tell me my good friend Ismail deals opium?"

I nodded eagerly.

"And Ahmad, right in front of me, sold three UZIs to those Palestinians the other day—"

"Impossible!" Hamid gasped. "I have been blind! We must stop this immediately. You and I, as partners, will clean this place out. What say you?"

"Like the partners we are," I whispered. I would have followed him to the Euphrates itself.

Hamid opened the door and gestured for me to lead. I stepped out, adjusting my sash. Before I could take the first step, his army boot connected with my backside and delivered a kick like none I had ever felt.

I flew down the three steps, crashed into two benches and landed face-first in the green, filthy water of the fountain, chipping two teeth on its spout.

The laughter was deafening, an ovation worthy of my father. Hamid still in the office, shut the door on his own amusement. I sat in the puddle, dazed, feeling my lips and tongue. The door opened again. Hamid's voice called out, light and natural, as if nothing had happened.

"Salman, bring the tea."

The clientele took the cue, barking for their orders. In that moment, everything became clear—to them and me. I was no longer a partner. No longer a storyteller.

I was a servant.

And Baba, you ask why did I not stand up to him? Why did I not complain?

I remind you again that we live in different times.

THE NARRATOR TELLS
THE STORY OF THE STORY

"Vengeance is mine, I will repay," says the Lord

Romans 12:19

Dear Ms. Vakil,

I don't consider myself a vengeful person. Even if I were, I lack the means—or perhaps the will—to exact punishment. And I certainly do not subscribe to the notion that "the pen is mightier than the sword." To me, the pen is merely a tool—an excellent one, yes, but one best suited for tallying the credits and debits in the ledger of life. As for justice, I leave that to the Lord.

It has been many years since you approached me, acting as volunteer editor of the newly conceived *Encyclopedia Persiranica*. If I recall correctly, it was at the Qajar Conference at the Copley

Place Marriott in Boston. You asked me to contribute an entry on my family, the Poonakis.

I still recall how delicately you tried to hurry me along by pointing out that the letter P comes not sixteenth, as in the English alphabet, but third, as in Farsi. I remember your left heel tilting back, your right hand absently chasing your Hermès scarf—an understated nod to the Islamists—as it slipped against your blue-black hair. I swear I heard the static crackle. You looked so young. I asked you if you attended a local school. Today, you would have taken it as a compliment; then you told me impatiently you had finished your dissertation in Edinburgh. My refusal to participate earned me a quick bite of your lower lip and a polite thank you. Judging by the silence that followed, I daresay we are well past P.

And yet a few months ago, I saw you again—entering the Charles Hotel in Cambridge. You looked different. Womanly. More harried, yet still charged with energy. You pushed the revolving door as though you were escaping captivity. You looked creamily rich. We, the moneyless old money, notice such things— distinctions marked by the smallest accouterments. Your vintage *Sac à dépêches* Hermès was a dead giveaway. I can't say I recognize your name as one of us.

Us is a strange pronoun. It suggests inclusion, yet we wield it like a fence, enclosing ourselves within an elite company. Please don't take offense. I am not in a position to be snooty and haven't been for some time some time. As a historian, you are familiar with the Thousand Family nomenclature. I count à *peine* forty families left—all interwoven, all cozy. An endangered species, no doubt. But are we worth saving? I haven't seen any protesters in Orange County holding posters in our defense. The ASPCA should take an interest, for there has been plenty of cruelty in our benighted country—but it has not been exclusive to us. In time, neglect will do what persecution once did. Soon, there will be little reason to hunt our not-so-shiny pelts.

Years have passed since your request. Decades have passed since our revolution. Writing something about my family has not been far from my mind. The regime has worsened in its brutality and corruption. You can appreciate my apprehension about setting down details of a family that believes in the separation of mosque and state. I needn't remind you of the fate of the Indian writer whose unwitting book ignited the wrath of an entire world—condemned by one old man whose legacy includes a regime adept at obfuscation. *Fluctus in simpulo*—a tempest in a ladle, as Cicero put it. I enjoy my modest cup of tea. I would rather not see it upset by ignoramuses.

Nevertheless, I will write the history of this family. I have taken certain precautions—casting our story as entertainment, a who-done-it, or, more precisely, a who-wrote-it.

Foreign names can be daunting. Think of the first fifty pages of *War and Peace*. So, I'll take a modern approach—rolling the cinematic credits immediately instead of relying on theatrical bows when all is said and done. I admit I prefer film over theater.

How to describe the Poonaki family tree? Diagrammatically, it resembles an hourglass. Identical twin princes form its pillars. One marries an aristocratic French beauty and has a daughter. The other weds the king's granddaughter and has a son. The cousins, in turn, marry, producing a final pair of fraternal twin boys—sterile, ending the Poonakis in three generations. A genetic palindrome. An ancestorial echo falls into silence.

You can immediately place my grandfathers in the historical milieu you know so well. Their father, Nasser al-Din Shah—the fourth monarch of the Qajar dynasty—ruled contemporaneously with Victoria for fifty years. Like her, he left his name to an era: the age of Nasseri. He fathered the twins after a summer afternoon stroll through his Harem in 1885, at a few strokes past three o'clock, with the daughter of his bootmaker. The royal bootmaker came from Poonak, a village near the capital. Later, when last names became obligatory, as a gesture of humility during difficult political times, my monozygotic grandfathers registered Poonaki as our shared patronymic.

Saleh Mirza, known as the Prince, is the more famous of the twin brothers. He had three wives. His first, the king's granddaughter, produced a son: my father, Nima. His twin brother, Sardar Mirza, lived willingly in his shadow. I intend to restore his reputation—his role in the constitutional revolution of 1906 deserves its due. He married a French countess who after many years, bore my mother, Lili.

My parents, Nima and Lili, were thus twice cousins; they were born a year apart on different continents. They married after the Second World War and waited eight years before producing the second set of Qajar twins. They named us Tari and Verdi. Family intermarriage is common enough, but I admit our genes have redundancy to spare. They could fit snugly within a single chromosome without losing information. It could have been tighter—my brother and I are fraternal. But I am happy to report we were born with all digits intact and no superfluous appendages sprouting from our coccyx.

Historians have used this compact genealogy of the Poonakis as proof of the Qajar degeneracy. Ms. Vakil, please do away with facile theories linking family intermarriage to some manifest genetic failing. Social taboos notwithstanding, the congenital risk from incestuous procreation doubles if some congenital disability already exists.

Your colleague has made the case for a pathological oligospermia—poor motility, in our lineage. Knowing of my paternal grandfather's well-documented philandering coupled with our family's low birthrate, I am inclined to agree. When I dutifully submitted my sample to the leering male nurse—his tongue pressed against his cheek into a crude bulge—I discovered my count fell far short of the required 20 million sperm per milliliter of semen. I mention this humiliating diligence of mine to demonstrate sincerity in searching for truth beyond mere facts.

As boys, my brother and I saw Dumas's *The Corsican Brothers* at the Alborz Movie House. Have you seen it? Douglas Fairbanks Jr. plays the Franchi Siamese twins, separated at birth. When one suffers, the other feels it. With us, the pain of one meant the laughter of the other. Our bookend twin grandfathers could not have been more different from us: they loved one another deeply, even though they lived apart most of their lives.

I love H. B. Warner (playing Dr. Paoli, surrounded by the adoring Dupres and Lorenzo, the rogue servant) when he says, "I have separated their bodies," as the camera zooms in on his silvery goateed head. The background orchestra swells and then lowers its volume like an acoustic quotation mark, making room for the dramatic question: *But what of their souls?"* His distant gaze contemplates a dark future. You can imagine the effect on us, sitting in the dark movie house, watching one Fairbanks watching the other Fairbanks die. Despite the ridiculous Farsi dubbing, the scene held a key to us. I can't remember who sat with us.

I have read your article on my twin grandfathers in the *Encyclopedia Persiranica,* and I can't fault the facts. You are right. Who am I to argue? They were born on the third of August of 1885. One held several essential cabinet positions; the other wrote essays and articles on modern early twentieth-century painting. But what of their souls, Ms. Vakil? What of their souls? Can you imbue this essence in your alphabetically arranged encyclopedia?

Before the rolling credits dwindle to an eye-straining font, one last person deserves mention with the rest of my family. Professor Dal—Dal, the letter D in our alphabet—a surgeon and our step-uncle, lived in our home for most of our lives. The Prince adopted Professor Dal as a child. Older than my parents, he acted as their elder brother during difficult times. A brilliant surgeon, he earned his professorship from Universitätsmedizin Berlin. You can guess who I am referring to, but to protect the names of the guilty, I have taken the pivot of this particular universe and rotated it by a few degrees at its root. I call this country Persiran. My country parallels yours, but I live in it more comfortably than I could in yours. In my country, they speak the same Farsi language as you speak in your objective country. My country contains all the same cities. The same crude oil bubbles out of the same fields. The wrestlers wrestle with the same grace. As in your country, our wolves are smaller than those in northern Europe. Tempted as I might be to blot them out, Persiran tolerates even the same clergy. I can see one difference. My country has room for the Poonakis.

Still, I can confirm, Ms. Vakil, that I possess a valise full of correspondence between my princely grandfathers. I would guess a history professor these days would kill or maim any human being—indeed another colleague—for original manuscripts not seen or touched by greedy hands. I promise the documents will be ample payment for your patience and diligence, a tasty treat for a still-active history professor hoping for fame. They belong to the objective country you so lovingly try to document. The valise in my care contains information going back to the creation of our constitution. It is like discovering new letters from the signers of the U.S. Constitution—if not from a Washington or a Madison, then from a young Charles Pinckney. Ms. Vakil. I have researched your background thoroughly. Your small publishing house in Tehran has put out quality work. Your precarious position at the university attests to your integrity. The papers will be yours in due time.

I chose a childlike simpleton you know well to narrate as my avatar; the story preserves the age-old tradition of telling stories through an innocent—and, more practically, gives me legal protection in a country respectful of the letter of the law.

Please do not be angry with me. I remember you in my mind's eye as lovely, intelligent and resourceful. Use our story with caution. I request you deal with the history of the Poonakis with the same energy you showed the day you pushed your way through the revolving doors of the Charles Hotel.

THE STORYTELLER
FINDS THE STORY

"When my head is off, set it on this plate and have it press down firm upon the powder to stop the bleeding. After that open the book. The least of the secrets being this: when my head is off, you turn three pages of the book, then read three lines upon the left-hand page, my severed head will speak and answer any manner of question."

One Thousand and One Nights

A few months after the kick that sent me sprawling into servitude, Hamid—this so-called revolutionary guard, local committee man, son of a jackal—decided, unbeknown to me, to take complete control of my tearoom. Why? I learned others had taken an interest in the tearoom. The local Mullah, Haj Rajab, had begun asking awkward questions. Never one to pass up a profit, the unscrupulous Hamid hatched a plan to eliminate me.

What had I done to deserve this? Hadn't I been an obedient son? Hadn't I memorized thousands of lines of poetry? Hadn't I rubbed Baba's feet when he came home exhausted?

The day before *Norouz*, business was hopping, the derelicts were in a good mood and Hamid hadn't been around for weeks. I had just emptied a basin of brown dishwater into the gutter in the back alley and was about to reenter the tearoom through the back door when I heard someone calling my name.

A small figure in a black chador came toward me, gripping one corner of the cloth between her teeth to prevent it from slipping.

"Mr. Hekaiatchi," she said in a low, timid voice, teeth still clenched. "I am your cousin. Your brother sends his regards and asks if you have any work for me in the tearoom."

"My brother?" I asked absently.

"Hamid Hekaiatchi," she said, certain of the effect.

I had forgotten Hamid had taken my last name since claiming Baba as his father. To her credit, she didn't gloat for too long.

"I work for modest wages."

"You will have to," I said, trying to be authoritative, though my voice implied she had the job. "How old are you?"

"Seventeen." At that, the chador slipped off her head with a faint crackle like silk on silk, revealing a face like a moon, two charcoal eyes aglow in a perfectly round face, and, from where I stood, the hint of a swell on her chest. In an instant, her chador was back in place.

"You start tomorrow morning. Kitchen work.

"Thank you," she said. "Hamid said to tell you he'd be grateful to you in the future."

A joke, in hindsight. "Grateful to you in the future." What a lark. The kitchen had plenty of work, but she did little of it. In a matter of days, her chador became the shifting frame through which she exhibited different parts of herself—a womanly thigh, a girlish calf, a milky chest—all revealed as if by accident, each glimpse designed to blind me to her domestic incompetence.

She had no shame in drawing my attention. I might reach for a rag on the floor, and there—her ankle, ready for admiration.

"Do you always stare at girls so insolently, Mr. Hekaiatchi?" she asked.

"I beg your pardon." My face burned.

She laughed, mirthless. "Put your eyeballs back in your head."

"I was reaching for the rag." I held it up like evidence in court. "I meant no offense."

"Your eyes find me a hundred times a day. I can feel it, even when my back is turned." She lifted her chador an inch higher, scratching at imaginary mosquito bites.

"It won't happen again," I muttered. How did her beauty make me so servile?

"Not for at least ten minutes, I'd guess." She turned with a laugh, unrepentant.

I was a fool. I was fooled by her looks, fooled by her connections to that bastard Hamid. But in my defense, biology was against me. No matter my mood or my burdens, the sight of a young girl makes me feel half my weight. What is the source of this uncontrollable desire? Simple. Twenty-nine years of virginity.

Yes, I, Salman Hekaiatchi, after years of travel, education and refined upbringing, had yet to experience the folds of a woman. An oversight? One easily corrected by a visit to a whorehouse. No. Virginity was merely the symptom.

I was in one of those light, half-my-weight moods when I entered the kitchen five evenings later. Fatmeh, the girl, squatted by the outside door, skirts pulled high as she scrubbed laundry in a basin. I watched from the doorway. She panted with exertion, strands of hair coiled against her flushed face. Her bare feet, pink from the water, planted wide apart, revealed the curves of her thighs like drawn bows. Her arms moved rhythmically against the washboard, her backside oscillating with each stroke. A magnificent sight. I imagined rolling beneath her like a mechanic under a car.

She looked up, caught my stare, read every ounce of my desire.

"Azizeh-del, darling, if you want to get between my legs, say so,"

No trace of shyness. Then, to my utter astonishment, she coolly pushed the tub aside, slid back against the wall and, with a single wriggle, pulled her skirt up to her hips. Her bare buttocks formed a milky heart against the brownstone floor. Knees bent, legs open, she lay back, her head awkwardly against the wall. Her matted, ageless, convoluted sex yawned, waiting to swallow me in one slippery gulp. She hushed me with a finger to her nose, motioning me forward with the other

"Come on, get your fill, and hurry before someone comes in."

"My God . . . my Lord," I stammered. I approached, fumbling. The heavens had opened, and I was about to step inside. I reached into my pants, but at the first gasp of open air—like a cheap water pistol—I sprayed her legs and clothing with four shameful squirts.

I hadn't even entered her.

I collapsed, my knees buckling under the weight of humiliation. And then she laughed—a deep, mocking laugh from a woman, not a girl.

"Easy peasy," she said.

She leapt up, wailing like a wronged child, and ran into the tearoom. Her cries had the bright tinkle of a girl in distress.

The kitchen filled in an instant—accusations, cursing, screaming, slapping, pinching. Always pinching. For some reason, people pinched me in moments of violence. They grabbed flesh and twisted it, as if to confirm my reality.

An ugly crowd for ugly times. I took the beating, curling under a table to protect my head. A couple of men pulled at my legs, uselessly. And, as the kicks rained down, a strange thing happened—I found myself looking forward to my demise. In a systematic beating, there comes a moment of lucidity before unconsciousness. I reached that stage.

And I laughed. A shriek of laughter burst out of my lungs. The beating stopped.

Taking their silence as permission, I laughed again, louder. The crowd hesitated. It dawned on them—they were in the presence of a madman. I rolled on the floor, giggling like a tickled child. It was no easy act, laughing as four or five men pulled me up. But it worked. They hauled me to the basement with a few farewell slaps and kicks. Compared to what I'd endured, it felt like angel caresses.

They threw me on a mound of coal. Someone upstairs called for the neighborhood committee.

We Muslims fear the insane.

I sat in the dark. I could see the door, framed by a thin, fading rectangle of daylight, interrupted by its hinges. Hours went by. The tearoom emptied. I could no longer hear the muffled din of customers above. The door had long immersed me in total darkness when I heard the lock turn. The authorities—three of my partner's cronies—looked inside with some trepidation. Each invited the others to go in and fetch me. I immediately increased my cachinnations.

(I can smile now as I sit in my cozy room above Mammad-Ali's store, remembering the three boys, barely eighteen, looking into a dark, dirty coal room and trying to discern a man with an incoherent mass sitting on a pile of coal. The high-pitched laughter reverberated in the empty basement.)

The three discussed their orders. They pulled straws. They dared each other. They argued, but Imam Ali couldn't drag these boys into the coal room to come after me. I wasn't in a mood to cooperate until I heard them discussing their options.

"Why don't we shoot him right where he is?" one said.

"Agha Hamid told us to take him outside the city," the other said.

"I say we shoot him right now and drag him to the car and dump him later," the first one said.

It was time for me to reduce their options and fight another day. I exited the room covered in soot, arms stretched out as if to hug the world, and let out an operatic laugh. The boys pulled the safeties of their Kalashnikovs, ready to slay the repulsive mother of the ogre Foolad Zereh. Ignoring their threat, I moved toward the stairs. The three of them—their guns pointing entirely out of fear, as in a scene from a Hollywood movie—followed me upstairs, their shadows on the staircase wall moving like cartoon monsters.

It was late at night; the great Tehran Grand Bazaar stores had rolled down their corrugated steel shutters. Only a few Afghani sweepers still worked with concentrated diligence. It recalled their unabated resistance to the Russian invasion of their country. The three guards shoved me into the back of an old, cream-colored Rambler with slippery, plastic-covered seats. All three sat in the front seat. We drove west, out of the city. I recall passing the unfinished urban apartments of the old Shah's regime; God bless his soul. We drove past the airport and headed toward the town of Karaj. The purple shadows of the mountains on our right moved behind us like an unending convoy train. The driver turned left onto a dirt road; the mountains cleaved away and disappeared behind us in a small, wheel-spun storm of dust. In front of us lay flat terrain lit by the hard light of the moon. In the middle of nowhere, broken brick walls adorned with faded, salmon-colored advertisements of lipstick and pressure cookers appeared under the headlights. I continued laughing until the driver took a sharp right onto a dirt road.

I began crying and laughing alternately as I realized how close I was to being granted an audience with my maker. I am embarrassed to say my bladder and my sphincter lost control and did their part, leaking urine and fecal matter in small spurts of panic, no matter how hard I tried to contract my anal muscles.

The boys in front began sniffing the air with the confused look of tracker dogs, silently questioning each other's body control. As the smell overpowered—or, more accurately, filled the small space in the car—it dawned on them this was not the result of a minor indiscretion for which everyone accuses the other of being responsible. As the mystery resolved in their not-so-bright minds, they looked at me. I was prepared, with my most dazzling smile plastered over my face. They pulled to the side of the road and, praise be to the Lord, a discussion among the three committee guards ensued. The gist of their talk was religious: Does Islam permit the execution of the insane?

Thank God superstition doesn't spare the criminal mind. The religious disceptation ended with an agreement to find a more learned authority. We headed back toward the city. The discovery of my soiled state brought about some more slapping, in the tradition of my mother reaching back from the front seat, which I withstood in good humor.

After an hour, all of us close to suffocation, we arrived somewhere in town, a few blocks (I realized) from the British embassy. We stopped in front of a pair of wrought-iron gates guarding a large house whose dark silhouette occupied the center of a spacious garden. The driver flicked the horn a few times. An old, sleepy man—no doubt the gardener or the doorman—opened the gate with difficulty by lifting it and dragging it through the gravel, marking a perfect quarter-circle. We drove along a path around the house. We parked under a covering before what was once a magnificent door, in which some ignoramus had cut a rough opening and installed a smaller metal door. The driver renewed his short bursts of honking. The offensive door opened. Two men in white walked out. A third man appeared close behind them, still pulling on his white doctor-like uniform.

The driver jumped out and kissed both cheeks of the half-dressed man. They whispered amiably. We could hear their soft laughter. I was out of steam; fortunately, the two guards sitting in the car were satisfied with an imbecilic smile and closed eyes. The driver returned. Not wanting to come closer than required, he prodded me out of the car with his Kalashnikov. He pushed me over to the first two orderlies in white, who quickly stepped back. The driver, glad to be rid of me, jumped into the car, grabbed his nose with his thumb and forefinger, shook his head in mock horror and waved a nonchalant farewell to his friend. They drove the car out of my life as the sun raised a wan, silvery light against a pearly sky.

I treasure those tiny moments from where I sit today, safe, roofed and cared for by the more than ample Zahra (Mammad Ali's daughter). They stand as pillars of my resistance. As I stood covered in black soot, caked shit, and a mixture of piss and sperm, for the second time in the night, the brave, bearded children of the revolution dared not approach me.

Outside the unknown house, the orderlies cleaned me with a garden hose. All the while complaining I had delayed their morning prayers. They escorted my wet, shivering and tired carcass inside. The plaque affixed to the small metal door said I was the guest of the Martyrs Foundation for Mental Health. We walked through several corridors with clean, well-lit rooms on each side. The rooms, once the setting of a wealthy family's life, had been repurposed to "take care" of war casualties, who sat on their beds with the gaze of holocaust victims.

I squelched down the corridor in my wet shoes. We arrived at a desk next to a door. The orderly picked up a set of large keys on a heavy ring and opened the unlocked door. It led to a staircase heading below. We entered a tenebrous corridor with cells on each side. One bare sixty-watt bulb hanging from the ceiling lit the area. We stopped at the fourth cell door on the left. One of the orderlies unlocked the complicated door, twirling the rough iron keys in the two massive, rusted padlocks with over-refined wrist motions. He opened the heavy door, revealing a vertical grave whose insides jumped at me. Instinctively, I leaned back against the other two orderlies. They saw that as a sign of resistance and instantly, in unison, swung me inside like a sack of rice. The door closed with a bang. The padlocks found their natural state with two consecutive clicks.

In the dark, my head cocked, my ears pricked. I could hear the rhythmic breathing of another. I waited. My heart knocked furiously against my chest, begging to be let out. Had I been caged with a crazed animal? Nothing happened. Gradually, reason reasserted itself. I probably shared a cell with some poor creature like myself. They wanted to teach me a lesson. In all probability, they'd release me in the morning and tell me to watch my step in the future.

I began to recover my mental balance. As my eyes grew accustomed to the dark, I discerned, high on the opposite wall, a small, rectangular window framing a watered-down, milky dawn. I could sense the floor, covered with straw. I quietly moved away from the metronomic breathing to sit in the opposite corner under the window. After a while, my courage returned—a paralyzing fatigue set in. I stretched flat on a thin mattress. It felt as comfortable as the fluffiest down-filled bedding. I fell immediately into a father-less sleep.

My thoughts were not unhappy ones. It had been the most eventful day of my life. A jailbait daughter of Eve had had me nearly within her, a mob had almost torn me apart for rape, three young Muslims had attempted to shoot me in the middle of nowhere and now, labeled a lunatic, I slept in a cage with some wretch. I had much to brag about and tell my listeners in the tea-room. Little did I know I'd be the owner of a story Gabriel himself would need to witness.

THE SECOND NIGHT: 0010

THE WRITER TAKES YOU
BY THE HAND

I promised to interrupt, and so I will. My princeling once described *One Thousand and One Nights* as an operating system—a metaphor from decades ago that still resonates. I, however, see it as a hyperlink system: a web of interconnected stories. Just as the king summoned Scheherazade to entertain him, we call upon Siri and Alexa in our modern age. Within the STEM framework of civilization, the number 1001 serves as the binary representation of nine—a fitting link. *One Thousand and One Nights* spans about 2.74 years, assuming no leap year, reflecting a slower-paced world.

In contrast, our fast-paced, techno-distracted lives might require only nine nights. Much like William Blake's poem, the narratives of nine dreamy nights unfold. Blake's dream state inspires our tale.

Two narrators have spoken so far: the princeling, one of aristocratic twins, and the fat storyteller. Mine excluded, three voices will come together eventually to weave a grand tale—an ambitious venture. Some confusion may arise; the princeling admits to creating the fat storyteller. In the spirit of an eighteenth-century book, I pause to address you directly, "dear "reader." You may object to the hackneyed expression "dear reader." I will drop the "dear" at once. I don't intend to patronize. Trust all our voices, reader. Trust them all.

THE OMNISCIENT NARRATOR INTRUDES

Houses have crumbled in my memory as soundlessly as they did in the mute films of yore.

The Stories of Vladimir Nabokov

Let my grand and gloriously fat storyteller rest in the familiar haven of my boyhood. Allow me to fill in the details he could never know. Indulge me, Ms. Vakil, in a moment of self-reflection. My mother gave birth to my brother and me on January 10, 1954, just seconds apart, echoing the biblical story of Esau and Jacob. Jacob followed Esau from the womb with his hand gripping Esau's heel. They were fraternal, as we were; the Bible tells us one was hairy and the other smooth, one clever and the other simple. When we emerged, one of us was frail and sickly, the other robust and healthy.

I entered this world the color of one giant bruise, choking—hardly a grand entrance, as you might agree. My father named me Allah-Verdi, meaning "God's gift" in Arabic. Since addressing me as Allah seemed inappropriate, they called me Verdi. Following me, my brother, Tari-Verdi, slipped and slid out of our mother with ease, taking full advantage of my missionary efforts—a trait he carried throughout his life. Tari-Verdi also means "God's gift," but in Turkish. The ignorant and pious, unfamiliar with the Turkish root for "God," and not wanting to call him by the same name, shortened his name to Tari.

Physical horrors awaited me. Drawing from the modern horror film genre—you've likely noticed my love of cinema—I envision a helicopter hovering over our country house, capturing it from above. The metallic blue glint of the camera lens gleams as the house's windows gently tremble from the helicopter's vibrations. A shot of the power generator shifts the focus, revealing the trustworthy source of the disturbance while hinting at the rural setting—a neat touch. It's a modest, one-story house. Inside the living room, the rural charm is further emphasized. A dim bulb pulses weakly in sync with the generator's cycles, like an optical metronome. In the corner, two infants lie bundled in identical cribs, their wrappings resembling open-faced mummies. The camera zooms in on a tear in one of the mosquito net canopies. The ominous beat of drums underscores the significance of this breach. Something is amiss. The shot moves closer. A gray tail hangs nonchalantly over the edge of a crib. The audience stirs with horror. A fitting title for this story? A Rat in the Crib.

The camera shifts to the bedroom, offering a sensual shot of the mother as she dreams. The audience knows it's a dream—the surreal backdrop of dull-colored geometric shapes makes it clear. Her eyes remain closed, an arm draped across her brow. The audience knows she can't intervene. The scene snaps back to the living room. It all happens in an instant. The music quickens as the rat begins its grim task. The mother stays lost in her dream while the rat gnaws at the baby's cheek, moving closer to the right eye.

The audience turns to the night watchman, Gorbun-Ali, a towering Turk from Azerbaijan, with pale white skin and piercing blue-black eyes. The seventy-year-old moves on a single leg, aided by two well-worn, crook-handled canes. Can a one-legged man tiptoe? Remarkably, he can. Careful not to disturb the household, he slows each hop into a deliberate, sliding motion. The music crescendos, rising higher and faster. The rat pauses at the faint sound, lifting its head to listen. The camera zooms in, highlighting its blood-streaked front teeth, squeezing every drop of tension from the moment. As the rat prepares to resume its gruesome work, the head of the guard's cane strikes in a swift, decisive blow. The rat lets out a final, unnatural scream—a distorted sound engineered in the studio by speeding up a tape of human laughter, unconvincing but eerie enough. The night guard has saved the baby. The other baby sleeps soundly, with no twin stories to relate.

The face-munching left me disfigured for much of my childhood. It started near my upper lip and spiraled outward toward my right eye. As I grew, changes in bone structure helped, though my face still bears a slight asymmetry. You've seen me, Ms. Vakil. I trust you'd agree I don't cut too shabby a figure.

Though my birth certificate claims I am fifty-eight years old, I consider my actual birth to have occurred sixteen years after the biological event overseen by my mother. I imagine a god—perhaps

Aeolus, like those depicted by Botticelli in the Sistine's cornice, cheeks impossibly puffed—placing my mother's navel delicately in his mouth, like the knot of a birthday balloon. Slowly, he expanded the amniotic membrane outside her body, engulfing us even as she gave birth to her beloved boys. This image captures how my brother and I viewed the world for the next sixteen years. Each year, another echoing puff from our guardian Greek god stretched the figurative balloon around us until one of us finally burst it, joining the bland society of other men.

No human law could have stopped us in our relentless pursuit of each other's ruin. The Bible offered a knowing nod to the patient reader, warning that evil would befall the hairy one rather than the clever. Poor hairy souls! It's this bias that makes the Old Testament so prejudiced. Our shared resolve to destroy one another was perfectly balanced; our interactions with the outside world were maneuvers to gain the upper hand until one of us emerged victorious. The outcome felt inevitable—and yet, it was I who won.

I do miss him. Forty-two years later, I yearn for the first sixteen years of my life, much like a gymnast reminiscing about her finest routines. I miss the sense of purpose that defined our existence. I still catch myself scheming and plotting, trapped in habits that now feel empty. The vibrancy of our lives was savage and thrilling, so much so that when I close my eyes, I can transport myself back forty years to the Valley of Poonak, where we spent our boyhood summers.

Our country home rested on the western side of the Poonak Valley, a green blemish against the dusty village of Poonak. Its flat, modern architecture faced east toward the city of Tehran. In our childhood, the town across the gulch didn't have the menacing cloak of smog that now looms over it. The gardens that once blanketed the valley in green, stretching for miles northward to the village of Farahzad, are mostly gone. They have been replaced by sprawling suburban travertine houses, poorly serviced with water and sewage. The once-small village of Poonak has grown into a town and become part of Tehran's suburbs. Today, the house stands repurposed as the administrative office for Beheshteh Zahra, the city's sprawling graveyard.

Can these petty officials even grasp what our lives were like back then? My mother's open-air lunch parties, where women basked in the sun, slathered in expensive lotions, gleamed in frilly sixties bikinis. The men lounged under the shade of oak trees, locked in endless backgammon matches, their laughter and the clatter of dice echoing like a joyful symphony. The soft clinking of ice in gin and tonic tumblers filled the air with tiny salutes.

Tehran, in those days, was an oasis of simplicity and comfort. Free of traffic and smog, it offered a charmingly unhurried urban life. On Shahreza Avenue, there was a modest shop where my father picked up French and English magazines. On Ferdowsi Avenue, the Bonamie shop—crammed with delights—provided every bit of un-Islamic charcuterie my mother could wish for.

I often wonder if I can be fair to the memories of my parents. How could a child ever be? A few scoldings might linger in his mind and overshadow all else, or he might bury a traumatic experience, refusing to hold a parent accountable. My clearest memories of my parents are rooted in the sixties, shaped by childhood distortions that clash with the accounts others give of them. I remember my mother as a mature, dignified woman. Like all Poonakis, my sibling and I arrived to grace our parents' middle ages; we weren't children of a young couple. I cannot reconcile my mother with her youthful photographs—the short-haired, chin-jutting rebel of a girl in those images transformed into an elegant Parisian woman. More French than Persiranian, she carried her sophistication with effortless ease.

In the 1950s and 1960s, we idolized everything foreign, and originality was highly prized. My mother embodied it completely. In our culture, she softened her blonde hair to a reddish-brown to avoid drawing excessive attention on the streets. She identified as Catholic, a conviction driven by her mother's determination and her father's indifference toward religion. To her, faith was less about God and more about the culture it inspired. She adored all things Catholic and dismissed Islamic traditions—not the faith itself, but its cultural expressions. She spoke fluent Farsi, although with a distinctly French accent. It reinforced her Frenchness, like the accordion in a film establishing a Parisian scene. Her humor was sharp and incisive. Like a perceptive foreigner, she viewed the country clearly, seeing the forest despite the trees.

Even in the sixties, she predicted the coming revolution. Whenever she spotted the young Shah's helicopter cutting across the city toward his palace, she would remark to the courtiers—by then, my father was a trusted confidant of the Shah—"How dependent we are on the flawless operation of a few mechanical parts."

She split her time between Tehran and Paris, with French being the primary language in our household. To place her vividly in your mind, indulge me in one of my cinematic musings. Surely, like everyone, you've seen *The Sound of Music*. No, Ms. Vakil, I am not referring to Julie Andrews as the guitar-playing peasant nun who charms Captain Georg von Trapp. When my brother and I watched the dubbed version of the film (with songs included) and first saw Baroness Elsa Schraeder—portrayed by the elegant Eleanor Parker—in her two-piece orange Chanel suit, paired with a chic polka-dot silk blouse and a bow tied gracefully at her hip, we couldn't help but giggle and whisper, 'Maman!'

My mother's wispy, circumflex eyebrows questioned more; her pupils had a tincture of green, as did my father's eyes; her body was thinner, not quite as womanly as Elsa's; her laugh was manly, loud, with occasional unladylike snorts. Yet, from that moment on, the film became incomprehensible to us. Why would an aristocrat throw over a woman with so much grace and humor for a guitar-playing, bandy-legged, manipulative nun? A noblesse-oblige fling in some Austrian auberge or haystack would have been more understandable, but leaving the Baroness? Unthinkable. There was nothing to dislike about her. She retained her poise even in defeat—something my mother certainly would not have done. Her glittering diamond earrings seemed to shimmer in sympathy with a nearly shed tear. That was something we never saw—not the earrings—we never saw my mother's tears.

In his later years, my father struck me as a pitiable figure, clinging to his place at the court of the young upstart, Moham-mad Reza Shah—the second king of the Pahlavi dynasty but the last Shah of the Persiranian Empire. What a burden to carry to his grave.

My view of my father has softened over time. He was a strikingly handsome, refined man, admired by all who crossed his path. Though he feared no one, he was not brave; fear did not register as part of his nature. In his youth, he spent a brief stint in the army and worked for only a few years. He lived by Montaigne's principle for noble existence: that one's lineage must avoid trade and taxes for three generations to maintain dignity. His loyalty belonged to a mediocre king who understood nothing of loyalty.

I see my father as a Lancelot born into the wrong era. His type wears the nonchalant pose of the heroic, one that is not easily mimicked or packaged by our marketing gurus. Modern society has little use for Lancelots. For the past century, governments have favored the Talleyrand archetype: adaptable, calculating, conspiratorial and unbound by principles. In the Darwinian order, Lancelots and Talleyrands emerge to meet the needs of their age. Yet, history has leaned heavily on the Talleyrands, leaving little room for the Lancelots as the spirit of heroism is steadily purged from humanity's gene pool.

While heroes now become athletic superstars, confined to the stark world of wins and losses, my father stood apart. Ill-equipped for petty rivalries and brutal politics, he waited for a King to demand everything of him. That moment never came. He embodied Churchill's adage of being born to success yet destined for failure. With no grand battles to fight, the slow drip of ordinary life wore him down. I knew him during that drip-drip phase.

Ms. Vakil, I hardly need to describe the smog and urban sprawl that have steadily crept up to blanket the towns and villages surrounding old Tehran. Every year, nearly 40,000 people succumb to pollution-related illnesses. But in my youth, a traffic-free, half-hour drive from the city's center to Poonak brought us to clear, starry skies. By day, the air carried the scent of ripe harvests, fresh dung from sheep and cows, and the sound of the river rushing below as snowmelt cascaded downstream. By summer, the river dried up, leaving behind large boulders in its bed, perfect for transforming into castles and fortresses in our games with the Poonak village boys.

The primitive irrigation system, a perpetual source of feuds among the peasants, nourished the valley's resilient fruit trees. Siah Mashad cherry trees offered their audacious red twin cherries, whose stems any boy worth his salt could tie into a knot with his tongue. Walnut trees stained our hands black for months after school began. The red and white mulberry trees beckoned us to climb their branches fiercely. My brother, the village boys and I raced to shake the branches while the village girls gathered beneath with blankets and their veils to catch the cascade of mulberries—a ritual woven with both competition and camaraderie.

And permanently, on the highest and thinnest branch, bathed in the sharp rays of sunlight, stood Hamid, the khadkhoda's (village headman's) son. More beautiful than handsome, he was still a boy, with bare, filthy feet gripping the branch like a parrot on its perch. Yet his sparkling black eyes radiated triumph. Hamid, who became the confidant of one twin and the lover of the other, refused to take sides but bore the weight of a guilty bystander.

Now, I live in a world stripped of the pleasures I once inherited by birth. In my most recent reinvention, I write technical software manuals for a high-tech firm in Boston. From my perch on a hill in Waltham, I watch the endless procession of traffic on Route 128 through the distorted lens of a vodka martini glass. The blinking red taillights weave like dragons in a Chinese carnival. My days are spent with engineers, crafting safety and legal disclaimers—words few will read but which appease management and sustain the legal ecosystem. I respect the corporate world; it inherited the mantle of the old feudal system I once benefited from. The difference is minor—today's elite relies on legal mechanisms to pass down wealth rather than the well-worn, washed-out blue genes.

I work in a cubicle designed with care to foster my well-being—a cocoon assembled by my employer with no hint of irony. The fuzzy walls, a blend of nylon and wool, form a corrugated cardboard-like barrier that traps every sound. The cubicle itself is an ergonomic haven. My monitor, mounted on an articulated arm, filters light through four bonded optical coating layers to shield my eyes from glare. A padded wrist support beside the keyboard disperses pressure, soothing my carpal tunnel and trapezius muscles. With its decal promising variable terrain, the floor mat encourages my feet to shift angles, stimulating the veins that circulate blood from my legs to my heart.

Amid these modern comforts, my over-weight Montblanc fountain pen rests on my desk—the same one my forgetful father left uncapped on a page in his petit salon—and serves as my time machine. Its presence conjures vivid memories, transporting me from my Waltham office back to our mansion, nestled in its city garden during the final days of our not-so-ancien régime.

February 12, 1979—this date remains etched in my memory. The swimming pool lies half-filled with brackish water, its surface rippling with necklaces of frog eggs. The cold wind nudges the wooden planks, meant to prevent icing, to thud gently against one another. Bakhtiar, the last Prime Minister of the monarchy, vanishes after thirty-six days in office. (He met his end at the end of a kitchen knife in a Paris apartment a few years later.) The four-star generals, eighteen regular generals, four division commanders and two admirals convene to declare the armed forces' neutrality in the conflict. Bazargan, Khomeini's chosen man, assumes control of the government. We all knew it was only a matter of time before they would come for people like me.

Beyond my garden walls, sensing the monarchy's total surrender, a crowd marches down Ferdowsi Avenue. Their chants call out the name of a peculiar old man who had been unknown to most of us mere months ago. Soon, an Air France flight delivers this "light of our lives" to Tehran, promising not paradise but la dolce vita right here on Earth. I had lived blissful years, freed from the shadow of my brother. During those years, petrodollars flowed abundantly. The nation, caught in an orgy of construction and industrial expansion, saw its fortunes rise faster than at any other point in the past two millennia. None of the familiar catalysts for mass revolution existed. On April 1, under the bright, gentle light of spring, 2,500 years of monarchy gave way to theocracy. By popular vote, the lambs had chosen their slaughter.

I heard the bus before I saw it. Its engine roared as it climbed the street outside our compound, heading straight for the gate. The front wheels screeched in a sharp turn, and the bus barreled through. The gates flew open, slammed against the walls, and swung back to strike the sides of the bus as it thundered into our courtyard. A mocha-colored Mercedes with tinted windows, lurched to a halt. I instinctively stepped back, hiding behind a geranium planter.

With a loud hiss, the passenger door threw itself open with abandon. Three boys, younger than me and armed with Israeli

UZIs, jumped out. None grasped the irony of the manufacturer of their weapons. Only culture could produce such contradictions, though it would take these boys generations to understand. They all sported freshly grown, fashionable beards, their eyes narrowing as they scanned for threats behind every tree.

To my astonishment, Hamid, the son of the village khadkhoda, and my childhood friend stepped out next. I hadn't seen him since my brother's death years earlier. He wore brown brogans, Western blue jeans and a red cotton shirt with untucked tails. A revolver thruzf into his waistband pinned part of his shirt into his trousers.

His face had shed its delicate beauty, replaced by sharper, more angular features, though his almond-shaped eyes remained unchanged. He held a bundle of documents, his mouth set in a grim line, his eyes blazing with determination. He thrust the papers toward me like a weapon. "By Ayatollah Khomeini's decree, this house and all its contents are now the property of the Islamic Republic, to be used for the benefit of the people in this neighborhood. Furthermore, by the same decree, the owner, one Mr. Poonaki, is under arrest, accused by multiple witnesses of conduct unbecoming of Islam." His tone was all business, without any recognition of our past friendship.

I stepped out from behind the geranium planter. One of the boys turned to a blue Lalejin ceramic pot and jabbed it viciously with his rifle, shattering it into pieces. "Stop that immediately," Hamid barked. The boy swallowed a smug smile but obeyed. A crow flapped its wings lazily, lifting off from a tree in the corner of the garden to perch on a higher branch. Behind the bus, a tobacco-brown dog darted past the gate. "You will sign the consent order immediately," Hamid said, his voice cold and commanding.

I read the decree. The Ayatollah—who could not have known of my existence—had personally signed the warrant for my arrest and the confiscation of my home. I extended a placating hand, searching for a reason. "Hamid, this is a mistake. My family has lived in this house for three generations." His jaw tightened, and red crescents formed at the corners of his mouth.

"How come he knows your name?" one of the boys asked.

"You've taken tea with my mother and father in this house," I whispered, softening my tone. "Surely . . ."

Before I could finish, Hamid's handgun flashed. In one swift motion, he struck my left cheek with the butt of the weapon. The impact dropped me to the gravel. He hauled me back up as I struggled to straighten, wobbling as I tried to regain balance. He smelled sharply of lye soap.

Hamid thrust a pen under my nose. "Sign it," he demanded. I refused. I watched as the bus emptied, and with it came people I had known my entire life. They met my small gestures of recognition with cold indifference.

In time, Ms. Vakil, I did sign away all my wealth—houses, land, bank accounts and cars. It took nine days. Parliament had already passed an act seizing the property of many families, naming each one. Those forced to comply signed a formulaic Islamic phrase to reframe this grand theft on God's balance sheet, moving it from the haram to the halal column. In the end, everyone surrendered. My turn came on the ninth day—more accurately, after nine nights.

After I signed, Hamid secured my release and drove me to the airport the same day. He handed me a passport, complete with the necessary stamps. I chose Boston because I owned a small apartment and had a modest bank account. Within days, I found myself branded as an immigrant. I will define an immigrant: We are tightrope walkers who perform tricks a few hundred feet in the air. We hear drum rolls. We look down, and to our surprise, the circus staff has removed the net.

Recounting my sixteen years of gestation requires no madeleine to evoke memory, but it does demand structure. Our tireless psychic laundress smooths out the wrinkles in our recollections; without her, we would all suffer the torment of chaotic, total recall, like Borges's *Funes the Memorious*. Yet even she could do nothing for the rips and tears in the fabric of my being. And so, my story will revolve around those rips and tears.

"It's a true story," you might hear a respectable elderly lady remark to her husband as they exit the cinema, her words brimming with misplaced certainty. I make no such claim. During nine candle-dark nights spent imprisoned in the basement of my own house, a sieve-like process removed all traces of privilege from me. Beyond detection, even by such a fine filter, it remains a goodwill that no accountant could ever write off the asset sheet.

The structure for this story came from Alex, my cubicle mate—a Russian programmer. We work in pairs: one programmer and one writer. One day, he noticed *The Book of the Thousand Nights and One Night* on my desk, rendered into English from the French translation by Dr. J. C. Mardus.

"That book," Alex said, "has the coolest operating system."

"What do you mean?" I asked.

"Think about it," he explained. "Look at how many stories you can plug in, nested like a named function defined within another enclosing block. It's simple. Scheherazade is the kernel—she facilitates communication between the hardware and software."

Inspired by this ancient nested storytelling structure, I summoned the storyteller who meets the yarn spinner, my surgeon uncle, who quite literally gave birth to me, the narrator. I require 1001 binary nights—or nine decimal nights. The truth will surely shake the branches of our genetic tree more violently than we ever shook the mulberry trees in Poonak. Let its fruits fall wherever they may.

THE STORYTELLER WAKES TO DISCOVER THE SPINNING SURGEON

"Omne ignotum pro magnifico:"
everything unknown passes for miraculous."

A few hours into my deep sleep, I woke to an eerie, ululating sound. Disoriented and unsure of my place in time and space, I sat up to find a hoary figure standing in the center of the cell. The morning sun streamed through the small window, casting a corridor of silver motes that illuminated the decrepit man like a natural spotlight. His long, white hair draped over his shoulders, framing a gleaming bald dome. His back bore two festering wounds, raw and angry. A dirty loincloth barely concealed his frail frame and heavily wrinkled skin. His face tapered toward the lower mandible as if gravity had pulled the bone and muscle downward to their lowest point of equilibrium. I might have mistaken him for a deranged Hindu fakir were it not for his pale blue eyes and milky white skin.

What struck me most were his actions. He threw his head back every few seconds, growling like a dog on the verge of attack, followed by a piercing howl. He seemed oblivious to my presence. I did my best to remain unnoticed. After several howls, I heard movement at the door. An orderly opened the small porthole and peered inside. The old man immediately ceased his screaming and turned his head sharply. Then, without warning, he shouted at me:

"What am I?"

"Pardon me, sir?" I asked, suddenly the focus of his manic attention.

"What. Am. I?" His voice trembled with intensity.

I stammered, unsure of what to say. "I . . . I don't know."

He removed his loincloth and ceremoniously revealed a small penis resting on ridiculously large testicles, like a turn-of-the-century bicycle with its outsized front wheels.

"And now, can you not see what I am?" he demanded as though removing his loincloth might somehow unveil the workings of his mind.

"No, sir," I replied cautiously, trying to avoid provoking him further. The metallic clanking of locks echoed through the room, signaling that the orderly had decided to intervene.

"You fool," he spat. "I am an oil well, don't you see?"

Each metallic scrape as the door unlatched amplified my unease. I fought the urge to cry out for help.

"Of course I do," I said, my voice steady despite the chaos.

"Shut up, you fat oaf, and watch." He directed his body toward me and urinated in my direction. He would have drenched me a great deal more if he had had the bladder of a younger man. He turned 180 degrees. To my horror, I saw his defecation oozing out from between his flaccid buttocks. The door opened, and a large, hairy orderly entered the room. In a frenzy of waste production, the old man lifted his arms akimbo, threw his head back as if in victory on the battlefield, and vomited. "An efficient oil well at work," he shouted, and, almost breathless from the vomiting, he managed to give a hiccup of a laugh.

The muscular orderly waited patiently and gave short encouragements, his hairy arms crossed across his white overalls. "That's right, Professor, get it all out, bring the oil price down. Yes, that's good, old man, more now." When it was over, the orderly approached the exhausted man from behind, picked him up in a bear hug, and carried him out of the room as if lifting a child. The old man went limp like a protester taken to the back of a police truck. Left behind in the cell was yours truly, praying to the Almighty for kindness and pity. The irony of my acts the night before was not lost on me. This old man operated at a different level. He could shit, piss and vomit at will to convince his captors of his insanity. It gave me hope for his sanity.

This first unnerving meeting with Professor Dal did little to prepare me for the second. In the afternoon, the same meaty orderly, accompanied by a much smaller, weasel-like colleague, brought him back, drugged and asleep. They threw him on the mattress as if he were a sack of rice. They also got a mop and a bucket of water mixed with a noxious disinfectant.

I started negotiations for my release. I dropped all pretense of insanity. I begged to be released and not to be left alone with this maniac sleeping in a drugged stupor. I explained I belonged to the bazaar class and posed no threat to the Islamic Republic. No amount of tears and supplication worked. They ordered me to clean up; they expected the cell to be cleaner than my mother's bedroom. "I know about your mother's bedroom because I have been there," said the hairy orderly, holding up his left arm as if checking his watch and pumping his fist back and forth in a crude representation of what he would do to my dear departed mother. They left in uproarious hilarity.

Dejected, I cleaned the mess. Hunger took over. In my life, no crisis has managed to diminish my appetite. On the contrary, my enormous hunger dictates my moods. In a single sitting, I have consumed two whole chickens, an entire rice pan and half a dozen eggs. and washed it down with a jug of doogh—the delightful, peppered yogurt-and-water concoction. As my stomach growled, I began my vigil for supper.

I sat on the hard surface, growing increasingly impatient. It had been fifteen hours since I last ate. I mentally cataloged my sins, searching for one so grave as to warrant this cruel punishment. None came to mind. At last, the jailer arrived—a grotesquely hairy man whose beard line crept unnervingly high, reaching above his cheekbones and forming a sharp angle near his nose and eye socket. I couldn't help but wonder if this man ever slept.

My heart sank at the meager portion when he handed over the food. Unable to mask my disappointment, I glanced up and he grinned, revealing a set of meaty gums.

"What's the matter? You don't like our food?" he taunted.

"The doctor recommends a strict regimen for you. We're concerned about both your mind and your body."

"No doctor has seen me,' I replied. 'Can I please see a doctor?"

The jailer smirked. "I am your doctor," he said with mock authority. "And I strongly advise you to shed the excess flesh hanging from you immediately."

I immediately understood there was no negotiation with this member of the animal kingdom. I held my tongue until he left. Then, I devoured the broth ravenously, dipping into it the stale bread I had softened in a water bowl. The unappetizing meal vanished in less time than it takes to raise an eyebrow. Only then did I realize, to my horror, that I had also consumed the old man's share. For the next two hours, I lay petrified on my bed, squinting my eyes to feign sleep. I prayed he'd remain oblivious until morning. I resolved to offer him part of my breakfast as penance.

In this agitated state, I drifted into sleep. I dreamt of the hand of God descending from the heavens, its flat palm covering my entire back. Each finger was as large as the butane tank I used for my tearoom stove. The hand blessed and caressed me, applying a gentle pressure reminiscent of my mother's soothing massages when she woke me for school. But then, the pressure intensified. One of the fingers curled around my body. It gripped my left side. The sensation turned painful, as though the Almighty Himself was displeased with His servant.

I struggled toward wakefulness, swimming through layers of sleep like a diver surfacing for air. At first, I thought it was Bakhtak—the ogre who visits me after a heavy meal. I muttered my short prayer for such occasions. I tried to return to sleep. The pressure persisted. Besides, I remembered I had barely eaten. I became aware that Bakhtak felt thinner and bonier than usual. "Baba, is that you?" I whispered. I didn't feel the fatherly tickle in my ear. As I spiraled up further into wakefulness, I felt the unmistakable, forceful jab of a metallic object against my ribs. It hurt.

"Quiet down, or I'll stab you this instant." The voice was unmistakably the old man's, but it had changed—its tone was now sharp, educated and laced with a ruthless edge. He had climbed on top of me while I slept. Was he prepared to kill me over broth and stale bread?

"Sir," I pleaded, my voice trembling. "I made an honest mistake. You can have my share of the food in the morning. Please, spare me."

'Quiet down,' he repeated, his tone calm but unyielding. "The food is irrelevant. You and I have much to discuss. I have much to say, and you have much to hear." His measured voice should have reassured me, but it didn't. I lay frozen, paralyzed by fear. I never considered shaking him off, though I could have easily thrown him halfway across the cell. The cold certainty in his voice kept me as still as my trembling body allowed. I felt the unrelenting pressure of a blade against one of my higher ribs, dangerously close to my heart. Where had he even found a knife?

"Who are you?" I whispered.

"All in good time," he replied. "But can I trust you to stay still and listen?"

"Yes," I stammered. 'But please, get off my back."

To my surprise, his voice softened, the menace evaporating.

He now spoke with the warmth of an old uncle. "No, dear boy, I can't do that. We need to form one silhouette. The guards often check through the peephole. I've made a straw man of myself," he added. I felt him smile at a private joke. "Since you can't sleep on top of me, I must sleep on top of you." With that, he eased the blade's pressure, which turned out to be nothing more than the handle of a spoon. He shifted, making himself comfortable on top of me. He lay supine with one leg crossed over the other as he stared at the ceiling.

What was it we were meant to do together? I feared some sinister intention, but I dismissed the thought. His demeanor was too composed, too deliberate. I couldn't decipher his purpose.

"Look here, boy," he said. "Do you know who I am?"

"'An oil well?' I asked. I dreaded a repeat of the previous morning's chaos.

He snickered a sound that was almost girlish in its lightness. I couldn't see him, but I imagined him covering his mouth as he giggled. "My name is Professor Dal. I'm a surgeon—though most know me as The Yarner. I could suture a wound with one hand. The nickname stuck." He didn't explain his bizarre antics during the day, and I didn't dare ask.

"The surgeon? The same Professor Dal who served as the Shah's doctor?" I said.

My cellmate was once the nation's most celebrated surgeon, whose illustrious career spanned half a century. He was a fixture at the royal court in the early fifties and sixties. But during the oil boom of the seventies, he dared to criticize the cartel. He fell out of favor and vanished from the public eye. I had only vague recollections of his reputation—nothing more.

Over the next eight nights, Professor Dal unfolded the saga of the Poonakis, a family whose legacy spanned only three generations. He recounted tales of the twin princes who founded the family and their twin grandchildren, whose mutual hatred consumed their lives. Each evening, after our meager meal of broth and bread, the Professor would crawl over to my mattress and, without hesitation, climb on top of me to get comfortable. From this perch, he spun stories—tales of love and vengeance. Sometimes, I suspected him of being a madman who found my body softer than his pallet. But then, his words would shift, revealing the wisdom of a man recounting the collapse of a family. Other times, he shared a stark and precise history of a nation marred by tragedy and brutality.

Listening to him, I marveled at his vocal dexterity. He was a master of voices—men's, women's, children's—effortlessly inhabiting the personalities of those he described. I did not know of his famed ability to suture with one hand, but I could attest to his unmatched skill in spinning a yarn, rivaling even my father's. On the first night, as I shifted my large frame to accommodate the weight of his bones, he said calmly, "Stop fidgeting, kind boy. We have eight nights to tell our story."

"How do you know that?" I asked, the spark of hope unmistakable in my voice. "Did you hear something from the guards? Are they going to let me out? They are, aren't they?"

"Quiet, boy," he replied firmly. "You must meet Tala, the Shah's umpteenth wife."

THE SURGEON, THE YARN SPINNER, TELLS THE STORY OF THE YOUNG PRINCES

Wednesday, I think. Thursday, I enjoy. Friday, I play. Oh, unhappy Saturday: my legs are bleeding from the strokes of cherry tree branches.

Nursery Rhyme

"All stories are stories of conception. In the West, they are called love stories. To explain how the second pair of twins came to spill out onto the surgery room floor, I must first recount four previous conceptions," Professor Dal began. "Let me introduce you to Tala—the ambitious daughter of the royal bootmaker, the king's concubine and the royal twins' mother. Stop me if I lose you," he added. "When you leave here, there must be no confusion."

Tala wore flowery housedresses in her later years, her white hair, hands and bunioned feet heavily stained with bright orange henna as if clinging to a youth long gone. She spoke endlessly, her conversations rooted in her earlier life before childbirth complications altered her course. She died in her mid-sixties, midsentence, while narrating the origin of a pair of earrings worn by a eunuch in the harem. Her triumph over destiny became her punishment— she replayed those formative years endlessly, as if trapped in time. Some believed that her monumental effort to bear the king's offspring left her equating that success with the very end of life itself. "In modern terms, she had a stroke during childbirth," the surgeon clarified.

What thoughts must have passed through her mind, at sixteen, as she stood by the intricately latticed palace windows, gazing into the garden? She would have seen patches of hyacinths and narcissi there—some with single blossoms touched with azure, others with creamy white petals encircling a golden, dew-speckled center. Marble pools, their fountains cascading mercury waves, shimmered in the sunlight as schools of gold and silver-finned fish glided in harmony. They moved as though guided by a single mind and body, swaying seamlessly from one direction to the next. She couldn't have dreamt or imagined the breathtaking spectacle."

In her fourth year of concubinage, she, the daughter of the royal bootmaker, prepared to receive the king of kings, the monarch of all Persiran, for the second time. She sat in his Room-of-Delight, adorned with luxurious carpets, rugs and brocade draperies in deep, rich shades of red. Plush velvet and cashmere cushions embroidered with pearls lined the walls, while tiny mirrors embedded into broad niches sparkled like precious gems, framing oil paintings of hunting scenes. At the center of the wall behind her hung a single frameless portrait of His Majesty the Shah, depicted at nineteen—the lord and master of the harem.

She had meticulously rubbed her body with Sadri, a specially perfumed rice, and tinted her lips with a vibrant powder derived from Shan-Djarf, a rare desert insect found in cracked mud. Her attire featured the latest fashion—a voluminous, flounced tutu introduced to the harem by the king. He had witnessed ballet dancers perform in Paris.

The city resonated with the sound of midday prayer. Her time had come. She bared her heavy breasts. Picking up a pair of copper tongs, she cupped her left breast and placed the nipple between its jaws. She pinched lightly. Then, in a quick, downward motion, she crushed the tissue. The instantaneous pain blurred her vision. She let out a soft moan. The bruised nipple stood erect, bulging, the color of a dead calf's tongue. Satisfied with the result, she repeated the process on her right breast. The pain now made her fall back on the cushions. The king loved thick nipples. "Ooh," I groaned. "It must have hurt?"

"Unless you need clarification, please keep your comments to yourself," Dal poked something painfully into my side.

No sacrifice was too great. Tala's childhood memories surged to the forefront—sucking on dirty muslin wrapped around shards of sugar; the salty tang of her mother's finger, with a minute scrap of opium nestled beneath the nail, lulling her into blissful sleep; the well-controlled cadence of her father's voice echoing in sharp reprimands. They had called her Tala, meaning gold, a tribute to her straw-yellow hair. Her golden locks—on her head and, more uniquely, in other places—became the fortuitous gift that shaped her destiny, securing her and her future twins' fortune through sheer genetic happenstance. The famous Poonakis lived for three generations in luxury thanks to the color of Tala's pubic hair.

"Professor, can I ask how you know these facts? After all, you weren't born yet," I interrupted.

"A good question, my fluffy friend," He rolled over me as quickly as on a mattress. His stomach flushed on my back, he brought his mouth close to my ear. I felt his lips brushing the hair on my lobe. "I am an orphan. The family adopted me. I am as much a Poonaki as the others. I will explain everything in good time," he said. He then rolled back to his original position, his back to mine, stared at the ceiling with one leg crossed over the other, and continued.

At twelve, her father gave her away. On a Wednesday, her mother walked her to the bathhouse. When they returned, she found the house filled with trays of assorted foods: fruits grown to perfection; nuts of every kind—walnuts, almonds, pistachios—on half a dozen trays with elaborate designs; boxes of nougats made of honey, pistachios stacked neatly in the corner; toffees, plain and nut-filled; fondants shaped like half-moons; Turkish delight. She had never seen so many sweets: peppermint lumps decorated with gold leaves, boiled sweets sticking deliciously to fingers. It all felt like an adventure. What child would not see the bright side of the bargain?

The next night, two women escorted her into the Room of Delight to await the Shah. Only twelve years old, she dozed in and out of imagined nightmares. Her mother and aunt had painted a bizarre picture of men's absolute right to insert into her body a part of their bodies without her complaint. A silky prepubescent tuft of yellow hair had recently covered her. The Shah arrived late. She awoke to see his rough outline quietly undressing. Her first clear sense of him in the bed was a heavy, clinging odor of salty sweat. He entered her scrawny body unceremoniously. Her yellow hair, her claim to distinction, mattered little in the dark. She bled excessively, which disgusted him. They replaced her immediately. She understood the look of pity on the faces of the other concubines.

She navigated a life steeped in deception, insults, gossip and intrigue within the harem for several years. This enclosed world—a tiny, self-contained city within a city—teemed with eunuchs, chamberlains, pages, courtiers, guardians, door listeners, sorcerers, interpreters of dreams, destined victims and manipulative witnesses. These individuals evolved into the realm's most cunning and sophisticated politicians, perpetually immersed in plotting and counterplotting through intelligence networks. The elders championed their favored protégés, employing diverse strategies. All shared one ultimate goal: securing the king's favor by providing him a son—a legitimate heir whose claim to the king's patrimony would guarantee their benefactor's stability and comfort in old age.

Through this treacherous web, Tala endured. The women, save for a handful of naïve younger rivals, grew to respect her as a formidable contender. Determined to reclaim her place in the king's chamber after her initial failure, Tala committed to rigorous discipline and meticulous preparation. She transformed into an embodiment of desirability, never veering too far toward thinness or corpulence. Instead, she maintained an alluring, skintight plumpness—the perfect balance of feminine allure. Her daily routine included oiling and massaging her skin to preserve its supple texture. Outdoors, she donned a thick veil to shield her delicate, fair complexion from the harsh sun and dust. And on this day, she would claim her reward.

The shrill, frantic voice of Djavaher, the eunuch known as Jewel, broke the stillness. His cries heralded the Shah's arrival, sending the women scattering in all directions. The Shah emerged onto the balcony overlooking the meticulously paved courtyard and descended the stairs, his presence commanding. His black hair swayed, his long nose gave him an air of sophistication and his dagger-like mustache accentuated his regal demeanor. Yet, his muddy, lethargic eyes, concealed beneath drooping lids, revealed a man at odds with the burden of his excesses.

The Shah wore a white linen shirt beneath a padded coat of fine cotton wool intricately quilted with silk thread. Over this, he wore a light blue jacket, cinched tightly at the waist, its pointed cuffs lined with cashmere and bordered with rare brocade. He draped over his shoulder a long orange cape. The finest sable lined it. Hundreds of small, fluffy tails decorated its fringe.

As he descended the stairs, Djavaher, stout and meticulous, leaped from the balcony into the courtyard. Falling to his knees, he passionately kissed the Shah's hand. The Shah smiled magnanimously, his head tilting gently from side to side, nodding in acknowledgment. In the dim corners of the courtyard, the single diamond on his lamb hat caught the light, casting wild reflections.

Before Djavaher could complete his effusive welcome, a commotion erupted. Djohar, known as Ink—the black eunuch rumored to be an Abyssinian prince—arrived in a whirlwind. His shaved head gleamed and his smooth, muscular frame resembled a seasoned pugilist. Djohar, proudly claimed descent from the prophet. He insisted, no, he knew, that he was the last of this sacred line. He pushed through the cluster of women to announce that the queen, Ghamar-ed-Dowleh, the Moon of the Empire, would receive the Shah. Flanked by Djohar on one side and Djavaher on the other, the Shah crossed the courtyard, smiling at the prostrate houris. He ascended the marble stairs at the far end and disappeared behind a cascade of jasmine into a small, tent-like structure on the queen's balcony.

The women, positioned at the lower rungs of the harem's rigid hierarchy, waited patiently. None harbored jealousy toward the queen. Instead, they exchanged insolent glances, some emboldened by their striking physical beauty, others by their noble lineage. They all awaited the Shah's emergence from his cultural visit. The queen was renowned for her literary and poetic prowess. The Shah, ever discreet, had already made his selection before entering the queen's chamber. It took only a subtle nod in the direction of his chosen. As a gesture of courtesy, the women lowered their eyes. Their expressions betrayed no hint of judgment or disapproval. The eunuchs, attuned to the Shah's gaze, would later inform the fortunate woman of her selection.

For three years, Tala had meticulously prepared for this moment. She knew the Shah had not selected her; he showed interest in another concubine, a slender figure reminiscent of a supple boy. Years later, with a grainy, coquettish laugh from deep in her throat, she'd recall the scene. If pressed, Djohar—for half of Tala's dowry—would apologize to the Shah for the error. There were many afternoons; a small mistake did not displease the Shah. After all, Tala would not disappoint. Nothing could deter her resolve. She had ordered exquisite sweets and sherbet. Two young servants arrived with colored glasses and a decanter. Once they left, Tala deftly flicked open the stone on her ring and emptied its powdery contents into the decanter with a steady hand. She understood the peril of her actions. To tamper with the Shah's food or drink meant a guaranteed death, one steeped in agony. The peasant girls returned moments later, carrying trays laden with zulbia, blushing and giggling as they placed them down. Feeling triumphant, Tala basked in the sound of their amusement.

The powder—a fertility concoction crafted by Sarah the Jewess sorceress—contained crushed pearls, a spice resembling pepper, a few hairs plucked from the upper lip of a living leopard, and the navel of a gazelle severed immediately following a lion's attack. The sorceress had recited talismanic incantations as the powder dried beneath the light of five moons. Tala sat back, her confidence unwavering, and patiently awaited her master.

They heard the approaching footsteps. A sudden loud sneeze—a divine warning halted the Shah in his tracks. Tala smirked, unshaken by the outdated superstition. Such tricks, likely devised by one of the younger concubines aware of the Shah's religious fervor, would not sway her. She reclined on her cushions, waiting. Then came the second sneeze—the signal to proceed—thanks to the professional sneezer she had hired for this very moment. Once more, she heard the Shah's footsteps resume.

On August 3, 1885, Tala gave birth to twin princes: Sardar Mirza and Saleh Mirza. The Shah bestowed upon them the honorific Mirza, elevating them as princes and placing them firmly in his heart. Tala's triumph didn't come without sacrifice. The complications during childbirth marked the end of her youthful vigor and, with it, we bid farewell to the younger Tala.

The two princes, Sardar Mirza and Saleh Mirza, spent their

early years together, with the women of their father's harem at Golestan Palace. Until the age of eight, the identical twins were inseparable. At four years old, their nurse, or tayeh, caught them in their shared bed, caressing, smelling and licking each other's heads like playful cubs in the wild—though the word "caught" implies guilt, which they did not feel. Their innocent behavior drew disapproval from those around them, who deemed it unnatural. Throughout their childhood, the twins navigated attempts to separate them.

Defying tradition, the Shah didn't designate a French monsieur or mademoiselle to tutor them, but an Englishman named Wilfred Sparroy. He taught them French, English, mathematics and gymnastics. He had previously tutored the Shah's grandchildren through his eldest son, Zell al-Sultan. Zell al-Sultan, not born of a royal mother, forty years their senior, couldn't inherit the crown. Mr. Sparroy, jovial yet linguistically flawed, spoke French with a terrible accent—a common conceit among the English that foreign languages should be spoken in an English manner. This accent haunted Saleh Mirza throughout his life, manifesting in his peculiar pronunciation: he pronounced *parler* (to talk) as "parlay," *bruit* (noise) as "brou-ee" and *oeuf* (egg) as "oaf." Sardar Mirza would enjoy circumstances that allowed him to perfect his French accent.

In the intricate politics of the harem, full brothers formed alliances against half-brothers, whose mothers, servants and eunuchs often fueled divisions among them. Saleh Mirza, a serious and focused boy with exceptional concentration, devoted himself to reading and translating newspapers. He meticulously rendered articles from French or English into Farsi, later achieving remarkable political success as an elder statesman. His brilliance was undeniable, especially in an environment where a Qajar prince had less chance of ascending in politics than a donkey driver had of becoming prime minister. Sardar Mirza, in contrast, was far more cheerful and carefree, demonstrating an innate talent for languages.

The tutors presented a detailed progress report on the Shah's children each year. Nasser al-Din Shah, revered as the pivot of the universe, eagerly attended these readings. He invited notable figures, including foreign scholars, missionaries and resident consuls, to witness the event. In preparation, Mr. Hoeltzer, the German from the Indo-European Telegraph Department, brought outdated mural maps of the world. They assembled a dais encircled by chairs. The few foreign guests sat alongside the Shah. Everyone else stood in a semicircle behind the Shah's chair, heads bowed and arms crossed over their chests.

One by one, his boys—aged five to sixteen—knelt on a small, square cushion before him. Their heads, adorned with tall astrakhan hats, remained down as they fixed their gaze on the ground. Regarded as miniature adults, the boys did not wear children's attire such as sailor suits or lederhosen. Instead, they dressed in traditional Persiranian overcoats made of cashmere with a straight military collar. The coat, fastened only at the neck, was tightly tailored at the waist then flared into plaited folds that fell below the knees. The open front showcased striking purple, brown, or ruby silk and velvet undercoats. The tuck of the legs and the natural drape of the overcoat's folds discreetly hid baggy white socks. No one, except the King, walked on a carpet with shoes.

The progress report had the air of an Olympiad. The competitive spirit reverberated through the harem. Radio-like, the eunuchs recounted details with vivid storytelling as the day-long affair transitioned from formal seriousness to lively chaos. The boys competed in poetry recitals and, chalk in hand, raced to solve arithmetic problems on the stones before the dais. Little boys stretched strings across the maps, their cheeks brushing against the brown, raised mountain ranges as they struggled to measure the distance between foreign capitals and Tehran—the center of the universe. Members of foreign consuls tested the children's linguistic proficiency, while the tutors, primarily French, fumed at their legations for slighting their favorite princes. The Shah watched with amusement, smiling and pointing as he alternated between complimenting and scolding his offspring. He rewarded victors with a gold coin and a kiss from the dignitaries seated on the dais. Those less fortunate risked the falak (bastinado), often carried out by their tutor or a eunuch.

On April 30, Nasser al-Din Shah, the pivot of the universe, attended his final report reading, just one day before a bullet from an old revolver brought an end to the forty-eight-year Nasseri era. It marked a monumental shift comparable to the transition from the Victorian to the Edwardian era. At sixty-four, the Shah leaned heavily on his cane. Despite his customary twenty-course meals, his figure remained relatively unscathed, thanks to his peculiar habit of chewing, savoring and spitting out each morsel. His signature Qajar bedroom eyes, which would become even more pronounced in his son, lent him a regal, chin-raised posture—not out of pride but necessity. It allowed him to see beyond his sagging upper eyelids.

On this significant day, twelve-year-old princes Sardar Mirza and Saleh Mirza vied fiercely in spoken and written French against three half-brothers, two of whom were much older. Spring was in full bloom, and the skies stretched out in an unbroken pale blue, unmarred by clouds. Around the courtyard, joubs—channels of spring water—burbled gently. Monsieur Rocha, a regular attendee and the consul from Rasht, used argot to confuse the boys and their English tutor, Master Sparroy. Thanks to his flawless pronunciation, Sardar Mirza claimed victory in the verbal examination. With his sharp intellect and diligence, Saleh Mirza outperformed all in grammar.

As they prepared for dictation, Monsieur Rocha read aloud from one of La Fontaine's fables. His precise, didactic delivery followed the rhythmic cadence familiar to anyone subjected to the rigors of the French educational system. Concerned about the Shah's notoriously short attention span, tutors hovered anxiously over the boys, ready to intervene at the first sign of error. These sudden-death dictations rarely extended beyond a few sentences.

Monsieur Rocha dramatically announced the title of the fable: *La Grenouille Qui Veut se Faire Aussi Grosse Que le Bœuf*—The Frog Who Would Make Himself as Big as a Bull. Seven-year-old Ahmad Mirza requested a repetition of the word "frog." He would one day graduate from the Theresianum in Austria and become a guest of Emperor Franz Joseph I. The word *grenouille* defeated him swiftly. His youth spared him from the routine falak.

The next casualty was Mohammad Reza Mirza Rokn es-Saltaneh, a striking fourteen-year-old with a unibrow. In a bold maneuver, he attempted to distract Monsieur Rocha by demanding a clearer repetition of the consul's words, citing difficulty understanding his regional accent. Taken aback, Monsieur Rocha turned toward the audience. Seeing his chance, the prince mouthed an appeal to his tutor, seeking the correct spelling of the word *bœuf* from the fable's title. The tutor, unimpressed by his audacity, glared sternly and remained silent. The consul's repetition of the word was no aid; either one grasped the French collé diphthong "œ" or one did not. Frustrated, the tutor seized the boy's ear in a harsh pinch, hissing the word "cretin" repeatedly under his breath. The Shah, observing the scene, erupted into laughter, prompting hesitant chuckles from the rest of the audience. The Shah favored Mohammad Reza Mirza. Over time, this roguish brother grew to be a trusted companion of the twins, often seen at the Poonaki house. His presence became immortalized in the daguerreotypes proudly displayed atop the grand piano and the small mahogany side tables. As a tribute to his infamous dictation mishap, his brothers affectionately nicknamed him le Bœuf.

Monsieur Rocha recited the fable: "*Une grenouille vid un bœuf, qui lui sembla de belle taille.*" The three remaining boys anxiously chewed the ends of their freshly sharpened pens, visibly straining under the pressure. The tutors closely monitored their progress, noting every slip. Sixteen-year-old Nosrat al-Din Mirza, another unfortunate victim of Mr. Sparroy's English-tainted French, mistakenly transformed the word *taille* ("size") into the English word "tie." Despite this blunder, he would become a fair painter, a skilled musician and a lifelong confidant of Sardar Mirza during their adult years in Paris.

As the contest continued, Monsieur Rocha recited the next lines for the remaining competitors—the twins: "*Elle qui n'estoit pas grosse en tout comme un œuf/Envieuse s'étend, et s'enfle, et se travaille.*" Out of brotherly affection, Saleh Mirza decided to let his twin, Sardar Mirza, win the prize. Feigning confusion over the tricky

French diphthong, he deliberately wrote *un oaf* instead of *un œuf* ("an egg").

His act of selflessness earned Sardar Mirza the gold coin—and the honor of a ceremonial kiss from their royal father. This decision would have far-reaching consequences in both their lives.

Sardar Mirza didn't have much time to rejoice in his victory. The next afternoon, an advance guard arrived to announce the assassination attempt on the Shah. He had been shot after prayer in Shah Abbdol-Azim Shrine in Ray, four miles from Tehran. The harem ululated from every window of Golestan Palace.

The Shah had sat inside the grand mosque, leaning on his silver-laden cane. A rivulet of sweat ran from his forehead; a servant dabbed at it with a handkerchief. It was hotter than the day before. The mosque was less protected from the sun. The famous sanctuary's prayers had always pleased the pious Shah. He planned to receive petitions in person afterward. As he completed his prayers, a man of average height—thin, wearing poor man's clothes and wrapped in a tattered blanket—approached him. As with all assassinations, people would marvel at the coincidences necessary for the act to succeed. It was the first time a crowd had been allowed to remain inside the mosque while the Shah prayed.

Mirza Reza Kermani carried a sheaf of paper. It looked like a petition, but it hid his rusty gun. He looked strangely modern in his wild, disheveled, proto-Islamic terrorist garb. His thin, white turban resembled a series of handkerchiefs knotted at the corners; his unkempt beard seemed a bit too well tended for a poor illiterate. He had close-set, otherworldly eyes. With his delicate, dark, bony fingers curled around the trigger, he approached confidently, never in doubt. He fired point-blank—three shots around the heart. Just a few gravestones away lay the Shah's real heart, the grave of his favorite wife, Jayran, buried there thirty-seven years before. Again, people marveled at the coincidence.

Mirza Reza represented the liberal view of society. He once remarked, "I had a chance to kill him before, but I didn't because the Jews celebrate their picnic after the eighth day of Passover. I didn't want the Jews accused of killing the Shah." This sentiment, undeniably progressive, reflected a complex moral calculation. In August, the courts executed Mirza Reza. They left his body hanging for two days—a grim spectacle meant as a deterrent. It would prove ineffective.

Calm and composed, Ali Asghar Khan Atabak, better known as Amin Soltan, took charge. The premier, who had faithfully served for nine years, maneuvered the Shah's failing body into the carriage. For the benefit of the onlookers, he loudly addressed the Shah, feigning optimism. "Your Majesty, let us return to the palace. Your shoulder is grazed and needs attention." The Shah, in his final moments, gurgled faintly back, "If I survive, I will rule differently," before succumbing to an irreversible coma.

In the carriage, Amin Soltan staged an illusion of life. He straightened the Shah's body and lifted the sleeve for a royal handwave. He tugged at the hair behind his head to simulate a royal nod. Little did the premier know he'd meet a similar fate nine years later. Abbas Agha, an anarchist, would assassinate him in front of parliament.

Amin Soltan acted swiftly, sending advance guards to Tabriz to inform the Crown Prince and dispatching couriers to foreign embassies to secure international support for the succession. This decisive action cemented his reputation for loyalty and strategic thinking, ensuring his place in the court for most of the new Shah's reign.

The Shah passed away at the palace. They announced his death a day later. The Russian and English delegations endorsed the Crown Prince, Mozaffar al-Din Shah, the second-eldest surviving son. The eldest son, Zell al-Sultan, born of a non-royal mother, yielded without a claim. Mozaffar, a middle-aged man long overlooked by his father, had waited far from the capital, in Tabriz, for the crown. Now it was his.

The harem's ululations quickly turned somber as hundreds of women awaited their fates. Most would be married off to merchants, as marrying one of the Shah's wives or concubines carried no stigma—on the contrary, it was a mark of prestige. Those with children received stipends to support them.

To the twelve-year-old princes, their second-eldest brother appeared more like a grandfather. At forty-four, after twenty-five years of waiting, Mozaffar al-Din Shah looked far older than his age. His drooping eyelids resembled tortoise shells sliding sluggishly across his face while deep furrows etched his forehead. His broom-like white mustaches, spread wide as if charged with static, added to his worn and prematurely aged appearance. Though outwardly kind, he was, in truth, detached and indifferent.

Within weeks, the new Shah called the twins to sit on his knees and discuss their futures. He decreed that they would inherit the village of Poonak, along with its lands and income, ensuring the family's comfort for generations. He granted their mother, Tala Khanum, a modest annuity. She returned to live with her father. Turning to the Premier Amin Soltan, who stood behind him, the Shah took a royal decree wrapped in gold ribbon. He gently asked one twin, "Which of you is Sardar? *Ah, je vois que votre français est excellent, n'est-ce pas?* Sardar's chest swelled with pride at the compliment. "We will send you to France to study with Monsieur."

Then, he swiveled like a turtle and faced the other twin. "And you must be Saleh Mirza?" he remarked with a faintly tragic smile at his deduction. "I hear you are an excellent scholar. You will remain here to study at the palace and later enroll at the Dar al-Funun." The prestigious polytechnic institute would prepare Saleh for a future in medicine, engineering, military science or geology. With a few strokes of the pen, the twins' destinies diverged. Sardar Mirza's journey to Europe and Saleh Mirza's education in Tehran would separate the brothers for ten years—a forced division they never forgave.

For Sardar Mirza, his time in Europe felt surreal, like a dream of sinking to the ocean floor and frantically swimming toward the faint light above, only to awaken gasping for air in his bed in Paris. The city's mechanical hum, the scent of bakeries and the melodic cadence of spoken French reassured him, anchoring him in the stability of a civilized world. His journey to Europe took months, beginning with a ride to Tabriz, via Qazvin and Zanjan, before reaching Odessa, the gateway to the West. A solemn farewell marked the departure. On a clear, cold morning, snow sparkled on the distant Alborz Mountains. The barren, gray expanse of stone and scrub stretched endlessly as the brothers rode hand in hand for the two-day journey to Qazvin.

Their fourteen-year-old brother, Mohammad Reza Mirza Rokn es-Saltaneh—known as le Bœuf—accompanied them, having been entrusted with carrying the seal to the new Crown

Prince, Mohammad Ali, a boy who, as tradition demanded, resided in Tabriz. The reigning Shahs didn't trust their sons.

Khodrat, Sardar Mirza's loyal servant, followed closely on horseback. He used his long, black beard to hide his tears. Tasked with ensuring the safety of the three princes, Simon Khan—a tall, ascetic Armenian with a fatalistic outlook—rode alongside them. A trusted confidant and polyglot fluent in French, Russian, Persian and Turkish, Simon Khan straddled both Eastern and Western cultures. Born in Odessa, his life would tragically end decades later during the Armenian genocide.

After a grueling day's ride, the travelers spent a wretched night at their first camp. Though the air was frigid, gusts of wind carried an overpowering, decaying stench that seeped into every corner of the site, thick as the soles of their worn leather shoes. The odor robbed them of appetite and left them restless while the relentless cries of hungry jackals and the mournful braying of a stranded donkey echoed through the darkness. The donkey's eerily persistent cries rose and fell in haunting waves throughout the night. Was it not the prophet who warned that the braying of a donkey signals the presence of Satan nearby?

By four in the morning, they had performed their ablutions with dirt and offered their prayers in haste. A sparse meal of tea, feta and bread readied them for the road. By five, they pressed westward. The oppressive stench worsened with every mile. The donkey's braying grew louder and more despairing. Wrapping their shawls tightly over their noses and mouths, they pushed forward until they found the source—a grim open graveyard where peasants discarded their aged and diseased animals. Hundreds of skeletal remains littered the natural pit in varying states of decay.

Among them, a dying donkey lay halfway down the slope, still breathing, its glazed eyes observing the commotion stirred by the riders.

Simon Khan gestured silently at a fellow rider, drawing his index finger across his throat in command. The rider dismounted, unsheathed a knife, and approached the suffering animal. As he knelt beside its head, the donkey brayed one last time, its yellowed, stained teeth exposed in defiance. With a swift, clean motion, the rider plunged the blade into the soft spot beneath its muzzle and withdrew it, sparing the creature further agony. The donkey gurgled and breathed its final sigh.

By sunset, the group arrived at Qazvin's outskirts, the dead of winter amplifying the city's desolation. Passing through the gardens and groves, the boys, accustomed to the palace's opulence, saw only a bleak terrain of gnarled, leafless woodlands—hardly reminiscent of the once-glorious Safavid capital. Peasant smoke rose from burning cow dung, winding through sparse trees like threadbare wisps. The party entered the town through narrow, frozen alleys, their horses' hooves slipping against the icy mud and snow with a sound like grinding stone. Unlike the wide streets their father had built in Tehran, Qazvin's alleyways seemed untouched since Genghis Khanh's era, exuding a sense of ruin and neglect. Half-starved, festering dogs chased the riders half-heartedly, responding to fading instincts. Fearing injury from the cramped surroundings, the boys lifted their legs, precariously balancing cross-legged atop their saddles.

Closer to the bazaar, the town showed signs of life. Dim lanterns illuminated modest workshops, their proprietors emerging to entice the travelers toward their wares. Late that evening, the royal party arrived at the grand Sa'd al-Saltaneh caravanserai. The largest of its kind in the empire, it was a marvel commissioned by the Shah and newly completed with the finest bricks—a veritable Ritz-Carlton of its era.

"What is a Reets Karton?" I asked.

"A luxury hotel, like our Hilton uptown," Dal replied with a hint of mischief.

Servants swarmed out from every corner to greet them. The travelers occupied three guest suites, or hujrehs, each elevated three feet above the courtyard. Inside, the room's bedding lay neatly on the floor, along with a felt skullcap, comb and toothbrush on each pillow. Though used, these amenities anticipated the toiletries found in modern hotels.

For the three princes, order seemed to return to their lives. After a restful sleep, they awoke to a princely breakfast. Later, they washed and rejuvenated at the Sadieh Bathhouse behind the caravanserai, preparing for their last day together. As they scrubbed the grime from their skin, the twins questioned why they couldn't continue traveling together to Tabriz. "Who would it harm?" they ask. Relaxing in warm, cleansing waters, their thoughts turned toward a solution. If le Bœuf planned to return to Tehran after delivering the seal to the Crown Prince, could Saleh Mirza not join him after a brief stay in Tabriz? They knew defying the Shah had consequences, but as they sweated away the last traces of weariness, le Bœuf, bold and cunning, reassured them. "Leave it to me," he said.

After their baths, le Bœuf summoned his servant and instructed him to fetch a professional letter writer. These scribes, easily found near mosques or official buildings, worked from small wooden setups displaying samples of their calligraphy. The samples were a mere formality, unnecessary for the illiterate customers who studied them like novices marveling at a work of art. Le Bœuf insisted on hiring the finest calligrapher money could buy. The chosen man resembled an Indian Maharishi, sported a toothless grin and a tongueless, gummy smile—a punishment inflicted decades earlier by a governor for a minor transgression. Sitting cross-legged on the floor, the calligrapher began to transcribe as le Bœuf dictated:

To Their Highnesses Mohammad Reza, Saleh and Sardar Mirza, my esteemed uncles: We welcome our uncles to Tabriz in the name of God and His infinite kindness. We have dispatched our courier to greet you and deliver our warmest regards. With great anticipation, we await your arrival. Having heard much about your inseparable bond, we would rather not receive the sad half if we could welcome the happy whole instead. We expect your presence at court by the end of the month. Signed and sealed by the Crown Prince.

Once the letter was complete, le Bœuf dismissed the calligrapher and unwrapped a piece of intricately sewn cloth, its velvet interior cradling the royal seal. The emblem—a lion proudly holding a sword with an irregularly shaped sun rising behind it—glimmered in the candlelight. Melting yellow wax, le Bœuf carefully affixed the seal to the letter, his tongue flicking at his lower lip in concentration. As the wax hardened, he smiled, satisfied with his handiwork.

Finding a suitable messenger proved trickier. Le Bœuf instructed his servant to search for a luti near the bazaar. The term, a precursor to the English "lout," denoted a blend of chivalry and cunning. After interviewing several colorful characters, le Bœuf settled on a robust Turk with a propeller-like black mustache, a manly stance, rudimentary riding skills and an infuriatingly smug grin. Le Bœuf quickly wiped the grin from the man's face with a few pointed remarks. The Turk's lack of riding expertise posed a problem; he flopped atop the saddle like a scarecrow. To compensate, le Bœuf had him walk the horse into the caravanserai. The prince then spent the afternoon dressing the man appropriately, and drilling him on to bow and present the letter. The man's accent worked to their advantage, given Tabriz's predominantly Turkish population. After generously paying the "messenger," le Bœuf ensured he understood the necessity of disappearing for several months after delivering the letter. As the evening fell, le Bœuf and Simon Khan smoked their ghalian (waterpipe) on the veranda, seated atop a Baluchi rug. The messenger, right on time, interrupted the tranquil moment. He called loudly for the prince, his tone suitably urgent.

"For God's sake," le Bœuf muttered, more bored than annoyed, "tell the man I am right here. Bring him to me—quietly." The messenger played his part well. He approached with the letter in hand. Le Bœuf broke the seal, read the missive, and handed it casually to Simon Khan. "This should please the boys," he remarked. Simon Khan read the letter carefully, his expression skeptical. "The Shah's orders are the Shah's orders," he said quietly. "Not even the Crown Prince can countermand them." Le Bœuf, taken aback, quickly masked his surprise. Simon Khan had accepted the letter's authenticity but questioned the Crown Prince's authority to override his father's decree.

"You are wise, Simon Khan," le Bœuf said smoothly. "We

face a predicament. Do we arrive with one prince devastated, crying his eyes out? Displeasing one master to placate another seems unavoidable. From what I've heard, the Crown Prince takes offense easily."

Simon Khan brooded briefly before suggesting: "If Your Highness permits, I will safeguard the letter to explain matters should we face inquiries in the capital."

"Simon Khan, you may keep it for as long as it serves you," le Bœuf replied with deliberate nonchalance. Yet, as he watched Simon Khan pocket the letter, le Bœuf knew a reckoning would come. For now, that thought did little to diminish his joy in sharing the "good news" with the boys.

The following day, the three princes, accompanied by Simon Khan, Khodrat and five riders, set out on a 120-mile journey to Zanjan. The trip took four days, buoyed by the twins' exuberant spirits. The group's high morale mirrored the sunny weather and shared camaraderie. The scenery shifted as they traveled north, the gray flatlands giving way to verdant hills and elevated landscapes. Simon Khan and Khodrat taught the twins how to hunt, chase hares and trust their horses in thick terrain. Le Bœuf's antics kept everyone laughing; one morning, he crawled beneath the horses to loosen the guards' saddles. When the guards mounted in unison, they toppled to the ground, prompting uproarious laughter from all. Each afternoon, three guards rode ahead with mules to set up camp. When the rest arrived, a skinned deer or plucked pheasants roasted over the fire. In the evenings, the group gathered around the flames, listening to Simon Khan recount tales of distant lands like Odessa and Erzerum. He spoke of Tatar races in the Caucasus and the bashi-bazouks who once roamed as marauders.

Years later, in Paris, Sardar Mirza would hang a painting of a bashi-bazouk by Jean-Léon Gérôme in his bedroom at the Hôtel Lutetia. Though Picasso teased him endlessly for his romanticized vision of the Orient, Sardar Mirza understood better than most—and certainly better than Picasso—the fine line between romance and reality. The joyful camaraderie of those four days would forever remain etched in their memories, though they could not foresee the events that would soon cloud those sunny moments.

Tanned, healthy and full of talk, the princes entered Zanjan on the fourth day. It wasn't a welcoming city for the Qajars; the Shah's premier had put several people to death in Zanjan for promoting the Baha'i faith. The Court viewed the spread of the Baha'i movement as a threat to the dynasty. Prudently, they crossed the city's twisted alleys at midday prayer. The ceremonial front guards refrained from the customary shouting of the royals' arrival. They stayed for the night at the caravanserai Sangi.

In a convivial mood, the party didn't see what Simon Khan saw: an aggressive mob with unformed intentions. He decided to begin the hundred-and-eight-mile journey toward Tabriz the following day, a between-fire-and-flame decision. Flurries of snowflakes stuck to their eyelashes; the day turned cold; the clouds grew thick. On the first day, they trotted briskly to cover thirty miles. They saw fewer riders and fewer men walking the road. Plenty of dirt-poor women, children swaddled to their backs in dirty rags or hanging onto their desiccated breasts, begged piteously as the royal party passed. A few women managed to grab a rider's leg and run alongside the horse for a few paces.

"Give me bread money. May God not take your children. For Ali's sake, give me a shahi." Shoeless, snot-nosed, filthy ragamuffins ran after them for quite a distance. The pursuers would give up, showing their boyish spirit in high-pitched whistles and throwing a few stones at the backs of the animals. Simon Khan threw change off the path but never slowed the pace. Snow and rain alternated all through the day. They spent a cold night; dampness seeped through their bones. It was impossible to keep the fire burning with any intensity.

They made good progress the following morning, but the wind had whirled the snow furiously by afternoon. The riders felt they had entered a tunnel of needles that cut their faces raw. They huddled on their saddles, wrapped themselves in shawls and rode closely. The guards encircled the boys' horses and the pack mules. Packs of wolves or jackals could attack isolated animals. By six in the afternoon, they couldn't see two horse-lengths before them. Simon Khan ordered the group to form a circle. They forced the mounts to lie in a circle around them. He had the animals' front and back legs tied together. He covered the nervous beasts and their riders with traveling kilims. The two brothers huddled beside one of their horses' warm, yielding stomachs. They ate dried bread. They hardly slept.

Simon Khan woke everyone up in the dark, around three in the morning. "Your Highnesses," he said, "we need to get the horses moving, or they will freeze to death." Inches of snow had settled on the camp. The wind had stopped; the frenzied flurries of yesterday transformed into large, patient flakes that settled demurely onto the ground. The men approached their hidden mounts to untie their legs. The thick snow had muted the universe. On Simon Khan's signal, the snow-covered camp abruptly moved. The horses, startled at the whistling and the tugging of the riders, rose awkwardly the way horses stand up. They shook the snow off the heavy gilims that covered them. The men began packing the mules. The movement revived the living.

They took a slow, deliberate pace on the third and fourth days. It snowed all day and night, not relenting until the afternoon of the fourth day. They stopped often to let the horses rest; the steeds tired quickly, plodding their legs in and out of snowdrifts. At the front, the mules, more agile than the horses despite their heavier loads, coaxed them to take the next step. On the fourth day, they made camp amid an abandoned group of hovels—an array of roofless walls of mud and straw. Simon Khan had grown quiet. With the passing of the storm, he knew that a cruel, pitiless cold would descend on them. His responsibility for the princes weighed heavily. The boys' teeth chattered, but they had held up well. Simon Khan ordered the men to make a shelter by tethering black tent cloth to the abandoned walls. They cut pieces of the mud walls to make crude, low-burning bricks from their straw. The "bricks" burned for a long time—with meager heat but plenty of smoke. Simon Khan understood they had to pick up the pace. They had brought food for five days and were running low: only dried bread and figs remained. He estimated another three days of travel.

They woke before dawn to a bitter cold. The twins' faces looked pinched and thin; their elder brother was in no better shape. The landscape, empurpled in the waning moonlight, looked unenticing; an untidy wilderness lay ahead of them waiting to sprout green, and the barrenness behind them seemed unending, a hopeless vista. A cacophony of jackals filled the silence. The wolves of our country don't howl. Their distant silhouettes stood on the circular horizon, a sharp reminder of their presence. The horses shifted their weight on a thin, crunchy layer of icy snow. It sounded like people biting into dozens of crisp apples. The sun rose orange-colored, without heat, but soon it brightened into a chilly, sunny day.

Before noon, they reached a shallow, frozen river. The sound of gurgling water beneath the ice revived them for no reason. Water ran along the river's shores, splashing against the smooth pebbles, appearing and then disappearing under the ice. After days of riding in the snow, Simon Khan celebrated privately. He believed they were northwest of Hashtrood, the region of eight north-south rivers. It meant the riders could reach Tabriz in two days. In the distance, among a few hovels near the frozen river, Simon Khan thought he could see some animals meandering. He ordered a quicker pace.

A pack of jackals sat in the middle of the river on top of the thicker ice, busily pulling and pushing at a carcass probably killed by wolves. The sound of the horses didn't disturb their feeding frenzy until the party was nearly on top of them. The jackals scattered at first but then held their ground. They sneered suspiciously, heads twisted and bloody muzzles low to the ground. They watched the riders from a hundred yards downriver. The remnants of the feast would haunt the memories of the boys; the half-eaten bodies of a woman and two children, their backs frozen to the ice, lay prone, their stomachs torn open and emptied. Their extremities were missing. Their faces were cleanly chewed. The stark remains gave the impression of cadavers shamelessly exposing their insides for all to see.

The horses circled the bodies awkwardly. Beneath the clomping of their hooves, beneath the ice and snow, the muted river gargled water to the choking point. The jackals growled, ever more distant. The men had eyes for the young boys, whose silent tears lay frozen on their sun-and-snow-burned cheeks.

Hearing the jackals slink back to finish their ghastly meal, the party pushed on with little rest and food all day—as if to put the most distance between themselves and the frozen bodies. The wind, pitiless and penetrating, picked up again. They spent their coldest night yet. Simon Khan and Khodrat sat up all night, the boys sleeping between their legs, swaddled in the gilims and any other wrappings they could find.

Sardar Mirza coughed all night and awoke in the morning with a low fever. Simon Khan and Khodrat understood the gravity. The ultimate punishment awaited them if any harm came to the royal princes. Khodrat asked the feverish prince to ride with him, but the boy refused summarily. They started in the dark again. Simon Khan pushed the horses harder. He knew the horses would be worthless after this trip.

An hour into their march, with the horizon a dull red streak, Sardar Mirza's horse lagged by twenty yards. One lone guard trailed the column. Out of nowhere, three wolves sprang into action, targeting both horses simultaneously. These light gray wolves, smaller in our country, compensated for their size with remarkable speed and powerful jaws. The startled horses thrashed and whinnied in panic, colliding with one another and nearly unseating their riders.

Two of the wolves concentrated their assault on the guard's horse. The guard shouted for help but kept his composure. Drawing his sword, he swung at one of the wolves, which had latched onto the back of the saddle with its teeth, hanging in mid-air. The blade struck the wolf's muzzle, slashing across its left eye and skull, prompting a sharp, canine yelp of pain. The sword's arc cut deep into the guard's horse, slicing just above the stifle joint. Reacting instantly to the injury, the horse lunged in agony, crushing the second wolf beneath its hooves as it attempted to sink its teeth into the smooth belly of the other mount. In its desperate struggle, the horse toppled over, throwing the guard headfirst into the deep snow, which mercifully cushioned his fall. The second wolf, battered but alive, squeezed out from beneath the fallen horse and retreated, conceding defeat.

The third wolf latched onto the hind leg of Sardar Mirza's horse, sinking its teeth deeply into the hock. The horse whinnied in pain. It thrashed its hindquarters to shake the predator loose. Sardar Mirza clung tightly to the saddle, his weakened body swaying precariously. Despite its fierce kicks, the wolf's unyielding jaws controlled the horse's movement. Exhausted by fever and the struggle, Sardar Mirza's strength gave way, his legs splayed in the air and he was nearly thrown to the ground. His horse, hypnotized by the trauma, gave up the fight. It sat back on its hind legs and looked philosophical as the wolf tore viciously at its leg. The hungry wolf's ferocious head, a blur, jerked left and right to rip a scrap off the leg. Simon Khan galloped toward the scene, revolver in hand. As Sardar Mirza slipped backward from the saddle, Simon Khan fired a single shot, instantly striking the wolf and killing it. Reaching out, he grabbed the boy and pulled him to safety just as the spent horse crumpled to the ground.

They bled the two horses to death using the same technique as for the abandoned donkey. Saleh Mirza rode with Simon Khan. Sardar Mirza, trembling violently, rode with Khodrat, who wrapped the boy warmly and held him securely. Despite his injury, the guard earned a gold coin for his bravery and continued the journey, his arm in a sling, astride Saleh Mirza's horse. By the next day, as the midday call to prayer echoed from the mosques, the party reached the broad highway to Tabriz. Known as Dar-il-Sultaneh, the abode of the kingdom. Tabriz had once been home to half a million people, boasting 300 caravanserais and 250 mosques before an earthquake reduced its grandeur. Now a bustling city of 150,000, its healthy climate earned it the nickname "the Fever-Dissipating City." From afar, the travelers could see the imposing Arch of Ali Shah, a thick-walled structure visible from all approaches. Simon Khan sent two guards ahead, shouting, "Make way, the princes are coming," and enforcing their command with firm strikes of their rods. His priority was to get the ailing prince to the palace quickly.

To avoid the city's congestion, they directed their route toward the summer palace, where Crown Prince Mohammad Ali had established his winter residence. Despite its location in the city's south, the palace sat on 75 acres of gardens curiously named the Northern Gardens. Entering a grand brick archway, they proceeded along a long double avenue leading to the palace. In front of a fifty-foot fountain, a waiting group stood assembled. Le Bœuf, weary and cold from the journey, began to sweat nervously. He sensed that reckoning was near, though its severity remained unclear. Upon reaching the fountain, Khodrat carefully handed Sardar Mirza to a waiting servant, who gently eased him to the ground. Saleh Mirza, eager to dismount, swung his legs without caution. Simon Khan, quick to act, caught his arm, preventing what would have been an embarrassing fall. Saleh Mirza immediately ran to his brother, wrapping him in an embrace and whispering words of reassurance. Sardar Mirza, barely conscious, seemed unaware of his surroundings or his brother's comforting words.

A tall, foreign-looking man stepped forward. Clean-shaven except for a meticulously groomed mustache, he wore the traditional tails of a tutor. Without turning, he addressed those behind him. "What they say about the Highnesses' devotion to one another is true. Our French Prince does look unwell, *n'est-ce pas?*" His atrocious Russian-accented French carried a note of derision. We meet for the first time the twenty-three-year-old Seraya Shapshal, known at court as Shapshal Khan. Born in Bahçesaray, Crimea, and of Karaim Jewish descent, he served as the Crown Prince's tutor. Within a decade, Shapshal would exchange his tutor's attire for the regalia of a court minister. Even now, he emanated thinly veiled hostility toward the young princes.

Addressing Simon Khan with disdain, Shapshal remarked, "Let's clarify this situation, Your Grace. I can't imagine any scenario where the renowned Simon Khan would disobey His Majesty's direct orders." He paused, his tone sharp. "We received an agitated and perplexing telegram last week from His Majesty's minister."

Unaware of the brewing storm, Simon Khan replied evenly, "When I received the Crown Prince's orders, I naturally assumed you had cleared it with Tehran." His genuine naivety pained Le Bœuf, who stood apprehensively behind the boys, anticipating what would come next

"What order?" Shapshal Khan rolled his eyes and stretched out his hand. "The telegraph did mention an order from the Crown Prince. We have looked through all our records. We didn't send such an order." Simon Khan drew the forged order from inside his jacket. As he read the order, the confusion on Shapshal Khan's face gave Simon Khan the confidence to look around. He gave the boys a reassuring smile. It stabbed at le Bœuf's heart.

"I wrote it—to keep my brothers together for a while longer," he yelled. He didn't want the charade to humiliate Simon Khan. "Simon Khan knows nothing. I have the Crown Prince's seal, with our brother's compliments. I used it to fool everyone."

Simon Khan's smile froze. He lost all color. "Your Highnesses—" he began to sputter.

"I asked him to do it," Saleh Mirza said. "We wanted to see Sardar Mirza off in Tabriz."

"*Mais c'est charmant* ça. *Tant de courage*," Shapshal pronounced. "We have clarified the misunderstanding. If Your Highnesses will follow me, the Crown Prince will await you in the interior court in the reception room." Simon Khan made to follow. Shapshal, with a curt hand gesture, stopped him. "We might need you later, Simon Khan. Right now, the Crown Prince wants to see his uncles in private."

"The boy is sick, and the other two are near exhaustion," Simon Khan whispered in the Russian's ear. "Let them rest first."

"It will be up to the Crown Prince, Your Grace," Shapshal Khan said.

Shapshal and the three princes walked to the large interior court lined with flower beds. They entered a circular building with a marble fountain in the center, empty in winter. Shapshal knocked at the heavy door. Someone said, "Enter," in Turkish. They walked into a small room adorned with paintings of foreign envoys who had visited Tabriz—the walls and ceilings covered with tiny mirror pieces typical of Persiranian and Turkish palaces. Erect behind a bureau, the Crown Prince looked younger than his twenty-four years. On each side of his puffed-up chest, a five-by-five matrix of medals adorned the smart black military uniform. He had the overweight look of a spoiled adolescent who frequents pastry shops. "Not your kind of size, my fluffy one," Dal added.

The Crown Prince looked angry. His lower lip hung out like a young boy about to cry. It made him seem less severe, but his trembling mustache displayed an angry person. The Crown Prince listened while Shapshal Khan whispered the circumstances. The Tehran court minister had sent several telegrams in their search for explanations. They accused the Crown Prince's court of incompetence. As clarity descended, the Crown Prince's mood improved. He talked to them first in Turkish. They did not understand. He switched to the Turkish-accented Farsi.

"Welcome, my uncles," he said. "Before putting this incident behind us, we must let Tehran know you have arrived. Thanks to God, you are alive. I hear you had a trying trip. You understand we need to clarify the circumstances of using our seal to our father and friends in Tehran. And we have a small problem. Once we send the telegram to Tehran, they will invariably ask what punishment I have ordered for the lèse-majesté. We ask you, why wait for the inevitable question? Don't answer. We have asked ourselves the same question. We come to the same answer each time. Let's not waste a telegram. Let us mete out your punishment quickly and be done with it." He rubbed his hands in satisfaction. He had considered the problem from all angles. "We will witness the bastinado outside immediately," he told the tutor.

"Your Highness," le Bœuf sputtered. "My young brothers had nothing to do with this. A bastinado could kill him"—he pointed to Sardar Mirza, who swayed, leaning on his brother. "Look at him, Your Highness. He is burning with fever."

"Don't overdramatize," the Crown Prince replied. "Take your punishment and be done with it. We want you and your brother to leave us immediately after it. Go back to Tehran. You are not welcome in this palace."

The cruelty of the order sank in. Besides the danger of the bastinado to Sardar Mirza, the order forced them to return to Tehran in February. A trip they had just experienced could mean death for Le Bœuf and Saleh Mirza, especially without Simon Khan as a guide.

Shapshal escorted them outside. The crowd of courtiers had gathered in silence. The courts, government offices, and schools regularly practice this vicious punishment. The beaten did not get debarred from their ongoing activities. Once inflicted, the Ministers and premiers returned to their duties. To punish three princes of the realm at once, two so young, was unprecedented. They had cleared a strip of ground of all snow. Silk carpets lay on the ground. The court showed full respect for the rank of the victims.

The three boys lay next to one another, a few feet apart. Sardar Mirza immediately fell asleep—or passed out. He lay with his hand outstretched in his twin brother's hand. In the middle position, Saleh Mirza turned his head toward his twin. It would be ten years before he saw his brother again. Two men bared the princes' feet. Both bowed deeply. A mustachioed man with a waspy, thin waist asked for their pardon. He placed a bamboo pole under all six feet, beneath the ankles. He placed another bamboo pole of similar size on top of their ankles. He firmly tied the two ends of the bamboo sticks. The feet stuck out between the sticks like *taftoon* bread.

They waited this way for a few minutes before the Crown Prince emerged. Shapshal Khan followed. No speeches. There were around forty witnesses, among them Simon Khan and Khodrat—the latter using his beard once again to collect and hide his tears. The Crown Prince made a sign. The two muscular servants picked up the bamboo poles and raised them from the ground. The six soles pointed to the sky. Three mustachioed men, including the wispy-waisted leader, picked out three long sticks from a bundle on the ground. They whipped each stick in the air with a deft wrist movement, listening for the pure note with heads aslant, like dogs before a chase. A pure note meant no internal cracks. Once each had found his perfect stick, two of them took their places on each side to flog away at the feet of Sardar Mirza and *Le Boeuf* sideways. The more expert leader placed himself in the middle to lash out the length of Saleh Mirza's feet—a more challenging position. It needed care not to break the toes.

It was January 28, 1896, a leap year, a Tuesday. It was late afternoon and cold. A soft northern light lent a tragic atmosphere. Three strong arms stretched into the air, and three sticks came past three men's shoulders, trembling gently with their own weight. The men waited for the Crown Prince to give the final nod. The young princes' frozen, reddened soles were about to get skinned. The Shah, a fleetingly kind man, was incensed at his eldest son's treatment of his royal brothers. His anger lasted a day.

"Professor, I prefer their lot to mine," I said.

"How so?" the Professor asked, leaning to the side to hear my explanation.

"In the last few days, I have been beaten up uncontrollably on several occasions. I have faced near death with little explanation. I sit in this prison without due process. A bastinado has structure. You know the outcome; it may be painful and will end. The torture comes from not knowing. " He patted my side like a rider pats a horse's neck.

"Wise words, my bag of lard. Don't we live ignorant of our death? Let me go on, and you might change your mind."

Saleh Mirza and *Le Bœuf* were escorted out of the city the same day without knowing whether Sardar Mirza would survive. They could not walk for days. They rode back in the cold. At the end of each day of riding, servants carried them from their mounts to their camp, a bitter humiliation for *Le Bœuf*.

Saleh Mirza barely survived the trip back to the capital. It took months to restore him to health. He survived by coddling his hate and anger. He nursed each moment they spent in the company of the Crown Prince as a moment to remember. He would mature into a taciturn man who saw life as a series of random events to bear without complaint. He formed a solid moral structure in his nuanced brain. He believed his travails had prepared him someday to redress unfairness through the exercise of power—but it was years before he understood what he meant by power.

Sardar Mirza came closer to death. He lay in bed for weeks with doctors in attendance. Fearful of the consequences, the Crown Prince kept the illness a secret. Sardar Mirza emerged with a lasting *joie de vivre*. He seldom placed himself in situations where life could deal him a lousy hand. He believed that by steering cleverly, he could avoid life's slurs. From this philosophy, he developed a habit of not thinking too deeply about the past; he saw no sense in it. Aesthetics attracted him. Ugliness repelled him. Yet he would suffer more than his brother.

After Norouz—the New Year, the first spring day—Simon Khan, Khodrat and Sardar Mirza began their journey toward Paris. They took what was then the most direct route up across Transcaucasia and the Black Sea to Odesa. From there, the railways gave them many alternatives to reach Paris. Thin and drawn, the prince had lost his boyishness, but his eyes brimmed with humor. The Crown Prince, improbably feeling a smidgeon of guilt, agreed to send an accompanying guard as far as Urumiah. There, they engaged a coach upholstered in thick, cerise-colored, buttoned leather and drawn by six horses to travel to Tiflis. The carriage, essentially a house on wheels, had a large box reserved for the ladies and a smaller one for the male passengers. Sardar Mirza remembered little of the other passengers; Simon Khan could sit in the male section, but the prince rode on the carriage next to the Cossack driver, a Taras Bulba type, who wielded his whip as if signing historical documents. The driver, who at every stop invited all sorts of men to punch him in the stomach, laughed aloud at everything Sardar Mirza said, even though he understood nothing.

With the return of spring, the cold now merely refreshed Sardar Mirza. They made good time thanks to their triple-crown padarozhuna—the Russian license which allowed fresh horses at every stop. They covered 350 miles, most of it through Russian territory. They traveled via Julfa and entered Russia, used a wire-rope ferry to cross the Aras River, passed through the ancient city of Nakhjavan and went on to Tiflis.

The road to Tiflis, teeming with life and activity, brought their carriage to a crawl. Homemade carts jostled alongside droshkies drawn by trotting horses. Oxen with sagging double chins plodded steadily while camel caravans and overburdened donkeys trudged forward, all making way for the grandeur of their passing carriage. Though poverty was evident, it lacked the same air of desperation they had observed during their winter journey. Even to their inexperienced eyes, the Russian villages along the route seemed more prosperous than the squalid settlements of hovels they had left behind.

The landscape retained its arid character, yet the abundant watermills lining the rivers hinted at greater fertility in the surrounding lands. Peasants, carrying buckets of milk balanced on sturdy shoulders, moved about purposefully. Robust women, vociferous and commanding, shouted at the flocks of sheep and goats milling at their feet. The cacophony of life—the braying, bleating and shouts—was ever-present, yet it carried a tone of vigor rather than the desperate, forlorn cries and pleading they had witnessed earlier in their journey.

On the fifth day, from the top of the carriage, Sardar Mirza beheld a molten silver line shimmering on the horizon. The driver pointed out Mount Ararat rising to their left, fifty miles away. But biblical Ararat held little interest for the prince. He had spent his life waking to the sight of the Alborz Range, whose peaks, crowning the land north of Tehran, were far more magnificent than lonely Ararat. The silver shimmer expanded, swallowing the horizon, and as they approached, it resolved into a vast lake encircled by softened volcanic hills. The lake enthralled him. Never before had he seen a body of water so immense. The group spent half the day picnicking on its shores, feasting on fresh trout bought from the locals and dipping their bare legs into the heart-stopping cold of the lake. At night, they lodged in two-room Russian post houses, free of charge. Newly erected English-made iron telegraph poles—symbols of progress and the reason for the princes' swift summons—lined the road, courtesy of Messrs Siemens.

They arrived in Tiflis at midday under a torrent of rain, which turned the city into a sea of mud. The Kur River split the town, creating an island in its midst. The rising waters nearly swallowed bridges, yet the people of Tiflis, unfazed by the weather, carried on with their affairs. In any other city, a royal traveler might have been received as an honored guest at the palace of Grand Duke Michael; however, the people of Tiflis harbored deep reservations about the Qajars. Sardar Mirza's ancestor, Agha Mohammad Khan, had sacked the city and razed its churches a century earlier.

Famed for its sulfur baths, the city was split into colonies. The Russian quarter, with its grand buildings, dominated all others. Beyond the city, 150,000 Russian Cossack officers, in their colorful uniforms, bunked in barracks sprawled across the hillsides—a deliberate show of force meant to intimidate the Turks to the west.

Only Constantinople and Odessa could rival Tiflis in diversity. The Caucasus, known in Arabic as Djabal al-Alsun, "the Mountain of Languages," was a patchwork of peoples. Ossetians conversed with Tajiks in a muddled Farsi. A Mingrelian beggar scoffed at a handout from an Abkhazian refugee. Over a shared hookah, a Talysh intellectual urged his Lezgian companion to resist Russian tyranny. Tatar peasants haggled over silver-stamped daggers sold by Persiranians merchants. German millennialists debated the Second Coming with Greek Orthodox believers. Talmudic Jews feuded bitterly with their anti-Talmudic counterparts. Turks eyed Armenian shopkeepers with the deep mistrust that would soon explode into bloodshed. Meanwhile, hotel-owning Frenchmen vied with stiff-collared English diplomats for dominance in the city's social sphere.

In his element, Simon Khan made straight for the American store, purchasing ready-made suits that required only minor adjustments. He filled a trunk with Western attire for them all— starched white shirts, waistcoats, silk socks, shoes and a pair of galoshes for each. Sardar Mirza, a born dandy, would later recall their first foray into Western fashion with peals of laughter—the notion of wearing off-the-rack American suits astonished his aristocratic French friends. They lodged at the Hotel de Londres that night, awaiting their train to Poti the next day. The first European-style establishment Sardar Mirza had ever encountered, the hotel introduced him and Khodrat to modern plumbing. The idea of bathing in a tub of water—stewing in one's dirt—elicited murmurs of disgust, and no amount of persuasion could convince them to sit on a porcelain toilet. For the rest of their journey, they squatted atop the toilet seats of various hotels, careful not to let any part of their bodies touch the foreign contraption. (Later, peer pressure at school would remedy his habits.) At dinner, no amount of aristocratic bluff could disguise their struggle with the potage du jour. The prince, unwilling to lower his standards, hesitated before resigning himself to the indignity of eating with a spoon.

It rained through the night. By morning, they had reason to thank Simon Khan for those galoshes. The streets had turned into a foot-swallowing quagmire. It forced those without proper footwear to go barefoot. Women in European-style dresses, their faces veiled in Eastern-style hijabs, perched on the backs of Albanian water carriers to cross the mire. Men lost their shoes in the mud. The prince and his companions took a phaeton to the railway station, a monumental structure and early precursor to Soviet architecture, standing miles outside town. Several times, Simon Khan tossed a few coins to bystanders to elicit their help to push the carriage wheels free of the muck.

The train to Poti, a port on the Black Sea, had run for twenty-five years, and little had changed. The prince settled into a window seat in the first-class compartment. His eyes drank in the scenery with the rapt attention of a child before a television. Accustomed to the arid landscapes of Persiran, he marveled at the lush beech and pine forests, the well-tended fields bursting with Indian corn, and the deep valleys filled with fruit trees and ferns. Mounds of thistles, adorned with red and bruise-colored berries, blurred past while ancient forts loomed on distant hills. He did not sleep for a moment during the seventeen-hour journey.

The well-provisioned train stopped frequently, filling the air with the rich, homey scent of food. Samovars on board brewed excellent tea, served in large glasses and refilled at each station. As the train labored up the Suram Pass, its three engines chugged steadily and deliberately. As they descended toward sea level, the Rioni River meandered alongside, now on the right, now on the left.

"Now, don't fall asleep yet, my living bed. We are getting to the good parts," the professor said. Indeed, my imagination had accompanied the little prince inside the rhythmic train, and my eyes had gotten heavy from sleep.

In 1897, Poti—built on a malarial marsh teeming with flies and frogs—bore more resemblance to an American gold rush town than a refined European port. The city's famous mayor, Niko Nikoladze, had begun his ambitious reconstruction efforts. It gave the city a raw, unfinished look. The travelers stayed three nights at the barely passable Hotel Jacquot before boarding a flat-bottomed steamer to cross the bar. From there, they transferred to another steamer for the five-day voyage across the Black Sea to Odesa.

The upper decks of the first-class cabins housed a pair of Russian generals, five wealthy Turkish merchants in red fezzes and half a dozen English diplomats. Next to the prince's berth, a French aristocrat and his family occupied a suite of two bedrooms—his wife and three daughters, all prettily dressed in muslin and lace. Khodrat and the other servants of the first-class passengers were lodged in second-class cabins, while the lowest deck, in third class, teemed with a chaotic mix of travelers, their makeshift luggage stacked around them.

Few places could match the Black Sea ports for their fusion of East and West, yet the separation remained stark. To Europeans, the Orientals were little more than savages needing Christian refinement. Simon Khan understood this well. To spare the young prince unnecessary humiliation, he took every opportunity to teach him Western etiquette.

The steamer set off, skirting the Abkhazian coast. Through the portholes, endless forests of towering timber unfurled in disciplined rows. Simon Khan spent the first afternoon walking the decks, cultivating acquaintances. He approached the first-class passengers with his customary charm. "I am His Royal Highness's secretary. Forgive my interruption, but HRH would consider it an honor if you would join him for dinner at his table." As the brother of a king—a duke, in English peerage—the prince had the privilege of inviting any of his fellow travelers to dine with him. To refuse would have been lèse-majesté. The Westerners had no notion that the Shah had scores of brothers and children, making the comparison to a European duke somewhat misleading. Simon Khan exploited this ambiguity at every turn, reinforcing Sardar Mirza's position whenever possible.

When selecting dinner guests, Simon Khan favored those fluent in French. Among them was Pyotr Alexeyevich Krasnov, a hearty graduate of the Junker infantry school in St. Petersburg, his chest gleaming with Crimean War medals. He was accompanied by his anxious wife. Mr. Scott, a stammering young English secretary, was on his way to England to make a suitable marriage. His superiors hoped to salvage his stalled career. Years later, as a middle-aged bureaucrat in the British Embassy in Tehran, Mr. Scott would prove invaluable to the twins. Simon Khan extended his most consequential invitation to Monsieur le Comte, the French aristocrat traveling with his daughters—each of whom would find a husband on this voyage.

Catherine, the eldest at fourteen, talked incessantly. In Odessa, she'd meet an Italian aristocrat whose questionable lineage was redeemed by rare financial solvency. The second daughter, thirteen-year-old Regine, the most beautiful of the three, married a Volkonsky from the famous Russian family. (We shall meet the Volkonskys in Yalta soon enough.) The youngest, Anaïs de Grandpierre, would cross paths with Sardar Mirza twenty-six years later at a party hosted by André Gide. The Comte would fiercely oppose his daughter's marriage to an "Oriental wastrel." All three daughters eloped. All of Paris compared the poor old Comte to Shakespeare's King Lear.

The steamer's first-class dining room, adorned in rich leather, polished brass and dark mahogany, was arranged in a grand design—six round tables encircling a larger central one, like the petals of a flower. Each table groaned under the weight of pink, hand-painted Sèvres plates, stacked in triplicate with delicate soup bowls balanced on top, their floral patterns spreading like a garden in full bloom. Baccarat cut-glass stemware caught the chandelier's glow, casting dancing reflections on silverware from Gorham of Manhattan. A gleaming black piano, nearly the size of a kidney-shaped swimming pool, mirrored the chandelier's soft radiance across its immaculate veneer.

I won't claim that two twelve-year-olds fell in love at first sight—awkward self-consciousness ensured a natural resistance on both sides. Simon Khan's relentless training in etiquette and the French language had nearly paralyzed Sardar Mirza. Like an over-polished Eliza Doolittle, he found himself tongue-tied, acutely aware of Anaïs. He suffered terribly. How did they appear to each other? Sardar Mirza, dressed in tie and tails, bore an unusual coloring. His mother's fair skin gave him a Western look. The fine, golden sheen of hair on his arms and face and his jet-black hair marked his heritage. Anaïs, wispy and elegant, would grow taller than him. Her deep, sorrowful eyes would one day give her a haunted look. Now, they brimmed with a heartbreaking sensitivity. Her curly brown hair—forever a challenge—she kept short throughout her life, an act of control. Even at twelve, she sat with one long leg crossed over the other, foot hooked behind her ankle in effortless poise.

The Comte greeted Sardar Mirza with a crisp, Germanic bow. The boy, trained for such moments, responded with a measured, aristocratic nod. His future father-in-law then introduced his daughters. Sardar Mirza, summoning his courage, managed a few carefully rehearsed phrases—his best attempts at "the rain in Spain stays mainly on the plain." He was not alone in his struggles. The future Honorable Mr. Scott attempted the same, but his pronounced stutter made the children, always prone to giggle, fall silent. They watched him with helpless dread. Would he make it to the finish line?

General Krasnov, a florid and jovial man who would die of a heart attack in a German beer hall within a month, had little patience for stiff formality. He greeted Sardar Mirza with boisterous affection, clapping him on the back, winking and making a coin disappear behind the boy's ear—a trick that delighted the children. Sardar Mirza laughed aloud before quickly restoring the practiced, inscrutable expression Simon Khan had drilled into him. The general's disregard for decorum melted the ice. Sardar Mirza's abandoned, with relief, his carefully cultivated, sphinx-like demeanor.

Simon Khan and the other adults recognized the shift and allowed the relaxed atmosphere, like the unspoken indulgence given to children on the first days of summer vacation. The general's endless supply of amusing stories even coaxed the reserved Comte into contributing a few of his own. Each time he did, his daughters cried, "Papa!" in mock scolding, delight shining in their eyes. Thus began five days of adventure—playful excursions into port towns, picnics in the countryside and explorations of palaces with seemingly endless corridors.

Their first stop was Novorossiysk, a northern Black Sea port nestled against the pale green waters of Tsemess Bay. The ten-mile crescent-shaped harbor never froze, though it endured the fierce bora winds in winter. They arrived on the eve of the first anniversary of Novorossiysk's designation as the capital of the Black Sea Governorate—the Russian Empire's smallest administrative division. General Krasnov, sentimental in his advancing years, reminisced about his youth as a dashing lieutenant. His rheumy eyes glistened with tears as he pointed down the coastline. "Down there," he murmured, "they ordered me to blow up a brand-new fort. Can you imagine? The war had barely begun, and we were already tearing down what we had built." He shook his head in disgust. His stout wife, recognizing the creeping melancholy, jabbed him sharply in the ribs and shot him a warning look, her eyes flicking toward the children. Krasnov cleared his throat and forced a smile. "But look at it now!" he declared, recovering. "Wharves, fortifications, esplanades, electricity, a railway terminus—God has blessed us! God preserve the Tsar!"

The evening's fireworks transfixed the passengers, bursting in brilliant sprays over the harbor. The Comte remained aboard, observing from the safety of the ship. Onshore, the city's brass band blared martial anthems, their melodies lost in the approving roar of the crowd, which swelled with each fresh eruption in the night sky. Sardar Mirza and the three sisters weaved through the revelers, trailed—at least in theory—by Khodrat. Their French governess, Mademoiselle Marte, was supposed to watch the girls but was far too engaged in conversation. She split her attention between Mr. Scott's halting, heavily French-accented English and Simon Khan's quietly disapproving yet intrigued glances. Her laughter was reckless, lovely and entirely distracting. As for Khodrat, the children gave him the slip without even trying. He towered over the crowd. With his thick black beard down to his belly, he cut an imposing figure. His presence made his passage in the crowd difficult; the curious onlookers pressed in, scrutinizing the giant, preventing him from moving freely.

Meanwhile, the three girls and Sardar Mirza found their escape—a perch on a seawall, far from the noise. They shed their shoes and stockings, giggling as they dangled their bare feet over the edge. With each crashing wave, the sea foam climbed the wall, stretching like an ominous shadow before spraying their feet in a cool, ticklish embrace. They shrieked, laughing harder each time. Sardar Mirza's attention never strayed from Anaïs, the quietest of the three. Within their small circle, the sisters understood the unspoken attraction. They did not tease, nor did they interfere. They let it be. That night, they all enjoyed themselves. Anaïs de Grandpierre and Sardar Mirza enjoyed it most of all.

At noon the next day, the steamer dropped anchor at Kerch, a quiet village nestled eighty miles up the coast. Sardar Mirza's anticipation quickly turned to disappointment—the Comte had severely scolded his daughters for their reckless disappearance the night before, berating them for thoughtlessly worrying Mademoiselle Marte. He confined them to the steamer as punishment, sentencing them to an afternoon of regret. There was no question of reprimanding the prince for the same offense. Instead, Mr. Scott, an impeccable guide, invited Sardar Mirza and Simon Khan to accompany him to the hilltops overlooking Kerch. From there, they took in a breathtaking panorama—Asia and Europe bound in their eternal embrace—alongside the ruins of an ancient acropolis where Mithridates, King of Pontus, had taken his own life to escape Pompey's grasp.

That evening, a lavish dinner at Sardar Mirza's table, followed by games, restored harmony between the children and the adults. By the next morning, warm spring rain kept everyone inside as the steamer approached Yalta, the crown jewel of the Russian Riviera. To the children's delight, Simon Khan, General Krasnov and Comte de Grandpierre announced a plan: instead of sailing directly to Sevastopol, they would travel the thirty-five miles overland, with the steamer picking them up a day later. During their time in Tabriz, Simon Khan had followed protocol, forwarding Sardar Mirza's itinerary to the Crimean offices of the Grand Duke of the Sublime Porte and the Palace Élysée. Conveniently, the telegrams had omitted the prince's age. Simon Khan relied on the weight European courts placed on the royal lineage. It assumed the due reverence given to the king's brother. The response came swiftly: the Grand Duke was unavailable in the spring, and the Grand Palace at Livadia was undergoing repairs. They graciously extended the hospitality of the Maliy Palace—Czar Alexander III had died there three years earlier. How long would His Highness be staying? The message bore the elegant signature of the Grand Master of Ceremonies.

As the steamer's engines cut, it churned into Yalta's artificial harbor around three in the afternoon, trailing hundreds of squawking gulls. A warm drizzle blurred the landscape into an impressionist tableau. Beyond the fog, the jagged peaks of the Yai-Petri Yayla rose in ghostly silhouette. Yalta had transformed from a sleepy village to a summer haven for three successive czarinas. Broad avenues now stretched beneath palm and lime trees, while stone villas and grand hotels, designed in Turkish, Oriental and neoclassical styles, dotted the rolling countryside. Fashionable visitors strolled along the promenades and quays each evening, soaking in the sea air. Two imperial landaus awaited beneath the cypress trees at the pier. The group, swept up in a festive spirit, walked three miles to Maliy Palace. The valet, Khodrat and Mademoiselle Marte oversaw the luggage transfer from the steamer to the landaus. Mr. Scott had fallen ill and remained aboard the steamer.

As they walked, a fine mist clung to the cedars, pines and wild chestnuts. Below the sloping mountainside, the sea scrubbed the rocky shores with rhythmic precision. The Comte animatedly described a new sparkling wine—now the toast of European vintners—produced by Prince Lev Galitzin just a few miles away. Simon Khan listened with polite indulgence. The three girls, dressed in fashionable naval costumes, darted into the woods, plucking mushrooms, berries and wildflowers. Sardar Mirza, his self-consciousness long gone, joined them—his French had improved considerably in just a few days. The general, ever the entertainer, strutted beside his wife wearing one of her silk scarves and gallantly shielding her from the drizzle with an umbrella. Then, through the mist, the palace emerged. One by one, their conversations faded. The general called for his wife; she merely smiled and gestured upward. There it stood—Ippolit Monighetti's Maliy Palace—like a colossal Spanish galleon, run aground centuries ago and now swallowed by an enchanted forest. Clematis, roses, wisteria and honeysuckle tangled through the intricate wooden fretwork, weaving across the light pink walls. Decorative pilasters and delicate embellishments lent the structure a fragile, timeworn elegance. Water gurgled through the gutters. Shards of crimson light, breaking through the southern sky, pierced the thick oak and chestnut canopy, turning the hundreds of windowpanes into molten copper. Towering above it all, half a dozen cypress sentinels stood watch. The air was thick with laurel, rhododendron and myrtle.

A handful of Cossack guards, dressed in long blue coats and bearskin hats, had already retrieved the minimal luggage from the landaus. Five stood at attention near the entrance, awaiting the guests. Then, from the shadows, a tall, silver-haired man stepped forward. Frail, stooped with age and bred for a lifetime of gliding silently over marble and parquet, he moved carefully on the gravel. With a practiced bow, he acknowledged the Comte—though an imperceptible shift in the Comte's expression, coupled with a discreet cough, prompted the man to pivot smoothly midsentence toward Sardar Mirza instead. "Welcome, Your Highness, to Maliy." His voice was low and measured, attuned to the slightest diplomatic misstep. "I am Ruslan Papkov, the royal butler at your service. May I introduce Count Volkonsky, a guest of His Majesty the Czar?"

Sardar Mirza inclined his head in casual acknowledgment, signaling his approval of the arrangements. Behind him, the three de Grandpierre sisters smirked behind their hands. "The Count Volkonsky?" The Comte's brows lifted slightly. Papkov, ever the master of courtly nuance, turned smoothly toward him. "The young Count Volkonsky, sire." A third shoe had dropped. The Comte was about to meet yet another future son-in-law—his third in less than a fortnight.

That evening, the young noble met the group at dinner. Shy and bookish, he had a slight build and wore delicate spectacles at fifteen. Unlike his father, who had embarked on a weeklong hunting expedition, the son had chosen to remain at the palace.

He blended seamlessly into the group, his gaze quickly drawn to the prettiest de Grandpierre sister. The children saw the palace as a children's paradise. The polished marquetry floors, made of contrasting woods, gleamed beneath their woolen socks, allowing them to skate effortlessly. Plush sofas covered in chintz and cretonne, lace-patterned silk chairs tied with moiré ribbons, and mahogany desks inlaid with gilded leather piled high with neatly stacked books filled every room. Bronze statues of turbaned slaves, grinning as they balanced platters of food, stood among gilded clocks depicting Greek wrestlers and mythical creatures and loads of trinkets—porcelain frogs, multijointed silverfish, ceramic Staffordshire greyhounds and glass ornaments of every shape—cluttered large and small tables. Heavy silver daguerreotypes adorned the walls, depicting generations of royal children catching butterflies, rowing boats or posing stiffly *en famille*. Maliy Palace was a dreamscape where history slumbered beneath a layer of dust, and the children glided through opulent halls, their laughter bouncing off gold-trimmed ceilings. For Sardar Mirza and Anaïs de Grandpierre, the enchantment had just begun.

Papkov proved to be the evening's greatest surprise. With a twinkle in his eye, he proposed games and delighted in the company of the young guests. During his years of service to Czar Alexander III, he witnessed the most unruly royal household in Europe. The unassuming czar, a man of simple tastes, and his Danish czarina, raised in the least pretentious court in Europe, encouraged an unusual degree of freedom among their children—much to the shock of the Russian aristocracy. The imperial offspring had earned a reputation for being the most ill-mannered royal children in the world. They pelted each other with breadcrumbs across the table, made rude noises during court ceremonies and mocked one another for indulging in such refined pursuits as reading or letter-writing. Alexander's nephews had even trailed the enormous czar through the palace, calling him "Uncle Fatty."

For the palace's maids and servants, the arrival of this lively new group of children was a welcome disruption. Since the death of the old czar, the halls had felt lifeless, a mausoleum of fading grandeur. The Comte, General Krasnov and Simon Khan paid the price for this lack of order. They endured a lackluster meal that bore the unmistakable imprint of the late czar's indifference to fine dining. When the palace's chef had departed, the butler had seen fit to replace him with a cook from a humble inn in Yalta. After dinner, Papkov suggested a game of hide-and-seek. General Krasnov, ever in high spirits, volunteered to be "it." As the children scattered, he promptly settled back into an armchair in the draw-ing room, a glass of cognac in hand, while his wife chastised him for his trickery. "Pyotr, you cannot leave them out there all night," she scolded.

"Ninety-eight," the general called out, then leaned toward her with a grin. "Oh, my dear, you forget," he murmured, sotto voce. He turned toward the staircase and bellowed, "Ninety-nine," before whispering, "All the fun is in hiding, n'est-ce pas?" Then, as a grand finale, he thundered, "One hundred!" Meanwhile, young Volkonsky had trailed behind the charming Régine. Catherine, who felt too mature for hide and seek, slipped into the library with a book. Anaïs and Sardar Mirza darted up the narrow stair-case and down the corridor. Laughing breathlessly, they ducked into a bedroom, oblivious to the black ribbon pinned to the door. Moonlight poured through the tall windows. It illuminated the bedroom where Alexander III had succumbed to chronic nephritis. The white walls and polished parquet floor gleamed in a creamy blue light. They giggled in hushed tones, reveling in the secrecy of their hiding place. Someone had etched a small white cross into the floor near an overstuffed armchair—the very one where the czar had spent his final minutes. Lovingly folded beside it lay his cream-colored cashmere blanket, the one used on his deathbed. A delicate Napoleon III chandelier adorned with black silhouette portraits on ivory hung from the ceiling, its velvet tassels swaying slightly in the still air. Oak-carved miniature cabinets, resembling apothecary chests of drawers, were fixed to the walls. Beyond the French doors, a small balcony overlooked the Black Sea, its dark expanse stretching forever.

Anaïs stepped onto the cross and, with a glint in her eye, turned to Sardar Mirza. "Stand in front of me," she whispered. The moment's weight settled over them as they stood bathed in the moonlight. Then, with quiet certainty, she asked, "You will marry me when we are older."

"*Oui*," Sardar Mirza answered.

All the prepubescent tensions of their journey melted away. They might have been, as they would be someday, a middle-aged couple in love. Like all lovers, they would revisit this moment repeatedly, the unconventional proposal spoken in the hush of a sacred space. Anaïs de Grandpierre—later known as the Countess—would never forgive Czar Nicholas II for razing Maliy Palace, replacing it with the imposing neo-Renaissance Livadia Palace that would one day host the Yalta Conference. All her life, she'd speak of the cross on the floor of that vanished palace, where she had foreseen their future union. Before any more words could pass between them, the doorknob creaked. Hearts pounding, they scurried behind the czar's capacious chair. They felt the delicious fear known to all children caught in forbidden places for a few endless seconds. Then came the soft voice of Ruslan Papkov. "Children, Your Highness," he said gently, "may I be so bold as to request you find a more suitable hiding place? The Empress will be most displeased if she learns I allowed anyone into this room—even distinguished guests such as yourselves."

The following morning, under a sky of profound blue promise, they departed for Sevastopol in imperial carriages arranged by Papkov. The palace staff waved enthusiastically from the grand entrance. Papkov smiled. Young Volkonsky looked forlorn. The maids fluttered handkerchiefs in farewell. The guards stood impassive. They followed the coastal road and climbed two thousand feet through subtropical splendor—pomegranate, fig and mulberry trees gradually yielding to towering magnolias, sycamores and lotus. Higher still, the lush vegetation vanished, replaced by the stark majesty of the Baidar Gate. Below them, the sea, kissed by a gentle wind, shimmered like molten silver beneath the scattered light.

As they descended toward Sevastopol, the air grew colder, the mountains austere and the landscape was more reminiscent of the Caucasus. A somber mood settled over the children; the adventure drew to a close. That evening, they sailed for Odessa, the steamer cutting through cobalt waters beneath a sky brushed with wisps of cloud. If anyone had cared to look, they might have seen Sevastopol's battered skyline bathed in a wistful pink glow, its white churches and houses momentarily lovely in the fading light.

In Odessa, their paths diverged. General Krasnov and his

wife remained in the city, where he would spend the final month of his life. The Grandpierre family continued to Trieste, then Venice, returning to Paris by late August. Mr. Scott departed for London. Simon Khan, Khodrat and Sardar Mirza boarded a train bound for the Gare du Nord. It would take twenty-six years for the betrothed to meet again. Mr. Scott would reacquaint himself with the twins within a decade.

"You must admit, my bed-boat," murmured the Professor, "this was a far more civilized union than that of the old Shah and golden-haired Tala." He fell silent at last. I felt him drift away. In my dreams, I mourned the two princes. In my dreams, I grieved their separation.

THE THIRD NIGHT: 0011

HELP ME, WRITER, FOR I AM CONFUSED

I counted at least five layers of nested storytellers in the five volumes of *One Thousand and One Nights*, each passing the baton to the next. Here and now, I make you this promise: I will not add another voice to my trio of narrators. I do not count myself among them—I am not a narrator but a guide, a help icon hovering in the top right corner of the screen. Am I shirking responsibility? Hardly. Each of my narrators is rooted in reality. I stand by them as one would stand by brothers and uncles. They are figures of history, their fatness, old age and disfigurements preserved in the photographs of their time. From this point forward, they will take turns, each stepping forward in order. No cutting the line. The princeling, the fat storyteller and the surgeon will work together, nightly, to weave the promised tale.

So far, my princeling has written to the lady historian about his parents—their once-fiery love now dulled—and his despised brother. He has reconsidered his earlier judgment of his father. He sees him as a man born in the wrong century. He recalls his ugly duckling existence as the weaker twin. He speaks of the horror of being gnawed by a rat—an experience not his alone, as reports exist of rats attacking babies in their cradles. He tells of his capture by Islamic revolutionaries in his ancestral home and of his middle-class life in present-day Boston.

Beneath him, like the supporting structure of this history, lies my fat storyteller. He reports on the surgeon—the yarn-spinner. The surgeon recounts the beginnings of the Poonaki family, a sex-for-security story. He tells of the arduous journey of the prince-ling's twin grandfathers and their few golden days, overshadowed by brutal attacks from wolves and the freshly minted crown prince. The twins' separation—a cruel, arbitrary decision by the new Shah, their elderly brother—sets the stage. One twin, a natural linguist, travels to Paris; the other, a promising and bright courtier, remains behind at court.

You will meet five Shahs. The first three were from the Qajar dynasty. The last two are from the new Pahlavi dynasty. You just met the father of the grandfather twins, the Pivot of the Universe Nasser al-Din Shah. To keep you centered, see him as the contem-porary Queen Victoria, in the same historical time and with more than half a century of rule. He died five years earlier, in 1896. (not 1996) You also met his rheumy son, Mozaffar al-Din Shah. He sends one of the twins to Europe and keeps the other. He ruled for eleven years and died in 1907 (1896). To keep up, Edward VII, Queen Victoria's son, ruled for only nine years and died in 1910. I can't quite keep the parallel going because King George V ruled a healthy twenty-six years before Edward VIII ruled for a year. George V upsets our thesis, Mohammad Ali Shah's two-year reign (in our recounting so far he is the Crown Prince) resembles the one-year reign of Edward VIII. In their short reigns, they exhibited the spoilt-child characteristics that might amuse a PhD student.

You can pinpoint the historical moment when the aristocratic group of travelers arrived at Yalta's newly built artificial harbor. Looking closely, you might glimpse a fair-haired woman of medium height, wearing a beret, strolling along the seafront and looking for her lost lorgnette, a white Pomeranian trailing behind her. What timing, right?

Have I made things more confusing? Let's get through the next night. I'll meet you at dawn to unravel the sleepless third night.

THE NOT-SO-OMNISCIENT NARRATOR
INTRUDES AGAIN AND AGAIN

"It can't be helped, I prefer my vices to my friends."

Marcel Proust

Dear Ms. Vakil,

Your suspicious questions warm my heart. They show me you are genuinely interested. I must have hit a home run, as my adopted country says. My grandfathers' roles in the Constitutional Revolution would make you proud.

For a brief moment, you dropped your veil of courtesy and questioned—too sharply—the authenticity and provenance of my documents. Let me assure you, they are no cheap fictional devices. My uncle stored them in one of my paternal grandmother's houses. You already know from your research that my grandfather,

Prince Saleh Mirza, had three wives. Like him, his first wife—my grandmother—was a direct descendant of Nasser al-Din Shah, his granddaughter. Our family tree resembles an ingrown toenail. I don't need to remind you of the science behind inbreeding.

My grandfather built three identical houses close enough to the primary residence to hear Gorbun-Ali, the doorman, sneeze: three large, hexagonal two-story pavilions facing the main building. Each had six walls of full-length windows on both floors. Behind them stretched narrow gardens with doors leading to the back street. One had to pass through the pavilions themselves to reach these gardens, ensuring complete privacy.

After the wives died—within a year of each other—the houses stood empty, untouched. Over time, my grandfather used them as storage space. By the time my brother and I came along, they had deteriorated beyond repair. The air inside was thick with the scent of decay. I remember wooden crates stacked in their centers, once filled with large, expensive, abandoned furniture. A few smaller, cheaper settees sat exposed, their upholstery rotted, their springs visible, rusted and broken. Water had warped the wood paneling; planks and bricks covered the shattered windows. Crumbling plaster from the ceilings coated everything with fine dust, like gauze over a forgotten relic.

And what relics? Closets filled with half a century's mildewed clothing. Hatboxes strewn about—some empty, others containing unworn hats with intricate netting. Stacks of trunks and suitcases brimming with official gold-braided court uniforms, morning coats and wedding suits. Soft, milky mold contoured the once crisp and black tuxedos. Rotting green and blue cardboard boxes still cradled their medals and decorations, some with miniature flags dangling beneath their metallic inscriptions. Lapel pins, delicate as flower buds or starburst-like, nestled in deep-mauve velvet, soggy with time. And there was more. Walking sticks, ceremonial swords, yellow-hued daguerreotypes, notebooks and old camera equipment spanning decades of technological breakthroughs. Even a German Luger. The abandoned houses were a paradise for children with an appetite for adventure.

One of those pavilions, cluttered with all this bric-a-brac, also hid the historical letters you now question—right under the noses of the revolutionary guards. A few days before my arrest, I concealed my documents and a handful of valuables in my maternal grandmother's abandoned house. Through a so-called family friend, I arranged to smuggle a suitcase out via the Spanish consulate's diplomatic pouch. Inside were my papers and two Qajar paintings that would have spared me the drudgery of technical writing had they reached me in time. The suitcase deemed worthless, arrived in Boston a decade later—long after I first met you. The paintings never did. Somewhere in Alicante, a thieving consul undersecretary now regales a roomful of friends with tales of how he met an art dealer on Manouchehri Avenue in the final days of the Shah and, with a Spanish shrug, boasts of purchasing *para nada*—for nothing—two priceless Qajar portraits. I cannot reveal how the suitcase eventually reached me. That would expose an innocent man to unnecessary danger. To put your mind at ease, I have mailed you the letter forged by le Bœuf and sealed with the Crown Prince's stamp. You must admit, the old street scribe was no amateur calligrapher. Consider it a breadcrumb on your path to academic fame.

As for my grandfathers' correspondence, it is rich with insight into their lives. Their separation was not merely a family tragedy but a momentous historical event. Ever the pragmatist, Saleh Mirza wrote about their harrowing trek to Tabriz with a cool detachment, only allowing emotion to seep in once he reached middle age. He was not a prolific correspondent; his letters came monthly at best. By contrast, his brother, Sardar Mirza, wrote extensively, pouring out his thoughts in weekly letters. He described his journey from Tabriz to Paris in near-reverent detail. Paris became the love of his life, a city that shaped his very being.

He did not write much about the preceding, more traumatic trip. His letters—those I still possess—refer only once, and in vague terms, to their journey before Tabriz. He describes the trip from Tehran as a collapse of sensation, a narrowing of perception to a singularity, a dimensionless point straight out of a geometry book. He claims to remember nothing. Then, using the same analogy in reverse, he describes Paris as an explosion of awareness, a bombardment of beauty that rekindled his senses. He recalls what should have been a brutal, harrowing experience as an adventure.

Reading his letters, one wonders if he had studied Gogol. Even Poti—a squalid, disease-ridden port—lingers in his memory, not for its filth but for the chorus of frogs that kept him awake at night. Had he already mastered the art of selective memory? Had he filtered out the horrors? Or was he merely honoring our custom—our reluctance to burden loved ones with unpleasant truths?

The brothers spare us the voyeuristic details of their beatings. But like a surgeon separating conjoined twins, the moment of their forced division is precise. It began with the crack of sticks against their bare feet. It continued with the different paths they followed as adolescents. Both saw this rupture as the defining moment of their lives. We can trace their trajectories from this brutal initiation. Whatever chemical surge coursed through their bodies that day carved deep grooves into their minds that would shape their decisions during the semi-glorious Constitutional Revolution. And yet, through it all, their love for one another remained untouched.

Ms. Vakil, I will help you reconstruct the long-overlooked reputations of these two men. Your profession has ignored them for far too long. Traveling westward had a profound effect on young Sardar Mirza. Those carriages, steamers and trains were more than mere transportation—they were time machines. The slow seepage of modernity eastward had kept the lands beyond the Caucasus isolated, insular and incomprehensible to his young mind. The first trains would not reach Tehran until a quarter of a century after his journey. From his privileged perch, he had assumed such marvels existed solely for men of his rank. The realization that the common masses also had access to them shattered his carefully constructed universe. His transformation—from an Eastern potentate in waiting to a budding Western gentleman—began in Tiflis.

Could there be lands where ordinary people's daily surroundings surpassed the splendor of his father's palaces? Raised by ignorant women and eunuchs, they convinced him, as they were convinced, that he lived in the most extraordinary empire humanity had ever known. But at every stop from Tiflis to Paris, his eyes gathered evidence to the contrary. By the time he arrived in Paris, speculation had given way to surrender. Nothing could have prepared him. In 1897, no city on earth could have had a more significant impact on Sardar Mirza than Paris. He arrived at the Gare du Nord at the height of the Belle Époque, a dazzling, chaotic, jubilant era in which the legacy of the French Enlightenment—revolution, anticlericalism—animated art, literature, and entertainment. The *Vent de Jolie*, the winds of beauty, carried him aloft like a kite.

Years later, he took his ten-year-old daughter, Lili, to see Monet's *Boulevard des Capucines*. The painting's electric energy, its pulsating café crowds, transported him back to that first overwhelming moment. He tried to explain it to her—the contrast between Paris's ordered, expectant crowds and Tehran's impoverished, ramshackle streets. But she, a Parisian child, had no frame of reference. Everything about Paris excited his voracious mind. In letters to his brother, he complained about schoolwork, referring to his teachers as tedious old men. But he relished writing. At first, he wrote in Farsi, peppered with French idioms; by age fifteen, he had switched to French. He sent detailed letters to his brother, who devoured every word, hungry for the world he described.

In the throes of the cult of "the right to be lazy," France had given birth to an explosion of art and entertainment. Every night, cabarets overflowed with singers, poets and raconteurs spinning tales of the dispossessed, the prostitutes and the rogues. The Folies Bergère democratized the café-concert, offering new forms of amusement to all classes. The elite indulged alongside the working class at roller coasters, racetracks, wax museums and music halls.

Sardar Mirza marveled at the spectacle of the Grands Boulevards. Any random swath of the crowd appeared more prosperous, more refined and better dressed than the most distinguished guests in his father's palaces. "Our palace mice are poorer than their church mice," he wrote wryly to his brother. He became obsessed with transportation. When the Métro opened at the turn of the century, he insisted that Khodrat take him repeatedly, despite his companion's deep-seated fear of the underground monster. He could not fathom the West's exaggerated belief in the riches of the East.

Another moment of reckoning arrived when he attended the 1900 Universal Exposition. At first, he was unimpressed. The grand Ferris wheels, escalators, talking films, Campbell's soup cans and Russian nesting dolls left him cold. But then he saw the paintings. After years of dismissal and ridicule, the French government officially recognized Impressionism for the first time. Manet, Pissarro, Renoir, Degas, Morisot, Monet, Sisley—all their works now hung alongside the grand masters of the nineteenth century. It was a revelation. It electrified him. Though he had no artistic talent, he knew he had to be part of this movement—to support, promote and write about it. He understood it. He would explain it to others.

The following year, Barnum & Bailey arrived in Paris to great fanfare. It failed to impress him. My maternal grandfather had no patience for cheap thrills. By seventeen, he had visited the pleasure dens of Paris with little enthusiasm. He confessed to his brother that he suffered terribly from post-coital melancholy. He sampled absinthe and opium with curiosity. He developed a passion for bicycles, purchasing one of his own and spending Sundays at the Vélodrome de la Seine. You see, Ms. Vakil, Sardar Mirza submerged himself in Gauloiserie—and he never reemerged.

As I leap forward seventy-five years, my focus on my eminent grandfathers remains unwavering. If you are to understand my family, I must introduce you to someone you know only superficially. I spent nine days imprisoned in my own home. One other stood out among the men who disembarked from the bus the day of my arrest: Professor Dal, the famous surgeon we all called uncle. With his bald, egg-shaped head and rows of teeth like planks, the man who had brought me into this world stepped off that bus. He looked at the house nostalgically. He had lived there longer than me. He embraced me firmly. He had loved my father like a blood brother—but from the moment he first saw her, he loved my mother like no sister.

Uncle Dal entered the house like a man reclaiming his throne. And he would remain there for the next ten years. For a brief period, the Islamic Republic repurposed my home, the Poonaki residence, to house high-profile political prisoners. But after the bombing of the parliament on June 28, 1981—when seventy-three of the regime's parliamentary leaders happily surrendered their earthly lives for heavenly residence—the flood of new political detainees made my house inadequate. Evin, Tehran's infamous prison, absorbed the overflow. The authorities repurposed my house yet again—this time, as an asylum. Uncle Dal adapted to his new role with ease.

He had spent his childhood in this house. My paternal grandfather, Saleh Mirza—the Prince—adopted him on a whim. Childless then, he had been drawn to the boy's fair coloring. Bright as a summer's day, Uncle Dal grew up modest and perceptive. Well-liked, quiet and kind, he never hurt a soul. His looks alone ensured him the effortless respect accorded to foreigners: Thick blond hair, blue eyes, and a narrow, equine face drawn by God with perfect symmetry.

At a time when few sent their children abroad—let alone an adopted son—my grandfather sent Uncle Dal to Germany for his education. The move coincided roughly with the birth of Saleh

Mirza's son, my father. Dal completed high school in Germany as the Nazis rose to power. Like many at the time, he sympathized with the movement—not out of hatred but as a reaction to British colonial ambitions and Russian land grabs. After medical school, he remained in Germany through the war, tending to the endless stream of wounded soldiers. By the war's end, any youthful enthusiasm for ideology had been scrubbed clean. He returned home to a warm welcome from my parents, who loved him dearly for the rest of their lives.

Our uncle soon entered the royal court as a close friend of Mohammad Reza Shah (also known as Reza Pahlavi), the last monarch of Persiran. He secured his place at the palace on February 4, 1949, when he treated the Shah's wounds after an attempted assassination. The first three bullets struck the Shah's hat before the fourth entered his cheek and exited through his upper lip. The fifth lodged in his shoulder. The sixth never came—mercifully, the assassin's gun jammed. Uncle Dal, ever wry, had joked with the Shah that his hat deserved medical attention more than he did. That service earned him a permanent seat at the Belote table. He never exploited his position—except, occasionally, to urge the Shah toward mercy when punishing his opposition.

Uncle Dal possessed an extraordinary gift for physical diagnosis. His manual detection of tumors and fluid buildups at medical school in Berlin had become legendary. Though too thick for a surgeon's, his hands moved over the body with uncanny precision, coaxing and massaging flesh until they found the cells gone awry. He could detect what even the best X-ray technology of the time could not. When he advised surgery, the second opinion—lacking his sensitivity to touch—often contradicted him. Those who ignored his diagnosis found themselves months later with inoperable tumors, their treatment now far more complicated. And yet, by the mid-fifties, something in him fractured. He reported that a woman—our mother, though he never spoke her name—had given birth to twins immersed in a black, viscous liquid. He identified it as oil. Present in the operating room were Dr. Malik, the surgeon on duty; Dr. Rasekh, the gynecologist, and two nurses. None denied the presence of some dark substance. But to them, the Professor had exaggerated its amount. A few months later, he noticed an unnatural thickness in my mother's milk. And while playing with us one afternoon, he swore that one of us—he never specified which—drenched him in black urine.

Dear Ms. Vakil, what can I say? We deal in fact-based history, not magical fiction. A sensitive man, hammered by war, had returned home to great professional success but with a fragile grip on reality. His mind balanced on a razor's edge. Did watching my mother give birth bring home, most viscerally, her inaccessibility to him forever? Did those grueling fifteen hours of labor unmoor him, triggering the hallucination of oil gushing forth? Who can say whether his diagnostic abilities sharpened with time, or whether they, too, began to slip from reality? He detected cancer earlier and earlier, recommending surgery wholesale—to men, women and children alike. By the late sixties, newspapers had begun questioning his competence. He chose to retire quietly. He had a luxury duplex apartment downtown, yet he spent much of his time with us. My father gave him a permanent room—Uncle's room, we called it. No, it was not in the attic. And no, I have no memory of him behaving like a madman.

Six thousand miles away and twenty-five years ago, night covered the land of a thousand and one nights. The Persiran-Iraq War had ended. My frightened storyteller picked up his tale once more.

THE STORYTELLER EYES
THE YARN SPINNING SURGEON
WITH SUSPICION

The stars, that nature hung in heaven, and filled their lamps with everlasting oil,
give due light to the misled and lonely traveler.

John Milton

My darling Baba, in my heart, your place remains empty. Yet, in these times, there are advantages to not walking this Earth. I do not know if the Almighty has granted you new corporeal eyes where you hover, but if He has, do you see the destruction left in the wake of this endless war? If not, borrow my eyes. Roam through my memories. And then tell me, Baba—how do you and I see the world so differently? The war has ended. The old man has admitted as much on the radio, saying he has "drunk from the poisoned chalice"—though it seems a weak brew since he continues to live comfortably in Jamaran. Eight years of trench warfare with our neighbor, and now our soldiers hopscotch through minefields, breathing in the stench of nerve gas. They eat and shit in dusty trenches under the blistering sun. When ordered, they rise in waves to be cut down by an enemy dug deep into the earth. A million lives lost—for what, Baba? One madman launched this war in a cynical bid to reclaim the imagined glories of the seventh century, with a bit of oil on the side. Another madman refused peace for a decade, yearning to drag the world's clocks back to that same blood-soaked time.

And so here we are, in the wreckage they have left behind. There is no law, no respect. They don't even have respect for the religious laws they claim to uphold. Look at the rascal Hamid—no one dares ask how he came to own the most famous teahouse in Tehran. Fear is the new order of things. I have not set foot outside Mammad-Ali's shop since I left the prison they call a madhouse—the madhouse they call a prison. You call me a coward, Baba? Have you forgotten that Mammad-Ali's shop is only two blocks from the teahouse? Through the broken shards of his storefront sign—a white, fluorescent letter shaped like a woman's breast, a semicircle with a dot in the middle, the letter N in our script—I can see the back door of the teahouse. If I stepped outside, draped in a black chador, they would instantly recognize me. My size alone would betray me. Instead, I sent Mammad-Ali to survey the teahouse. He reported back that the enemy remains entrenched, surviving now in filth. The war's end has slowed their arms business but not their grip on power.

"What can I tell you that I would not tell your father?" Mammad-Ali lamented. "These rascals have drained the sparkle from life. They have destroyed beauty, music and poetry. They have destroyed our country." I had never known him to wax poetic. For now, I will wait. But I will keep my promises—to my master, my Arbab, the mad witness and my Professor. I will tell you the story of my third day.

I woke to Professor Dal's screams. Bathed in morning light, he stood in the center of the cell, clad only in a loincloth, his head thrown back like an old wolf howling at an unseen moon. His upper body bore the marks of his torment, his bruises forming a moiré of light and shadow, like the stripes of a zebra. I faced him, meeting his gaze. I winked, nodding as though we were co-conspirators in his absurd performance. He acknowledged nothing. "What am I?" he demanded, his voice raw.

By now, I was at ease in his presence—but irritated by his persistence. "It's me, Hekaiatchi," I whispered. "The guards aren't here. What are we doing? Do you want me to howl?" Slowly, like a Kung Fu master, he turned to face me. His hand lifted high, moving with deliberate grace. I watched an idiot's smile on my lips. Then, without warning, the hand descended—a flash of movement, a brutal slap. Pain exploded through my face. Only the sheer weight of my body kept me from crumpling to the floor. My neck cracked; the taste of blood flooded my mouth.

Gingerly, I ran my tongue along the inside of my cheek—it felt like chewing gum mixed with cookie crumbs. "What am I?" he repeated.

"An oil—an oil well?" I stammered. I scrambled toward the door, screaming for help. Professor Dal reenacted the same scene as the day before. He removed his loincloth and defiled the cell. The guards arrived, hauling him away for the rest of the day. I cleaned the mess as best I could, relieved to be rid of him. By late afternoon, they brought him back without explanation.

I begged the guards not to leave me alone with this madman. They laughed at my fear—what harm could a frail old man, barely a hundred pounds, possibly do to me? He slept deeply. I tried to stay awake, but exhaustion took me.

I woke with a start. He was on top of me, straddling my stomach like a crab, his face inches from mine. He smelled faintly of vomit. "Wake up, my bag of feathers," he murmured. "The night is young. We have much to discuss. The agonies of birth, the manias of motherhood, the twins' sex lessons . . ." Just like that, he was the considerate old man of the night before.

"Get off me," I snapped. "I want nothing to do with you or your madness. Go back to your corner and let me sleep."

"But, dear boy, what's the matter?" he asked, his voice laced with feigned concern. "I thought we had reached an understanding. A comfortable arrangement."

"Comfortable?" I scoffed. "This morning, you slapped me and pissed on me. Who are you?"

"That," he said, "is what I am about to tell you."

And then he began his story, a wise beginning. As my Baba used to say, the storyteller must first earn the listener's trust—lest the audience dismiss him as nothing more than a gossip monger, or a charlatan..

THE STORY OF THE SURGEON

"There is nothing either good or bad, but thinking makes it so."

Hamlet—William Shakespeare

I have brought and will continue to bring to life the stories of countless souls upon this celestial expanse of yours. Women whispered their secrets in my presence as if I were their son; hard-drinking princes carelessly revealed state matters as if I were their brother; opium-smoking servants confided in me as if I were their ward. You cannot verify my tale, and I will provide only the barest details—but you will believe me.

Let me retell the circumstances under which my mother cast me away, as they were relayed to me by Prince Saleh Mirza. We called him the Prince. We capitalized him. He stood apart as the most capable among a thousand lesser princes. Until I turned eleven, I knew nothing of my surname. My mother had left me at the mansion as an infant, my fate wrapped in a few soiled sheets bearing her careful script. She had pinned the pages to my swaddling. I bore the Prince's coloring. He took me in. In this land, people prize paler skin. "My pliable one, as you can see, my skin had the amber glow of fine scotch; my hair, though you find no trace of it today, was as yellow as the sun a child draws. It was a source of pride and a mark of my foreignness." I held a special place in the household for eleven years, sleeping in my room within the main house. The Prince once told me the woman who entrusted me to him was no beggar, but he revealed little more—until that fateful summer when I turned eleven.

In 1905, the Russians and the English divided our country into zones of influence. The Russians longed to claim the northern provinces outright, while the English coveted the oil that bubbled from the southern regions like water from a spring. We saw it as the betrayal of the century. We understood the savage Russians. But the English? Their betrayal soaked into our national soul. During those years of the Constitutional Revolution, the Great Powers maintained the flimsiest pretense of our independence. By 1915, the year of my birth, the English and the Russians—now allies—were embroiled in a desperate war. They no longer even feigned diplomacy. Administrations came and went, their survival dependent on their ability to anticipate the whims of the Allied embassies. Conspiratorial plots festered in every corner. We credited the Allies with omnipotence, believing they controlled all human events.

The Prince endured the most challenging and lonesome years of his life. His second wife had borne him no children in three years of marriage, and court gossip questioned his manhood. A sober man, he revered tradition as steadfastly as Cato the Younger, his favorite philosopher. That summer day, seated in our country garden in Poonak, he told me how he had come to adopt me. "A lady in rags approached my horse at the governor's gate," he said. "One could tell at a glance that she was no common beggar. She did not step into the street like the others. She extended the infant to me from the sidewalk. Her chador, though worn, was of fine make, concealing her features. She had wrapped the child papoose-style, white-skinned, blue-eyed, with a shock of blond hair sticking out. 'Your Highness, take your son,' she said. The crowd hushed. Our coloring matched, and—quite honestly, not knowing who stood beneath that chador—I had a moment of doubt." Here, he let loose his abrupt guffaw, the laugh that delighted all who heard it. He claimed this was the truth. Though I might have quibbled about the details, I believed him. He let me read the heart-wrenching letter. It haunted my life.

> I, Zoleikha (my maternal family name is unreadable, obliterated by a stain of what appears to be baby excrement), set down this account so my son will not go into the world nameless. May those who read these words take pity on me. As God is my witness, I write the truth as I know it in my heart. I dip a sliver of wood into my cloth-soaked China ink. They beat me senseless. Then, my father threw me out of the house like garbage. They struck me again and again to force a miscarriage. You held on, my son. I hope you prove to be the fighter your lineage demands. The little money left to me came from my widowed aunt, who sheltered me in her home, one of the few untouched by the English bombard-

ment of Dilwar. She lived alone, sustained by my father's generosity. When she sent word of my condition, my father's response was simple: Whores do not belong in your house.

I will not waste ink recounting the horrors of my journey to Shiraz or the months I survived in its streets. At times, kindness fed me; at others, I resorted to the basest means available to women. Tomorrow, I will take my child to the governor's house. I have heard that a Qajar prince of great repute rules over us. I ask for nothing in return. Life has nothing left for me. My son, you are of the Tangestani tribe, fierce and free, dwelling near the port of Bushehr. Our village, Dilwar, was known for its pirates. Yes, your grandfather was one of the greatest among them. I will not tarnish his name further. I have earned his wrath, but if not for you, I would have proven my mettle by ceasing to exist. My father trusted me above all others. He had a tutor teach me to read and write when he could not. No other woman in our tribe had such knowledge. He used me as a messenger to his captains, confident in my discretion.

More Arab than Persiranian, we lived in Bushehr under the protection of the noble Rais Ali, the Tangestani chief. A few years before my disgrace, the British navy bombarded Dilwar to force my father's surrender. They demanded that Rais Ali hand him over. An honorable man, he refused the mighty British. In retaliation, they razed our village, destroying every dhow at the port, leaving fishermen without a livelihood. One English officer likened the floating wreckage to matchsticks. My father escaped. We fled to Bushehr.

I first saw the German Wassmuss in Bushehr two years after the British attack. My father, brother and I traveled to Shiraz to meet him under the governor's protection. The Alharab Al-Azmi, the Great War, had begun. The stars aligned, and Rais Ali sensed destiny's hand. He dreamt of driving the English from our lands. For six months, I carried messages between Wassmuss and the resistance. The British never suspected me—a woman—as a courier. Their arrogance blinded them. The night before the battle, I shared food and water with the men crouched in the Mashalah, waiting for dawn. We struck before first light. We caught them unprepared. My brother fought fiercely, but the English guns overwhelmed us. A bullet felled my brother. Rais Ali carried his body from the field.

The English retaliated by massacring our village. My brother's wife and children—your cousins—were slaughtered. They erased our birthplace from the material world. The resistance crumbled. The English lit the night with their infernal machines. They hunted our men like animals. A bullet found Rais Ali. He lingered for three days before succumbing without complaint. Now, the infidels rule us again. My father mourns in silence. My son, if I leave you with any wisdom, it is this: Never trust the English. Live with honor.

You can understand, my fluffy one, why reading that letter at eleven affected me so profoundly. Imagine a boy who dreams of an imaginary mother every night, only to receive—out of the abyss—a letter addressing him directly as "son." Worse still, she speaks of her ultimate sacrifice to secure his comfort. The Prince watched me as I read. His chin rested on his cane. When I lifted my head, our eyes met—his were bloodshot, weary and sad. Constitutional politics had long decayed into the arbitrary intrigues of dictatorship. With his reluctant blessing, a once-in-a-century event—the demise of his dynasty—had already unfolded. The Prince had helped negotiate the exile of a second monarch, his nephew's son. Another king had joined the procession of dethroned royals, condemned to wander Europe's spas and sanatoriums. How civilized it all once seemed.

Reza Shah had launched his two-Shah dynasty. He placed the peacock crown upon his head with his own hands. In my naïveté, I wanted to tell the Prince that the letter changed nothing—that I would always consider him my father. But he didn't let me speak. He leaned in, his face close to mine. "Do you understand the import of the letter, boy?" he asked. I nodded, though questions swarmed in my head. A Rolls crunched up the driveway. The Prince lifted his head as two men exited the chauffeur-driven car, removing their hats as they approached. Both were attachés from the British embassy. I recognized Mr. Scott—he and the Prince had been friends since the Constitutional Revolution's glory days. The other, Mr. Nicolson, agemate to the Prince, looked ten years younger. Dressed in a brown three-piece suit, he observed me through protuberant eyes. The Prince introduced me strangely. "Mr. Nicolson," he said, "meet Dal. He has been under my protection since birth." They examined me like a specimen under a microscope. The Prince continued, "Mr. Nicolson, my young ward here is a legitimate Per-siranian national. Despite rumors and appearances, I can assure you he is not German." Even then, I sensed an agreement had been struck among the three men long before I arrived at the table. They nodded and did not ask a single question.

The Prince gripped his cane with both hands and rose to his feet. He did not wait for a servant to assist him. "Hear me all," he declared, his voice echoing through the garden. Everyone straightened. "The Almighty has finally seen fit to bless me with a child." The entire household emerged, along with a few snot-nosed peasant boys and their fathers, laboring in the gardens below, eager to offer their congratulations. The two Englishmen muttered inanities: "Well done, old boy." The Prince, ever prepared for the ceremony, distributed coins from a womanish red velvet purse. I forced my face into a pale imitation of joy. The Prince noticed. He always noticed. He didn't try to soothe me. He did not utter a single kind word. Coins dispensed, he turned back to the Englishmen. "Mr. Nicolson, I trust your audience with His Majesty went well yesterday."

"Tolerably well, Your Highness. He was full of praise for you." (Mr. Nicolson, never a fan of the new Shah, had once warned his first minister, "I don't like Reza Shah's sly look.")

The Prince tapped his cane. "Would you make a wager with me?" Mr. Nicolson, a soft, civilized man, shook his head gently with a noncommittal smile. No diplomat answers an open ques-tion. "What are the odds I will live to see my child grow to this young man's age?" He gestured toward me with his cane. One of them would lose that bet within months.

"Your Highness has a strong portfolio in His Majesty's new government," Mr. Scott said.

The Prince exhaled. "Mr. Scott, you and I feasted in our youth. We would let *le diable* caress our buttocks to sit at the table again, wouldn't we?"

"There is talk of reviving the constitution," Mr. Nicolson said. The Prince sighed. I remember little else from that afternoon.

Over the next five years, he treated me fairly—yes, even with kindness—the kindness one offers a friend's son. Never again did I sit on his knees as he chattered with guests, nor feel the absent-minded stroke of his fingers across my head as he passed, nor the light touch on the nape of my neck. His natural neglect eroded my standing in his household. They moved me from upstairs to down-stairs to make way for the nursery. Guests who once acknowledged me with polite chatter now passed me by, stone-faced. Small slights from the servants flourished into the ultimate slight: pity. Can one be a former son and yet still live? I had lost and gained a family in a single afternoon. My childish imagination scrambled to repair the damage. I built a new world around the soiled pages of the letter. I placed Wassmuss—the distant adventurer—at the center, envisioning him as a Sinbad perched high on the lateen sail of a great ship, commanding his piratical in-laws to make haste, for they needed to rescue me. We lived six hundred miles inland.

I don't want to paint myself as a male Cinderella, shut away in an attic, whispering to rats. You don't know who Cinderella is, my ample comforter? From your story, I'd say she is someone much like you. My education continued with the same severity as before. I gained some freedom to explore. And as I matured, I grasped that no flying dhow would sail inland to rescue me. I needed to take matters into my own hands. My fascination with German history deepened, fueled by my growing commitment to finding my father. Duly noted, a German tutor appeared. The Prince worked in mysterious ways. Herr Lorentz, a dapper young man in a sober dark suit, did not live with us. A birdlike figure with abrupt, tiny movements, he arrived every day at four and stayed for three hours. I always tried to keep him longer.

He was mild-mannered, generous and patient. He tried to instill in me a love of literature. Specialization had yet to narrow the twentieth-century mind—he had studied the entire field of Persiranistik, from *The Avesta*, the Zoroastrian scriptures, to Kurdish dialects, encompassing religion and culture. By the time he arrived in Tehran, he had traveled through the valleys of the upper Oxus, recording ancient languages. Later, he gained renown in Hamburg as one of the last encyclopedic scholars of our country. For two years, he made me read Goethe, pacing around the table, holding the book at arm's length, pince-nez in hand. He corrected my pronunciation with the patience of an old nun. He patted my head like a pet when I did well. His eyes teared at the passage where young Werther and Lotte read Macpherson's *Poems of Ossian*.

Herr Lorentz's deep learning in Persiranian literature didn't interest me. My hunger for German culture left no room for anything else. I wanted to learn about Bismarck, who had captured my imagination as he had once captured Paris. That the Prussian chancellor was Queen Victoria's "bitter enemy" was enough for me. Herr Lorentz tut-tutted at my militaristic leanings and steered me toward Rilke. I waxed heatedly on the unfairness of the Versailles Treaty. He suggested to the Prince that I study in Germany. The Prince agreed at once. Perhaps it solved a problem. Perhaps it salved his conscience. And so, they arranged my departure with my enthusiastic consent.

Herr Lorentz wrote to Berlinisches Gymnasium zum Grauen Kloster, his alma mater, highly recommending me to his former headmaster—who happened to be his uncle. For the last nine months of his stay, he rigorously prepared me for the demands of a German gymnasium. During this time, I devised a plan to find my putative father in the south, where newspapers had recently reported his presence. Meanwhile, I had matured into—"Why be modest, my springy one?'—a striking young man. At five-foot-ten, considered tall and well-built, I drew stares wherever I went. My blue eyes and light hair, juxtaposed with my dusky complexion, made me an exotic presence in a land of black hair and dark eyes.

I traveled to Europe via the western route through Luristan and Kurdistan, which surprised no one. After the communist revolution, the northern road through Russia lost its imperial allure. Many now journeyed by car through the rugged terrain to Khaniquin on the Persiran-Iraq border, from where they could take the train to Baghdad. I planned a detour. I requested permission to stay in Baghdad for a few weeks before proceeding to Europe, but I never planned to make that journey. Instead, I intended to use those weeks to travel a thousand miles south to Bushehr to join my father. With ample funds and no one monitoring my movements, I dreamed of father-and-son adventures.

I had no guarantee he still lived in Bushehr. The Prince received daily newspapers, and I scoured them for news of Wassmuss. He had gained a folkloric reputation among us and the English, whom he had dazzled with his success against them. Strangely, the German press remained silent on the subject. I knew

that, after the war, his tribal support had faded. The British imprisoned him for a time. After his release, he lived in Berlin until 1926.
Then I read in *The Times*: "Herr Wassmuss, the famous German
spy, has returned to Bushehr. 'I want to live in peace among people
I love. I am now retired from the German government. My life's
adventures are behind me,'" the paper quoted.

The Prince arranged for me to travel with the English consul
in the Trans-Desert Mail—a large, mud-splattered Dodge with
black sacks of mail affixed to its mudguards. It ran biweekly from
Tehran to Beirut. Letters painted white on the hood gave it an
official air, likely to deter robbers. I sat in the front beside the
driver, a Scotsman named O'Rourke, though everyone called him
Arak, after the anise liquor popular in the region. I never saw him
drink during our four-day journey. He was a seasoned driver, fluent
in Russian and Persiranian, albeit with an accent that made him
difficult to understand. He confided that his wife lived in a lunatic
asylum in Beirut. The job paid well, but he longed to return to
Russia, where he had worked on the railways before the war. He
had served in the Russian army and loved the Russians more than
the English. He looked younger than he was, but after hours on the
road, the dust, like fingerprint powder, highlighted the fine wrinkles around his eyes and mouth. Two English ladies, likely mother
and daughter, sat in the back. Both were matronly and had made
this trip several times. The younger visited her husband at the legation once a year. Her mother accompanied her as a *dame d'honneur*.
They covered their mouths with handkerchiefs for hours, lowering
them to address Arak with the haughty familiarity reserved for
servants. He understood his place and didn't seem to mind.

We departed late in the morning. I had provisions for four

days. There was little fanfare as the car pulled out of the compound; most of the British legation had already moved to the summer residence. The Tehran-Hamadan highway was serviceable but crowded with livestock and horse-drawn carriages ferrying goods to the capital. Tiny donkeys marched under towering loads of brassware. Flocks of sheep sashayed in the road, their bells ringing lazily. Our deafening horn, coupled with gentle nudges from the bumper, eventually persuaded them to part. We arrived in Qazvin early and completed our paperwork. The ladies chose to rest instead of pushing on to Hamadan. Arak and I slept in the car—he was in the front, and I was in the back. In the morning, the ladies, revived, wrinkled their noses at the stale scent of our shared quarters.

Beyond Aveh Pass, the road emptied. The air lightened, a breeze cooling us as we zigzagged up the steep incline. I stretched out my hand, making gliding motions. The two women whispered and tittered. The arid browns of the landscape gave way to greener undergrowth. By afternoon, we descended to Hamadan, one of the world's oldest cities. We stayed in a small, clean hotel where the owner served a fragrant Persiranian stew of lamb, chickpeas, white beans, onion, potatoes, tomatoes, turmeric and dried lime in a traditional stone crock. I slept like a child. Before dawn, we continued through white-trunked poplars alongside a river, then parted from the water to climb a road cut into the mountain. Arak maneuvered the hairpin bends with careful back-and-forth movements, the metal gears screeching with each shift. We reached ten thousand feet. At nine in the morning, the sky was cobalt blue, the air crisp. We stopped for tea by the roadside. I won't forget that moment— the sense of possibility, freedom and adventure. The world lay open before me as I sipped hot tea and ate bread and cheese. At seventy-five, I can count on one hand the moments when all emotions coalesced into the pure understanding of the future.

We descended ten thousand feet in less than seven miles, met by a patient, dry heat. The car pressed on toward Kermanshah through red, brown and copper hills. Twice, we stopped to replace the driver's front wheel tube. The Kurds we passed wore baggy trousers secured with twisted sashes. The men, fine-boned and chiseled, carried themselves with grace. The women layered their colorful garments, their smiles gummy, faces weather-worn. Tied to their mothers' backs, infants peeked mischievously over their shoulders. Pressed for time, Arak accelerated—the heat cut at our faces. Without a word, the elder Englishwoman handed me a scarf. I nodded my thanks. We paused at a caravanserai, one of many spaced twenty miles apart—the distance a camel walks in a day. The proprietor warned us to stay the night, not for commercial interest, Arak assured us, but because of genuine concern for the marauders. Arak dismissed the danger. "As long as we're prepared to plow them down with the car, we'll be fine," he said.

I observed Arak's method more than once that night. Silhouettes of riders appeared in the distance. He stomped on the accelerator. The car surged. At the last moment, the riders wrenched their reins, their startled faces glimpsed briefly before darkness swallowed them. Arak chuckled and slapped his thigh. I pondered a single question: what if the car broke down? Past midnight, we reached Kermanshah. The British consulate, a large but unremarkable brick building, awaited us. A tall, sleepy Englishman greeted the ladies, escorting them inside without a glance in my direction. Stung, I fumed in the car with Arak all night, who merely chuckled, "Looks like it's just you and me again."

The next day, the country opened up before me. The car moved steadily, eating up the miles. The vastness of the landscape and my sleepless night lulled me into a dreamlike state; I would drift off, only to jolt awake as my head fell against my chest. We crossed Kurdistan under an unforgiving sun, its brilliance leaching the color from everything. Arak wore thin gloves to grip the wheel—it was too hot to touch. More and more camels appeared in the distance like mirages from the tales of *A Thousand and One Nights*. Late in the afternoon, we arrived in Khaniqin, a Kurdish city divided by the Dyala River. I bid Arak a warm goodbye and boarded the train to Baghdad.

I entered the first-class carriage, and my two English companions glanced up; surprised they appraised me anew. Then, like taut elastic bands, their expressions snapped back to the supercilious look bred into colonial wives—heads held high, eyelids at half-mast as if surveying the world from a lofty vantage point. The train took ten hours to cover the hundred miles to Baghdad. At the station, our parting was perfunctory—a nod as they hurried onto the platform.

I passed through Baghdad twice in a fortnight, both times distracted. I should have been in awe of the metropolis that made Tehran look like a village. Instead, my impressions were other than visual. I remember Baghdad not through my eyes but through my nose and ears: the asthmatic wheezing of the locomotive, the scratchy music of gramophones in cafés, the pungent aroma of spiced food, the shrill cries of beggar boys as they chased after me. I stayed at the luxurious Claridge Hotel on Rashid Street, parallel to the Tigris—the first real luxury I had ever known.

I boarded the Pioneer—the same steamer my father, Wassmuss, had traveled on in 1915. As a German consul, he had taken this route to launch his operations against the British. I saw it as a good omen. "Boy, never believe in omens," Dal admonished.

The Pioneer had seen better days. It had served both the Turks and the Royal Navy during the war. Now, under the management of a Turkish firm—one of the last remnants of the Ottoman bureaucracy—it had turned into a shadow of its former self. First-class accommodations amounted to little more than a shared berth in what had once been an elegant stateroom. Three Jewish Baghdadi couples occupied the sitting room, unbearably stuffy in the summer heat. We partitioned it with curtains to afford the women some privacy. During the day, we lounged in deck chairs beneath the shade of the pilothouse. My companions, seasoned travelers who worked for British banks, spoke three or four languages apiece. With my German and halting French, I followed their sophisticated conversations. They took me under their wing.

The deck below resembled a bazaar more than the orderly space of a marine steamer. Families sprawled on carpet squares, leaning against portable beds, chattering loudly over their cooking utensils. Acrid smoke from inferior oil curled into the air, drifting up to us all day. Small, fragile shelters shielded passengers from the punishing sun. The Turkish captain, a hulking man in a soiled military uniform adorned with unimpressive tin medals, strutted about, a tarboosh perched precariously on his oversized head. His mustache curled comically at the ends, like a propeller. He treated us courteously but barked contemptuously at the passengers below, bellowing threats against potential fire hazards. He swore on the Koran that he would fling every last one of them into the river. After each outburst, he would turn to us, seeking validation, his eyes pitying us for having to endure what he considered the scum of the earth.

The pilot, Al Hamdi, was a tall, ascetic-looking Arab. He skillfully navigated us out of the port. Low in the summer, the river revealed small, protruding islands where Baghdadis swam and lazed in the afternoon heat. Gramophones blared from the shore, and passengers leaned over the railings to call out to friends and family on these islets as we passed. Comical little gufas—circular boats made of reeds and bitumen—bobbed around us like moons orbiting a planet. Within a mile, the lively scenes faded. The world flattened into reeds, bushes and an unchanging horizon. The monotony made it feel as though we were standing still. Only the occasional stork or a flock of pelicans disrupted the landscape. We passed the ruins of Ctesiphon, the ancient Persiranian capital, and my new friends filled in its history with colorful anecdotes. I could have reconstructed the palace in my mind. Then came two days of unbearable boredom. I thought the heat was insufferable—until I learned that worse was yet to come.

At Qurna, near the confluence of the Tigris and Euphrates, we anchored in what was said to be the Garden of Eden. Aside from a scattering of date trees, paradise was disappointingly barren. The next day, we reached Basra, a filthy town overrun with vermin, where my companions disembarked. Their hearty farewells left me alone in first class, free to dwell on the looming meeting with my father. The excitement of seeing my mother's land and confronting my swashbuckling father gripped me again as I neared my destination.

Would I recognize him? Would he embrace me as his son? How would I introduce myself? As I agonized over these questions for the thousandth time, the landscape changed again. The final sixty miles to Al Faw were lush, the riverbanks painted in fresh greens despite the heat. The Karun River merged with the Tigris and Euphrates, its current propelling us toward the gulf. The steamer announced our arrival at Al Faw with a two-short, one-long blast of its horn. To cross the gulf, I would have to rely on luck—I hoped to hire a dhow for the hundred-mile journey to Bushehr, my family's battleground. Fortune favored me. A medium-sized dhow, crewed by twenty men, was set to sail for India with a cargo of dates. I set out at once, riding an ass while another carried my luggage, its burden balanced in two swaying suitcases. The herdsman followed, murmuring encouragement to the beast.

By afternoon, I boarded the topsy-turvy vessel. Dressed in my suit, the African crew from Zanzibar met me with mocking, red-gum grins. We sailed into a spectacular sunset. The journey took two days with a strong wind. The coast was always in sight. The heat was staggering. Here, the air temperature surpassed body temperature for half the year. My skin peeled like potato shavings, flayed raw by the relentless sun. God knows how I would have survived a more extended voyage.

The crew, an incurious lot, shared their food, which I paid for without protest. They advised me to stay below deck, but I could endure no more than an hour in its suffocating dark. The rolling ship had me vomiting in gut-wrenching fits, much to their amusement. The overpowering stench of overripe dates numbed all sense of taste and smell. I have not touched a date in fifty years. By the time we reached port, I was semi-naked, my skin beet-red from head to toe, my vision nearly gone. I woke in a decent hotel, feverish and disoriented. The bellboy had heard of Herr Wassmuss. In my delirium, I scrawled a note in German:

Dear Herr Wassmuss,

I am the ward of Prince Saleh Mirza. A letter from my late mother, Zoleikha Tangestani, revealed your relationship with her during the Great War and, thus, your connection to me. With no expectations on my part [a lie] and no obligations on yours [another lie], I request to meet you tomorrow at the Semiramis Hotel at six in the afternoon.

Your son, Dal Wassmuss

I collapsed into my hotel bed, the darkness a reprieve from the pounding in my skull. The outcome would not have changed with a more gradual approach, but the shock tactic triggered an explosive encounter. Never had I considered an aggressive response in any version of my dreams. I cannot swear by the accuracy of my recollection of meeting my supposed father. A dream, tangled with all others, whispered to me: Someone's knocking on your hotel door. Minutes, or perhaps hours, had passed since I had sent the note—I could not tell. The knocking did not stop. It dragged me from sleep to a sitting position. I heard a man say to the bellboy in local Farsi (instead of the Arabic dialect), "Open this door, or I will kick you down the stairs." A heavy man with grizzled hair suddenly loomed in the doorway, blustering and raging in German. Unable to see his opponent in the darkness, he strode in and flung open all the window shutters, pushing out with both hands as if unleashing the sun's energy. He was still ranting when I saw him clearly for the first time—a heavy, angry, middle-aged man of no distinction. He stopped dead. His head tilted slightly like a dog trying to make sense of an unfamiliar sound. Was it my blue eyes, blond hair, or the feverish confusion in my gaze that stunned him? The silence held for mere moments before he erupted again. The entire hotel must have heard him.

"Do you think I would consort with a peasant woman from Tangestan? The British had a $500,000 bounty on my head! Do you think I trusted a mere peasant"—the word dripped with disdain—"to run my operations? You Persiranians are the scum of the earth with your conspiracies and theories. I live in a miserable country." He spat the word 'theories' with a thick German accent as if the notion disgusted him. "I bought this farm to make some money. All you people do is try to cheat me. Little men, squabbling, selling me down the river. I am sick of all of you." He came closer to the bed. "And now they send me some parentless"—he used the Persiranian insult for a nobody—"kid from a village? Is this the best they could do? You don't even look German. Answer me! Did the English send you? It won't work, you know. I am retired. Not that they believe me—these shit Anglos! They think I am here to stir rebellion. I am done. Done! I tell you, I am going back to Germany as soon as I sell this wretched farm. What do these people want from me?"

His tirade now turned directly to me. He stepped closer, his left hand clawing at my shirtless torso, slipping, then moving up toward my throat. He pushed me hard against the headboard. I could smell the acrid sweat of a man long unwashed; his soaked shirt outlined wet ship-shaped stains beneath his armpits. His eyes were cruel, capable of harm. "You signed my name in the hotel register!" His outrage turned fixated now. He switched to enraged German. "You dare use my name? My name?" He repeated it, spitting out the words. "You are not fit to bear my honorable name." With his right hand, he slapped me. Hard.

The impact blurred the edges of my vision. Before I could fully register it, another slap followed. My mind teetered on the edge of consciousness. Then, the hotel manager and two waiters seized him from behind, dragging him away as he screamed dire threats at me. The manager summoned a doctor. I had traveled a thousand miles to meet him. I didn't say a single word. To this day, I cannot stand hearing anyone call me by his last name. The encounter lasted all of a couple of minutes. What was the truth? He admitted to knowing my mother by denying that she played a role in his operations. It didn't matter. I wanted nothing to do with this filthy man, so unworthy of my imagined construct of a Superman. He returned to Berlin in April 1931. In a small paragraph in the *Vossische Zeitung* that November, I read that he had died a broken man—forgotten and impoverished. I did not shed a tear.

In the Bushehr hotel, an Egyptian doctor of extreme kindness bathed me in cool water and applied a thick layer of tropical lotion over my sun-scorched skin. He instructed the staff to keep me cool with wet towels and assigned an orderly to guard my room. But he could do nothing for my psychic pain. After the war, I met him at a medical convention in Vienna. He didn't recognize me. I introduced myself by thanking him for his kindness to a teenage boy. By then, I had made a name for myself as a surgeon. After dinner, we sat in a stateroom drinking Marillenschnaps. Every few minutes, he slapped his forehead in disbelief, trying to reconcile the renowned doctor before him with the burned, broken boy in Bushehr—the "hellhole of the Gulf," as he called it. I returned to Baghdad and boarded the Orient Express from Istanbul to Berlin. I decided to get on with my studies.

My train glided into Berlin in late summer. To my surprise, Harold Nicolson waited for me on the platform. Steam enveloped him, parts of him appearing and disappearing like a specter. He smiled warmly. "Hadjit, your servant, has come to pick you up," he said. He looked older and stouter. Like Sardar Mirza arriving in Paris, Berlin overwhelmed my senses. In the 1930s, Berlin called itself the third-largest city in the world. It was a city at war with its own identity—its structure eroded by the collapse of the monarchy, the rise of hyperinflation, attempted revolutions and ruthless political assassinations.

We stopped before a Gothic abbey, the Berlinisches Gymnasium zum Grauen Kloster, the city's oldest and most prestigious gymnasium. The vaulted arches reminded me of a caravanserai. Harold laughed at my analogy before dropping me off at the Persiranian embassy, where I would stay on and off for three years. As he prepared to leave, he grabbed my shoulders, looking deeply into my face. "I know you admire the Germans, my boy. There is much to admire. But I beg you, do not fall for Herr Hitler's antics. Do not fall for it," he urged. "I promised my good friend Saleh Mirza I'd watch over you. Call me if you need anything." He pressed a large, pearly visiting card into my hand, the royal coat of arms embossed on it. Quickly, he turned me around, using my back as a writing surface to jot his London details. Then, without another word, he jumped into his car. As he drove away, he shot a hand out the window in a vague, parting salute.

I lived in Berlin for three years with the ambassador and his aristocratic wife, a Qajar princess. She treated me like a son. A thoroughly modern woman, she resembled a Rossetti painting. The ambassador, a quiet and dignified diplomat, worked tirelessly to convince the Germans of our Aryan heritage. It was he who suggested to the new Shah that we change our country's name to Persiran to align with the Germans' racial theories. This effort ultimately earned us honorary recognition. He had no illusions of superiority, but he understood diplomacy. Reza Shah lacked subtlety, overplayed his hand and sealed his fate before the decade's end. I spent those years conjugating Latin and Greek verbs, translating Horace and Virgil. Despite Harold's warnings, I fell for the Nazis. I caught the last echoes of Berlin's wild 1920s before the Nazis, scrubbed the city clean. We visited cabarets, indulged in expensive women and drowned ourselves in the distractions of youth.

And then, with my Abitur passed and my medical career set, I walked into the world of German surgery—a disciple of the great Herr Doktor Sauerbruch.

The small window in the cell, now a dark gray, signaled the approaching daylight. Professor Dal fell silent.

THE FOURTH NIGHT: 0100

THE WRITER CLARIFIES
THE EMERGING PATTERN

"Why three narrators?" you ask. Because each one offers a unique perspective on the history of their time. This book is an oral history, and like all oral histories, it requires multiple witnesses to capture the full scope of the story. The princeling writes from Boston to the historian in Tehran, recounting the turmoil his family faced during the last Shah's reign. His account, rich in historical documentation, offers insights into the lives of his grandfathers—men whose positions in the hierarchy ensured their lives were well-documented. With this material abundance, the princeling reconstructs the remnants of two dynasties. His narrative lacks the intimate details of everyday life. To fill this gap, he introduces his uncle to the lady historian. You would agree that the Surgeon Yarn-Spinner, an eyewitness to history, provides a personal and vivid account.

On the third night, he shares the story of his adoption, his German father's life during the interwar period, and the mounting disappointments that began when he was eleven years old—disappointments that would shape his future. His role as an eyewitness is crucial; he connects the lives of the pairs of twins across three generations, linking the past with the present. I did not elaborate on Wassmuss. Numerous historians have written about his life. Historians cover the English bombardment in the South of Iran in a few footnotes. It deserves better.

The princeling and the Fatman converse with Ms. Vakil and Baba, while the Professor speaks only through the Fatman. The Fatman, our imagined King Shahryar of *1001 Nights*, sprawls on his bed, always eager for more stories from Scheherazade, the skeletal surgeon. He is our most reliable oral historian, yet a mad, broken man.

THE CIRCUMCISED NARRATOR DOES
HIS FORK-SWALLOWING TRICK

Fork: An instrument used chiefly for the purpose of putting dead animals into the mouth.

Ambrose Bierce

Dear Ms. Vakil,

I live in a small, modest one-bedroom apartment. The building, with its fourteen units, has seen better days. Since arriving in Boston, I've moved twice, each time downgrading to a less desirable neighborhood. I've reached some form of economic equilibrium—I'm where I belong now. I have trouble focusing on your email. The overwhelming smell of garlic, ginger, peanuts and chili peppers from my Szechwan neighbors suffocates me. The woman—likely an imported wife from mainland China—talks incessantly as if she's constantly haggling for produce. Her husband, a natural-born citizen, takes offense at the slightest provocation with the skill of a seasoned diplomat. I endlessly argue with my Irish neighbor, whose age is indeterminate. She wears a permanently disapproving expression. She threatens to punch the chattering Chinese woman. We have reached an impasse.

I detected your personal question, no matter how indirect. By sending your regards to Mrs. Poonaki, you indirectly ask if there is a Mrs. Poonaki. Neither of us is innocent; there any many layers to that question. I should jokingly ask, "What are your intentions, younger-than-I lady?" But forgive my humor. I won't sidestep the question. No, there is no Mrs. Poonaki. I misunderstood your questions about the documents. I appreciate your trust in their authenticity. Your interest is in Mr. Hekaiatchi, my fictional storyteller. I must be cautious in how I answer. I admit a more solid version of Mr. Hekaiatchi exists beyond my creation. I've never met him in person, but after the Persiran-Iraq War ended in the eighties, I began receiving letters from him. He claimed to have been a cellmate of my Uncle Dal and demanded compensation for "critical information" about my family.

Since my forced exile, I've received numerous, shall we say, "petitions" from family members of former servants, all soliciting money. Once, a woman wrote claiming to be the third wife of old Nemat, my grandfather and father's lifelong servant. She requested a monthly stipend. I was unaware Nemat even had a first wife, let alone a third. He had been a bachelor all his life. Jenia, the daughter of our Armenian driver, who I remember as a thin little girl, sent me a letter in broken English asking for a U.S. visa. Naturally, I was in no position to help financially or with visas. Over time,

the letters stopped, but Mr. Hekaiatchi continued his correspondence for some time. I haven't heard from him in at least thirty
years—the idea to use him as a storyteller came from details in
those letters. I admit, I'm disturbed that you know the man. May I
ask how you came to be acquainted with him? You've unwittingly
stepped into my story, Ms. Vakil. My storyteller—or should I say
our storyteller?—will portray himself as you describe him to me.
Our connection now feels more personal.

I know which generation of twins interests you. I warned you
before that your focus on the older, historical twins must involve
many intertwined threads, each twisted and knotted with a noose
at both ends. I've found a strange symmetry in the history of my
paternal grandfathers and their twin grandchildren—us. That
particular twist, which occurred decades before my birth, reached
me in my prison cell on the ninth night of my imprisonment
and nearly strangled me. I might not have recalled the following
event if not for a chance meeting with a man named Golchin
in Boston a few years ago. Ms. Vakil, you must understand how
often one encounters fellow immigrants—far too frequently to be
mere coincidence. One Saturday morning, I ventured out into the
harsh Boston winter, my mood as grim as the icy layers coating
the plowed snow. Each breath of air was a stinging cut. I cursed
the day I chose Boston as my destination. I entered a hair salon for
a haircut—an ordinary place with linoleum floors. A thin upper
level had a dozen hair-cutting stations, while the lower level had a
row of molded plastic chairs for waiting customers, separated by a
wrought iron railing. A middle-aged woman in bifocals observed
me from behind a lectern. "Got an appointment?" she asked. "No?
At least have a name, honey?"

I told her my name and the smell of herbal shampoo filled the
air. "Please take a seat. Someone will be with you. Andre, music.
A customer." She spoke the one-word sentences with a whine. A
girl in tight jeans and a tight T-shirt, with a coffee cup in hand,
swayed her hips to no music before stopping. A man, who I immediately recognized, walked over. "My name is Andre. Would you
step this way?" It was Golchin—parading as a seventy-year-old
homosexual with a faux French accent. Despite the makeup and
years, I recognized the blotchy face. He removed his red velvet
jacket with flair and slipped into a sea-green surgeon's tunic. I sat
at the station closest to the window. A diploma in Latin hung on
the wall, with his assumed name in bold Roman lettering. Outside,
I saw the shop sign swinging in the wind: Adam and Eve's, Get a
Head Start, Andre LaTour, Consultant Hairstylist.

He picked up a pair of scissors and began snipping at the air,
his usual nervous chatter filling the silence. The sound was unmistakable, a signature of sorts. Back in Tehran, Golchin had been
our neighborhood barber. His small shop was two blocks from
our house in Ferdowsi Square. He had more than just the title
of barber—he fancied himself an amateur M.D., making house
calls, assisting in deliveries and even performing circumcisions. He
believed hair was part of the body and that cutting it was as vital a
skill as any doctor's. My father had a soft spot for Golchin and was
a regular at his shop. Two weeks before my seventh birthday, during
his weekly haircut, my father arranged for Golchin to perform my
circumcision. I can't explain my father's actions. A man who prided
himself on modernity, who counted the country's top surgeon as an
elder brother, entrusted this task to a barber. It was nothing more

than patronage for him. My father believed in staying connected with the working class, equating it with democracy and generosity.

He set a date for January eleventh, the day after our birthday. The gifts would make the pain more bearable.

It was a cold, sunny day. A crow's cry echoed through the garden, a reminder of the winter chill. Dozens of wide trays filled with cooked plums sat out to dry, their juice ready for the picking. They circumcised me in the dining room, using a large white towel to cover a metal cabinet from the upstairs bedroom, the makeshift operating table. My mother held my hand, trying to comfort me. I was naked, my belly button sticking out. I remember the fear as my mother tried to distract me, swinging me playfully in the air, but it didn't work. The smell of fresh bread from the kitchen did little to soothe me.

Then, my father walked into the room with Golchin, who removed his shoes before stepping onto the Turkoman rug. Tall as a thief's ladder, he wore a white uniform with a priest like collar. His thin face had been ravaged by smallpox; his combed-back hair revealed tiny craters on his forehead. His black hair shone with the latest pomades. One long, clumpy strand always adorned his forehead. He swept it back at regular intervals with a simultaneous motion of hand and head. Full of charm and respect for the parent, he poked his index finger once too often into the head of the child. That poking finger revived memories.

Neither my brother nor I liked Golchin. Under his arm, he carried a rolled brown leather pouch, like the complimentary tool-kit, in the trunk of a new car. He set up his tools on the dining table and explained the procedure to my father, emphasizing its delicate nature. Meanwhile, I sat crying, sneaking glances at him and my father, feeling the weight of his impatience.

Golchin chose a twenty-inch bamboo stick from among his tools. He split it lengthwise with his penknife, extending the crack eight or nine inches to the middle of the stick. He walked to the operating table, pulled at my foreskin, and slid it down into the crack in the stick. I began to cry and struggle. Golchin held the end of the stick with one hand; with the other, he fished a piece of red and white string from his back pocket—the type used on pastry boxes. He wrapped it tightly around the makeshift bamboo clamp. He returned to the dining table, chose a shaving razor and opened the blade. His eyes narrowed to slits. He approached me like Bela Lugosi would. He waved the razor. My father glared at him. All of a sudden, Golchin clapped his hand to his forehead. He walked quickly back to his bag. He found his bottle of alcohol.

A ridiculous image persists in my memory, a primal distillation of fear, shame and humiliation. I see myself leaning back in my mother's tight embrace, with the end of a bamboo stick pointing out—a propeller centered on my piddling penis. Servants stand ready to immobilize me.

Golchin quickly disinfected his razor with a cotton swab drenched in alcohol. He swung one leg over the table as if mounting a horse. Someone standing behind him held my legs pinned to the table. Golchin's elbow angled high. He pulled in earnest at my trifling foreskin, sticking out from the crack in the bamboo stick. His razor hand emerged like a sparrow poised to fly from its branch. The hand descended, disappearing from view below my mother's hugging arms. I looked up at my mother, who turned her head in a grimace of pain. I don't remember any physical pain.

The afternoon of my circumcision, my brother and I played with an assortment of birthday toys in our room. I sat on my freshly made bed, a bandaged package between my legs, while my brother sprawled on the floor, rolling a small Matchbox ambulance toward me. Its white back doors, with a red cross, stenciled in, swung open on tiny hinges, revealing a red interior and a plastic stretcher inside. Have I transformed an ordinary Corgi car into an ambulance in my memory? I can't say, but it feels too convenient. My brother mimicked engine sounds, lulling my suspicions as he guided the toy toward my bed. I clutched my toys, wary. He could seize the moment to snatch one away. But I never imagined his intent—to pounce and squeeze the gauze package.

I muffled my cries in the blanket, shielding us both from our father's temper. Our fights remained between us. We watched as blood seeped to the edges of the gauze. He stared, fascinated, then shouted, "Mummy?" The single word was implicit: "Look what I've discovered. Parents, come investigate." Our mother and father rushed in. They questioned us—him sharply, me gently. My mother wrapped me in a blanket. We drove to the hospital. Over and over, she berated herself for letting Golchin into our home, for warning my father against allowing a quack to perform surgery and for failing to prevent this. My father's eyes burned with fury for the second time that day. My brother and I remained silent. Neither of us admitted how the bleeding had started.

My father never spoke of it again. Golchin vanished. The neighborhood buzzed with rumors. Someone claimed they saw him being forced into a car. A neighbor swore they heard him pleading his innocence. A correctional officer whispered of a brutal beating, saying Golchin's feet had been flayed raw. Others recounted stories with shifting protagonists, their imaginations feeding their memories. No one believed Mrs. Haratunian, the Armenian widow when she insisted she had lent Golchin money to escape the country. In time, my father gained a reputation for brutality. Long after his death, the revolutionary courts heard testimonies implicating him in similar crimes.

Golchin squirted farted water from a plastic bottle to dampen my hair. He trimmed around the edges. He sneezed—a slight, stifled sound, like a tissue yanked too quickly from its box.

"Ms. Vakil, do you recall that scene in *The Great Escape*? When Gordon Jackson, the intelligence officer, automatically thanks the German officer who cunningly wishes him good luck in English? Rather like Jackson, I instinctively blessed Golchin's sneeze—in Farsi."

"Thank you," he replied. "You remembered me, Mr. Poonaki."

"Yes. You haven't changed. But how did you remember me?"

"I didn't. You gave your name to the receptionist." He said it pleasantly, making me feel doubly foolish. His fingers tightened their grip. I raised my head. Without sarcasm, he inquired about my father, just an old barber making conversation. "His Excellency did me a disservice long ago, you know." He cocked his head as if sifting through memories. I said nothing. "My condolences regardless," he added. "Do you live in Boston? I moved here over forty years ago. Thank goodness. What would I have done if I had to emigrate at this age?"

"Have you got your citizenship?" I asked, steering the conversation to a favorite topic among immigrants. He answered with a joke about Khomeini. We chatted about employment, the prime rate and Googoosh's new singing career. When I reached for my wallet, he waved me off. I left, feeling strangely relieved.

You interpret the ambulance incident as an innocent grab for a toy, free of malice. But, dear one-woman jury, I intend to prove beyond reasonable doubt that my brother and I sought to hurt each other at every opportunity. Due to our difference in size and strength, he favored brute force; I preferred the psychological counter. In photographs, we appeared as funhouse distortions of each other. To make my case, Ms. Jury, I must stretch our professional boundaries. I adhere to the subtleties of taarof, our polite verbal dance that shields us from confrontation. I once pitied the Americans—of whom I am now one—for their openness, their naked exposure to direct interrogation. How did English lose the distinction between you and thou? Why blur politeness and intimacy, familiarity and disrespect? We Persiranians dance a long dance before moving from *vous* to *tu*. I know elderly couples who have never used the intimate thou; their lovemaking must be silent, for otherwise, in what circumstance might one employ the plural you in bed?

Indulge me: I must peel away layers of taarof to describe my parents' lovemaking. I hear your sigh, but trust me, it's not gratuitous. It clarifies that my brother and I, even as children, did not play games lightly. During our thirteenth summer, our father, Nima Poonaki, decided to educate us in the American way: total openness. He gave us a book on the facts of life. The cover depicted a girl in a frilly dress, holding a Japanese parasol and a straw basket, leaning to kiss a ragged boy in lederhosen, his sock drooping at the ankle. Tiny hearts bubbled off the blue cardboard cover. Anatomical outlines lay bare the bladder, uterus, urethra and fallopian tubes. The male figure, shown in profile, had a placid penis resting on his scrotum. The female displayed frontally, bore a dark triangle for genitals and two dotted semicircles for breasts—a clinical depiction of reproduction.

The second chapter replaced outlines with blue-hued photographs of fetal development. But science couldn't extinguish the mystery surrounding entry and penetration. We asked our father the inevitable question: Had he practiced entering our mother? His response was gruff: Focus on the other chapters. And yes, the act was practiced occasionally. How else did we imagine we came to exist?

To us, the series of photographs felt incomplete. The author should have added one more bluish image to the sequence of fetal development. We still felt enclosed in our shared, imaginary sack of consciousness. Within that sack, we wrestled with one another while everyone else remained outside, their noses and pale lips flattened against an invisible barrier as if pressed against a window. The book had cracked open the door to sexuality. It would never shut again. Our glands whispered to us, urging us to ignore the book, its author and even our father, whose brusque manner had only deepened the mystery. Instead, they compelled us to seek proof, satisfy curiosity and remove doubt.

I made the first attempt. I associated nighttime with penetration—a reasonable assumption, though my parents happened to be the exception. Night after night, I listened for their footsteps ascending the stairs after giving the final orders to the servants. Then, as the house quieted, I would hear the doors shutting. Distant traffic murmured through the walls like an inverted acoustic telescope. Nearer, much nearer, was my brother Tari's rhythmic breathing. I would tiptoe out of the room, race across the hall and peer through the crude but generous keyhole. Night after night, in the dim light, I saw nothing but their still outlines in bed. The urgency that the book had stoked waned, as did my nocturnal forays.

Everyone napped on summer afternoons without exception. One day, I woke with a start from our forced siesta. My brother's bed was empty. I cracked open the bedroom door and saw Tari hunched at our parents' keyhole. At first, I didn't connect his actions with my nighttime explorations—until I noticed his gray, English-style shorts and gray socks, one falling to his ankle. The image snapped into place: the girl with the Japanese parasol. I watched him, transfixed by his concentration. His hands were clasped between his thighs, rubbing together absent-mindedly. Suddenly, he straightened and bolted back toward our room. I had just enough time to leap into bed and feign sleep before he entered. He buried his face in his pillow and whimpered softly. I had to know why.

A few days later, I waited for the house to settle into its afternoon lull. I listened for my brother's breathing to settle into sleep. Then, as quietly as possible, I positioned my eye at the keyhole, its shape reminiscent of a question mark. As my vision adjusted to the dimness, my mind flooded: my first encounter with hard-core pornography. Slanted bars of light filtered through the wooden shutters, illuminating the floating dust of summer. On the bed, a couple—no longer young—made efficient love. The man methodically shifted the woman's position, dividing time into near-perfect intervals. It was a performance, a film that supplemented the book. Then the phone rang. The actors, unrecognizable to me until that moment, lifted their heads. The man, still on his knees, still inside the woman, reached for the receiver. His paunch distorted under the pressure of her backside. "Hello. Poonaki," he said, his voice level, utterly undisturbed. In full glory, my father conducted a phone conversation as though seated at his desk rather than embedded in my mother's body. "I will call you back." He placed the receiver back onto its cradle. More movements, more sounds. Then my mother sobbed. She cried—not in pain, but pleasure. I could tell the difference. My brother hadn't. But the realization didn't soften the shock. I watched her experience an orgasm in a graceless position—an unthinkable sight for a child, especially of one's mother. She growled, an animal sound from deep in her throat. She told my father to stop. She cried again. Her face contorted with raw emotion, completely departing from her refined poise. No child should witness the mechanics of their own creation. No parent should ever learn what their child has seen. How could an eleven-year-old make use of such knowledge? And yet, I did. And I didn't wait long.

On a dusty Sunday, we sat in the playroom, having lunch on a square table that often served as a bridge table. In our parents' absence, the cook had served ratatouille, his easy favorite. Prepared à la niçoise, it looked revolting. Bored, we picked at our food. I began the needling. "What were you watching last week?" I asked, playing the innocent. My fork rested on my tongue. I tapped it lightly on my upper teeth. I had one leg tucked under me; the other swung like the pendulum of a grandfather clock.

"Last week?"

"You know. In the afternoon. When you watched Mummy's bedroom." He hesitated. As far as he knew, I had only caught him spying, not discovered what he had seen. We glanced up to see the maid listening, alert.

"Pas devant les domestiques, Verdi. Es-tu devenu fou? he hissed. "Not in front of the servants, Verdi. Are you mad?" He needed time to fabricate a story.

"Not in front of Fatemeh, your favorite maid?" I switched back to Farsi.

"I wanted to see if they were asleep so I could go out and play," he said, pretending reluctance in his confession.

"Is that why Mummy cried?" I mimicked his innocence.

Tari's face flickered with confusion. He was speechless. I pressed on. *"Pourquoi maman pleurait?*—Why was Mummy crying?" I teased. "Do you know Daddy does that to her every afternoon? Do you know why she cries so loudly?" The words tumbled out, unplanned but inspired. Tari leaned forward, desperate for an explanation to resolve his weeks of bewilderment. "Because," I said, delivering it like a nursery rhyme, "she doesn't want to have any more children like us."

It was a revelation. The pieces clicked together in his mind: his love for our mother, the sex manual, the scene through the key-hole—all reframed in this new theory. His intellect had no choice but to resolve the contradictions at the expense of our mother. I watched him, my leg stilling, my fork tapping the ratatouille in measured beats. Tari stood, his expression stunned. His cheeks were wet. He walked out without a word.

"Is Master Tari all right?" Fatemeh asked, concerned.

"Oh yes," I said. Had I miscalculated? Had I gone too far? As I lifted the fork to take a bite, I noticed Fatemeh's conspiratorial smile. Behind her, Tari had crept back into the room, grinning wickedly. He must have signaled that he was about to make me jump.

Then, in a blur, he lunged from behind my chair, seizing my relaxed hand—still holding the fork—and, with a violent thrust, jammed the four prongs deep into the soft tissue at the back of my throat. The fork tore through the top of my tongue, shattered a molar, and ravaged my lower gums. As the blood rushed down my throat, Tari held on to the fork. He conjugated in my ear: "I hate you, I've always hated you and will always hate you. I hope you die." He then had the first seizure of his childhood; he collapsed behind the chair while I choked on my blood. Fatemeh's grin twisted into horror. Her muscles tensed, her eyes darting between Tari, who had collapsed into a seizure, and me, choking on my blood. From that day forward, I carried the mark of that moment in my speech—its defect, its permanent reminder. And Tari? He had no recollection of what he had done.

Dr. Fararat diagnosed Tari with temporary amnesia. At first, he remembered nothing of the past, but over time, his memories returned—except for the fork-swallowing incident. I had become a collector of physical afflictions. This time, I acquired a permanent speech defect. English suffered the least; the hard "g," as in "garlic," shifted to a "k," giving my words a clipped, mechanical edge, like horse hooves on cobblestones instead of earth. But Farsi, my native tongue, bore the worst of it. The language's natural guttural sounds, formed deep in the throat, were replaced by softer ones closer to the mouth. My speech took on a foreign tinge, an unnatural cadence. Saliva pooled in unfamiliar recesses when I tried to pronounce those lost sounds. It produced an awkward gurgling, accompanied often by an embarrassing spray. Strangers mistook me for an outsider—one of those rare foreigners who had mastered the language.

Ms. Vakil, I sense you turning away. Have my recollections revolted you? Don't lose interest. Let me wake my poor Hekaiatchi. Though he sleeps deeply during the day, he forgets nothing whispered to him by my unfortunate uncle, Professor Dal. They have mistreated him. I see your eyebrows lift, Ms. Vakil. How do I know of my uncle's mistreatment? I want to remind you that we met on the first day of our stay as guests at my house. To my battered eyes, he looked an even sorrier sight than me. Let me set the scene. The revolutionary guards had seized my house. They hadn't yet refashioned it into a prison. During my grandfather's time, they used the basement as a refuge from the heat and a storage space for food. A small fountain-fed pool acted as a natural air conditioner. Its gentle trickling echoing off the walls. My grandmother kept an army's worth of provisions down there—hundreds of glass jars, their handwritten labels trembling with age, held tomato paste, citrus juice, vinegar, fig-mint-prune chutneys, eggplant relishes, pickled red onions, sour grapes, even whole eggs suspended in brine.

In those days, the servants slept wherever they could find space, spreading their bedding in quiet corners, their rhythmic snoring blending with the hush of the house. But as modernity arrived and the staff dwindled, they demanded privacy. My father responded by constructing a maze of rooms around the basement, each pair sharing a half-window that offered only a glimpse of passing ankles. The central, windowless rooms—once used for storage—became administrative offices when the Revolutionary Guards moved in.

After a long day with my "persuasive" interrogators, two young guards dragged me back to my cell. My legs had given up hours earlier, after they had beaten the soles of my feet. They trailed uselessly behind me, twitching like the needles of a seismograph recording aftershocks. In another corridor, I saw two other men hauling my uncle. The hallways curved, and for a brief stretch, we were parallel—two bodies being dragged side by side, like debris caught in the same current. He was naked, his body a canvas of bruises. One eye was swollen shut, his bald head gleaming under the fluorescent light. He turned toward me with great effort, his large, toothy grin still intact. "Join me in a drag race?" he asked. A hand came down hard on his skull, snapping his head back like a broken marionette. His body went limp. And just like that, the corridors split, and we parted ways. I cannot fathom how he survived ten years.

FAT STORYTELLER SCRIBBLES
AWAY FROM HIS HIDEOUT

"Your tale, sir, would cure deafness."

The Tempest—William Shakespeare

I wake with a start. Baba's voice sings in my ear like a cuckoo clock. The room is cold, yet sweat clings to my sparse body hair. I crack my neck. Am I still in the loony bin? But no—the light pouring into the room is from the wrong angle, right to left. Shards of sunlight reveal the neatly stacked sacks of rice and turmeric from Mammad-Ali's store. Shadows stretch like propellers from my head to my toes. My little room above the store holds all I need: a roll of bedding, a small table, a pencil, and paper all courtesy of Mammad-Ali.

I have been thinking about my predicament. Scribbling away in this safe, aromatic upstairs cave, I realize I have not considered my long-term safety. Even in this benighted country, writing leaves a trace. Professor Dal gave me the name of a woman named Vakil. She teaches history at Tehran University. I can't imagine how she could help me. I can't risk contacting her now. How could I make my stories public despite my promises? I don't even dare leave my hideout.

Zahra brings me breakfast, her face flushed like a peasant woman working the rice fields. She wears her chador like a woman accustomed to labor, the shiny black fabric crossing her crown and cascading back in a semicircle, like a cape. She takes the two ends and wraps them snugly around her waist. She ties them above her belly, freeing her hands—and revealing a robust upper body. Her ample breasts, snug beneath a red sweater, jiggle as she climbs the stairs. On her way down, I glance at her generous hips, which no chador can conceal. I notice her crossed eyes less and less. Baba, don't worry. I have learned my lesson. You needn't buzz in my head whenever something of mine stirs in sympathy. I want to tell you about my fourth day in the loony bin. I woke up at midday, refreshed. I must have missed the oil-well act. Professor Dal was gone. The noon sun streamed through the top window, casting a prison-bar pattern on my clothes. The midday call to prayer always makes me hungry. Within five minutes, the food arrived. This prison wasn't so bad after all. I had heard a man speak of kings and princes as flesh and blood. I wanted more. I wanted to hear how the young princes fared in life. And Professor Dal himself—was he the son of the German spy? Had he eaten and slept among princes, grandees and Englishmen?

To my surprise, he entered the cell unaided, wearing a strange smile, without the guards pushing or shoving him. He lay down on his thin mattress without a word, staring at the ceiling. I started to speak, but his eyelids shut slowly, like a machine powering down. He fell asleep, leaving all my questions unanswered. That night, as I drifted asleep, he climbed on top of me.

"Get off my back!" I said.

"No choice, my boy. We don't want the guards coming in," he said.

"Can you at least let me know before you climb over me? My heart nearly gave way." I pouted.

"Should I knock or ring the doorbell?" he chuckled, his shaking body making mine tremble in rhythm. "Perhaps telephone for an appointment?" He tittered some more. "Listen to me, boy. We don't have time for your petty sensitivities. Tonight, I will skip sixty years to tell you about the other pair of twins."

I protested. It violated every rule of storytelling. Baba had always said, "Don't confuse the listener by rushing or skipping. Let them follow you, one bread-crumb at a time." But Professor Dal continued as if I hadn't spoken.

"Listen well. The first time you see Lily, she will be giving birth. It's not the most flattering way to meet a woman, but I will do her justice. I want to introduce her to you as the remarkable child she once was. You will see her beauty, her loveliness. She is a Poonaki by birth and by marriage. Through our nights, you will learn to love and cherish her. You will cry for her. You will understand why we were all in love with her."

I turned over reluctantly. The Professor stretched against my back, his head inches from my ear. His long white hair, encircling his bald dome, surrounded my face, making me want to sneeze. "See her in her twelfth hour of labor, on the tenth of January,

1954," he began. "See her ensconced in a world desperate to right itself. In the waiting room, her husband and cousin, Nima Poonaki, paces for those twelve hours. She labors mightily. Sometimes, she raises herself on her elbows, bares her gums, and then collapses, exhausted and afraid. From between her knees, a dark puddle oozes onto the sheets. She imagines giving birth to rotten, dead flesh nurtured inside her for nine months. But no. Twins emerge, shrouded in a thin, glossy film—not translucent, but black as ink. Their bruised-purple limbs are dough-like; one has a shock of clammy hair. She produces more of the black substance, soaking the bed and dripping onto the carpet. It will darken her milk, swirling through it like a storm. It slicks the latex gloves of the horrified surgeon, who stands frozen behind his cotton mask. He watches the woman he secretly loves as she brings forth two boys—and half a gallon of crude oil.

The oil oozes out, covering life—first seeping between toes like mud, then surging like the molten lava of an angry volcano. It will smear the heads of the wise so that the bald become indistinguishable from the hairy. It will drip from the eyelashes of seers onto the tongues of the thirsty, from the braves' chests to the fanatics' phalluses. It will mold the world into high-density polyethylene, disguising nature under films, coatings, foams, signs and displays. Politics and religion will merge. Wars will be the means, and heaven will be the end. The surgeon pulls down his mask and spits out a cotton thread. The taste lingers on his tongue like a phantom limb. Pthew, pthew. He tries again. The elusive filament finally falls onto the soaked sheets. The oil seeps into it like tea into sugar. Soon, it disappears."

"Elusive filament?" I scoffed. "You weren't in the delivery

room. And must you go on about the oil? My father always told me: don't get wedded to allegory. Listeners see through it. It makes the story predictable and dull."

"You gelatinous sack of human dung, do you dare judge the truth of my story? I have no time for silly allegories. The truth of my story surrounds you. Don't you understand that truth merely masquerades as facts? One must twist, distort and wrestle with facts to catch even a glimpse of truth. I was the surgeon in that operating room. I helped the love of my life give birth to my best friend's children."

I met his furious tirade with my truth. I told him about my childhood, circumstances and the winding path that led me here. I wasn't always obese; being overweight would be a fairer description. Like any ordinary boy, I entered puberty with confusion and anticipation, imagining the conquests that awaited me. I dreamed of riding prehensile thighs, of licking the salt of light sweat, of sinking into a yielding breast. I believed all this imminent. Instead, my treacherous glands launched a five-year reign of unchecked secretion, impervious to medical intervention. Now, at 320 pounds, I bear the consequences. But that wasn't all. My voice retained something of its boyish purity; my manhood never reached its full potential; my beard remains a mere fuzz upon my chin.

"I want you to know, Arbab, I studied my numbers and spelling diligently for nine years," I said. I left out the part about retaking subjects at the end of each summer. I spoke of my family. During the first true revolution, I told him, my grandfather abandoned the legendary tales of the Shahnameh and instead regaled the teahouse patrons with political news from the papers. I told him about you, Baba, how you took Hamid under your wing, how it hurt me because I knew. Baba, I knew you did not think me worthy of our family's name. I knew you did not believe I could carry on our tradition. So you brought in the jackal, Hamid. And it cost us the teahouse. I surrendered my full attention back to the Professor with humility. I called him my arbab, my teacher, my revered mentor. I begged him to continue. I cried. Months of frustration and fear spilled out of me like oil from a ruptured tanker.

"Calm down, my soft, fluffy friend. Everything will turn out for the best." He repeated the words, patting and stroking the nape of my neck. "You'll see. The Hamids of this world will not win. Their evil world is doomed. Calm down. I will show you lives that make yours seem serene." And so, fused like an oxpecker to his hippopotamus, the professor and I launched once more into the night. With its youthful timbre, his voice belied the old man on my back. My Baba would have said he had arrived at the crux of his story. "Son," Baba would declare after afternoon prayer, "women are the crux of all stories. It is always about women." And in the weightless realm of Professor Dal's tale, an entire world took shape upon my back, lighter than a Zoroastrian pastry.

THE SURGEON DISSECTS HIS
LOVE FOR THE LOVERS

"There is love of course. And then there's life, its enemy."

Jean Anouilh

At five in the morning, no one slept in the Poonaki house. The French windows glowed like lanterns, their square panes of lamplight diffused by lace curtains. Every room blazed with light. Outside, fat drops of rain slid from the bare cedars. The house itself—quicksilver pooled in licorice-black puddles—shimmered and dissolved under each drop, only to reform with a quiver in the January wind. A small portal within the massive front doors cracked open. An old man peered at the sky, made a quick decision and hurried across the garden toward the gate. His gait alternated between a short trot and quick, cautious steps. He picked his way over the puddles on tiptoe, his feet sinking into the thin crust of snow. He held a brown bag at arm's length in one outstretched hand as if it reeked, though more for balance than aversion.

Nemat, the eldest servant of the Poonaki household, reached the small room by the gate, winded. His Turkoman features bore the etchings of time, his face a web of cracks and furrows that met and parted like estuaries—the ideal *National Geographic* subject. He was seventy-three, or so he believed and still wore the stiff, white uniform introduced by the English for their colonial servants. He didn't bother knocking. The gatekeeper, Ghorban-Ali, was famously hard of hearing. Instead, Nemat flicked the light switch twice. The hulking man on the cot stirred, sat up, and blinked at him expectantly. The bare bulb above his head cast a glare on his shaved skull. He was early Nemat's age, yet his face bore no wrinkles. Nemat spoke loudly. "Two boys. The master has two boys."

Ghorban-Ali frowned, confused. Nemat repeated himself, holding up two fingers, then making a fist with an extended thumb to signify male progeny.

Ghorban-Ali's expression darkened. "Again?" he grunted.

Nemat nodded. "The hand of Ali be with them," he bellowed in the tone of the deaf.

The giant swung his legs over the bed and hopped onto his single foot as smoothly as a hydraulic piston. He propelled himself around the small room in a practiced dance, preparing for ablutions. His single foot carried him in swift, weightless bounds, a wind-up toy set in motion. Nemat left the bag of sweets and hurried back to organize breakfast.

Outside the gates, the daily commerce had already begun. In the cul-de-sac, two men took up their usual spots. Ali the Beggar had occupied his corner for over twenty years, swaddled in layers of rags arranged with care. Afflicted by the misfortune of having no visible affliction, he relied on a plaintive, high-pitched wail designed to extract sympathy but rarely shook loose more than a few coins. His companion, Ali-Shisheh, was a shy madman. His mismatched eyes lent him a fierce look, though he was harmless. He spent his days wiping windshields at traffic stops, misunderstanding the world's colors—red meant fortune, green meant evasion. Motorists tossed him coins to ward off the streaky mess his rag might leave. When paid, his face flushed beet red, his palm clenched around the coin, and his legs carried him in ecstatic bounds through traffic, bouncing off car fenders like a delighted pinball. The regulars paid him more for his wild antics than his dubious cleaning skills. The birth of the Poonaki twins guaranteed them both a lifetime of lunches. Every night, they returned to their places, curled up on the marble platforms flanking the gate—like stone lions before an Achaemenid palace.

Nemat considered them omens of good fortune. By some unseen logic, he thought that the beggars absorbed any misfortune meant for the twins. The beggars, oblivious to this assigned fate, prospered.

The Professor paused. A long silence stretched between us.

"Arbab? Master? Have you fallen asleep?" I asked.

"No, my boy," he murmured. "I mourn my family. Everything changed after the twins' birth. They drained the love from the house. I think about our dreams for them. How nature took its own path instead." With scientific certainty, he had assured Mrs. Poonaki of her pregnancy. "You'll have your puppies on the tenth of January," he had joked. She obliged.

"I can't overstate their effect on all our lives. Their very existence steeped us in misery. Nature stages a grand spectacle for the billions of desperate sperm. Sometimes, she twists the ending—allowing two to win. The twins weren't victors, merely co-finalists. For nine months, they lay curled together. If either had possessed a flicker of awareness, he would have wrapped the umbilical cord around the other's throat and strangled him. It's a perfect crime. No witnesses."

Verdi entered the world first, flailing like a trout on the deck of a trawler. He arrived in the sterile glare of the operating room, his oversized epiglottis choking his first breath. I forced a tube down his purple, gaping mouth and thrust him into an incubator before surgically correcting the defect. Behind him, Tari emerged—a healthy, rosy seven-pounder. I circumcised him on the spot. Verdi was too frail for such an unnecessary procedure. They were aware of each other early on, like flickering neon lights of consciousness. But this race did not start evenly. A single moment of neglect—common in those days—left permanent consequences. Verdi bore the disfigurement through childhood. God only knows what it did to him inside.

No one would have guessed they were twins. They shared a resemblance, but Verdi appeared sickly, his face crumpled like a discarded parchment. I could have repaired it surgically. I showed him before-and-after photographs of fire victims. He refused. He wanted to bear the burden. Tari flourished—a sturdy, golden boy who paraded his health, beauty and joy. We tried everything to bring them closer. We orchestrated elaborate birthday parties with meticulous fairness. We banned competitive games; whenever they played on opposing teams, it ended in a savage fight. Tari always won, beating Verdi mercilessly. Verdi never surrendered, no matter how long the blows rained down. By age six, their enmity had infected the entire household. Arguments split us. "This time, he started it," or "He had it coming—he's sly." I moved out.

I want to tell you about the happier days, before the birth. They didn't feel like happiness at the time. Before the war, the three of us met in Paris for the first time. I had known Nima as a child but not as an adult. He had been four or five when I left. He was born during my eleventh year, an adored miracle. The only child of a forty-one-year-old prince, he arrived with divine favor. I am neither religious nor superstitious, so I credit good genes instead. "Stay awake, my soft sofa."

Besides money, power and position, Nima had natural charm. He was at ease in his skin. People instantly liked him, oblivious to class distinctions. He required no lessons to choose the moral path—until he picked the wrong one. He never warmed to academics, but athletics carried him through. He set school records, playing volleyball and football—any game with a ball. The Prince's letters grew increasingly frustrated.

Dear boy, [he wrote to me in Germany]

Your grades arrived, along with the headmaster's report. Your acceptance into Europe's most prestigious medical school—perhaps the world's—makes me proud beyond words. I have also received my Nima's report. The only common thread

is the teacher's effusive excuses for my son's ineptitude.
He has not yet purchased his books, though school began
two months ago. I ordered a bastinado as a reminder of his
duties. Not one servant would comply. The boy lay back, legs
pointed skyward, whispering to each servant: "Do it, or my
father will be angry with you." Even Behruz, who can lift a
donkey, knelt before my window and wept. I gave up.

Your loving guardian,
Saleh Poonaki

By then, he no longer signed with honorifics. Reza Shah
reigned brutally. His reforms made princes irrelevant. Deep in the
throes of my internship, I heard nothing about the intrigues and
fears back home. Then, in 1938, out of the blue, I received the
following telegram from the Prince.

Sardar Mirza gravely ill with consumption. Arrive Berlin
2nd of May. Arrange a trip to Paris for the four of us. Nima,
Nemat and you will accompany me.

Saleh Poonaki."

Sardar Mirza was dying of tuberculosis in Paris. The disease
had claimed thousands, and I knew the grim reality—medicine
had yet to find a cure. Selman A. Waksman had spent years searching for one. I sent a telegram to him at Rutgers University, asking
about any experimental treatments. He replied with a friendly but
resigned note: "In hot pursuit, but wily bacteria." It wasn't until

late 1944 that he finally purified Streptomycin from Streptomyces griseus, but for Sardar Mirza, it would be too late.

And so began the whirlwind month that changed my life. I first saw twelve-year-old Nima as he disembarked at Lehrter Bahnhof Station, the jewel of French Neo-Renaissance architecture and the envy of Europe. I stood waiting beneath the great barrel-vaulted roof amid a growing sea of Brownshirts and uniformed soldiers—though their swelling presence had yet to strike me as unnatural. A thin, straight-backed boy, already showing the first hints of lankiness, walked toward me with effortless confidence ahead of the rest of his party. He smiled ear-to-ear as though he had always known me. Without hesitation, he stepped into my arms. "Brother," he said, kissing my cheeks three times.

Behind him, the Prince watched with pride. Then, with uncharacteristic emotion, he approached and regarded me with something close to awe. His eyes glistened behind his round spectacles. "You have grown into a remarkable-looking young man."

"Don't look so surprised, my muddy mattress. I was handsome once, too."

The Prince had aged. He leaned on a thick wooden cane, its simplicity starkly contrasting his past grandeur. At fifty-three, his hair was snow white, his once-vital face now drawn and gray. He had lived through the reigns of five Shahs across two dynasties, orchestrating the exile of two of them. Surveying the station, he murmured, "This country is ready for war."

As Nemat kissed my hands in greeting, I felt something stir deep within me. Five years had passed since I last saw them, yet their embraces reminded me of a truth I had not admitted to myself—I had missed them all. Despite the Prince's special affection for Nima, I could see his fatherly love also extended to me. He considered me family. And in that moment, standing amid the din of the station, I realized I had long since accepted them as my own. We settled at the Adlon Hotel on Pariser Platz, in the heart of Berlin's diplomatic quarter—next to the British Embassy, facing the French and American Embassies, mere blocks from the Chancellery. The Adlon was a hub of foreign dignitaries, journalists and celebrities. Over dinner, as we took in the opulence of Europe, the Prince marveled at the sheer weight of its wealth. "Even the doors of ordinary buildings look like palaces," he mused.

Then, over dessert, he shocked me. He proposed adopting me into the Poonaki family.

"I would be honored," he said. "If you took my name." The adoption, he clarified, would not include an inheritance—only some property, which he intended to transfer immediately. He and his brother had always had their assets in common, which was how he secured my future. "As a surgeon in our country, you will never lack an income."

"Your Highness," I began.

"Call me Father, like you used to," he interrupted. "I don't know why you stopped during your teenage years. It hurt my feelings, you know."

"Father," I corrected, "I thought that with Nima's birth, you had made it clear—you had one son." The Prince studied me as if I had grown horns. I pressed on. "And now, with Nima grown, shouldn't he have a say in this?" At that, the Prince threw back his head and laughed.

"My boy, the idea came from Nima himself. Until recently, he believed you were his blood brother. When I explained the truth, he asked why you didn't share our name. Before we left for this trip, he insisted I adopt you. I told him I had considered it years ago but knew you were searching for your roots."

I lowered my gaze. "I found nothing but dead ends." I told him about my journey, my desperate search for my German father. I described how I had confronted Wassmuss, only for him to deny me outright. And that I had not attended his funeral after he had died a few years later. The Prince had known. His agents had sent him reports from Baghdad. He had watched my quest with quiet concern.

"I suspected you might seek him out," he admitted. "I cannot say whether he was your father or not. We will never know. But if he was—there is no shame in being that man's son. Wassmuss was extraordinary." We spoke of my studies and my ambitions. He listened intently. Then, he turned to darker matters. "Reza Shah rules now absolutely," he said. "Much has changed for the better. But as always, we have placed our leader on a pedestal. He listens to no one. Only his son can influence him. The Crown Prince Mohammad Reza has returned from Switzerland. He is now in military training."

"Are you in danger, Father?"

"I cannot say," he admitted. "Years ago, when I was governor and Reza Shah a lowly officer in the Cossack division, he was assigned to me. He and his men rode as my escort. I treated him well. I invited him into my tent for dinner. We spoke often. I think he remembers those times fondly. Even now, he uses me for delicate diplomatic affairs. That is why I am here. Tomorrow, I meet Chancellor Hitler. The Shah has asked me to deliver some difficult messages."

I was mesmerized. The Prince, in direct negotiations with the Führer. At the time, I had been swept up in Nazi ideology, believing it to be the future.

"And what do you make of him?" I asked.

The Prince sighed. "I fear we have much in common, our two nations. An obsession with glory. A desire to rewrite history. And a dangerous leader whom no one dares question."

The next day, a telegram arrived. Khodrat, Sardar Mirza's faithful servant, pleaded with us to hurry—his master's condition had worsened. The Prince delayed his departure by a day to meet Hitler. We then boarded the overnight train to Paris.

We arrived at the Gare du Nord on May 5, 1938. The Prince, tense and impatient, moved swiftly down the platform. We scrambled to keep up. Nemat, bewildered and overburdened with satchels, struggled behind us. Then, we saw good-old Khodrat, towering at six-foot-four. He waited in the crowd. He had aged into a dignified figure, dressed impeccably like an English valet. The Prince's voice rang out across the station. "There he is!" he bellowed, pointing his cane like a general rallying his troops. Khodrat spotted him. Without hesitation, he shoved past a protesting guard and rushed forward. He reached the Prince in seconds and, to the astonishment of the onlookers, collapsed to his knees, kissing the hem of his master's coat. The Prince bent to lift him. The crowd watched in silent awe, trying to gauge the importance of the man before them.

Then, from the corner of my eye, I saw her. Lili stood beside her mother, the Countess, her arms wrapped around her waist. She watched us with quiet amusement, her delicate features framed by the light. She wore a white summer dress, a thin sweater over her shoulders, and a cloche hat that covered her fashionable, boyish haircut. And just like that, my life changed forever.

Lili's mother, Countess Anaïs de Grandpierre, was the daughter of the Comte de Grandpierre. Though not strictly entitled to it, she had adopted the title during the more relaxed conventions of the Third Republic. She stood ramrod straight, watching us with sad eyes, one hand resting lightly on her daughter's shoulder as she waited for Khodrat's embarrassing display of devotion to end. She looked older than her years, her hair arranged in a swept-up coiffure by the famous Antoine, topped with a slightly askew Suzanne Talbot hat. A half veil covered the left side of her face. She wore a cream-colored Schiaparelli two-piece ensemble, the blouse adorned with a barely discernible embroidered woman's face on the shoulder. The woman's hair, done in intricate gold filigree, cascaded wildly down the sleeve to the cuff.

As we approached, Nima, despite years of French tutors, suddenly grew as timid as a scolded puppy. His command of the language was shaky at best, and in the moment, it failed him entirely. I stepped forward, my French fluent—if marred by a heavy German accent. I introduced myself to the Countess, who acknowledged me with a slight nod and a smile so unexpectedly sweet that it startled me. The Prince finally freed himself from Khodrat's grasp. He turned to greet his sister-in-law. Khodrat saw Nemat under the weight of satchels and umbrellas. He descended upon him with a fervor that suggested seeing someone returning from the dead.

"How is my brother?" the Prince asked, his usual courtly manners forgotten in his distress.

"Not well, Your Highness," the Countess replied, reading his bluntness for what it was—deep concern for his twin. "You will see for yourself. We are not hopeful. Mirza is at peace with it." (All of Paris knew him simply as Mirza.)

Lili stepped forward and dropped into a soft curtsy, lifting the sides of her skirt in a girlish gesture. In a stilted, overly formal voice, she declared, *"Cher oncle, cher cousin, permettez-moi de saisir cette occasion permettez-moi de saisir cette occasion pour vous souhaiter la bienvenue à notre belle patrie."* We all stood awkwardly for a beat, unsure how to respond to her rehearsed welcome. Then, with a mischievous glint, she flashed her mother's sweet smile and broke into flawless Farsi, her French-accented Rs adding a charming flourish. "Really, family, you didn't fall for that, did you? Baba would have loved to see your faces." She winked at Nima. Astonished by her fluency, we laughed, and the tension between East and West melted away.

"Lili, vous êtes vraiment fatigante," the Countess sighed, playing the exasperated mother.

But Lili's expression softened as she slipped into her uncle's arms without hesitation. "You smell like him," she murmured, enchanting the Prince to his socks. I won't pretend I wasn't fascinated by the two cousins. Charm, more than intelligence, ruled their world. As Pindar said, "These enchanting creatures were created to fill the world with pleasant moments and goodwill."

As we stepped outside, we encountered a soft Paris spring day. The chauffeur took us to 12 Avenue George Mandel in the 16th arrondissement while Nemat and Khodrat stayed behind to see to the luggage. Nima, back to his usual exuberant self, chattered comfortably with Lili. I watched her closely—her candid blue eyes filled with wonder as she took in her newfound Persiranian family. I cannot tell you when my fascination with Lili began. My tastes do not lean toward prepubescent girls, but even then, she held the promise of the woman she would become. Despite the sorrow during those days, they had a peculiar brightness, and I credit Lili for it. She carried energy with her, filling any space she entered. Even the Prince, burdened as he was, could not help but be charmed. After that Paris visit, I did not see her for five years. I waited for her to grow up. Who waits for a twelve-year-old to grow up? I did.

We pressed together in the narrow French elevator. Lili and Nima giggled at the closeness. As it ascended with its steady clicking, we glimpsed each floor through the scissored brass doors. Marte, the Countess's maid, waited at the entrance, the apartment doors open behind her. She spoke into her handkerchief, mindful of her ill-fitting dentures and the risk of unseemly spray. Though no soubrette, she wore the traditional black dress with a crisp white apron, lace trim and cap. Inside, a nurse in white approached us, pressing a finger to her lips. "His Highness is resting," she whispered. "It was a difficult night." The apartment occupied the entire fourth floor, its polished parquet floors squeaking under our shoes. Floor-to-ceiling windows overlooked Avenue George Mandel, and Nima saw the Eiffel Tower rising behind the Trocadéro.

The Prince, impatient, turned to the Countess. "May I stay in my brother's room?"

"Of course," she said with quiet generosity. "My apartment is on the other side if you need anything." He thanked her and entered Sardar Mirza's room. He did not leave until his twin drew his last breath. It took four nights and a day. In those final days, I saw Sardar Mirza often. When we first entered his room, we wore white surgical masks. The Prince, stubborn as ever, refused.

Sardar Mirza sat propped against a mountain of pillows, draped in a black silk dressing gown. The stiff collar of his ironed pajamas flopped neatly over the robe. Above him, a Monet landscape of Giverny bathed the room in dappled violets. Lili ran to his side and curled against him, his fingers immediately moving to stroke her hair. He was medically blind. A large magnifying glass lay at his bedside, his only tool for examining the world. His coughing was the deep, unmistakable rattle of chronic tuberculosis. I saw the handkerchiefs in the small cloth-lined basket beside the bed, stained with bright, blood-tinged sputum. His skin was waxy with fever, his brow glistening, and his frame had withered—where once he and the Prince were identical, now the Prince looked twice his size.

Yet Mirza, ever the raconteur, remained as animated as his failing body allowed. He was full of stories—of the Constitutional Revolution, the artists he had known and the Paris he had lived in. He had gossiped with Proust, taken tea at Hôtel de Crillon and thrown wild parties with Jean Cocteau. He had debated art with Roger Fry and dined with Diaghilev. Picasso had sketched him once—bent over, inspecting a painting with his ever-present magnifying glass. The caricature hung on the back of the bedroom door. Through it all, the Prince remained by his side.

Late at night, I would check on them and find the Prince curled in bed with his brother, holding him in his arms. I pleaded with him to wear a mask to take precautions. "If I wear a mask," he said, "it would mean life still matters to me—when it does not."

"But Nima—" I started.

The Prince cut me off. "I cannot reach the world Nima lives in. He doesn't need me. I am not sure he needs anyone." He hesitated, then gestured toward Lili. "He will need her. Exceptional, isn't she?" Across the room, Lili sat with her father, laughing, oblivious to how little time they had left.

Fifty years later, I still recall my surprise at my anger. Angry at the Prince's presumption—that he saw them as a pair, rather than her and me. "You see, my floating balloon, I had expectations. I swear to you, I had no carnal designs on a twelve-year-old. I cannot explain it, but I had already envisioned her as a grown woman worthy of my lifelong devotion. And when I saw her five years later, she had fulfilled all my expectations. I was a handsome man—you may scoff, that is our human tragedy—but I tell you, women threw themselves at me. And I had my fill. But I swore Lili would never see me with another woman. She never did. You may think me absurd, but she expected it of me. People say marriages between cousins are written in the heavens. Perhaps. But a single event stole Lili's heart from me."

Sardar Mirza died on May 15th, a bright and sunny day. The servants drew the curtains, readying the apartment for a week of mourning and the endless parade of the Countess's friends and relatives. The Prince didn't emerge from his brother's bedroom. He suffered what I can only call a breakdown. A cry—a raw, animal sound—echoed through the apartment every few minutes. I am sure the neighbors heard it. Then came the Countess's soft murmuring, helpless in the face of such grief. In the servants' quarters, each of the Prince's howls shattered Khodrat, who wept without stopping. The young cousins, white-faced and silent, sat in the overstuffed living room, surrounded by paintings stacked carelessly against the walls—works by the greatest masters of the twentieth century, which would form the foundation of the Poonaki fortune in the years to come.

The Countess remained with the Prince all afternoon. To spare the children from his violent mourning, Nemat and I took them for a walk in the Bois de Boulogne. We wandered along an artificial lake, the world shimmering like one of the pointillist paintings in Sardar Mirza's library. Our reddened eyes struggled to adjust to the bright day. Families picnicked, children played, dogs ran free. I shouted warnings at the cousins, afraid they would step into the path of cyclists or galloping mares. A spirited thirteen-year-old, Nima would dart off to examine something, then return breathless, eager to show Lili his discoveries—a flower, a polished stone, a ladybug. *"C'est une coccinelle,"* I heard her marvel.

They bent their heads together, counting the insect's black spots as it crawled across their hands. Giggling, they built a staircase with their palms, guiding the ladybug up and down, up and down. Tired of the game, the insect finally abandoned them as it lifted itself impossibly into the air. They shaded their eyes in unison and watched it vanish into the sky. At that moment, my mind captured them as if in a photograph: two children, their faces upturned toward the sun, their delicate jawlines tracing a silhouette against the blue sky. They looked like a brother and sister whom God had washed in different dyes—milk and chocolate, one with Prussian blue eyes, the other with warm hazel. My heart melted for them. They were exquisite together. I envied their effortless beauty, their innocence. But I also loved them for it. I promised myself I would do anything to protect them. My powers would prove inadequate.

Beyond the lake, we came to a grassy clearing sloping into a soft embankment. Nima ran ahead and disappeared from view. In the distance, a black boxer dog circled its owner, leaping at a toy bone held just out of reach. Suddenly, it lost interest in the game. It froze, ears pricked, one paw lifted, its tongue hanging out in an absurd grin. Then it spotted us. The dog took off like a shot. Nemat called out a warning. I dismissed it. "Muslims don't like dogs," I thought. Behind me, a Doberman strained against its leash, eager to meet the oncoming boxer. I assumed that was the dog's real target. The boxer charged straight at Lili who stood between the dogs. She remained calm—she had grown up with dogs. I saw her bend slightly, ready to greet the animal. I shouted at her to stand still. She hesitated, stiffening at the sharpness of my voice.

At that moment, Nima appeared at the top of the embankment. He saw the dog racing toward Lili. And he ran. That boy could run. He reached the boxer just feet from Lili and crashed into it, sending them both tumbling. Boy and dog rolled together in a mess of limbs, dust and snarls. The boxer growled, barked and bit Nima four or five times in those few seconds. Shaken, the boxer stumbled to its feet. It looked bewildered, as if it had never meant to attack a human. Then, it remembered its original prey. It bolted past Lili, Nemat and me, aiming for the Doberman—though with far less enthusiasm. The Doberman's owner was ready. He cracked a short whip twice across the boxer's side, sending it yelping away.

We ran to Nima. Lili reached him first. By the time I reached them, he had managed to sit up. He collapsed back onto the dirt, cradling his injuries in silence. Blood trickled down his face. She threw her arms around him and wept. He had a torn lip. His nose bled. A deep bite marred his eyebrow and the corner of his eye—he would use artificial tears for the rest of his life. His right arm had a deep gash, his stomach was lightly wounded as his clothes had given some protection. I pressed a borrowed handkerchief to his eyebrow. "Lili, hold this." She obeyed, kneeling uncomfortably on the ground, cradling Nima's head to her chest. I cleaned his arm with lake water and bandaged it with another handkerchief. The boxer's owner, a blond man in a tweed jacket, apologized *mille fois*—a thousand times. He offered to take us to the American Hospital. Nima, through split lips, asked if the dog would be coming along. Everyone laughed. The laughter softened Lili's tears. She bent low and whispered something into Nima's ear. I wasn't paying attention—still tending his wounds—but I glanced up in time to see the shock pass over his face, followed by a smile. A smile that not even stitches or a tetanus shot at the hospital could erase. A thousand years later, over a drink, when there was nothing left to lose, Nima told me what she had said. "Mother chose Father as her husband when she was twelve in Russia," Lili had whispered. "I will choose mine in Paris."

"You see, my airy fundament, as the Persiranian proverb says, I wasn't even in the same garden. How could I have known how far ahead of me they had planned our future? The rising sun slanted golden rays through the high, grimy window. Professor Dal fell silent.

THE FIFTH NIGHT: 0101

THE WRITER TALKS ABOUT STRUCTURE AND CHOICES

Unfolding this story peels back the layers until we reach the raw, naked core of hate. Violence—its reckless offspring—lashes out with the impulsiveness of a child. And our twins, after all, are children. When I first heard of a brother committing an unspeakable act against his twin, I shuddered. My mind instinctively sought blame, pointing first at the parents. But then I remembered the nature of parenting in the wealthy households of the fifties—a modernity that was more performance than practice. Even in the West, the veneer of responsibility was paper-thin. The Surgeon saw the parents as a pair of ego-driven binary stars, locked in their own gravitational dance, leaving little space for anything—or anyone—else.

I have searched, with great effort, for the love stories buried within this history. But again and again, hate, violence and death force their way to the surface, refusing to be ignored. They dominate the narrative. Don't mistake this for a spoiler—fiction is bound by plot, but history remains unruly, open to infinite futures. What has happened cannot be undone. We tell these stories not for the sake of neat conclusions but to grasp at straws of understanding.

Meanwhile, the fat storyteller's misfortunes have shaped him, turning him from a flat character into a rounder one—though not yet as round as his own body. We have rounded him out, but have yet to breathe life into his nostrils. But calling him a "character" does not strip him of his reality. I hold a photograph of him and myself, both of us smiling awkwardly—a silent, undeniable testament to his existence.

THE NARRATOR'S DISCOURSE ON
POLITICS, SOCCER AND LOVE

"If God had wanted me otherwise, He would have created me otherwise."

Johann von Goethe

Dear Ms. Vakil,

It is 5:45 in the morning. I sit in my tiny apartment, over-looking the early traffic on the elevated Route 93. Trucks shake the building's foundations with rude insistence. A cowardly smear of yellow sun hesitates against my fourth-floor window, too weak yet to reflect from one object to another. On the floor, piles of books on early twentieth-century constitutional history teeter pre-cariously. Weathered black ribbons bind stacks of brittle papers, their seals of cracked red wax—pressed by my grandfather's strong hand—lending them, forgive the cliché, a literal air of legitimacy. Limou, my Tintin-like wire fox terrier (her name means lemon in Farsi and is an anagram of Milou) sits beside me, dejected. I trained her with my bark to stop pulling at the ribbons, keeping the manuscript rolls intact. Progress is slow. Reading handwritten documents requires practice, especially in Farsi, where words lean at impossible angles like weary travelers.

I am astounded by your revelations about Mr. Hekaiatchi, my fictional storyteller. You must understand the peculiar predicament this creates for me. Have I conjured a Golem? Has a character of my invention stepped into the world? The man who claimed to be my Uncle Dal's cellmate wrote to me two decades ago, detailing their time together in prison. His letters carried the air of authenticity, yet I could not verify them. His pecuniary demands were modest, but skepticism held me back. If his claims hold, then he and I have unknowingly bracketed my uncle's ten-year imprisonment—I, at the start, and he, at the end. For my purposes, I confined them together for nine nights and days. In reality, I do not know how long they shared that cell. I supposed Hekaiatchi was mad. He spoke of his father living inside his ear—a detail I shamelessly appropriated. Yet, at times, his letters conjured my uncle so vividly that I felt Dal's presence in my Boston apartment, with all his quirks and contradictions intact. He described a youthful detour to Germany I had never known about. I learned of his reckless venture into the Gulf only through a letter from Saleh Mirza to his agent in Baghdad. Hekaiatchi's voice rang true, but who could tell? And then, abruptly, his letters ceased. I regret not paying him for his troubles. At the time, I was struggling to stay afloat. Today, I am in a better position. Have you kept in touch? I would be willing to pay a fair price for the rest of his story.

For weeks now, each morning before work, I have labored to reconstruct the crucial days of our constitutional revolution. Your profession proves more difficult than I expected—it requires a precise and judicious mind, neither of which, I fear, are my strongest qualities. I can hear your frustration: "Let the professionals handle it, Mr. Poonaki." Rest assured, I am not attempting to write a magisterial history. That task belongs to you. My obsession is narrower: I mean to ferret out my grandfathers' contributions. I am puzzled. Puzzled by the decision of Ain Dawleh, the reactionary premier—a royalist to his marrow, cousin to the old king, a man as rigid as his name implies. Three weeks before Shah's total capitulation to the constitutionalists, Ain Dawleh dispatched a twenty-one-year-old Qajar prince—one whose sympathies he knew lay with the constitutionalists he opposed—as an envoy to an aging cleric who dreamed of a Sharia-based constitution. Why? Why pit an inexperienced aristocrat against a sixty-three-year-old jurist revered in Shia centers from Najaf to Tehran? What was the play?

My apartment is drowning in books—or, at least, up to Limou's ears. Her ears, pricked and alert, catch something beyond human perception. She lets out a low growl, quickly escalating into the triple barks that have united my neighbors against me (especially the Chinese couple next door). Deep in my reading, bifocals perched on my nose, I call to quiet her. She ignores me. I lift her onto my lap and continue. I have read and reread my grandfather's diaries. Notwithstanding the tears, it is worth peeling back the layers of our fine Persiranian onion—more layered than its

Western counterpart. Here, for your consideration, is my amateur historical interpretation.

The dying Shah—Mozaffar al-Din Shah, my grandfather's brother—plays ball (hello, America) with the 1906 constitutionalists. Despite the intrigues of his court physicians—French, English and local—it was the overbearing Dr. Schneider who had long ago diagnosed him with gout. It leads to Bright's disease and, finally, to congestive heart failure. The entire court knew the Shah tiptoed toward death. The Qajars, if nothing else, were masters of intrigue. Three figures opposed constitutional rule: the Crown Prince Mohammad Ali, awaiting his brief reign; Ain Dawleh, the stubborn old premier; and Sheikh Fazlollah Nouri, whose passion for divine law prefigured the theocracy we now endure. Each took a different approach. Please memorize these names.

The Crown Prince, raised by the Russian tutor Shapshal Khan, remained proudly illiterate. You remember, Ms. Vakil, this was the same man who had my twelve-year-old grandfathers' feet flogged raw in Tabriz. He believed his divine right was as absolute as Nicholas II's. When the clergy and merchants first demanded an independent judiciary, he scoffed, "A House of Justice? I am the House of Justice." But the tides shifted. Eight months later, he watched his father waste away. He had no desire to inherit an uprising. Letting the old fool grant a constitution served the Crown Prince better now—he could always undo it later. Let Mozaffar al-Din play the feeble reformer. When the time came, the son would be made of sterner stuff.

At first, the premier, Ain Dawleh, baffled by the defections of Nouri and the Crown Prince to the constitutionalist side, soon saw the longer game. He aligned himself with them. Together, they feigned support for the revolution while quietly betting against its survival. Ain Dawleh returned to power twice more but faded rapidly into history. The Crown Prince took the throne in January 1907. By 1909, the populace deposed him. Losers leave only minor ripples in history.

But Sheikh Nouri—his ripples became waves. You, Ms. Vakil, drive daily on the highway built in his honor. The man's fatwa against cinema silenced movie houses until his death. It is no surprise that Khomeini revered him. I urge you to stay laser-focused on him. His name meant nothing to me—until my arrest thirty-five years ago. Since then, I have pinned his photo to my mental board, drawing lines between him and the men who shaped our fate in the modern era. His strategy was simple, righteous and terrifying: to bring forth heaven on earth by force.

Let me take a breath. By now, you recognize my pattern. I tell the story from both ends: a first generation that builds, a third that fritters away. Do not rush to judgment. In the end, the Prince's gains were modest, as you know. And the fritterings—ah, Ms. Vakil, aren't all good family stories about the fritterings? Let's leave my three reactionaries behind or more accurately let my fatman bear witness from my uncle's mouth to the reader's ears sometime in the future.

My earliest memories of the drive to Poonak remain in chiaroscuro. The paved road from Mehrabad Airport turned to a dirt track stretching north for ten miles, cutting through scraggly land dotted with the occasional cluster of mud dwellings—barely even hamlets—huddled around the neglected gardens of absentee landlords. The light still burns bright in my mind. I remember no shadows except for the trembling shadow of our car, dancing beside us on the bumpy road. Behind the village of Poonak on a bright spring day, you could pause to rest on a thresher bench—a rough wooden plank perched atop the central hub of four shafts, each ending in a wooden wheel, pulled in a steady circle by a pair of oxen. Round and round, your weight would aid the weathered peasant as he separated the golden grain from the chaff. The high-pitched squeal of crushed wheat stalks—like nails scraping across a blackboard—sent shivers up our spines. From there, we would take two sharp, right-angled turns in the pale green, lemony Vauxhall, following the high mud-and-straw walls that enclosed Poonak. A cluster of filthy boys—Hamid among them—kicked a deflated plastic ball in the dust. Our car rolled past them, its tires crunching over loose gravel, before stopping in front of a large green wooden gate, later replaced by an automated metal one.

Our driver, Ovanes, nicknamed Mussio, a first-generation Russo-Armenian émigré, would sound the horn—two quick bursts. Silence. A few longer honks produced no better results. Somewhere in the depths of the garden, perhaps half a mile away, Nadali, the gardener, was likely bent over his flowers, watering them with his two large tin ewers. Mussio, the stoutest man in our world, would mutter curses under his breath—sometimes in Armenian, sometimes in Russian. A sophisticated man and a master mechanic, he spoke several languages. Years earlier, in an era before excess, he had saved for months to buy a Rolex watch, a craftsman's tribute to another craftsman. Now, with his usual grumbling, he would leverage his bulk from the car to perform a feat that my brother and I never tired of watching. He could create enough gap for a much thinner man to slip through by pushing both gates inward. With Houdini-like precision, he would bend his knees, lower his head sideways through the gap, and then—still gripping the outer edge of the gate—coax his belly through, a close shave every time. From the backseat, we'd peel our sticky thighs from the vinyl to watch in fascination.

In a letter, my mother once referred to those double green gates as the pearly gates of heaven. As they swung open, dappled shadows from the fruit trees spilled across the ground, a sharp contrast to the relentless brightness of the last hour's drive. We'd pass through the orchard, where cherry, sour cherry, fig, pomegranate, walnut, mulberry and white berry trees stood in careful rows. Among them, rows of strawberries and cherry tomatoes peeked red beneath dusty green leaves. The sound of water gurgling through the joubs, open waterways, and the smell of freshly cut grass still visit me in daydreams as I sit in my cubicle, drafting endless, mind-numbing safety instructions. The road turned into a shaded, graveled avenue lined with tightly planted sycamores. Their roots intertwined dangerously beneath the soil, tripping careless walkers, while high above, their bowed crowns met in secret conferences, sealing out the sun. The car stopped at the base of a wide stone staircase, its slabs worn thin by time. As we climbed, the trees opened to reveal a sunlit platform.

To the left stood the modern house our parents built, where once the Prince had sat, handing Uncle Dal a letter from his mother. To the right, a rough-hewn pool, murky and black, served as the main reservoir, feeding the gardens in the valley. My mother replaced it with a modern swimming pool within a few years. You could see the city sprawled far across the valley to the southwest. In those days, the divide between Tehran and Shemiran—where aristocrats and foreign diplomats escaped the summer heat—appeared distinctly. To the far left, the mountains stretched endlessly, punctuated by the snowy peak of Mount Damavand, its top blown off in some youthful moment of volcanic recklessness. Below us, a low stone parapet ran along the edge, marking the drop into the valley of terraced gardens that sloped gently down to the river. The highest terrace was a sheer ten-meter fall. The gardens ran for miles along the river (already drying), north to the village of Farahzad. Back then, poverty and rural simplicity still had a nineteenth-century texture. Today, if you Google Poonak or Farahzad, you'll find kite surfing venues, single women looking for dates and hookah bars.

We spent our summers here, from the last day of school until the night before it reopened. I can't recall exactly when we began mixing with the village boys. Privilege dissolves when boys compete, but you can never entirely ignore it. We brought a leather ball to replace their misshapen plastic one. Do I remember the first time I met Hamid? No, not exactly. But our first real interaction must have been after our thirteenth birthday. He acted deferential and defiant. Dirt clung to him from head to toe. Taller than us, his shaved head revealed the scars of old wounds—gashes from sticks and stones. His cocoa-colored face was sharp and wild yet startlingly open, as if his gleaming black eyes reflected the entire curved world. His voice had already cracked. His plastic sandals exposed splintered toenails. He wore pajama-like trousers that flapped around his ankles when he ran. Later, he would wear our hand-me-downs.

I don't recall him laughing. People considered themselves fortunate to receive even a tight smile. The other village boys—poorer, dirtier—faded into the dusty alleys of memory. But Hamid remained. I remember how we became friends. A brutal fight with Tari, ending in broken bones, cemented Hamid's bond with him. Something else would bind him to me. We played soccer on the private dirt road leading to our gate. The gate itself served as one goalpost; at the other end, where the road met the main thorough-fare, we marked two short wooden posts. The field was a rough, rock-strewn rectangle enclosed by mud-and-straw garden walls. The walls were considered the twelfth player. They always passed the ball back at an equal angle on the opponent's other side. An unspoken rule prohibited kicking too hard against the walls—chunks of dried mud could loosen, damaging someone's property.

I didn't play. I was still delicate yet strong-willed. My brother, stocky as a bull, played hard. Some boys wanted to be on his team; others remained loyal to Hamid. I made suggestions. Logical ones. It pleased everyone. One afternoon, I proposed clearing the field of rocks. Another day, I suggested building a stone outcrop for spectators. And then I started making rules—for every conceivable situation. What if the ball rolled into the gutter? What if it crossed the goal line? And what if Mussio, in one of his idle moments, decided to join in and unpredictably booted the ball halfway to Farahzad? My new role pleased everyone—except my brother. He seethed. A rivalry simmered between him and Hamid. I had wedged myself into it. The boys looked to me to settle disputes, and, whether I admitted it or not, my calls favored Hamid. My brother challenged me—sometimes publicly, sometimes back at the house, where arguments ended in bruising physical fights. He was well-liked and charming, even though his smile always seemed patronizing to me.

I am enjoying a crisp New England autumn day as I write to

you this Sunday. The sun lingers warmly on the skin before a cool breeze reminds it who's the boss. I walked by the ocean this morning, past the high school fields. The baseball diamond, meticulously maintained, gave way to half a dozen neatly lined soccer fields. Hundreds of little girls in full uniform shrieked and laughed as they chased pristine blue-and-white leather balls. Adults in referee uniforms watched over them. When did the world get so rich? Forty-five years ago, our dust-covered game had a seriousness I don't see here. We played at battle. Back then, I was the impartial referee. But I wasn't impartial, was I? I fell for a peasant boy. For his elegance, his beauty. How could a child, caked in dirt, walk with such grace? It makes one believe in a deity.

And then came the slap. I remember a larger-than-usual crowd at the game. The villagers stood behind my stone fence. It was dusk, and people were back from the fields. I remember women and young girls, some wearing chadors, others with open faces, their hair dirty and tangled, their noses snotty. The game turned into a ferocious, competitive match, with everyone sweaty-wet and short-tempered. My brother scored a contentious goal. The ball crossed over the short stump of a post at the other end of the field. He and Hamid ran instantly to my doorstep; the crowd peered, cow-like, over my shoulders as the rivals quarreled. Calling it for Hamid, I disallowed the goal. The crowd murmured their approval, their hearts with their kind. My incensed brother looked at me for a few long seconds. Then, without warning, he slapped me hard. Hamid grabbed Tari's hand to prevent him from hitting me again. "Bebakhsesh, agha. Forgive him, sir," he said it to me, not him.

A shadow swept across my brother's face, the way a cloud momentarily dims the sun. His jaw tightened. "You impertinent peasant," he spat. And then the fight erupted. My brother—shorter, heavier, with a low, bulldog-like center of gravity—lunged at Hamid's midsection like a wild beast. They tumbled into the dirt, a blur of flailing limbs and guttural grunts, kicking up dust clouds as they wrestled like rabid dogs. The other boys formed a tight circle around them, shouting, their voices shrill with excitement. Hamid was quicker, but my brother was stronger. In seconds, he had Hamid pinned beneath him, knees pressed into his ribs, fists hammering down in a flurry of blows—an unusual method in a country where fights were settled through wrestling, not striking.

Then, something shifted. From the corner of my eye, Mussio stepped out of our garden door, drawn by the commotion. But just as quickly, everything froze. The shouting stopped. The movement stopped. Even breath seemed to hold still. Hamid had Tari's index finger in his grip. His knuckles went white as he twisted it back with all his strength. The boys watching held their breath, their faces locked in that wince of anticipation—the one you make when a balloon is about to burst. I can still see it, though I know I couldn't possibly have—Tari's reddened fingertip vanishing inside Hamid's clenched fist. Then came the crack. Everyone heard it. "Ach!" My brother yelped, leaping off Hamid's chest, cradling his hand, cursing, and spinning in frantic circles like a wounded animal.

Hamid sprang up as if released from a spring trap, his face smeared with blood. His matted hair, streaked with dust and sweat, clung to his forehead like the bloodied feathers of a beheaded chicken. He bent double, hands on his knees, panting. Then, as only he could, my brother shattered the tension. He threw his head back and laughed—a wild, full-bellied laugh, cutting through the stunned silence. Still clutching his injured hand, he slung his good arm around Hamid's shoulder. "You've got guts, you lucky bastard." Hamid, still dazed, flicked a glance in my direction as if seeking permission to accept this truce. Slowly, he allowed one of his rare, tight smiles. The boys erupted in cheers. Everyone clapped except me.

How much more girlish could I feel? A boy had fought over me. My body betrayed me with an exasperating erection. Mussio loaded them into the car and drove to the hospital, where Professor Dal set their noses and reset their bones. By the next day, both patched up, swollen but victorious, their battle wounds had become trophies. Don't blush, Ms. Vakil. Boys will be boys—and sometimes girls. The fight erased the humiliation of the slap. People remembered the spectacle but not its cause.

And now, let me take you back to the era you love best. Let me shake awake the flabby, out-of-shape Hulk who slumbers uncomfortably in our shared experience.

THE FAT STORYTELLER STICKS
HIS COVERED HEAD OUT

"He will run into any mould, but he won't keep shape."

Middlemarch—George Eliot

Scribble, scribble, Baba. What a miserable excuse for a pencil! I
have filled three thin, wobbly-ruled exercise books. As with all
things local, I suspect the manufacturer replaced proper graphite
with a cheap carbon substitute. My handwriting appears in faint,
blond strokes. I wet the tip in my mouth to darken the lines, so
now my lower lip bears a permanent mark, like a tattoo. I can't fault
Mammad-Ali's generosity amidst the Persiran-Iraq war. We live in
difficult times. War profiteers, charlatans, politicians and mullahs
blur into one another. They collude seamlessly. They petition the
government for factories. They secure preferential exchange rates

for dollars. They swap out raw materials for cheaper alternatives, pocket the difference and resell the surplus currency on the black market. The next in line repeats the scam, though on a smaller scale, and so it goes.

My concerns grow with this manuscript. It sits dangerously on my table cum desk. I have written several letters to the sole surviving member of the Poonaki family, Mr. Verdi Poonaki. I promised Professor Dal I would contact him once they released me from the loony house. I asked Mammad-Ali to mail the letters with the utmost discretion—these days, you wouldn't want anyone to know that someone in his household is corresponding with the United States. Mr. Poonaki never answered. I have no way of knowing if he even received them.

Instead, I will visit the offices of Vakil Khanum, the Professor of Qajar History. The thought of it quickens my pulse and dries my mouth. What if she reports me to the officials? What if she doesn't believe me? What if—

First, I sent Zahra on a reconnaissance mission. The office is on the fourth floor of a building near Palestine Square. Not much frightens my Zahra. She climbed the stairs and knocked on the gilded door, then, without waiting for a reply, walked right in—a government office protocol. Inside, she found a modest suite of three or four rooms where seven or eight neatly kerchiefed young women, seated behind small tables, worked collegially at their computer screens. The eldest among them raised her head with a polite smile. "May I help you?" Zahra, quick on her feet, asked if they needed a charwoman. The woman declined but remained courteous. Unfazed, Zahra pressed further—could she see the boss? "On Tuesdays and Thursdays, Ms. Vakil teaches at Tehran University," came the reply. Zahra returned the next day.

What impressed her wasn't the orderly office, brimming with computers. Nor was it the women's unexpectedly gracious manner toward a chadori (a veiled woman). No, what struck my clever Zahra most was that they continued working in their boss's absence. "They are Takhoutis," she told me. She meant the rich—the remnants of the Shah's regime. Like a forked stick dowsing for water, my darling has a nose for money.

"No unwiped-ass official commits like that," she reported excitedly.

I thanked her profusely. I also noticed that, for my benefit, perhaps, she had traded her dark chador for a handsome scarf. A stray lock of hair, accidentally on purpose, draped across her face, partially obscuring her crossed eyes. Her dark brown skirt molded against her curves, the silhouette reminiscent of a Persiranian vase. She descended the stairs, her sturdy, stockinged calves steady with each step, leaving me alone with my thoughts—thoughts I now uncomfortably share with you, Baba.

I wetted my depleted pencil against my lower lip to distract myself from unholy musings. Then, gripping it awkwardly in my fat hand, I resumed writing about my fifth day and night. I woke to the usual chorus—Professor Dal's shrieks. I kept my distance but watched him. He asked his question. I answered correctly. It made no difference. He carried out his ritual. The guards recited their lines, then hauled him off. Where to, I could not say. But this much I knew:

I shared my cell with two people. The man who kept me company at night was not the raving lunatic who woke me every morning. I was stuck with a diurnal schizophrenic.

On the fifth night, he asked politely. "Could you accommodate me on your back?" I answered by rolling onto my stomach. He climbed over me like a child mounting his father or a horse rider settling into the saddle. He lay on his stomach, his breath close to my ear. Tonight, his voice carried. "Tonight, I will recount the most glorious time in our history," he whispered. "You may think I exaggerate, but it took bravery, luck and the crazy logic of a few to make it happen."

THE SURGEON HAS THE TWIN PRINCES PAY DEARLY FOR THE RIGHT BILL

There ought to be a system of manners in every nation which a well-informed mind would be disposed to relish. To make us love our country, our country ought to be lovely.

Reflections on the Revolution in France—Edmund Burke

On the eve of the Constitutional Revolution, Sardar Mirza returned to Tehran a stranger in his own land. A decade abroad had stretched into what felt like a century. His passage through Russia had been wretched—his arrival coinciding with the near-revolution of 1905 and a -winter so cruel that it leeched the spirit from even the most jubilant Russian aristocrats he had known in Paris. He spent time traveling Russia.

His hair—wild and curling—was a relic of Montparnasse. A toothbrush mustache perched neatly on his upper lip. His Parisian suit, tailored by Creed, hugged his frame; a fine silk Charvet tie adorned his neck; a fedora shaded his eyes. His Farsi was rusty, his rs rolling like a Frenchman's, his accent settling on him like a beret. He laughed too often, too loudly—an echo of too many nights at Café de Paris and Les Deux Magots. How does the sparkle in one twin's eyes fade, only to gleam in the other's?

Sardar Mirza arrived in Tehran in early July 1906 as the court retreated to Shemiran, nestled in the foothills of the Alborz Mountains, for the summer. A message had reached him from his maternal grandfather—Usta Taghi, the humble bootmaker of the late Shah. A car would collect him Friday morning and take him to court. His brother would be there to receive him. Sleep evaded him that night. Dawn delivered an unexpected pleasure. Too early for his liking, a Rolls-Royce purred to a stop in front of his lodgings. He saw it as an auspicious start after the arduous journey. The driver looked less promising—a hulking peasant with thick arms, clad in a grimy uniform, his cap too small for his freshly shaved head. Under closer scrutiny, one might discern a younger Ghorban-Ali—the same Poonaki doorman who, half a century later, would be left deaf by influenza, his gait reduced to a peculiar hop after a bullet shattered his thigh. Amputation awaited him. For now, young Ghorban-Ali gawked. Was this man a Qajar prince? The brother of Saleh Mirza, the court's rising star? No—this was a filthy Christian faranghi, foreigner. The upholstery would require a thorough scrubbing. In the back seat, the dandy prince—shy of twenty-one—lit his first morning cigarette. He leaned back, savoring the ride, eager to see his brother. The Rolls-

Royce wove through the garden of the Sahebqaranieh Palace, the road curving along the white-walled compound. A crowd had gathered at the entrance, where the Rolls stopped. His first thought was of his brother. He stepped out brimming with enthusiasm. "Mon cher frère," was on his lips when—CRACK. A sharp slap. The force sent him sprawling onto the pebbled ground. His mind raced to make sense of the moment. *Merde.* Did someone slap the back of my neck? Then another concern—had the fall torn his bespoke trousers?

A gravelly voice thundered above him. "Bow to the Shadow of God, the Shah of Shahs, you miserable princeling." From somewhere else, another voice—Turkish-accented, measured, amused: "Don't be so rough on our French brother." Mozaffar ad-Din Shah stepped forward, bending down to lift Sardar Mirza by the shoulders. "My young brother, modernity is upon us, but I remain your sovereign." The Shah examined him, tilting his shoulders as though inspecting a gemstone for flaws. Then came the sound of another car rolling through the gates. The Shah's attention wavered. It was a fortunate distraction. Sardar Mirza seized the moment to study the man before him, the fifty-three-year-old Shah, with five months remaining on earth.

The Shah looked dreadful—sallow and sickly, his eyes rheumy, deep purple bags sagging beneath them. He moved with the gait of a man twenty years his senior. His mustache—cartoonishly overgrown—had yellowed with age. Still gazing toward the arriving car, the Shah finally said, "Welcome back to court, brother. Now, go and greet your twin. He has been a thorn in our side these past few weeks, waiting for you." Later, Sardar Mirza learned that his arrival had, by pure chance, preceded that of the acting English chargé d'affaires. Hence, the grand reception. Thus, the Shah's presence at the door. Evelyn Grant Duff, the British diplomat, had come to warn the Shah of his Prime Minister's dwindling favor.

Saleh Mirza awaited him inside the building. Conservative in dress and manner—if not in thought—he wore full traditional garb: a flowing abba, a lacquered kalamdan penholder tucked into his cummerbund. A black lambskin kolah rested firmly on his head. His thick mustache stretched his face wide, dulling any resemblance between the twins. But their high, chipmunk-like cheekbones betrayed them—their features pushed upward, sharpening their Mughal eyes. He stepped out of an office. The brothers melted into an embrace, hidden from the onlookers. "I see the Shah remains friendly to us," Sardar Mirza muttered, still smarting from his humiliation.

"Yes," Saleh Mirza chuckled. "He practices the friendliness of Auntie Bear."

They both laughed, recalling the old tale. A man and a bear become friends. Despite warnings, he trusts the beast. One afternoon, a fly lands on his face as he naps under a tree. Auntie Bear, meaning well, picks up a rock and, with great force, smashes it down to rid her friend of the pest. The fly escapes. The man's skull does not. "You're lucky you weren't given a foot whipping," Saleh Mirza grinned. The last time they had seen each other, they had been boys, flat on their backs, staring at one another. Now, they embraced once more. Through the hot July days, they kept each other company, speaking late into the night. Saleh spoke of the electric energy coursing through the city—the cries for political freedom echoing from every street corner. Sardar Mirza described the intoxicating artistic revolution in Europe, the Montparnasse salons, the writers, the painters, the composers. "Brother," he said, "France is changing. Prime Minister Aristide Briand has done the unthinkable. He passed the law of laïcité—the republic no longer recognizes or subsidizes any religion. The state is now entirely secular. Can you believe it? Anything is possible."

Saleh Mirza, equally impassioned, spoke of the uprisings in Tehran and Qom. "That same December, when France severed church from state, two thousand people sought refuge in the Shah Abbdol-Azim Shrine—merchants, clerics, all demanding a House of Justice. The Shah and our cousin, Ain Dawleh, had to concede. They yielded." His voice quickened with excitement. "And now, as the government reneges on its promises, the clergy have returned to the sanctuary. If the Shah fails to honor his word, even Sheikh Nouri might join the opposition." He shook his head in wonder. "Sheikh Nouri. Can you imagine? Anything is possible."

A week later, on Thursday, July 19, the two brothers attended an open lunch hosted by Premier Ain Dawleh. Dozens of courtiers reclined on multilayered carpets in the long room adjoining the Premier's office at the summer palace. In the center of the room, a beautiful cashmere carpet bore an array of dishes: colorful rice, light brown stews, skewered lamb kebabs, and feta cheese nestled among heaps of parsley, basil, tarragon, fiery radishes and scallions. Around the dishes, the cook had scattered soaked walnuts and almonds, while at the center, fresh from the royal baker, servants stacked dozens of large, steaming oval nans, each marked with a matrix of burns from hot stones in the oven. Feeling better than he had in months, the Premier cajoled his guests to eat and enjoy.

At sixty-one, the Premier was imposing, with a striking, cotton-white walrus mustache contrasting his thick, black eyebrows. Dressed in his gilded, bemedaled uniform with wide gold-leaf epaulets, he bore more resemblance to a stern, fatherly German Junker than an Eastern potentate. A wily statesman, he had mastered the English tactic of divide and conquer—though he divided more than he conquered. A congratulatory, festive air filled the room. His Excellency had secured a victory over the sit-in by sending his Cossacks to blockade the mosque. They had exchanged a few stray bullets, but there were no casualties; the opposition blinked. Ayatollah Tabataba'i and Behbehani agreed to return to Qom under Cossack protection, accompanied by a few thousand supporters. "Your Grace, have we seen the end of this matter?" asked the Foreign Minister's son, his tone more calculated than curious. The Foreign Minister, a constitutional sympathizer, commanded broad support among the clergy and merchants, and many viewed him as the future Prime Minister. His son, a Russian-trained political scientist and a friend of Saleh Mirza, was eager to make his mark in the volatile political arena.

"I doubt it," the Premier said, scooping beef stew onto a piece of bread and tucking it under his mustache. "But the bazaar spoke—or remained silent—last Sunday. I can handle the mullahs. I can handle the merchants. Together, they can make trouble."

"Then Your Grace has not heard?" interjected Mushir Molk, the younger.

"Heard what?" The Premier's gaze sharpened.

"The merchants have asked Evelyn Grant Duff, the acting chargé d'affaires, to allow the British compound to serve as a political asylum while the British Legation summers in Golhak." The British staff moved to their northern summer residence each year, leaving the large compound in Tehran deserted. Fifty people had sought sanctuary there under the age-old Persiranian custom of bast, or sanctuary.

The Premier visibly relaxed. "Oh, I know about Sayyed Behbehani's letter to the chargé. The British Foreign Minister, Lord Grey, assured me their gates will remain closed."

"No, sir, I am not referring to last week's letter," the young man corrected. "My sources tell me that fifty merchants, the Bonakdar brothers and several religious students have taken refuge in the compound. Mr. Grant Duff reportedly told them that while he lived in a country with a strong asylum tradition, he could not, in good conscience, deny its people the same right."

The Premier, ever astute, did not waste time debating. The young man didn't spread unsubstantiated rumors. "Did Mr. Grant Duff use the phrase 'in good conscience'? If we had granted his country a share of our custom excise tax instead of favoring our Russian friends, we might have seen a different outcome," he sniffed. "They will not rid themselves of me without a good fight. Now, to practical matters—" The crowd at the British Legation had swelled to a thousand while they ate lunch and continued to grow by the hour. His gaze settled on Saleh Mirza. "Prince, my cousin, I have a small assignment for you. It requires the utmost delicacy." The Premier ordered Saleh Mirza, accompanied by two escorts, to travel to Qom and meet the reactionary religious leader, Sheikh Nouri.

Saleh Mirza arrived in Qom the following day. He left the car behind a mile outside the city, approaching Sheikh Nouri's house traditionally, mounted on horseback. The sun was beginning its descent, casting long shadows across the land. A large, rough-hewn wooden door in the mud-and-straw wall surrounding the house, stood like an ancient sentinel. Within that door was another, smaller one—barely large enough for a child. This exaggerated display of humility, a well-understood gesture among the mullahs of old, equated moral virtue with physical discomfort.

In front of the door, a crowd of ragged people gathered—some hoping for a free meal, others presenting petitions and still others seeking legal advice. At the time, the religious establishment oversaw all matters of law. Sheikh Nouri had secured the royal court's lucrative business, making him a figure of influence and wealth. Two men, with the appearance of seminary students but a rough edge about them, stood guard at the entrance. There was no question of making the prince wait. He had sent word ahead of his arrival time. The two men bowed. Saleh Mirza removed his shoes outside the door. Though not tall—five feet five inches in his socks—he had to bend down to pass through the door within the door. The modest, turn-of-the-century house had four rooms built in a row on a four-foot-high platform. Each room had a door to the front veranda, a simple tiled platform resembling a stage. Below the platform, a small, square, flagstone yard had a pentagonal pool for the five daily ablutions before prayer.

The Sheikh sat in a lotus position, at ease on a worn carpet and leaning against a large cushion. His elbow rested on his knee, with his palm propping up his head, giving him the appearance of casual indifference. A large, salt-and-pepper beard framed his face, and his simple, pale abba hung loosely over a less-than-clean shirt. His gaze, fixed unblinkingly on Saleh Mirza, conveyed a deep-seated contempt.

With a dramatic "Ya-Allah," the Sheikh pretended to rise

in greeting, but Saleh Mirza, well-versed in Persiranian etiquette, rushed forward, urging the Sheikh to remain seated. This delicate dance of deference, designed to compel greater respect, ended with the prince arriving just in time to assist the Sheikh back onto the Kashan carpet—a fine piece dating from the early 19th century. They settled into their seats, murmuring a stream of formal greetings, exchanged in the manner of finely crafted Baroque rhetoric. A rough-looking seminarian served them tea.

Imam Khomeini would later describe the Sheikh as the "rose of the Shiite clergy," but today, he was more focused on a pressing matter. "Your Highness," he began with a deep bow, "you've traveled far to visit this humble abode. We hear troubling reports from the capital."

This wasn't the Western "royal we." Even today, those of lower social standing speak in the plural. For a high-ranking religious figure, it was an effort to show humility. A skill the newer generation of mullahs had sadly lost.

The premier had instructed Saleh Mirza to remind the Sheikh of the favor granted to him years ago, when the royal court had transferred the flow of court cases from Sayyed Behbehani—his religious rival—to Sheikh Nouri. The favor could easily be withdrawn, redirected toward a new spiritual leader—or even back to his rival. Behbehani, it seemed, had already aligned himself with the constitutionalists, plotting to restore the previous premier and reclaim the lucrative court cases.

Saleh Mirza had protested. "Your Highness, such a crude threat will only insult the Sheikh," he warned. The threat would be an empty one. The most likely successor to the premier, the liberal Mushir Dawleh, was a close friend of the Sheikh's. "The mullahs know the power of money," the premier insisted. "Tell the Sheikh that if he joins the opposition, he will see none of the royal favor."

With this in mind, Saleh Mirza relayed Prince Ain Dawleh's greetings: "His Highness inquires about your health and whether you have ruled on the Shah's request for a loan from the Russians. His Majesty's health necessitates a trip to Europe. Does Your Grace consider the loan halal?"

The Sheikh took a deep breath. "In the name of God the Almighty, I have thought long and hard about a loan from the infidels. They have committed atrocities against our Muslim brothers in the north. God has taken revenge, letting the yellow race loose to ravage these barbarians. Now the Russian infidels wish to bleed us financially."

"Your Grace's wisdom is vast and unassailable," Saleh Mirza replied. "His Majesty's disappointment will also be vast and unassailable." The Sheikh's demeanor shifted, though his voice remained level, almost detached—as though expounding on religious dogma. Yet beneath the surface of his words, political intrigue simmered. The bedding by the door told the Prince the Sheikh's true intentions: he was preparing to align with the constitutionalists, even though this was an alliance of convenience rather than true ideological unity.

"I sense you face contradictory goals, young prince," the Sheikh said, his voice slightly more pointed. "I suspect your newly arrived foreign brother preaches the gospel of commoners voting for laws. Let me warn you," he paused for effect. "We will not negotiate Islamic law. Islamic law remains a perfection, for the Koran hands it down. It exists like a spirit among us. The clergy might clarify minor points for the ignorant, but we do not question its divinity. We do not put God's law to a vote. Do you not see the blasphemy in your proposed democracy?"

"Your Grace, the talk is only of a House of Justice, grounded in Shiite precepts," the prince countered.

"You've missed the latest developments," the Sheikh replied. "Since the morning, demands for the House of Assembly have escalated. The British have allowed three thousand people to gather in the gardens of their legation. I hear that your brother and my dear friend's son, Mushir Molk, hold classes on the grounds of the infidels. Are you still a Muslim, Your Highness?"

"Your Grace knows of my absolute devotion to the Prophet, Ali, his son-in-law, and his successors. You misunderstand my intentions, Your Grace. I am a loyal subject to my royal brother. The protection of the crown compels me to act as the times demand. May I say with the greatest respect, doesn't your Holiness's joining the sit-in at the Friday mosque with the seminaries contradict your goals?"

"Your goals and mine differ, but God has granted us the same tools to compete for His glory." The Sheikh's gaze narrowed. "How often does a humble servant of God have the chance to build an Islamic kingdom to the glory of God?" The Sheikh's eyes glittered with malice. The man's ambition startled the Prince. The Sheikh saw the crown as a barrier, the chaos as an opportunity. His vision of an Islamic state laid its first bricks right then, seventy-five years before its completion.

"You asked if I am a Muslim. May I ask if Your Grace remains loyal to the throne?"

The Sheikh's patience at an end, "Do not test me, young pup." He coughed loudly, his eyes narrowing in frustration.

"Not my goal, Your Grace," Saleh Mirza said, rising to his feet. "If you permit me, I shall now take my leave and shorten my shadow from your presence." As Saleh Mirza hurried back to the capital, he was troubled by the Sheikh's comment about his twin. What had led a Qajar prince to enter the gardens of a foreign embassy without the court's permission? By the time he returned to Tehran, the number of people at the British Legation had swelled to 5,000. The crowd grew until, by early August, it reached 14,000. The people came from all walks of life, but the most prominent group was from the Bazaar. Instead of returning to court in the north, Saleh Mirza went to his house in town. He could throw a stone from his home and hit the British embassy nearby. He lived in a modest, traditional house. It stood in the center of a large plot. He only had the idea of building the large house and the surrounding gazebos.

Prince Saleh Mirza's grandfather never stopped working as a bootmaker. Saleh had set up a small workshop for him at the far end of the modest garden, which later became home to Ghorban-Ali, the one-legged doorman. Upon seeing the Prince's arrival, his mother, now thirty-seven, rushed to the door with an unexpectedly youthful prance that never failed to take him by surprise. She had lost her youthful beauty—her features had hardened into a square shape, her skin cracked and weathered. Her once-lighthearted chatter now seemed at odds with her more matronly demeanor. The Prince reassured her gently and, with the cook's help, sent her back to her routine. He then found Nemat, the manservant, helping his grandfather stretch leather hides behind the house. The stench of the tanned leather made him gag. He had allowed his grandfather to continue his trade in the home as a sign of personal humility, but now he wondered if he'd overextended his goodwill at court. Nemat, squatting on his haunches, tugged at the hide with all his might, securing it in the vice.

"Nemat, leave that. I need you here right away," he called irritably. Nemat, youthful and quick, looked up. His face was fresh and unweathered, a 23-year-old Turkoman with the strength and agility of a horseman. He rose swiftly and trotted over to the Prince, a cheeky smile lighting up his features.

"Your Highness, how can I serve you?" he asked, his tone unruffled and confident, unfazed by the Prince's royal status but ever-loyal. Seeing the Prince's tense demeanor, he asked, "Is something wrong, Your Highness?"

"I need you to take a message to my brother at the British Legation," Saleh Mirza replied.

"Your Highness, His Highness told me to tell you not to worry. He'll be back shortly." A commotion erupted at the front of the house as if on cue. Saleh Mirza rushed inside to find Sardar Mirza and four young grandees, two sets of brothers, excitedly discussing the day's events. The Shah's son-in-law, a Berlin mineralogy graduate, spoke incessantly while his former polytechnic professor brother sat quietly. The two sons of the upcoming premier, Mushir Molk, a Russian-trained political scientist, and his brother Mu'tamin, a French-trained lawyer, rounded out the group. At the sight of his brother, Saleh Mirza's heart softened with affection. Sardar Mirza dashed toward him, eager to hear about his meeting with Nouri. "Will he join us?" he asked.

"He's already taken refuge at the Friday mosque with Behbehani and Tabataba'i," Saleh Mirza replied. As his companions broke into congratulatory remarks, he raised a hand to stop them.

"Brother and the rest of you understand this: he will never join us. We have a most improbable marriage of convenience. He will never agree to a justice system that isn't under the clergy's control. Never." Saleh Mirza, who had never left Persiran, understood the hurdles. Later, they would all grow disillusioned; some would even change allegiances. "Now," he continued, "explain to me what possessed you to enter a foreign legation without the Shah's permission. Last I checked, you are His Majesty's brother, are you not?"

"Brother, you must see it yourself," Sardar Mirza answered. "The entire working class of Tehran has gathered in the compound. And who do I see among them?" He paused dramatically. "Mr. Scott. I wrote about him when we were in Paris ten years ago. He was with us then. Now he's the chargé d'affaires at the British Legation. Mr. Smart, Major C.B. Stokes and Colonel J.A. Douglas, the military attaché, have joined the sit-in. They teach with us in open-air seminars on how to build a democratic infrastructure."

"The English look as excited as schoolgirls," Mukhbir al-Saltaneh observed.

"Brother, you must come with me tomorrow. It will convince you of the movement's pure intentions," Sardar Mirza urged.

"I'm the trusted advisor to our ailing brother, the Shah. If they see me conspiring with the English, I would hurt him irreparably," Saleh Mirza said.

"Your loyalty is misplaced, Prince," Mu'tamin al-Mulk interjected. "I have it on good authority that HRH has requested a loan for another European trip." His "good authority" was his father, who would soon inherit the government.

"I have higher authority telling me it will not be approved," the Prince said, his tone resolute. "One way or another, it changes nothing for me." Deep down, he wanted to experience the excitement the others described. The times were heady, and the possibilities felt limitless. He couldn't break the unwritten laws of tradition—mos maiorum—the ancient rules that dictated his actions. These laws didn't change, no matter who sat on the throne.

Later that night, as he prepared for bed, Saleh Mirza explained to his brother, "I want to help, but my hands are tied." While the Prince slept, Sardar Mirza, unable to rest, grinned in the dark. He had a plan. It was time to borrow a page from Le Bœuf's book of tricks. The following day, Sardar Mirza asked Nemat to fetch the barber immediately. Saleh Mirza narrowed his eyes. "What are you up to, brother? You have that devilish grin again."

"Nothing," Sardar Mirza said, still smiling. "I've ordered the barber to give us both a good shave."

"Us? My beard is in full bloom, and the court admires my mustache. I don't need a shave. Well, maybe a trim."

"I have more than a trim in mind. Don't you agree that a man must witness and hear things firsthand to make a sound judgment? How else would you advise those at court?"

"I do not argue with your logic," the Prince said, casting a wary glance at his brother. "But how does my shaving—oh, no, you don't!"

"Yes, brother. We did this enough times as children. If you wear my European suit and—impossibly—try to emulate me, looking brighter and livelier, you—"

"I get the idea." The Prince grinned. "But I can't risk it. You can live in Europe, but I can't afford to get exiled. More than that, you can't afford me to live in Europe." He referred to the enormous funds needed to support Sardar Mirza's princely lifestyle.

The barber waited patiently, sipping tea while the brothers debated the plan's merits. By eleven in the morning, Sardar Mirza had convinced the Prince to sit for the barber's razor. The Prince would never wear a beard again. Under Sardar Mirza's meticulous guidance, the barber gave the Prince the most refined cut of his career, shaping him to resemble one of the Parisian Left Bank crowd. Using a hot iron rod, their mother added subtle waves to the Prince's new haircut. When he donned Sardar Mirza's gray Creed suit, the two brothers looked so alike they could pass for twins. To make the Prince's entrance less noticeable, they waited until dusk. They enlisted the help of their four friends to accompany him, keeping an eye out for anyone who might try to speak with Sardar Mirza—especially the Shah's spies.

Nervously, the Prince begged his brother to stay behind. "Please act with gravitas if anyone comes unannounced. Make sure you wear my full Persian garb. I know you don't like my plain black hat, but wear it, please." The rimless Astrakhan hat covered his new haircut. "And if anyone comes, send Nemat to fetch me from the legation."

Sardar Mirza, half-joking, warned him, "Stay away from foreigners. They'll surely tell from your atrocious French accent that you're not the real deal."

The entrance to the compound had a festive atmosphere. People milled about, chatting and laughing like they were at a fair. The setting sun threw a soft blue glow over the light brown dust. As the Prince entered, he saw that the once beautiful lawn had disappeared under large vats. They sat on coal fires, throwing sparks into the air like fireflies. The smell of cooking rice filled the air, and dark, mustachioed men fanned the coals while kebabs sizzled on pomegranate tree skewers. The bazaaris, the merchants of Tehran's Grand Bazaar, funded it all.

The Prince heard speeches from every corner of the compound. The courtiers scattered around the compound, proselytized and educated eagerly. The guilds had set up dozens of enormous tents housing the most influential guilds. One tent, where the butchers, tanners and chicken sellers stood, featured a thin man speaking from a wooden box in European clothing. Another tent housed the grocers' guild, where their leader, known for his integrity, spoke with surprising clarity. He would become a steadfast member of the Majlis, Iran's future parliament. The Prince lingered, listening intently. Not for the first time, he was in awe of the grocer's straightforward thinking. In contrast, he, a graduate of Dar al-Funun, found himself tangled in endless disputes with courtiers who had long since abandoned their morals.

A well-dressed man in traditional clothing eyed him from the entrance of another tent. From how the man looked at him, Saleh Mirza knew he was familiar with his brother. Trying to slip past, he hoped to lose himself in the crowd, but the man stepped forward, blocking his way.

"Your Highness," the man said, "have you forgotten your servant, Ibrahim Khaiayatbashi?" Representing the guild of tailors, he was a rich, resolute man and now a parliamentarian bound for the first Majlis.

"Not at all, Ibrahim Khan. I am savoring the different points of view." He tried to sound jovial like his brother.

"You must come tomorrow. The chairman will recognize the Central Society of Guilds meeting promptly at ten in the morning. Your Highness won't forget yesterday's promise when this is over?"

What had Sardar Mirza promised the man?

"Refresh my memory, Ibrahim Khan," he said.

The man whooped. "I hope Your Highness doesn't forget our petitions as easily as my simple request to have your elegant suit copied for our clients."

Relieved, he promised to lend his suit for a measuring. He walked on. Heavy smoke emanated from one tent—the cigarette seller's guild, represented by Ali Sigari. Not interested in politics, he had seized the opportunity to promote business. He had dozens of hookahs set up in the tent. He offered passersby reedy hand-rolled cigarettes. Smaller guilds had set up tents to watch for any new development. Walnut sellers, tinkers, straw plaiters, quiver makers, peddlers, galloon weavers and tailors talked animatedly. From afar, he saw his old friend, Valiullah Khan Nasr, the guild master of medical doctors. Forgetting his new persona, he joined him for a companionable chat about what he was seeing. Valiullah Khan watched with confusion as the mannerisms of his young friend, so familiar to him over the years, emerged from the shape of another man he had met yesterday. Unable to keep up the farce, Saleh Mirza sheepishly confessed to the doctor and swore him to secrecy.

Saleh Mirza met the head of the sugar and tea sellers. He listened to the pleas of the booksellers' representative, who lobbied for an independent judiciary. He tried convincing the leader of the guild of blacksmiths of the incompatibility of Sharia law with an independent judiciary. "Then the mullahs have to go back to Qom," replied the blacksmith. To his surprise, he realized the merchant class, so far without a voice, had taken voice lessons in liberal ideology—a voice he might not be able to support. He believed that, without any preparation or experience, quickly veering the country toward constitutionalism would be dangerous. Nothing in his experience squared the Sharia with secular laws, the approach championed by all the Euro-returning grandees—including his brother.

From afar, he saw the three British officials, Messrs. Scott, Stokes and Smart. They gave enthusiastic lectures on democracy and parliamentary tradition to packed crowds. Even the calculating British had lost their heads in the moment's enthusiasm. Saleh Mirza kept his distance from them. It dawned on him he needed practice in the art of democratic politics. He would have enjoyed the present opportunity, but his meddling, he knew, could have capricious consequences for his brother's life. The sky, a black velvet pincushion, was dotted with thousands of twinkling silver pins. The moon detailed the escarpments of the Northern Mountains, shrouded in a purplish blue. Small fires burned here and there. The compound looked like an army on the march—which it was. In each tent, a storyteller recounted the Shiite Kerbala tragedy, the *Rozeh Khani*. They squeezed their audience's last drop of tears.

I had to interrupt the Professor. I shook like a dog with a bone. "Arbab, I heard all this when I was ten. My Baba told me his Baba—the finest rozeh khan in the country—joined the tent of the goldsmiths' guild. He declaimed the murder of Imam Hussein every night for three weeks. He gathered the biggest crowds." On top of me, the Professors' gentle laughter tickled me into my laughter.

"I am not finished, my rubbery padding," Professor Dal said. "Have you lost weight? I can't make myself comfortable on top of you."

"Arbab, I haven't eaten a proper meal in four days. I am wasting away," I complained. "Can you talk to the guards when you are out in the morning?"

"Are we going to start with your cheekiness, my boy? Yo=u know I haven't left this cell in years. Now, quiet down. I will tell you what happened in the next few weeks."

The next day, the Prince, again disguised as his brother, walked from his house to join the meetings in the compound. Ghorban-Ali, acting as factotum, carried his lunch wrapped in cloth to present a more humble picture. People enjoyed Sardar Mirza's easygoing ways. His friends saw him as a young lightweight,/ but as the brother of the Shah. The constitutionalists had hoped to use him to shift the position of his influential brother, but he had made it clear that he intended to keep his channels open to both sides.

"The place where we lie in this prison, my boy, now derided by the rich as the "old" downtown, was the uppermost part of the city in those days."

As the Prince and Ghorban-Ali walked down Ferdowsi Avenue, the legation walls stretched along the right side of the dirt-packed street. The crowd outside the entrance, larger than the night before, wore the involuntary, permanent grins that went with the hot temperatures of midsummer—the equivalent of the hanging tongues of dogs. They looked impatient and possibly unruly. Ghorban-Ali, in the lead, pushed the crowd apart with his body, holding the small picnic bundle above his head. He hollered to make way for His Highness, Prince Sardar Mirza. It spoiled the desired effect of humility but successfully created a passage for him.

As the throng propelled the Prince forward, it cleared the entrance and formed an arch-like tunnel to the legation garden. Sweat ran down every crevice of his body; his brother's suit hung heavy and inadequate against the weather. The trees behind the walls promised welcome shade. Above the entrance, a small decorative tower mimicked the pattern of the walls and their balustrades.

As they entered beneath the arch, a man dressed in a Western-style coat and tie, with a barbered mustache and goatee, walked out of the legation grounds as if out of a grave. He shouted at the Prince, "Take this, you dirty foreigner!" Meeting the sudden glare of the sun, the man raised a hand to shield his eyes. Saleh Mirza, who received military salutes, didn't connect the man's gesture with his hostile words. The man fired a shot. He missed the prince and his servant. Ghorban-Ali threw his bundle of food. It hit the man's shooting hand. But not before he got off another shot. The bullet hit Ghorban-Ali on the inside of his thigh, splintering his thighbone but missing the artery. Blood quickly spread. The crowd rushed toward the assassin. He disappeared from view among a thicket of legs. He didn't survive the beating.

The Prince kneeled on one knee, aware of the crowd. His status kept them at bay as a circle formed around the fallen Ghorban-Ali. Men peered at them from every angle. He could hear the beating of the assassin. The Prince pushed the fingers of his left hand into Ghorban-Ali's wound. With the other hand, he jerked at the linen wrapped around his lunch; the silverware made a racket as it spilled on the stone floor. He fashioned a tourniquet on the upper part of Ghorban-Ali's thigh. Switching back to himself, he shot orders around like a machine gun. "Call Valiullah Khan Nasr from inside, now!" he told one man. "You, hold this tourniquet and twist hard," he commanded another. "Don't concern yourself if he screams." And then: "In the name of the Shah," he shouted at the crowd behind the circle around him, "stop beating the man." Ghorban-Ali watched the foppish prince become a warrior, much like his master. "Well, they *are* twins," he thought before he passed out. The Prince didn't miss his 10:00 meeting.

In all revolutions, there comes a magical time when the most disparate groups come together to move heaven and earth. These magical three weeks had no precedent in our 2,500-year history. The numbers gathered at the legation grew by the day—merchants, princes and guilds. Ninety miles away, the clergy sat in sanctuary at the Friday mosque in Qom: All of one mind. "You might ask yourself, my ball of feathers: So what if these mullahs sat on their haunches in some mosque? What could come of that? Think of it: all judiciary matters in the country came to a squealing halt. It may be hard to imagine, but the mullahs once had a practical function." Couriers went back and forth, ensuring the government didn't manipulate the clergy against the guilds. Small fissures might quickly turn into tectonic faults. The alliance made its first unanimous tactical demand: remove Premier Ain Dawleh. He lasted ten days. The Prince reverted back to his own persona on the odd days of the week. He traveled to the palace to work with the courtiers and the premier. He sought an audience with the Shah. He endured some ribbing for appearing clean-shaven but kept his hair hidden. On the other days, he visited the legation as a stand-in for his brother. He joined as many of the committees as he could. Sardar Mirza filled in on the odd days at the legation. They didn't want to miss any critical decisions.

The Shah rested most of the time, and waste accumulated in

his blood and body. His kidneys needed dialysis, but its invention would arrive twenty years too late. On the odd days, the frustrated Prince sat cooling his heels at the Shah's summer palace, up at Niavaran village in the foothills of the Alborz Mountains. Built by their father, French and Persiranian architecture combined to make this modest palace an aesthetic delight. Two towers on each side pushed the entrance back, giving it an understated elegance. Tall balconies with unobtrusive pillars traced the facade. The Shah's favorite wives had houses built pell-mell around the palace grounds.

When the Prince finally secured an audience, he thought it too late. He borrowed a driver from the Turkish embassy to drive him to Niavaran as Ghorban Ali's driving days had ended. The surgeons had amputated the leg. The prince walked up the red-carpeted stairs to enter the Shah's office. It resembled a pharmacy. Heavy brown bottles on a silver tray rattled on top of the desk; the room, stuffy and hot, smelled of chemicals. He approached the Shah's chaise longue, placed next to the desk. The Shah sat dressed but semi-recumbent, an intricately embroidered brown cashmere shawl on his lap. He watched Saleh Mirza's approach like a trapped animal with lugubrious eyes. Since childhood, whenever the Prince saw the Shah, he saw a scared, shy man, utterly unfit for the responsibilities thrust upon him. A thin veneer of bombast scarcely sustained the illusion of power. The Shah had once ordered he be photographed every half hour.

Saleh Mirza made a deep bow. He began the customary extolling of the Shah's many embodiments. "May God make luminous your proof—"

The Shah waved him to stop.

"What news of town?" the Shah asked wearily in his thick Turkish accent.

"You Highness, our brother reports—"

"Not *our* brother, *your* brother," the Shah whined. "A traitor, like all the princes who have joined our enemies." He remembered the so-called assassination attempt on the Prince's brother the day before. He stopped. "You know, I didn't have anything to do with the . . ." he let the words hang. "I hate blood. I can't even bear the Eid al-Fitr sacrifice of a camel; I hire someone to impersonate me." The Shah threw Saleh Mirza a knowing look. "It is my impersonator who drives the spear in the throat of the caparisoned camel. Not me."

The Prince believed the Shah, but the impersonation comment worried him. Was this a subtle warning? Had the Shah uncovered their schoolboy prank? Had he heard of him and his brother impersonating each other? The Shah could order the assassination of his brother without witnessing blood. To the King's mind, however, worthier personages at the legation needed killing than his twin. This Shah didn't like confrontation. Hints, insinuations and tip-offs were his style—the strategy had the court second and third-guessing the Shah's every utterance.

"You, at least, have more gumption than all the others," the Shah said.

"Your Highness," the Prince urged, "the committees have debated a constitutional monarchy. We can control the course of events if we meet their demands by replacing the premier before it's too late. We could agree to establish a committee to study the judiciary's independence—without rushing into anything irreversible. We can shape its mission over the coming months. The clergy will stand with us; they will never accept a secular judiciary."

The Shah scoffed. "They want me to remove my beloved cousin Ain Dawleh. For what purpose, we ask? To impose Mushir Dawleh upon us, along with his two traitorous sons? Are we to welcome serpents into our bosom of trust? Yes, we know. They conspire behind our backs with the dastardly English."

"Your Highness, the premier will step down if we make it worthwhile," the Prince pressed.

The Shah, sallow skin tinged the color of faded egg yolk, turned his rheumy eyes on the young man. "Look at us. What do you see? You see a dying man. The choice of a premier is my prerogative. If we remove him under pressure, those cannibals will devour us alive." And the Shah was right. They would eat him alive.

"Your Highness, I beg you to reconsider."

Without lifting his arm from his lap, the Shah flicked the fingers of his right hand toward the door—languid, dismissive. The audience was over. The Prince never saw him again. As he stepped from the room, the Shah's chamberlain appeared—tall, severe, his face as expressionless as a death mask. He loomed over those he addressed, bending ghoulishly toward them. In a whisper, he bade the Prince to attend the Crown Prince. The Prince had never heard the man's natural voice. He only ever spoke in that hushed murmur—an ideal courtier. He followed the chamberlain through the palace's dim corridors to a vast, wood-paneled chamber known as the War Room. Two newly installed electric chandeliers burned overhead, their glow stifled by the heavy gold lamé curtains drawn tight. The Crown Prince did not offer a seat. He stood at the far end of the oversized, polished mahogany table, his customary haughty air about him, his brows knotted in thought. The Prince hesitated by the door. "I hope Your Highness is in good health?" he asked, more out of formality than concern. "I want you to know no one knows I am here," the Crown Prince said. He prided himself on his cunning—a belief nurtured by the obsequious figures who thrived in the clandestine world of the court. "Did your meeting with our crowned father go well?"

The Prince hesitated momentarily before deciding to ask for his help. To his surprise, the Crown Prince immediately grasped the gravity of the situation. All of the court knew of his disdain for the premier. He had even funneled money to the clergy's sit-in to oust him. He despised nearly everyone associated with his father's administration. "I will convince my father to remove Ain Dawleh," the Crown Prince declared. Two days later, he succeeded.

On July 30, Mushir Dawleh, a more liberal figure, accepted the premiership. But by the time Mushir Dawleh took office, the conversation had evolved. Was it already too late, as Saleh Mirza had warned? Or had the masses—the beast—sensed weakness, as the Shah had predicted? And how far had the argument moved? To his horror, the Prince saw delegates speak of republicanism, especially those from Tabriz. To him, this was nothing short of treason. He rushed back to the palace. Again, he sought an audience with the Crown Prince. "Give them anything they ask, but not a republic. Our father cannot give away our rights," the Crown Prince declared. "Give them their precious parliament. I will persuade my father to consent. But remember my words: I will not go down the path Czar Nicholas took last year. Once I am Shah, I will not let a single morsel of my Allah-given power slide down their greedy throats. Imagine it—walnut sellers presuming to make decisions on my behalf. It will never do. So long as I live, I will never consent to a constitutional monarchy."

"As Your Highness well knows, they will have His Majesty and Your Highness swear on the Holy Koran to uphold the constitution."

The Crown Prince regarded him with a stony glare as if a foolish child had just requested a stable full of Arabian horses.

The Prince hurried to secure an audience with the new premier. "The Shah has conceded," the premier said with a smile. "I will negotiate language acceptable to both sides. Tell my son. He and I have crossed many great rivers to get here; now, we have only to step over a narrow joub"—he gestured toward the ancient open-sewer channels that carried water through the city and its gardens. With the Shah's reluctant approval secured, the constitutionalists now had to bridge their divisions. For three days, they debated the wording of the proclamation.

In a wiley move, before final approval from the Societies, the government prematurely released the document to the public—bearing the dying Shah's signature. Sardar Mirza and Mushir Molk, the premier's constitutionalist son, stood before the legation walls, reading the posted proclamation. "There is no mention of Persiran as a unified nation," Sardar Mirza noted, frowning. "And the Majlis—Parliament—will pass laws according to 'the sacred Sharia'?"

An admirer of the secular French system, he was appalled. Outraged, the constitutionalists demanded the government remove all posted copies and immediately submitted revised language. Mushir Dawleh planned to officially release the corrected proclamation on the Shah's birthday, the fifth of August. He swore to his son there would be no sleight of hand, no tricks. The second proclamation addressed the first concern by inserting the phrase Persiran nation. But on the more crucial issue of Sharia law, it made matters worse. Instead of removing the reference, it formally declared the Majlis an Islamic parliament. The premier's postscript read: We are an Islamic nation, are we not? A final version On August 8, the Shah signed the third draft of the proclamation. He backdated it to the fifth, ensuring it linked his birthday forever to the declaration. Nouri hadn't won but hadn't disappeared in the last signed version.

"Wake up, my tiny whale pond," Professor Dal murmured. "Have you fallen asleep in the most optimistic time of our 2,500-year history?"

"No, Arbab—just resting my eyes," I replied.

But darkness had lost its battle against the light. Professor Dal fell silent, discreetly closing his eyes to rest.

THE SIXTH NIGHT: 0110

THE WRITER AT A
TROUBLED CROSSROADS

Allow me to pause here—a deliberate intermission—so the reader can fully appreciate the essence of Iran's 1905 revolution. I choose not to adopt my princeling's term, "Persiran." While I understand the allure for an aristocrat to unite Persia and Iran into an idealized, private utopia, the 1905 revolution was not about privatization but democratization. It was a rare moment, a missed opportunity that continues to resonate.

For many Iranians, 1953 is the historical marker of misfortune—the year when British and American forces orchestrated the coup to unseat Mossadegh. We often indulge in finger-pointing. Don't get me wrong; I am not here to wash and disinfect the hands of the West. Instead, I desire to jolt my fellow countrymen awake, to cry, "Don't you see the bigger cause?" In 1905, we achieved something miraculous—a rare alignment of forces akin to an anti-perfect storm. Religious leaders, bazaaris, aristocrats, the Shah and even the British (of all parties!) shared an uncommon harmony. Yet, we let it slip through our fingers.

Mohammaad-Ali Shah, the vengeful and reactionary heir, is the antagonist of this narrative. After his coronation, he fiercely resisted the tide of change. He ultimately lost his throne and the Qajar dynasty, but not before sowing chaos and disunity that left the nation reeling. Reza Shah then rose to establish a new dynasty, systematically dismantling the constitution to render it toothless and replacing it with rigid authoritarian controls.

He is our Henry VII. He wins the crown by force, establishes the Tudors, but his legitimacy questioned. Winning a crown in battle counts in our monarchical system. Keeping it is a different question. The Pahlavis (no possessive) Tudors.

So, I pose the question: who bears the blame for our collective failure? Where is the mirror that forces us to confront ourselves?

Fifty years after the 1905 revolution, the infamous rivalry between the brothers and Hamid ended in physical confrontations. Now, a different test looms—the clash of intellects. Let the battle begin.

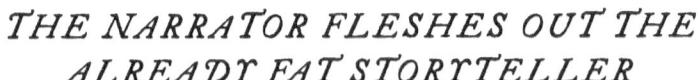

THE NARRATOR FLESHES OUT THE
ALREADY FAT STORYTELLER

"There should always be some foundation to the most airy fabric."

Lord Byron

Dear Ms. Vakil,

You've long been aware of the existence of these papers. I assume the real Mr. Hekaiatchi learned about them through my uncle. Are you suggesting these documents should have been delivered to you rather than to me two decades ago? Despite your diligent efforts and relentless investigation, you must concede that I am the rightful heir to these papers. I admit that Mr. Hekaiatchi—the genuine one, not my fictional storyteller—sent them to me freely.

The plot thickens. After failing to capture my interest with his meandering letters, Mr. Hekaiatchi, as you've informed me, sought you out to recount the tale of his imprisonment. Admirable persistence, wouldn't you agree? He believed leaving a story untold was akin to taking it to the grave—a crime against fictional characters, punishable on judgment day. I, on the other hand, have done the opposite. Like a god, I've breathed life into a Golem. With every word I write, I shape him further, molding him into a reflection of the real man—a living, breathing individual whose story, as journalists might say, "checks out." I confess to feeling guilty. I regret treating him poorly. Please continue your search for him. I'm not opposed to offering a modest sum as a gesture of gratitude.

Thank you for your corrections. I acknowledge that I may have taken some liberties, perhaps attributing a few undeserved IQ points to both the outgoing premier and the Crown Prince. I've noted your concerns. Rest assured, our new Shah, the unintelligent and uneducated Mohammad Ali, will fulfill his role with unerring foolishness. I'm also well aware of the debates among historians about attributing words to historical figures. I claim the storyteller's privilege, much like my fictional fat man's father. While I may not have always been a direct witness, I grew up at a dinner table where the protagonists—or those who knew them firsthand—discussed the events now reduced to dull history books. Unlike my brother, who often rolled his eyes in boredom, I listened intently, captivated by their accounts. I worked tirelessly to reconcile the inaccuracies of memory, relying on letters and historical sources.

I acknowledge the scarcity of candid records. Self-preservation often silenced even the most natural writers. In your meticulous commentary, I sense a scholar indulging me. For all I know, you've dismissed my words as the ramblings of a wistful middle-aged man yearning for a bygone era. By definition, the bygone existed. Whether I long for it is a matter we can debate.

While investigating my narrative structure, I thumbed through the *1001 Nights*—not reading it all, mind you. No sane parent should let a child near that book. Back then, cuckolded men enjoyed a terrifying amount of leeway. Did you know that three years before Scheherazade began spinning her tales, King Shahryar—having witnessed his betrayal—slept with and then beheaded 1,096 virgins?

And did you also know Scheherazade skipped twenty nights of storytelling? She paused discreetly midway through a tale as the 699th morning broke. Twenty days passed. She resumed, pretending nothing had happened. Only in the final pages of Volume Four do we learn why: she had given birth to twins. Twins, Ms. Vakil. And on the last night, she introduces to the slow-witted Shah, a two-and-a-half-year-old boy, claiming—proud as a peacock—that she had never missed a single night. Please don't take offense, Ms. Vakil. They don't make women like they used to. But my question is: what happened to the other twin?

My French grandmother was a tough cookie in her own right. She had an absolute disdain for anything natural. The more human hands intervened—twisting, reshaping, manipulating the world—the more she approved. For her, culture was humanity's last stand against indifferent nature, which, as she liked to say, "doesn't give a hoot for our existence." She viewed childbirth quite differently from our Scheherazade. "An inhuman process for making humans," she said. "Why couldn't we pluck them from the earth like tomatoes? After all, we shove them back in when they die."

Sardar Mirza lies buried in Montparnasse. He bought three vertical plots—forward-thinking, as always. The Countess and my mother Lili rest beside him. My maternal grandmother, the Countess, and my paternal grandfather, the Prince, mourned together. They grew unexpectedly close in the weeks before the Prince's return to Tehran. He confided in her: Nima—my father—was slipping in his studies. More troubling was Reza Shah's increasingly erratic authoritarianism. By the late 1930s, his paranoia had peaked. Public figures vanished, died of mysterious illnesses in prison, or committed suicide. The Prince didn't believe Nima was in immediate danger, but he worried about the boy's future if anything happened to him. The Countess offered sanctuary—an extended stay at her home in Paris. But the Prince couldn't imagine adapting to European life. She suggested enrolling Nima at Le Rosey, the Swiss boarding school that had shaped Crown Prince Mohammad Reza.

"You know," she told him, "Europe is no less dangerous. *Tout cela finira mal.* But the Swiss—well, the Swiss know how to take care of themselves." And so Nima remained in Europe. As you already know, the Prince returned to Tehran—to meet his end, Ms. Vakil. He died half a year later, in mid-winter 1939. The Countess stepped into the role of guardian with stoic grace. She took Nima to Le Rosey.

the Crown Prince, the last Shah of the Persiranian Empire, had been a diligent student and gifted athlete. My father, however, became a legend. He ran the 100-meter dash in around eleven seconds and held the national record for the 110-meter hurdles for a decade. His long legs devoured the track with effortless elegance. Critics said he didn't even try his hardest.

Then the war arrived. As the Countess predicted, the Swiss stayed neutral, and Nima continued his studies. On June 5, the Germans launched Operation Fall Rot. Seventeen days later, France fell. The Countess despised the Pétain government. "This is what happens," she sniffed, "when a peasant becomes a general." By 1943, life had become intolerable for her. She began funding the French Underground and offered shelter in her ancestral home to its endangered members. The Germans questioned her once, with polite, chilling efficiency.

My father graduated *à peine mais juste à temps*. "Barely," said the Countess, "but just in time." She decided to move them all back to Persiran. Reza Shah had abdicated in favor of his son two years earlier. The Allied forces now occupied the country. The English occupied their favorite area, the south's oil fields, while the Russians moved 60,000 men into the north. A puppet Soviet government ruled Azerbaijan—highly sympathetic to the communists and utterly disdainful of the central government. You heard Stalin licking his chops. He waited to inherit the north, the country's rice basket, along with the Caspian and the oil fields in the bargain.

The Countess regretted her move from the moment she stepped into the Prince's house until the day she left, two years later, when the war had ended. It marked her deeply. "*Sale gens, sale pays, sale culture,*" she declared of our beloved nation: "Dirty people, dirty country, dirty culture." She said it with such conviction no one dared challenge her.

None of this touched Nima or Lili. They had entered a state of blissful self-containment—impervious to worldly misery. My parents wore their invisible glitter lightly. When the time came to decide whether my father should pursue higher education at the Dar al-Funun—the technical college—he chose, instead, the Officers Cadet School. It was a rare choice for an aristocrat. Modeled by Reza Shah on France's military academy at Saint-Cyr, the school attracted the sons of Iran's new middle class—men who owed their rise to Reza Shah himself. The new Shah, his son, had graduated from Le Rosey and attended the Cadet School. Once again, my father followed in the monarch's academic footsteps. Thanks to well-placed favors, he was allowed to return home a few nights a week—relieving him of the dormitory's tedium.

He met our last Shah on the day of his graduation. Their social stations should have brought them together sooner, but my parents had no interest in society. Whatever free time they had, they spent together—traveling to the furthest corners of the country. A few months after the war, Uncle Dal arrived from Germany, close to death. Skeleton-thin, hollow-eyed, his hair thinned to wisps, he looked like a survivor of the Holocaust. The Countess nursed him back to health before turning to Lili. She asked her to return with her to Paris. When my parents announced their decision to marry, she smiled and embraced Nima with the warmth of a mother. They married with little ceremony. Uncle Dal and the faithful Nemat served as witnesses. A handful of cadets attended. The Countess then left the country.

Nima graduated soon after. He won several physical courage and sportsmanship medals. Wartime had diminished the pomp. A thin brass band wheezed through its crescendos. The Shah, impatient, waved the music to a halt and strode across the field toward the cadets. He had greater concerns than pinning ribbons on young officers. Soviet forces still occupied Azerbaijan. Stalin's puppet party, the Tudeh, had grown more potent in the north. The English, drained from the war, had withdrawn from the Gulf. Hope rested now with the Americans—and the U.N. Yet Washington's hostility toward the Soviets had not fully hardened. The Shah conferred the rank of Second Lieutenant on my father. General Razmara stood a respectful step behind, formally presenting the young officer: "Second Lieutenant Poonaki."

The Shah raised an eyebrow. "The Poonaki?"

My father answered calmly. For a moment, the specter of the Prince's death—the oddness of the circumstances—hovered in the air. The Shah turned to the General and murmured in polished French: "We have to watch this young man." It was ambiguous. Did he mean: watch him—he might be dangerous? Or: watch him—he has promise?

"I am at His Majesty's service," my father replied, also in French. Amused, the Shah asked where he'd learned the language. "Your Majesty, I followed your footsteps—from Le Rosey to here." Delighted, the Shah asked for the latest gossip from the Swiss school. They spoke briefly before the Shah moved on.

Let me stress, Ms. Vakil—my father was not ambitious. Ambition belonged to the lower classes. But he was smitten with the young Shah—as the Shah, in turn, was drawn to his Lancelot.

My father's first court invitation came soon after for a Friday volleyball game. As usual, he impressed both players and spectators. His young wife made a different kind of impression.

Few recall the first contest between the superpowers. Before the Russians sealed Eastern Europe behind Churchill's Iron Curtain, Stalin staged a practice run to our north. He propped up a puppet regime in Tabriz and refused to withdraw Soviet troops. Truman, newly elected, pushed back hard. The U.S. ambassador delivered the necessary threats. Stalin blinked. When the Soviets retreated, the Shah struck the separatist Tudeh forces. The Shah involved my father in the operational planning. Surrounded by grandees loyal to the old Qajar dynasty, he needed someone trustworthy. He saw my father as his discovery, conveniently overlooking his Qajar pedigree. My father, for his part, held romantic notions of noble service. He envisioned himself as a vassal to the king. He became the unofficial link between the Shah and General Razmara, who prepared the northern campaign. Razmara, fond of my father, sent him ahead—covertly—to scout the mountainous region of Azerbaijan. The work was dangerous, but my father thrived on it. He learned the terrain intimately, stayed with villagers and passed as a modest landowner. He returned unshaven, filthy—and exhilarated. He and the General spent hours poring over tactics. My father reported that the communists had lost local support. "We need to act now," he told the Shah.

In a clever maneuver, the Shah ordered nationwide elections. The constitution allowed Imperial troops to guarantee fair elections—including in Tabriz. With the Soviets gone, the separatists faced the army alone. Textbooks exaggerate the scale of that provincial conflict, but give it this: a paralyzed nation, beaten down by war and allies alike, the country almost lost its wealthiest province. Stalin's puppet regimes were on the brink of handing over Eastern Europe. The boldness of the Shah's move—small in scope, perhaps—saved Persiran's integrity. Imperial forces moved in three columns under General Razmara's command. The Shah flew overhead in his plane. My father, guiding the western column, advanced toward the highlands. They captured Mayaneh—Azerbaijan's third city, an ancient stronghold of the Midian Kingdom.

They met fierce resistance from General Daneshian, a KGB asset entrenched with well-fortified lines. He had vowed to fight to the death. The men had something to prove. Five years earlier, Reza Shah's army had evaporated at the first sign of Soviet aggression. Now, battling cold mountain passes, they pushed forward. Some soldiers, unfamiliar with rocky terrain, broke their ankles. Organized medics took care of the wounded behind the lines. But the planning held. Daneshian had ordered the old bridge destroyed. My father, relying on local knowledge, bypassed it entirely. He found a place downstream to cross the river. The western column pressed forward. They fought for a day. The support of the planes and artillery worked with precision. A stray bullet grazed my father's lip—but not before he saw the communists break ranks. They disappeared along the porous frontier into the Soviet Union. General Daneshian, disregarding his orders to shoot deserters and stand and fight, stole the cash from the local bank and disappeared behind the new "Iron Curtain."

Ms. Vakil, I swear to the truth of these stories. My father told them often and consistently, leaving little room for doubt. Yet I'm also aware that children rarely grasp the full weight of their parents' youth. I am burdened by the fragments of memory I have of them—two people so consumed with each other that their children were, at best, a faint afterthought. If my severe, composed father ever had a playful or daring side, I know of it only through others. My mother, whose aloofness from all things Persiranian eventually extended to us, faded from my memory long before she physically disappeared.

Still, I know this: they felt guilt. For selling out their class. Their heritage. And perhaps most of all, for selling our birthright. My brother and I came of age in a different Tehran than theirs—a city awakening, gleaming, impatient. We tasted the first wave of imported modernity: Hotshop, the American burger joint with its baby-blue vinyl seats and panoramic windows; the Ice Palace skating rink, dressed in deep brown leather for a child's wild imagination; the newly built bowling alley where teens lounged beside professional Scalextric tracks. Cinemas multiplied. Gone were the velvet-draped screens of my parents' time. Films opened with the Pahlavi national anthem blaring through massive 70mm and Cinerama projectors, bringing *How the West Was Won* and *The Sound of Music* to a dizzying life. This destroyed the underground culture of motorcyclists, who once darted madly through traffic with film canisters to ensure the same movie could play in two theaters simultaneously, with a lag of one reel. We enjoyed it all, always accompanied by a driver and a French governess. The world shimmered with artificial polish, feeding a blind optimism that Iran's ascent would never falter.

But I remember the first fracture. We were fourteen. It was a spring afternoon, sunlight spilling over the streets. We sat in our lemon-yellow Vauxhall, waiting at an intersection for the light to turn. I leaned on the window, chin on the elbow, only half-present. Then came Ali-Shisheh—the deaf, mute beggar who danced between cars, always pretending to clean windshields. His antics were familiar, even funny. We laughed as he approached, and I dug in my pockets for change. The light turned green. Mussio, our driver, accelerated. Then braked hard. A motorcyclist had run the red light, loaded down with film reels. Ali-Shisheh, unaware, stepped into the intersection.

I don't remember the moment of impact—only that he was in the air in a flash, like a puppet cut loose. The motorcycle tilted, then shot forward in a burst of silver sparks, slamming into the underside of another car. Film canisters scattered across the street. Somewhere, someone would miss *The Bridge on the River Kwai* that night. Both Ali-Shisheh and the motorcyclist died instantly.

This, Ms. Vakil, is where memory gives way to reconstruction. I don't remember seeing the usual street beggars after that. Perhaps the city banned them. And the practice of transporting film by motorcycle stopped—maybe because it had become cheaper to import duplicates. In the name of modernization, two tiny changes marked a rupture in the life we knew.

Thank you, Ms. Vakil, for your candor. After your last email about Mr. Hekaiatchi, I've revised "Our Storyteller." I've allowed him a more profound, more grounded moral authority. I hope I've captured your encounters with him faithfully—and I've taken the liberty of having him speak a few well-earned words of praise for Vakil Khanum, who matches you in every respect. Your tireless work deserves more recognition than it receives. You are a Khanum, a lady, in the truest, most gracious sense.

THE FAT STORYTELLER SWAPS
PENCIL FOR MICROPHONE

"It even tempts him to blurt out stories better never told."

Odyssey—Homer

Baba, I can feel your pride in me. With Zahra's help—may the good Lord bless her bold spirit—I finally visited the esteemed Vakil Khanum, editor. She holds a doctorate in history, though I sometimes wonder if history isn't simply ill and needs a physician. We played spies for the day. Zahra ordered a phone taxi—those have replaced the orange-striped Peykans of yore. No, Baba, I'm not being reckless. These new cars are discreet, the kind that blend in, not the matchbox clunkers we grew up with. We slipped into the car just past 2:00 when Tehran's traffic only pretended to move. I wore a chador—better safe than sorry. Zahra held my hand beneath its folds. I couldn't tell if it was for reassurance or something else. Like aftershocks of an earthquake, the pitter-patter of my heart conveyed my sentiments through the tips of my fingers.

Doctor Vakil awaited us behind her desk, flanked by six typing virgin houris—a striking woman, though thin and worn. Still, Baba, she's no match for my Zahra. Did I say my Zahra? I swear to you, Baba, nothing untoward has passed between us. Not even last night. Ah, last night—you won't believe how she startled me. I dreamed I was back in our garden in Karaj. You were there. The sun warmed the stone steps, and I sprawled across them like some contented crocodile. Then I woke with a jolt—terrified. I heard creaking on the stairs. Someone lingered long between each step as if weighing their intentions. I whispered like a revolutionary guard, "Who goes there?"

A head appeared. Zahra's. She laughed softly. "Hush, you'll wake Agha-joun, my dear dad."

She tiptoed into my bed—fully clothed, Baba, I promise—and nestled her back against me. I felt like the grandest man alive. Not grand like you, Baba, but grand in a small, happy way. I think I smiled in my sleep until morning when I woke to find the bed empty. I couldn't be sure she'd been there—until she reached for my hand in the taxi beneath the shared cover of our chadors.

We giggled like schoolgirls. It caught the attention of the mustachioed driver, so we quieted down to protect our little disguise.

Now, back to Doctor Vakil. She received us politely, though a faint irritation simmered beneath her composure. She wore a simple scarf perched lightly on coiffed black hair, with a single lock of white falling across her brow. It gave her gravitas. I was confident in my material and asked for a more private setting. She nodded and shut the milky-glass doors behind us, sealing off the clatter of keyboards. She gestured to the chairs before her desk. Zahra, suddenly transformed into a deferential serf, refused to sit. She retreated into a corner, whispering nonsense, until Doctor Vakil, without raising her voice, said: "Beshin, Zahra." That one word brought Zahra comfort. She sat stiffly, barely touching the edge of the chair, chador clenched in her teeth, eyes fixed on her shoes.

I've always hated chairs with arms. They make me aware of my body's spread. I sat awkwardly, then removed my chador. Vakil Khanum blinked, shook her head, and bit her lip. "What is the meaning of this?" she asked, lifting one elegantly arched eyebrow even higher—just like my old school principal when she doubted the legitimacy of our existence. I mumbled an apology, then steadied myself.

"Vakil Khanum," I said, "my name is Hekaiatchi. I was in prison a few months ago—with Professor Dal." That eyebrow jumped again.

"I know, I know," I rushed on. "Everyone assumes the Professor died after the revolution. But he didn't. He passed only recently." The eyebrow rose with less force.

"He'd been living in a . . . well, not a hospital. A mental institution. No, more like a prison masquerading as one." I felt absurd. There I was, dressed as a woman, admitting to being institutionalized, not exactly the makings of a credible witness. But Doctor Vakil surprised me.

"Mr. Hekaiatchi," she said, "I'm sorry for your imprisonment. Please know I don't doubt you. We live in farcical times." She gestured at my chador. "Let me say this first—I knew Professor Dal. I met him several times in my twenties before the revolution. I had just returned to Tehran to teach Qajar history at the university." She paused, weighing whether to say more, then chose restraint. "You'll also be pleased to know I once visited the Hekaiatchi tea house in the bazaar—back in better times. I presume you're the son of Abol-Hassan Hekaiatchi?" Oh, Baba—she knew you! I nearly melted into my creaky chair. After all these years, someone still remembers and values your art. "Mr. Hekaiatchi," she continued, "I'm not sure I understand how your experience relates to an ostracized professor of history."

At last, I found my footing. I told the lady how I ended up in that strange place, how I met Dal, how, by day, he raved like a madman, and, by night, spoke lucidly, mournfully, about history—his history, and the Poonakis, how he saw those last ten years as penance for staying silent during the war, for witnessing atrocities and doing nothing. I told her about Tala's struggle to conceive the twin princes. I recounted word by word about the boys' adventure to Tabriz, the wolf attack, the Crown Prince's bastinado and the tender moment with the French count's daughter in the czar's palace. When I spoke of the twins' part in the Constitutional Revolution, she began to write—not obtrusively, but quietly, respectfully.

My memory impressed her. She interrupted occasionally to ask for clarification but let me speak otherwise. I could see it in her eyes—I had her full attention. That a relatively unschooled pumpkin like me could discriminate the subtleties of ayatollahs and prime ministers of a century ago had impressed her. I lost all sense of time. I spoke for hours, oblivious to the changing light. By the time she finally cut in, the office had darkened; the girls had left long ago. Zahra dozed in her chair, lips parted in an O, her soft snores the only sound besides our voices.

"Dr. Vakil," I said, "I've written down much of what I just told you. What you heard is only half. There's more."

"And I want to hear the rest," she said.

"Would you consider publishing it, Khanum?"

She didn't answer right away.

"Khanum?" I prompted again.

"I heard you the first time, Mr. Hekaiatchi," she said. "And I want to answer without giving offense. You come from a long and noble oral tradition. You and your ancestors passed down stories from one generation to the next. The details may shift, but the core endures. In our era, details have taken on disproportionate importance. Today, a single word can provoke academic warfare. Scholars attack footnotes as if they were fortresses. From what I've read and studied, what you've shared rings true—but truth is not always enough for history as it's practiced now." She folded her hands on the desk. "Let me read what you've written. Better yet, let me record you. You have a rare gift, Mr. Hekaiatchi. One day, in a freer time, researchers may study your tapes as guideposts to larger truths. Do you understand?"

I sank back into the creaky chair, weary, disappointed—but also curious. Perhaps I didn't need to scrape ghostly marks onto paper with a chewed-up pencil. Maybe my voice could carry the tale farther than my hand ever could. Something struck me as she gathered her papers into a worn brown satchel. "Wait," I said.

She looked up. "Yes?"

"There was something strange on the sixth morning. Professor Dal returned to the cell different."

"In what way?"

"Normally, after cleanup, he'd slink into his corner and say nothing. But that day, the guards brought him in like always, and he sat upright on his cot like some Indian yogi—rigid, staring. I avoided him. I had learned my lesson. I didn't speak during the day. Then, out of nowhere, he said, 'I don't know who you are. I've been watching you. You're not one of them.'

'It's me, Arbab—Hekaiatchi,' I replied, falling again for his daylight madness.

'Shut up. Just listen.' His voice was sharp. 'My days are numbered. You don't know where you are. This house once belonged to a great man. A great man,' he repeated, eyes burning. 'You must promise me you'll find his grandson.'"

"I knew he meant the Prince," I told her. "So I said, 'You've told me plenty. I won't forget. I've got a memory made for stories like this.'" She nodded.

"But he scoffed. 'Stories? What stories, you servant's son? I sit beneath the earth, the fount of the nation's wealth. If I clench my asshole, oil prices rise by two points. But no one listens. For ten years, not one soul has checked my predictions.' He sneered at me. 'Who would believe you?'"

I paused. "Until today, my anger at being called a servant's child blinded me to what he said. That wasn't fair, Vakil Khanum."

"No, it wasn't," she said quietly. "But what did the Professor say?"

Like any proper storyteller, I wanted to build suspense. But one glance at sleeping Zahra—now stirring—pushed me to go on. "He pointed through the barred half-window. 'You see that wall, boy? That was one of the Prince's garden houses—he built one for each wife. That one belonged to his first, the daughter of Mozaffar al-Din Shah—his niece and wife both. The Poonaki papers are in her house.' I must've hesitated—maybe I raised an eyebrow—because he added, 'I put them there myself, just days before my arrest. Ten years ago.' Then he collapsed onto his bed and fell asleep. He never brought it up again."

Dr. Vakil sat up straighter. "We have no choice. You must retrieve those papers."

I laughed. "Of course. I'll return to my captors and ask for help loading the truck."

"I'm not joking," she said. "If you can get those documents, I'll authenticate them. Then, we'll release your oral history. Simultaneously, a university in the U.S. or U.K. will receive a generous archival donation from an anonymous source."

"We have to get them," Zahra said, fully awake.

"And how exactly do I do that?" I asked. "What happens when they trace it back to me? I was locked up in that asylum."

Dr. Vakil looked at me steadily. "From what I heard today, you're finished in this country anyway, Mr. Hekaiatchi. You and your wife could live in Turkey. Even the U.S." At the word wife, Zahra and I looked at each other, startled. I realized then that these ancient papers could separate us. Zahra, I think, saw it differently.

"Either way," said Dr. Vakil, "I want to record your story. But not here. Come to my apartment, Mr. Hekaiatchi." Baba, I traded my stubby pencil for a fat microphone. As we stood to leave, she stopped me with a nod and motioned for me to sit again. "You can't go without telling me about the sixth night." I smiled—wide, childlike as if I'd finished all my chores and could play outside. "Vakil Khanum," I said, "I'll spare you the uncomfortable details of how Professor Dal wormed his way back onto my back. . . ." He had grown frail, skeletal. He shuffled toward me like an old man searching for his cane. I lay on my stomach to help him mount me, as always. But he couldn't manage alone. One of his legs hung limp; I had to help him swing it over me. His long, grimy, puke-scented hair fell across my shoulders. They hadn't cleaned him properly. For a while, I thought he'd passed out. I called his name. He didn't move. I feared I carried a corpse on my back. Then suddenly, he chortled. "Did you think I'd died, my boy? You'd need a better trick than that to escape. You think you're Dantès now?" I was baffled. "You've never read *The Count of Monte Cristo*?" he cried, horrified. "What kind of storyteller hasn't read the Count?"

Since then, I've bought a translated copy. Now I understand. Unlike Dantès, I couldn't slip myself into a body bag and escape disguised as a dead man. I'm far too hefty for that kind of drama. And I've long since lost my patience for fat jokes. But that night— on the sixth night—he spoke in earnest.

THE SURGEON PROVES ALL IS
UNFAIR IN LOVE AND WAR

"*Post Lux Tenebras:* After the Light, the Dark."

I can't pinpoint the exact moment Nima and Lili became lovers. Somewhere, sometime after that afternoon with the dog bite, their flirtation began—a playful game that, years before their physical relationship began, signaled what was to come. The first time I heard it, we were still in Paris, not long after the dog incident. Lili made a curious cooing sound—"Ou, ou"—initially it struck me as childish nonsense, perhaps an imitation of a French owl. Only later did I realize she was asking, in French, "Where? Where?"

"Where the dogs meet," Nima replied. "It won't do," she said, shaking her head with a grin. Then came that wild, unmistakable, full-bodied, unrestrained laugh. The next time I heard the phrase was in Gstaad, Switzerland a year later. We had gathered to mourn the death of the Prince. A telegram had arrived with the news. The Countess and I, receiving it around the same time, agreed to meet in Gstaad, where Nima's school held its annual winter term. When I arrived, the Countess had checked into the Hotel Palace. Lili was with her.

It was a crisp, sunny day around midday. Unlike most destinations, Gstaad matched its postcards' perfection: the bluest sky, snow so white it seemed lit from within, icicles like hand-blown glass. The air was so clean you almost forgave the doctors who believed it could cure anything. The Hotel Palace loomed above from the train station like a white fairy castle perched on a hill. People in dark wool gathered on terraces for lunch; others carried skis over their shoulders and men hauled wooden sleds packed with shrieking children. It was my first ski resort. The Countess greeted me in the lobby and offered lunch. I declined. I was eager to find Nima—delivering bad news was something I never liked, despite my profession. The Countess understood. Together, we walked out to the skating rink to find Lili.

She had grown to match her mother's height. On the ice, she moved awkwardly, her arms crooked in front of her like the limbs of a delicate insect. In her black pants and turtleneck, she looked as fragile as a foal—newborn, wobbling. She skated toward us, panting, cheeks flushed, and threw her arms around my neck, trying to kiss both cheeks without falling. The effort pulled me down onto the ice. She laughed—a loud, unfettered laugh, like her uncle's, masculine in its force. It made me laugh, too. The Countess, ever more restrained, looked embarrassed. We walked to the school's chalets at the edge of town. Two large buildings stood side by side, traditional gabled roofs with broad eaves covering balconies that ran their length. A few smaller chalets completed the campus—an elite school even by those days' standards.

The Countess had alerted the headmaster. Inside, the halls buzzed with adolescent boys, their post-sports shouting bouncing in several languages. One glanced at Lili as we passed; I stopped him, asking in German if he knew where Nima was. He answered in French, eyes still fixed on Lili. "I saw him in his room five minutes ago," he said, and with a shrug that was more flirtation than indifference, added, "Follow me." Lili turned to her mother. "I can't wait to touch him," she said—not a trace of sexuality in her tone. The Countess and I understood. Lili had a gift for warmth, for transmitting affection through words.

On the third floor, the hallway swarmed with boys sliding on socked feet. Our guide gestured to the last room. The Countess knocked lightly. "May we come in, Nima?" He stood in the center of the room in white long johns, his bare chest rising above them, ski socks pulled high. He had grown to six-foot-two, a man's body with a child's face. Curls of hair trailed from his waistband to his navel, and though his physique was well-proportioned, his expression was all innocence—like an Italian sculpture of a boy in a man's form. He looked at us in confusion. Then, instantly, his face lit up and darkened just as fast. "Is it Father?" he asked.

We looked down. "A heart attack," I said, repeating the telegram's message. Tears slipped quietly down his face. Lili walked to him. He buried his head in her shoulder, his sobs muffled in her hair. The Countess and I stepped out, giving him privacy. I wished the Prince had seen how much the boy loved him. Nima's pain was harder to express but no less deep. He packed a bag and returned with us to the Hotel Palace. Once again, tragedy drew us together. And again, despite mourning, we found happiness in each other's company. Our laughter never felt like disrespect. We sledded. We shared dinners. The cousins got tipsy on wine and laughed uncontrollably—*fou rire*, that mad, contagious laughter. The Countess and I were infected, and soon we all roared. She and I argued endlessly about Hitler. She'd punctuate her opinions with glasses of grappa. "I lost cousins and friends at their age," she said once, pointing to Nima and Lili playing checkers by the fire. "No one remembers what they died for. They missed out on this." She swept her hand around the beautiful sitting room. "And the world continued—people drinking and laughing like nothing happened," I replied with bits of Nazi propaganda I knew she hated. She'd shake her head and sip her drink.

Those days blurred together in a kind of fool's paradise. On one bright afternoon, I remember Nima and Lili sitting on the balcony, lazily devouring crêpes soaked in Grand Marnier. Then, without a word or glance between them, they'd leap up in unison and bolt toward the mountain, racing until they collapsed laughing in the snow. The same laughter would catch them again—*fou-rire*—infectious, irresistible. From the balconies above, people watched and smiled, envious. It seemed apparent to everyone but me: these two puppies, as young as Romeo and Juliet, were destined to become lovers. I saw only children at play.

There are moments I'll never forget. One evening, stepping out of a restaurant into falling snow, the Countess suddenly shoved a handful of it down my back. The four of us exploded into a no-holds-barred snowball fight under the streetlights. When it ended, her eyes sparkled, and she gave me a shy, secret smile. That night, she came to my room. I understood what she needed. I was dazed but honored. The night before I left, I found Nima and Lili huddled around a bubbling bowl of raclette, their heads almost touching as they skewered chunks of bread and stretched strings of cheese between them like golden webs. She looked up at him and asked, "Where? Where?" He smiled down at her, indulgent, like a man twice her age.

"Where it snows and the wolves gather," he said.

She looked out the window thoughtfully, considering. "No, it won't do," she said at last. He nodded. When they noticed me, there was no guilt, no secrecy—just a simple, joyful welcome. She waved her skewer in the air, offering me a cheesy morsel. As I moved it around my mouth, trying not to burn myself, I asked, "What game is this?"

"Game?" Nima asked.

"Oh, not a game," said Lili. "We're planning where we'll make love for the first time."

I spat out the cheese, pretending I'd burned my tongue. They laughed. "Not tonight," Lili said. She punched my arm lightly. We moved on to other topics. But something lingered.

Only then did it dawn on me: these two, whom I loved like family, whom I envied and protected, paraded their tenderness before me, oblivious. Their joy—so unselfconscious, so complete—would become a kind of private torture in the years ahead. I remember no sorrow in our parting. We lived only hours apart. We were too young to imagine the fanged monster that awaited us just a few months down the road. My cushy cushion, my airy pouf—how hard it is to recognize happiness when you're soaking in it. We parted after that glorious week. We wouldn't see each other again for six years, except for briefly during the war. But before I speak of love, I must talk about war.

I returned to Germany with my heart aching but my spirit intact, ready to finish my medical studies. I foolishly believed that Europe stood on the brink of a new era. My dear, soft perch—my ignorance is no excuse. Half of Europe felt the evil rising. I didn't. I won't disguise my guilt. I won't pretend an apology wrapped in an explanation is anything but cowardice. I was young. I was naive. I was also complicit. I never witnessed the experiments later attributed to Herr Doktor Sauerbruch. I saw only the surgeon. In the operating room, he ruled like a tyrant. He barked orders, belittled staff and once even slashed an intern's hand with a scalpel so he'd never forget his mistake. He'd work on three patients at once. He expected us to open the chests, insert the pressure chamber he had invented and call for him when it was time for the decisive cut. He wore no gloves—he believed they dulled his touch.

In those days, no one dared to question a surgeon, especially not a German surgeon. Patients had no rights. Families received cold, brutal honesty: "Your boy won't make it through the night— pay the cashier on your way out." Or "Your wife will likely die, but she'll teach my students something." His arrogance was terrifying—and contagious. We followed him, experimented and pushed boundaries; in doing so, medicine advanced. But some of what we did blurred the line between boldness and recklessness. And while we weren't monsters, we did not always behave like men of conscience.

By 1942, Sauerbruch was Surgeon General of the army. I saw little of him after that. I didn't know about the mustard gas work. But I saw the statistical tables, the data in his neat hand.

The nurses whispered about a place called Natzweiler-Struthof. I chose not to ask. I thought myself a pure surgeon—above the mess of ideology. I wasn't. During those years, I operated on thousands of soldiers. At first, they came from the front, later, from across the river. In the final days, they arrived from the next street over. I aided and abetted.

How can I describe Berlin in those last months? The Allies bombed us daily. We operated under the open sky. When they destroyed one building, we moved to another. Still, we cut and stitched, even when starving and dehydrated. Outside, the city had become a wasteland. A bakery got bombed one morning—limbs decorated the trees like ghastly Christmas ornaments. The Nazis executed old men conscripted into the Volkssturm if they couldn't carry a weapon. SS officers shot wounded soldiers in the hospital for resisting. Hundreds hung from lampposts and signs around their necks declared them cowards. People held suicide parties. Wild animals roamed free—monkeys perched in trees like surreal spectators.

When Zhukov's army arrived at Charité, we were lucky. He named Sauerbruch Berlin's public health chief. He insisted on discipline in his ranks. Malinovsky's men, elsewhere in Berlin, unleashed horrors—mass rape, destruction. They spared the nurses, but only because we were in a hospital. I lived in the Charité basement. One doctor used a meat cleaver for amputations, believing speed was mercy. He killed dozens before we stopped him. My pride in being German, my disdain for the English—those childish vanities crumbled. Each day, I rode through the ruins on the bare metal rims of my bicycle, a red cross flapping from the handlebars. I wore a filthy white coat and a stethoscope as armor. The only possessions that mattered in my black bag were my surgical tools. Berlin had become a city of ghosts. Silence blanketed the ruins. Streets stood waiting for a gust of wind to bring them down. The Russians dismantled the city factory by factory, bolt by bolt. They packed it all into trains bound east. Russians stole from the Germans what the Germans had stolen. Much of it sits unseen in the Hermitage's basement.

I survived by offering what skills I had. Most of the time, I performed abortions—dirty, dangerous ones—for women raped by soldiers. They came to me hollow-eyed yet with a ferocity that frightened me. I begged them to reconsider. I warned them of infection, hemorrhage and death. But nothing I said could match the horror they had endured. They wanted the foreign thing out of them—violently, decisively. Their blank expressions never changed. They just stared straight ahead and opened their legs.

At night, we huddled in the hospital's basement and listened to the BBC on a crackling wireless set, ears tuned for any news of the advancing Americans. Rumors swirled of a race for Berlin, but we saw no sign of the Allies. A handful of officers passed through to meet with Russian generals, but their presence felt ghostly—insubstantial. The race had been a myth. We soon understood that Uncle Joe had outwitted Roosevelt at Yalta, to Churchill's thin-lipped fury.

Then came the message. During the BBC's cryptic segment—meant for hopefuls across enemy lines—I heard it. The correspondent, Lewis John Wynford, repeated it for three nights. "Hadjit will pick you up at the same place he left you—if you will let a bear hug you." I knew it was meant for me. Harold Nicholson, my old protector and now a high figure in Churchill's wartime government, had seen to that. Later, I learned that Nima and Lili had been working to find me. It was Nima who reached out to Harold. I knocked, absurdly, on the shell of our old Embassy. The Russian army had set up camp all around it—pitched tents, laid fires and occupied the streets with their brutal competence. Wherever the Red Army landed, they knew how to survive.

I felt ridiculous exposing myself to their unpredictable moods, but went anyway. Five soldiers confronted me at once; a tall, bearded youth with round spectacles—likely the local Party enforcer—asked in broken German what I was doing there. I pointed to the Red Cross on my bicycle, then at the Embassy and introduced myself as a Persiranian doctor stranded by war. He translated for the others, which set off howls of laughter. These were Russian peasants—cruel, generous, cunning and gullible. I'd seen them kill a man without a flicker, as casually as one steps on a beetle. A huge, red-faced soldier poked my chest and then pointed at my head.

"Otkuda u tebya zheltye volosy?" To my astonishment, a small Tajik soldier translated into Farsi: "He wants to know where you got the yellow hair." I lied in my best, formal Persiranian: "Tell him I'm from the Caspian coast. I wouldn't be surprised if the blond hair came from over the border—maybe from one of you." The man raised an eyebrow, impressed by my fluency and relayed the joke. Another round of laughter broke out.

I lingered in the area for days, tending to their injuries. I set bones, lanced abscesses and yanked infected teeth. In return, they fed me. On the fifth day, making my usual rounds of the makeshift encampment, I saw a man in civilian clothes walking toward me. He smiled broadly, arms outstretched. "Davno ne videlis', tovarishch," he said, pulling me into a bear hug. Then, in a whisper: "I'm Alexander Werth, BBC correspondent. Harold sent me. Time to get you out of here." In theatrical Russian, he stepped back and said, "Tovarishch, you look much thinner than the last time we met." I said nothing. Switching back to English, he said, "Don't fret, old boy. There's an Allied truck leaving Berlin tonight. I can get you on it. Are you game?" I nodded, my eyes stinging. "Leave the bike. Come with me." I picked up my medical bag, my most treasured possession—still lined with my surgical tools—and followed him as he jabbered in loud Russian. I was too dazed to speak. It felt as if God had sent the Archangel Michael in the guise of a BBC reporter to pluck me out of hell.

Professor Dal went quiet. The light leaking through the cell window was faint, a smudge of blue. I sensed time slipping.

"Arbab," I whispered, "what happened to Nima and Lili?"

He smirked. "Ah, you voyeur. You want to ask, 'Where? Where?'" Then, sing-song, "Where flowers carpet the earth and butterflies gather."

After they parted in Switzerland, the war scattered the cousins. They wrote—briefly, flatly. Neither had the gift of putting their feelings into letters. They existed for each other only in the flesh. When apart, they were siblings. When together, the rest of the world disappeared. They met again mid-war. The Countess sent me a note through military channels. She needed help getting home. My rapport with the German ambassador was strong enough to secure her and Lili's passports. They traveled as civilians. The Gestapo's claws must have been near. The Countess had spent a fortune aiding the French Resistance. Here, I have nothing to regret. Despite my Nazi sympathies, it never occurred to me to act dishonorably. They stayed in Berlin for only a day. I managed to spare a few hours from the grim parade of amputations, burns, broken bones and shrapnel wounds. The Battle of Stalingrad was grinding to its hideous end.

We met for lunch in a small, miserable restaurant—Berlin's worst days still ahead. All three wore sensible wartime clothes. The Countess had visibly aged. Fine wrinkles now traced her face like ripples on a wind-touched sea. Gone were the fashionable dresses; she wore a matronly tweed suit, oversized on her shrinking frame.

The cousins no longer looked alike. Lili had grown into a woman of startling beauty. She wore a gray skirt, practical shoes and a garçon haircut. A military-style cap sat low on her head— perhaps to hide that beauty. Nima wore a soft white shirt under a sleeveless gray sweater and dark brown corduroys. He looked more like a Spanish partisan than a Persiranian aristocrat. Still, something in their movement—the long-limbed, casual gait—revealed their blood. They walked ahead of the Countess, who strolled behind at her own pace, calling them her gazelles. The Countess urged me to join them on the journey back to Tehran. I wish I had. But I couldn't leave—not while the injured filled the wards.

After lunch, Nima and the Countess waited outside. It had begun to snow, the flakes settling in delicate patches on their coats. Through the fogged restaurant window, I watched them. I waited for Lili to return from the bathroom, her coat draped over my arm. She came out and slipped into it like a boy—both arms at once, quick and careless. I couldn't help myself. I grinned like a fool and tossed her the cousins' private phrase: "Where? Where?" She paused, startled. Then, a sad smile crossed her face. She stepped close, cupped my cheek and kissed the other. "It's no use, darling

Dal," she said softly. "Find a better woman than me. He and I are bound in ways more complicated than love."

Thirty years later—upstairs from this cell, in a room where she no longer lived—I asked Nima the same question. An old man asked a middle-aged one: "Where? Where?" He looked at me, stunned—as if suddenly seeing. I didn't care anymore who knew. What surprised me was that he didn't. "A woman always knows her rival," I said. "A man is the last to know."

"You loved her too?" he asked, still dazed.

"You were never the perceptive one," I said.

He gave a generous nod. "True." Then, after a pause: "Where flowers carpet the earth and butterflies gather," he said. "Lili and I were never in a rush. In 1943, Tehran was a sleepy town. No one bothered us. The Allies had taken over. I came back to inherit a sprawling household. The Countess, once settled, transformed into a grumbling concierge. She missed her countrymen. She hated the dust, the noise—everything. Oh, by the way—did you sleep with my mother-in-law?"

"Yes," I said without hesitation.

It struck me then how age peels us down, layer by layer, until nothing remains of the person who once dared everything. The woman who, in her youth, was all generosity now hoards pennies. The man who once charged through artillery now hesitates before an elevator. And you, the young, will remember us not for our passions but our petty conceits.   What became of the bold girl who once proposed marriage to a prince in a Russian palace? Or the tender, commanding woman who guided me inside her with quiet grace, murmuring what she needed without a hint of emasculation?

"Gstaad, wasn't it?" Nima asked. I nodded. "Lili was always the more perceptive of us," he said.

"She knew?" I asked.

"She guessed. When we arrived in Tehran in the middle of the war, the Countess turned on even Lili. So we roamed—partly to escape her, partly to be alone. But we couldn't find the 'where.' Nowhere felt right. Until one weekday in early spring, we climbed Tochaal."

I stared. "Tochaal? Everyone climbs that."

He smiled. "Exactly. Lili found magic in the ordinary. We kept pushing upward, beyond the usual paths. It was warm and windy. We reached a yellow valley around two in the afternoon, sweaty and dust-covered. Hardy sunflowers and daisies and a few wild orchids dotted the slope. On one side, a smooth rock wall shielded us from the wind. Meltwater trickled nearby. You could hear it gurgling in the rocks. "She walked to the stone face and peeled off her top. Put her palms on the cold rock. Pressed them to her cheeks—left prints in the dust. She squealed like a child. Called for me. I stripped down and joined her. We pressed our freezing hands to each other's bodies, laughing as our handprints ghosted the dust like children drawing on a fogged mirror. Then, something shifted. Our curiosity gave way to desire. And then the miracle happened. As I stood facing the rock, my palms on her breasts, her eyes widened. She stared past me. I turned—and saw them. Thousands of butterflies of every color over the flowers, skimming in that random jerky way they have. She ran into the middle of the field, waving her arms among the blooms—half-naked, her short hair tousled, her skin damp, her breasts bare, her face radiant. Butterflies everywhere. I have never seen anything more beautiful in my life. We didn't need to ask the question. That was the where."

By then, the sun had risen. A brilliant shard of light turned the window into a diamond. Professor Dal fell silent—indiscreetly. The old man's body trembled against mine. His tears slid down my neck like snowmelt off mountain rock. And pressing into my back, unmistakably, was his erection.

THE SEVENTH NIGHT: 0111

WHERE ARE WE? ASKS THE WRITER

Our Surgeon recalls his war years with a heavy heart; his regrets cast a shadow over his memories. Through his recollections, we glimpse the cracks in his mental stability forged in the crucible of those harrowing experiences. The night also weaves together tales of love and acts of devotion. Lily and Nima—what a fitting title for a romance novel. I adore my Lili and Nima, self-absorbed as they may be. I wish I could have cast them as the protagonists of a novel. Their love melts like spring snow at the cusp of middle age, yet an avalanche of emotion remains with our septuagenarian Surgeon—a reminder that unfulfilled love endures for eternity.

But history books do not operate on the rhythms of romance. Sadly, our couple serves merely as parents and children to pairs of more intriguing twins. We relegate the love story to a footnote. Like all astute readers, you keep an eye on the book's thickness in your right hand or the dwindling page count on your Kindle, realizing that more pages remain than the consummation of their love would suggest.

Did you catch my princeling's remark about Scheherazade's twenty-day maternity leave? I made the same claim in the opening paragraph of this history. I've adhered to a few of S. S. Van Dine's twenty rules for writing detective stories, particularly the one that insists all clues must be plainly stated. On rereading, the breadcrumbs should lead the reader to the conclusion, rendering the final chapter almost superfluous. But alas, like Hansel and Gretel, we find ourselves lost in the forest when the birds devour the crumbs. As promised, I will guide us out—but not before we endure more cruelty.

The sixth night shines a spotlight on our fat storyteller. He recalls the Surgeon's revelation: hidden just a few hundred yards from the basement, in which he is imprisoned, lies a valise of papers, coveted by all the narrators, including me. Let me lay it out plainly. We know the princeling eventually obtains these documents, but the mystery lies in how he acquires them. He promises them to the lady historian, and we hang on the edge of our seats, eager to uncover the details. And yes, I, too, have access to these papers.

Now, we suspect that the fat storyteller is more than a passive listener, a fleshy tape recorder. He is an actor, a doer. He doesn't merely swap pencils for a microphone; he begins to act, move and make difficult decisions. He comes alive not through descriptions but through his choices, for a man's decisions reveal his true character.

There is a slight chance, reader, that you might flag under the weight of names as we slug through the seventh night. Like a wrestling coach, after the first three-minute period, I have thirty seconds to whisper in your ears to persevere. Pronounce the names in whatever accent you prefer or recognize them as ideograms. The ironies of history await you. You have completed more than half.

THE NARRATOR HELPS WITH A
PIECE OF THE PUZZLE

"To die before being painted by Sargent is to go to heaven prematurely."

The Complete Short Stories of Saki—H. H. Munro

Dear Ms. Vakil,

Thank you for sending me the four digital recordings of Mr. Hekaiatchi's oral history. I never imagined his reedy voice would have such a high pitch, reminiscent of an old recording of Alessandro Moreschi, the castrato. I am truly overwhelmed by your generosity and trust. I will repay you in kind. I have hired Digiscribe, a local scanning company, to digitize all my documents, and I will make the originals available to you. From your letters, I understand that you frequently visit the local universities.

I have just returned from a yoga class and am full of ideas. The yoga studio is tucked away in a narrow strip mall, dwarfed by a gigantic Toys 'R' Us with its black corrugated wall that rises to the blue sky, resembling a two-dimensional Hollywood set. The yoga studio sits on the second floor, just above a Build-A-Bear Workshop selling tinsel-covered artificial Christmas trees. The store holds birthday parties every hour so efficiently that it's almost unsettling. They observe a brief moment of silence when the children carefully place a plastic red heart inside the cotton stuffing of their teddy bears. Then, with profound reverence, they stitch them up. But soon, the sounds of jubilant children whooping interrupt the quiet, breaking the spell of our meditation.

Today, I had a "madeleine" moment in that reflective yoga space. The sight of those tinsel trees transported me back to a childhood Christmas. My mother would put up a gigantic tree every year, adorned with the most exquisite ornaments. It stood proudly in the corner of our grand entrance, visible to all visitors for a month. Funny-looking hens made of blown glass in shades of orange clasped each other with their feet. Miniature Fabergé-like eggs, dangled heavily from the branches. Tiny Waterford crystal bells, silver yet translucent, hung from the pine needles and chimed delicately whenever the front door swung open. Small glass clown faces in Christmas red and green were suspended in a basket. The tree became a vertical village, covered in antique watches with italic faces, angels kneeling on scrap snow, Dresden paper medallions, Swarovski edelweiss blossoms that twinkled in the light and what seemed like hundreds of hand-painted, blown-glass globes adorned with glittering crystal in red, green, gold and silver. Instead of the usual star at the top of the tree, there was Papa

Noel. Lone Ranger-like, he rode a goose with a lemon-colored beak. Goose and rider, affixed to a globe, announced *Joyeux Noël* in jubilant italics.

My mother orchestrated all this with her managerial, take-charge skills. First, the servants would bring in hundreds of leather boxes. Unclasping these boxes was a treat, revealing each object in its cut velvet bed. Some had small fleur-de-lis clasps; others had hook-and-eye clasps made of bone. I was particularly fond of the boxes with a magnetic, stainless-steel bead fastened to an alligator leather strap, which clicked into place with satisfying confidence. The servants brought in old ladders, rusted and worn, from every corner of the garden to surround the tree like ancient scaffolding. My mother directed the household staff confidently, often changing her mind mid-task. She would bark new instructions with even more authority. She might demand an object moved to the other side of the tree. When the staff didn't move fast enough, she would rush to a ladder herself to do the job, causing a commotion. Everyone scrambled to stop her as if her life would be in danger should she climb even two rungs. Our devout Muslim household treated her like a rare and delicate bird. When we finished trimming, they brought in the gifts. They piled high beneath the tree, spilling on half the open parquet floor.

1963 stands out in my memory as particularly special. That year, our Parisian grandmother, the Countess, visited Tehran under protest—it was her first visit since the war years. I only remember her from this time. She refused to leave her bed during the day and never set foot outside, but she treated us with excessive affection. Christmas in Tehran felt natural to us: a glittering, mountain-like tree surrounded by colored packages, with the scent of pine and polished parquet filling the air. It feels unimaginable today. These were the most liberal years in our modern history.

I can think of only one other period in our history that was so tolerant of different beliefs: the glorious twenty months of the first Constitutional Majlis in 1907 and 1908. Sardar Mirza, the fun-loving twin, ran for election to represent the estate of nobles and landowners in the Majlis. He immediately allied himself with the liberal radical faction. During its brief existence, the Majlis angered many but also achieved much. It sought to curtail the Shah's power and limit religious leaders' authority. But no one understood the Majlis' inevitable failure better than the Prince. He deliberately kept his distance from the democratic set. The debate in the first Majlis centered around the supplementary 125 articles, four of which were particularly contentious. Article 2, written by the reactionary Sheikh Nouri, proposed the creation of a council made up of the highest-ranking religious leaders, who would sit as judges above the senate—a Shiite supreme court with the power to invalidate any parliamentary actions deemed contrary to Sharia law. Nouri called it "clerical constitutionalism" (naming streets after him was the least Khomeini could do). His proposal sparked mass demonstrations and forced Nouri into sanctuary in a mosque.

Nouri opposed vehemently Articles 8, 18 and 20 copied from the Belgian constitution. They protected the rights of minorities, mandated compulsory public education and guaranteed freedom of the press. The liberal faction eventually succeeded in enacting these three fundamental rights but conceded to Nouri on Article 2, establishing his religious supra-parliament. (As I'm sure you know, Ms. Vakil, in my adopted country, we paid for the beautiful Bill of Rights with the slavery compromise.) And so, Article 2 was enacted. The liberals were confident that other religious leaders wouldn't share power with the despised Sheikh Nouri. Article 2 remained dormant for over seventy years, a ticking time bomb that successive governments ignored. An old man with a good memory reawakened it in 1979. Little insertions have a way of biting with poisonous fangs.

I often shout from the rooftops to enlighten my American friends. They believe that the Constitutional Convention was the product of natural evolution. But no! The American republic was a miracle, the most remarkable fluke in Western civilization. At the time of nation-building, this country had a handful of civic geniuses who were fortunate enough to be reasonable. I don't want to lecture. But every time I sit down to write and connect a century of my family's history with the nine days I spent confined in my own house, I realize I need to add another jigsaw piece to the puzzle.

Jigsaws played a prominent role in our lives. A giant wooden jigsaw puzzle hung for many years in the petit salon, a Christmas gift from our maternal grandmother, brought during her visit to Tehran. It depicted a young woman from around 1910, wearing a large white hat. The gauzy scarf tied under her chin formed a perfect isosceles triangle with the edge of the hat. Within this triangular fabric frame, my grandmother's twenty-year-old face stared out with sarcastic, arched eyebrows. Impressionistic strokes defined the large, curved forehead my brother and I inherited. Her saucer-like eyes—daubs of yellow paint against dark pupils— resembled deep pools reflecting an unseen chandelier. Thin lips set firmly in a straight line betrayed a smirk at the left corner.

We opened gifts in her presence as she sat in an armchair in the hallway, her legs twisted around one another in her usual pose. She wore a Chanel ensemble and a tear-shaped sapphire locket on her orange cashmere sweater. Even at midnight, she carried her Hermès bag as if ready to step out onto the Rue Saint-Honoré. Everyone else exclaimed as we unwrapped our presents. When we opened the heavy wooden puzzle box with the picture of the puzzle on top, our grandmother, Anais de Grandpierre, looked up at her daughter but addressed everyone in the hallway: *"Mais voici ma jeunesse, imaginée par Belleroche."* She repeated the line countless times with a bored air: "Here is my youth, imagined by the famous artist Albert de Belleroche." The portrait of our grandmother, a luminary of the Belle Époque, wasn't as impressive to us as the puzzle itself. Each piece had been whimsically shaped—into birds, rabbits, swords, angels and snowflakes.

My grandmother's bespoke jigsaw puzzle, an older woman's attempt to preserve her youth, wasn't meant to be difficult. It easily captured the imagination of a seven-year-old. The artist had centered the painting on the tear-shaped, sapphire locket between her young breasts on its bed of white muslin. The puzzle was perfectly round, with the bright azure stone as the central piece, completing the image as my grandmother became the center of attention. Guests gathered around her, admiring her beauty and the puzzle.

The following day, my brother and I delighted everyone by solving the puzzle in under half an hour in my grandmother's bedroom, with both parents present, drinking tea. With dramatic flair, I placed the central piece—the locket, cut to match precisely its painted form—between my grandmother's painted breasts. It slid into place with an almost magical precision. It felt like the promise of a lifetime of shiny moments. Reclining in her bed, dressed in a negligee, her skin mottled above her drooping breasts and her blue-veined wrists adorned with jangling gold bangles, the living woman clapped to congratulate our success. I remember the sensuous, satisfying fit of the locket in its rightful place.

The excitement was not due to our puzzle-solving skills but because my brother and I cooperated for the first time without quarreling. My ever-optimistic mother saw this as a model for future gifts. For the next three years, she bought us increasingly complex puzzles with themes like the *101 Dalmatians* or irregular shapes that looked like the chalk outlines of murder victims. One year, she bought us the world's most challenging jigsaw—Jackson Pollock's *Convergence*. A few days after Christmas day, I slipped into the petit salon. Using the tip of a silver letter opener, I gently pried out, with some difficulty, the centerpiece of the puzzle—its jewel, the locket.

With my grandmother still in the house, the household panicked. Cool as ever, my mother ordered the local carpenter—a filthy, half-shaven man with sockless feet in plastic sandals, an early prototype of today's Islamic bureaucrat—to fill the missing piece with glued wood shavings. There was no question of him creating a new piece; he didn't have the skill. My mother then used her thin paintbrushes, reserved for New Year's egg painting, to complete the illusion. She instructed Reza Khan to glue the assembled puzzle onto a background frame. She hung the puzzle high on an inconspicuous sidewall, where my grandmother's weak eyes couldn't detect the changed piece.

The reasons behind my theft remain unclear. Why do boys keep tins filled with shoelaces, coins and stones? I hid the locket in an unused chimney hole covered by a tin lid. Some nights, I took it out and slept with it tightly gripped in my fist. I considered it the most perfect, magical object in the universe. Years later, I pretended to "find" it. By then, my grandmother had passed away, and the sixties were in full swing. The glued-together jigsaw sat forgotten in the basement. My "discovery" sparked excitement at lunch; my brother looked suspicious. I drilled a hole in the wooden piece—it no longer resembled a locket, and the paint had worn off like a cheap decal. I strung it on a leather cord and wore it as my lucky charm, my security blanket, fitting seamlessly with a teenager's style in the sixties. My mother saw it as a sentimental tribute to her mother.

A year later, I gave the charm to Hamid during the holy month of Muharram. The memory of the soccer game had faded, as had the contoured purple shapes around his eyes. The bump in the middle of his nose had transformed his boyish face. During Ashura, Shiites commemorate the martyrdom of Hussein, the grandson of the Prophet, who was slaughtered in 680 AD, along with his family, after ten days of extreme thirst and heroic resistance. Villages organize ta'ziyeh plays depicting the last days of the third Imam. These performances are interactive. The actors and audience collectively experience grief, which culminates in a procession in which participants beat their chests with their hands or chains. The village of Poonak had its ta'ziyeh stage built on land my father had donated. We and the villagers attended it annually. We arrived early in the afternoon. One of the villagers, caught up in the frenzy of grief, had seriously injured himself by repeatedly slashing his forehead with a poniard. My father and Hamid's father, the village head, immediately issued a joint order, warning of severe consequences for anyone who allowed or participated in such self-mutilation. Ms. Vakil, let me not get carried away with the absurd practices encouraged by our religious leaders. Self-flagellation exists in many religions, but our soft-skinned mullahs encourage the poor to beat their backs raw with chains. I never saw the mullahs use chains on their bodies.

My father listened to serious complaints about water rights in the valley. A group of agitated farmers from the lower valley approached, shouting their concerns. Peasants, by nature, are con-frontational. They always talk loudly to authority, as if they speak a different language from the landlord. But when the dispute concerns water rights, their loudness is not just a form of pro-test—it reflects their desperation. A severe drought had turned the once-green valley into dry yellow fields. The river had dried up, and farmers upstream had dammed the snowmelt, rerouting the water through the upper gardens. I don't recall the river ever running again after that. The gentle flow had ceased in our garden's small water canals. Tired and dusty petitioners leaned on their long-handled shovels and pickaxes, angry but primarily miserable. My father enjoyed solving concrete, local problems. No detail was too small, and he quickly resolved issues with wisdom and populist candor. After a lengthy discussion, the still somber but thoughtful farmers left.

We retired to the schoolhouse to eat refreshments while waiting for the play. In the evening, we walked through the vil-lage's dusty alleys between the houses' low clay-and-straw walls. The takieh, a simple square structure made of cement, sat a hun-dred yards beyond the village. Behind the stage, large vats sat on stacks of loose bricks, cooking white rice. Our cook, old Nemat's nephew—whose Mongolian features were even flatter—served the rice by burying a plate in the mound. It emerged with a pyramid of rice. With a magician's flourish, he twisted his wrist, offering the rice to the peasants who stood transfixed in awe. We offered free stacks of fresh sangak bread to the villagers.

The village women sat along one side of the stage, all wearing long black veils. The men stood at the corners. My father sat in the only chair while I stood among the villagers a few feet behind him. We faced the stage, with the mountains in the background. A warm wind from the desert caused the gaslights to whistle. Jackals howled beyond the valley.

There was a quick, nervous beat of the drum, followed by silence. Then came another burst, lingering in the air. The professional storyteller spoke in a clear voice, narrating the tragedy in a light rhyme. As he described the army of the caliph encircling Hussein and his seventy-two followers, I felt someone close behind me. Turning, I saw a dark, smiling boy of ten. I placed my hand on his shoulder and returned to the play. Then I felt him against me. At first, it seemed innocent, but soon he began to grind slowly against me. I feigned inattention and steadied him, but he moved back again. I glanced to the left and caught the yellow smile of an old man standing a few feet away, elbowing another man into the joke. I quickly moved before the man's eyes could find us. With a swift blow, I struck the back of the boy's head. He stumbled, falling to one knee beneath a gas lamp, then quickly stood and disappeared into the crowd. My father, raising an eyebrow, turned in his seat. The men in the audience interpreted his look as a signal to quiet down.

"The perverse tickle smites the boy," I heard Hamid say behind me. I turned and saw him smiling. I smiled back. "I had heard he had the disease, but I am surprised by his impudence," I replied.

"Is it a disease between two grown friends?" he asked.

"It is certainly not impudence between friends," I said, avoiding his gaze. The noise from the takieh grew louder. On one side of the stage, the actors celebrated the marriage of one of Hussein's nephews, while on the other, the Caliph's army mutilated the other nephew. The women sobbed. I retreated from the crowd and walked down the valley through a portal. I descended the giant stone stairs made of flat rocks from the riverbed and sat beneath a large mulberry tree. Even in the weak moonlight, it casts a shadow darker than the night. The ta'ziyeh continued, the drums silenced by a woman's hysterical sobbing. The wind sighed softly.

I heard a rustle nearby. "Who is it?" I called.

"It's me, sir," Hamid's voice answered, and I saw his silhouette just a few feet away. There was no shadow of the future or memory of the past—only the pure present. Head down and silent, he stepped forward: two confident steps. The gaslights above sounded like dragons breathing fire through copper vocal cords: too much light. I retreated deeper into the tree's shadow, my feet awkward on the protruding tree roots. He walked forward again, head down, eyes downward, less confident. I felt his hand on my belt. Only then did he look up. I felt his sweet breath. My palm felt the bristle of the shaved head. I heard the sobbing of the humans above and the screaming of the jackals below as I shed all rules and taboos. We listened to the procession march above us, making its way back down the village alleys. The sound of hands slapping against bare chests and chains clinking against flesh filled the air. We lay curled up together. At that moment, I felt an astonishing clarity—suddenly, I knew what I liked. I gave him the centerpiece of the puzzle then. He tucked it under his shirt.

Ms. Vakil, I know I've shared more than I should have. A love story, particularly a first love, gives us the illusion of believing in a soul. Forty years later, those memories have become my foundation. I trust you will keep them to yourself. Your sharp, intellectual mind might wonder if I chose Hamid, in part, to hurt my brother—to wound him psychologically. As a side benefit, I admit that Hamid's presence among us altered things. But love conquered hate. I knew I could devastate my brother with this revelation. He loved Hamid as a true brother; they shared every daring adventure. Like a woman, I instinctively understood that Hamid belonged to me. I would never lose him just to hurt my brother. The thought never even occurred to me.

Listening to the tapes now, I understand "our storyteller" better. I see him as someone who could grow beyond childish self-absorption into a more mature mind. He shows sympathy for my uncle. Have you found any trace of him yet?

THE FAT STORYTELLER
EXPERIENCES WAR THROUGH HIS
FUTURE FATHER-IN-LAW

"I have spent more than half a lifetime trying to express the tragic moment."

Marcel Marceau

Baba, my outing to Vakil Kahnum did me good. I step out cautiously, always expecting the worst, as though my head might be chopped off any day now, but still, I can't help but rejoice in my newfound freedom. I make sure not to draw any attention, not even from two blocks down the street. I wear a ragged American baseball cap and keep my head down. When Mammad-Ali has his hands full, I help behind the counter. He's a tiny man, wearing pajama-like pants and a dark blue shirt that hangs untucked. His small wrists, ankles, hands and feet stick out like the talons of a sparrow, but he lifts weights like a porter at the shipping docks. He'll throw a fifty-pound sack of rice over his shoulder and climb a ladder with it as casually as a construction worker.

Thank God he sees me as your son. He treats me with the old-school respect your generation commands. He never asks me to carry a heavy load—I'd shame myself if I tried. Since the war ended, Mammad-Ali's little shop has come alive again. Business is brisk. Zahra tells me the shelves sat empty for years. "We sold old batteries and scrap metal," she says, clenching her fist. Now the place bustles. She works in the back, sharp-eyed, watching over accounts like a hawk. I've grown fond of this shop with its rich smells and overflowing shelves. The refrigerator hums as it lights up rows of Cokes, Fantas, dooghs, butter, milk, and eggs. The fan flutters the newspapers and magazines. You can smell the halva stuffed with pistachios, the sharp yogurt, the salty feta—it makes you want to grab some sangak from next door and dig in.

I sweep the floors, dust the shelves, and feel something like ownership. Occasionally, I toss a gold foil chocolate or a packet of gum to a kid from the neighborhood. I do it like Mammad-Ali once did for us—without lifting his head, pretending to be busy so he wouldn't have to endure our gratitude.

One evening, Zahra and her friend Khadijeh walked through the bazaar and left me to close up. I heard a strange murmuring from the back room and investigated, thinking it might be mice. I found Mammad-Ali sitting on a rough stool beside boxes of soap and detergent, his head cradled in one palm. He cried—softly, discreetly. I rushed toward him. He looked up, startled, forcing a smile too late. "I lost two boys in the war with Iraq," he said.

"Fifteen and sixteen. Angels walking this earth. I tried to hide them—I wished they'd inherited my crossed eyes, like Zahra. They ran off and signed up with the militia, with those cursed Passports to Paradise. It was early in the war when Saddam agreed to restore the old border." He paused, then looked up at me with something like reverence.

"You went to school. I only finished three grades. And that old man—Khomeini—he rejected Saddam's offer within twenty-four hours. That one decision cost us six more years of war. We didn't gain a single pebble." He shook his head. "My younger son, Mohsen, died first. He volunteered to run across the minefields during Operation Ramadan. His brother, Ali, sent a letter—full of joy. They couldn't even find his body. When I got the news, I shut the shop and left Zahra with the neighbors. I boarded a bus to the front lines, hoping to find my boy, maybe even save him." His eyes took on a faraway glint.

"I arrived in Khorramshahr. It was hell on earth. We had taken the city back, but only rubble remained. The place belonged to Djinns—creatures with frog eyes and square muzzles. The soldiers walked around caked in mud, training for who knew what. Children, bandaged and limbless, played as if in some twisted schoolyard. People carried bodies on old carpets, on sheets of plastic, on scraps of cardboard." He spoke with the steadiness of someone who had relived it too many times.

"No one knew where they had sent my son in this chaos. I volunteered as a water carrier so I could eat—two buckets balanced on a rod over my shoulders. I worked the rear lines for a month. In my search for Ali, I passed through a prisoner camp. The Iraqi captives were half-naked, left in the dirt with no shade.

They looked no different from us. Same sunken eyes, same cracked skin." He glanced up again, gauging my reaction. "One morning, I stumbled on a mud-and-straw stable guarded by two men. They yelled at me to leave. But when you have children, you forget about danger. I kept walking. They pointed rifles; I played deaf. When I got close, I offered them water. They hesitated—maybe it was my small frame or the stupidity people assume comes from my crossed eyes. They drank, and I saw four white horses—majestic creatures behind them. Like something from the stories your father used to tell at the tearoom. I wish I had never learned why they kept these horses." He paused, then exhaled slowly.

"As time passed, I got closer to the trenches. Boys sat waiting, praying not for safety but for time to pass faster—so they could die and be done. Children, really—nine, ten years old. And then, during one of the human wave attacks, they sent one of those white horses into the storm. On its back sat a man in white robes, green turban, and green sash—made up like Imam Hussein himself. The soldiers didn't speak. The boys lit up. They believed what they saw. When the bugle sounded, he raised a sword—one of those storybook blades—and rode into the dust. Undoubtedly, he veered off once out of sight, sparing the horse. But the boys followed him. No weapons. Just faith. The mines tore them apart. I saw it. Little puffs of dust where there had been feet. Men rushed to carry back the injured so the next group wouldn't see." His voice was thin now, unraveling.

"It was about then they tried to capture Basra. I couldn't pray anymore. I lost faith in God. I spent a month looking for Ali. Then I saw him—my heart nearly exploded. He wore an oversized uniform, a standard helmet that swallowed his face. But I knew my boy. Even from a distance, I knew his posture. I ran to him. But he turned his face away. I called out. He wouldn't answer." Mammad-Ali fell silent, his shoulders shaking with sobs. Eventually, he continued.

"He told me he'd seen me weeks before but hid. He knew why I had come. I had the right to bring him home—I was over sixty, and he was my only surviving son. But he said he wanted martyrdom. He told me—eyes shining—that he had seen Imam Hussein with his own eyes. And something strange happened. I believed him. I saw my mistake. God's work is not the same as man's lies. I had seen the horses. I had seen the theater. These were not miracles. These were stories—our stories—misused, distorted." He looked at me with a mix of shame and resolve.

"I lost faith, but not forever. I regret those weeks. God may punish me for them. But I understand now the power of knowledge. Didn't He put us here to use our minds? For the first time, I regretted my ignorance. I regretted not educating my sons. When I came home, I made sure Zahra went to school. You're my witness, Mr. Hekaiatchi. Isn't she a demon with numbers?" He smiled through tears—his grief momentarily eclipsed by pride.

"You couldn't convince your Ali?" I asked.

"I couldn't tell if anything I said mattered. Ali told me his life now belonged to his comrades. 'They protect me, and I defend them,' he said. As long as the war continued, he would not come back. I threatened him—I said I'd file the official paperwork to have him released on account of my age and his being my only remaining son. He looked at me then with the calm, resigned eyes of someone three times his age."

"'Agha Joun—Dear Sir,' he said. 'That won't change a thing.

The day you claim me back, I'll run away again. Can't you see the chaos here? No one would stop me. There are ten-year-olds here—no one knows where they are or who they belong to.' I saw the truth in his words. I returned on the next bus and told him to be careful. Miraculously, he survived two more years. He died during Operation Kheibar, not long after turning eighteen. By then, the professional army had absorbed the militia and volunteer brigades."

"I still have his letters. The last one came in late February. He wrote with pride—told me how they fought through the marshes in southern Iraq and captured the Island of Majnun, forty miles north of Basra. After that, I heard nothing. Then, on New Year's Day, the first day of spring, they sent me his body. They told me to rejoice in his martyrdom. They forbade me to cry. I found him in the back of a truck stacked with corpses. He hadn't worn his gas mask when the Iraqis retaliated with mustard and nerve gas. They say it was quick. I thank God his mother didn't live to see this. No one should bear what I have."

Baba, I wept from the deepest part of my soul for Mammad-Ali. And worse—shamefully worse—I had never once asked about his children. I stayed in his house. He cared for me like a son. I never thought of asking what had happened to the boys. I vaguely remembered they were younger than me by several years. Neither he nor Zahra ever brought them up. Always attentive to my needs, they kept my comfort at the center of their lives. I cried for someone other than myself for the first time in years. Touched by my sudden grief, Mammad-Ali fell into my arms like a child. He tried to pat my back and comfort me but couldn't reach me. Instead he patted my stomach over and over. "My son," he kept whispering. "My son." We stayed like that for a long time.

Zahra and I prepared to begin recording my oral history a few days later. I abandoned my disguise as a woman. With Zahra by my side, I felt braver. A light snow had fallen the night before. It caught soot and pollution particles as it descended. It left the air sharp and clean. A chill wind swept through the city. We hailed a taxi and gave the driver the address: the Saman apartment complex—specifically, the older of the two towers known as Lower Saman. The buildings were among the first luxury high-rises built in the city. They made an impression on poor Zahra. We crossed the open plaza, entered the second tower, and passed through the gleaming lobby. Behind a polished desk sat a man with a skeptical look. "Mr. Hekaiatchi here to see you," he said into the phone. From the receiver came the faint mosquito whine of Vakil Khanum's voice. She permitted him to send us up. The man never looked up again. Zahra had never ridden in an elevator. She entered cautiously, clinging to my arm when it jolted to life. "God protect us," she murmured as the light above each floor flickered sequentially. The elevator opened directly into an apartment.

The view alone could stop a heart. The snow-covered Alborz mountains gleamed against a cobalt sky through the massive windows. To the northeast, Mount Damavand wore its white skirt like a queen. Zahra stared as if it were a palace. Even I was taken aback. A white-haired woman in tailored modern clothes greeted us softly and asked if we'd like tea. Even the maid—dressed in crisp linen—looked wealthier than anyone Zahra had ever known. She returned with tea and delicate cream-filled cones on a silver tray. "Khanum will be down shortly," she said.

Down? I thought. Zahra missed the significance, but I didn't. An upstairs in an apartment? "A house inside an apartment building," I whispered. In the center of the living room sat a large tape recorder with twin reels waiting to spin. I liked it immediately. I'd practiced your craft, Baba—the careful telling of a story—and now I could begin it right—enough of pencils. When Vakil Khanum entered, she did so without a scarf or veil. She looked radiant. Her thick black hair fell in straight, heavy lines that swayed with her every step, like the hair of a fairy-tale princess. Her dress ended below the knee. Zahra gasped. "You can remove your chador," said Ms. Vakil gently. "No men will enter. I assume you're comfortable with Mr. Hekaiatchi."

Zahra hesitated, then lowered her chador to her waist, keeping it ready, always alert to the threat of a man's sudden appearance. Ms. Vakil approached the recorder, holding a metallic microphone shaped like an ice cream cone. "This little switch here—slide it back and forth to stop and start the tape," she said. Her calmness settled my nerves. "Shall we begin, Mr. Hekaiatchi?" she asked. "Zahra and I have nothing better to do than listen to your fascinating story." I switched on the tape recorder.

Professor Dal, ever dramatic, had done his usual morning performance, flinging his head back like a man on a crucifix. I'd had two different cellmates. At first, I feared the daytime version of Dal for his madness, then the nighttime version for his discipline. By the seventh day, I feared neither. I had accepted both. By day, he ignored me. By night, he became the storyteller. And what prisoner doesn't welcome a tale to distract from the walls? I had barely slept the night before. I had stomach gas pressing me downward. But on the seventh night, when he climbed on top of me . . .

Here, Baba, I had to stop the recorder. I ate one of those glorious cream cones instead. I couldn't say what happened aloud—not with two women present. As he mounted me, I let out a long, pathetic fart. It fluttered out like an off-key accordion under his insubstantial weight. He burst into laughter.

"I must be quick, or your payment for my storytelling will fly away," he said, still laughing.

Then he asked, "Don't you know the tale of Caliph Harun al-Rashid and his Persiranian vizier, Barmaki?"

"I don't," I said, mortified.

He grinned. "Well, once the Caliph and his vizier, traveling in disguise, came upon a poor man on the road to Basra. They asked where he was headed. 'To find a doctor,' the man said. Barmaki, ever the showman, offered him a cure: 'Take three ounces of wind and three ounces of sunlight. Mix it carefully in a bottomless mortar. Let it sit in the air for three months, pound the mixture, sieve it and leave it in the sun again before applying the remedy.' The old man bent over, farted—not as magnificently as you, of course—and said, 'Be quick and gather the wind, Doctor. That's your payment for such a windy cure.'"

"I imagine the Caliph laughed just as hard as I did," Professor Dal said.

Baba, do you understand why I left that part out of the recording? Once I finished my cream cone, I clicked the switch and resumed the tale—clean, proper and poised.

THE SURGEON EVOKES THE
REVOLUTIONARY GRANDFATHERS

*"Then went the jury out whose names were Mr. Blindman, Mr.
No-good, Mr. Malice, Mr. Love-lust, Mr. Live-loose, Mr. Heady,
Mr. High-mind, Mr. Enmity, Mr. Liar, Mr. Cruelty, Mr. Hate-
light, Mr. Implacable, who every one gave in his private verdict
against him among themselves, and afterwards unanimously
concluded to bring him before the judge."*

—*Middlemarch*—George Eliot

After eighteen months, the first constitutional period ended in the
sound of cannon fire. As the Prince liked to say, "I told you so."
That year marked the only rift ever to come between the brothers.
It began with the coronation of thirty-eight-year-old Mohammad Ali Shah in 1907. The old monarch, Mozaffar al-Din Shah,

had signed the constitution and died within a week—leaving the throne to his petulant son.

The coronation fell on the 19th of January, two weeks after the old Shah had gone to meet the Almighty. The Prince, dressed impeccably in court attire, searched the crowded hall for his brother. Instead, he saw foreign faces peering out from behind the stage curtain. He saw Shapshal—always present, always preening—the uneducated, self-indulgent Russian tutor whose prim smile broadcast smug satisfaction. His investment had paid off. And he basked in its return. A shadow stirred in the background. Colonel Liakhov stepped forward in full Cossack uniform, bearing Russian-style epaulets and the groomed mustache and beard favored by his master, Czar Nicholas. Chin high, one hand behind his back, the other resting on his sword, he stood like a man convinced of his superiority. He commanded the Persiranian Cossacks, a regiment the Prince's father had formed in 1882—paid for by the Persiranian government, meant to serve the Shah alone. Any contact between Liakhov and the Russian command was, technically, treason. Yet the Shah had empowered him.

The Colonel's Russian masters had broken every promise. They sent orders from across the border, and the Prince's agents intercepted Liakhov's letters to the general staff in the Caucasus. But is it treason, the Crown Prince once mused, if the Shah knows and encourages it? As the ceremony approached, the Prince searched the ranks of bemedaled guests again. His brother was still absent. The new Shah had opened his reign by rebuffing the Majlis—against the Prince's advice—and had refused to invite a single member to the coronation. Sardar Mirza had received a courtesy invitation solely due to family ties. The Prince had begged his brother not to boycott the event. "Don't burn unnecessary bridges," he'd warned. But he also understood that his brother stood in solidarity with his colleagues.

The Prince had also urged Mohammad Ali to delay the coronation: "Your Highness, haste will make you seem insecure—and that will cause the people to doubt your divine right. Begin your reign with confidence." The Shah had smiled as if biting into a lemon and ignored the Prince's advice. At court, the Prince found himself increasingly isolated. The new regime rejected him. Beyond the Russians, the Shah surrounded himself with die-hard reactionaries. Among them, Amir Bahadur Jang swept in with gold-encrusted regalia and aristocratic disdain. His manteau hung across his shoulders like that of a Prussian Junker. The Prince respected the man—except for his contempt for constitutionalists, whom he dismissed as vermin. The Prince held firm. He believed in the monarchy. "Which of us cockroaches," he thought, "will be the one to interrupt 2,500 years of monarchy?" He understood the modern world. He hoped for a compromise—a viable constitutional monarchy.

His gaze rose to the throne, where his aging nephew had taken his place on the peacock seat. The oversized crown sat on his pudgy head like a bucket. His brows scowled permanently—a poor imitation of gravitas. His mustache drooped, failing to conceal the petulant lip. He gripped a curved, jewel-encrusted sword, its tip resting on the mirrored floor between his legs. "He sits on the peacock throne like a dumpling," the Prince thought. Compared to his grandfather, with that trim waist and heroic gaze fixed on the horizon, this new Shah looked anything but majestic. "*Une sacrée sacre, n'est-ce pas, Votre Altesse?*" Alliteration oozing from every syllable, Shapshal sidled up like a cat brushing against a trouser leg. "A sacred ceremony, is it not? *J'ai entendu dire que le frère de Votre Altesse est entre les griffes d'une petite grippe.*" His eyes roamed the room without ever resting on the person he addressed. I heard your brother has the flu. "I believe His Highness, my brother, is in excellent health. Who starts these rumors, Shapshal?" The Prince dropped the honorific—addressing him only by surname, as a commoner.

"His Majesty searched everywhere before the ceremony. He hoped to grace both Highnesses with a few words," Shapshal insisted.

"I'm sure something important detained my brother," said the Prince coolly.

"You mean something more important than his nephew's coronation?" Shapshal's brow arched like a predator about to pounce. "The last time your brother was detained, *je me souviens vaguement, mais je vous assure vraiment vaguement . . .* " He pressed his palm theatrically to his forehead. "I remember vaguely, I assure you. And yet . . . *tout cela s'est terminé très mal, non?* It ended badly, I believe?"

"What ended badly?" came a voice from behind. Sardar Mirza approached, smiling calmly.

"Ah, brother," said The Prince, "I was about to send this man to look for you. Remember him?" He turned to Shapshal. "His Majesty has been looking for us."

Sardar Mirza gave Shapshal a blank look. "Are you not one of His Majesty's servants?"

"We met many years ago, Your Highness," Shapshal said evasively.

Sardar Mirza turned to his brother and, with his back to Shapshal, muttered, "I've never seen the man before." He had forgotten the beatings they'd received as boys. The Prince, who remembered every lash, took satisfaction in his brother's confusion—proof that the incident held no significance to him.

"What made you come after all?" The Prince asked. "You look tired. People might mistake you for my older brother." As they walked away, Shapshal fumed behind them.

"I came to see that man over there," Sardar Mirza said, pointing to Sa'd al-Dawlah, the parliament president. "The Majlis is furious. They can't believe their president allowed this insult to stand. The Shah has not invited one representative. Sa'd al-Dawlah has changed. We work night and day drafting the supplemental fundamental laws—but he doesn't care. He dislikes Hakim Molk, avoids his house and skips the nightly sessions." The meetings, led by the late Shah's doctor and a rabid constitutionalist, drew liberals who debated until dawn.

"Be careful," The Prince warned. "The Shah opposes the provisions. He received a letter from Sheikh Nouri this morning—congratulating him, then warning that he'd fall into the hands of the Babis and the infidels." The Prince already knew Sa'd al-Dawlah had changed more than his brother realized. The radicals had pushed him too far. He drifted toward the conservatives, resigned by May and within a year became a reactionary.

"Wait until you see the size of the cuts. The Majlis slashed the royal budget. He'll be furious," said Sardar Mirza. He glanced at the Shah on the throne. "We also blocked his foreign loans. I even voted to cut our allowance." The Prince sighed. His brother had no sense of money. How did he think he could afford his European clothes?

"You make enemies too easily," the Prince murmured.

Sardar Mirza nodded politely to passing cousins and courtiers. "There goes His Highness Azudul Molk," he said, pointing at the fierce leader of the Qajar clan, whose black eyebrows and piercing gaze menaced every guest. "Is he to be the next premier?"

"No, not him," said the Prince. "But tell your Majlis friends to compromise. The Shah wants to recall Atabak from Europe."

"Atabak?" Sardar Mirza laughed. "The same premier who served our father and our brother? Why do we keep going back to the same stable? Are we short of racehorses? The northern states will revolt before they let him return."

"Nevertheless," said the Prince, "the Shah wants a man of his own. He believes the Great Atabak will slow the Majlis."

"Slow us? For what purpose? He swore on the Holy Book to uphold the constitution."

The Prince leaned in close. "The Shah also swore to abolish it. Never believe otherwise, brother."

"What weighty matter engages Your Highnesses so intensely?" asked Cecil Spring-Rice, the British chargé d'affaires, as he approached with arms wide in greeting. His court uniform gleamed in the light: a dark blue jacket with a high collar and gold embroidery, white breeches striped in gold, and long tails that swayed behind him. Under one arm, he carried a cocked hat adorned with white ostrich plumes. Sir Cecil, now forty-eight and a Balliol man, bore a resemblance—especially in his tweeds—to a kind-eyed, middle-aged Sigmund Freud. Behind him followed a lean man in a black tailcoat, smiling with the shy restraint of an English spinster.

"Your Excellency honors us with your presence," said the Prince, bowing slightly.

"I wonder if you've had the pleasure of meeting Mr. Scott. He has only recently joined our mission," said Sir Cecil.

"Mr. Scott!" Sardar Mirza's face brightened into a wide smile.

"Indeed, Your Highness," Mr. Scott returned the smile, his stutter almost gone. "It's a pleasure to see you after so many years, Your Highness."

The Prince and Sir Cecil exchanged vague, pleasant smiles, each aware they were outside the private joke.

"Brother, Mr. Scott traveled with me through the Caucasus. I mentioned him in my letters," Sardar Mirza explained. "Mr. Scott, you must come visit us next week."

"I'd be honored," said Mr. Scott. "Did Your Highness ever reconnect with the delightful De Grandpierre family?"

"Your Highness," Spring-Rice said quietly, drawing the Prince aside, "His Majesty appears quite satisfied upon the Peacock Throne."

"Yes," replied The Prince, recognizing the English art of speaking through implication. He waited, as patience was the required currency.

"Forty years of practicing as a crown prince does keep one young," the Prince said.

Sir Cecil laughed, then adopted a more serious tone. "Still, it seems His Majesty regards England with less affection than your brother or father did. Better, perhaps, to follow their example—

flirt with all suitors, love none." His lips smiled primly. His eyes did not. "Even adversaries need breathing room."

The Prince took the warning in stride, though its precise shape escaped him. "Your Excellency knows well my influence at court is diminished. I could count my remaining days on one hand."

Spring-Rice chose to misread the remark. "God willing, Your Highness has half a century of service left to offer." The Prince sighed, reflecting on the English habit of thinking in centuries. He longed for the end of ceremonies.

"What's the most duplicitous country in the world, boy?" Professor Dal's voice broke through my reverie of royal pageantry.

"England," I replied without hesitation. No campaign of anti-American propaganda had ever dislodged Persiran's deep suspicion of the British.

"Good boy," he said with a chuckle. "But we didn't resent the English quite so much back then. We understood the Russians were grasping, brutal and naked in their ambition. We saw ourselves in them. Had we possessed their resources, we might have acted the same. Their uniforms fooled no one. But the English . . ." He paused. "We expected more from them. Please don't ask me why. Perhaps because they let us into their legation, or we imagined we protected their path to India. We weren't the main prize—that's why the betrayal of 1906 cut so deep. That quiet understanding between Britain and Russia—it scarred our psyche. We expected more."

In late June, the Prince traveled several miles south of Tehran to the Shah Abbdol-Azim Shrine under the sweltering summer sun. It wasn't the annual pilgrimage to his father's tomb. He went, for the second time, to meet Sheikh Nouri.

As the Prince had predicted, Premier Atabak had returned from Europe. He had asked the Prince to open a dialogue. The Great Atabak—unexpectedly moderate—sought compromise. The Shah had envisioned him as a loyal hardliner. Parliament expected a relic of reaction. But Europe had softened Atabak's edges. He returned liberal-minded and keen to exploit the divisions within the clergy. He courted both camps: Sheikh Nouri, the Shah's religious ally, and the reformist clerics seated in Parliament. His strategy: use each side to temper the other.

The old cleric Nouri sat in yet another sit-in. He had transformed the shrine into a bustling sanctuary of protest. A thousand followers crowded the mosque's courtyards. The shrine's golden dome shimmered between two tiled minarets. Over three hundred seminary students had left their studies to support the Sheikh. Along the walls, hundreds more sat—many in rags, waiting for free meals. The Prince entered the shaded mosque, the sudden coolness offering a welcome reprieve. The students bowed as he passed. Nouri's sit-in had become a resounding success: eighteen senior clerics and thirty mid-ranking scholars had joined him, forming a powerful bloc against the government.

And so the Prince, long a believer in balance, found his place beside this pragmatic premier. "Sheikh, you look at ease here," said the Prince, noting the composed air of command around the white-turbaned cleric. Nouri sat cross-legged, surrounded by his circle—five senior clerics scribbled notes behind him. A cluster of young seminarians stood by, eyes downcast, ready to act as couriers or scribes. Petitioners entered in turns, posing complex theological questions. It felt like a quieter, grayer rendering of a Mughal court painting. The heart of the operation beat around the struggle with the Majlis. Denied space in the capital's newspapers, the Sheikh's lieutenants had created a bureaucracy within the mosque. The Shah had secretly granted him use of the state's telegraph lines. In a corner, a printing press clattered, producing pamphlets and declarations.

The Rulings of Sheikh Fazlollah Nouri now thundered from the mosque's shadows—denouncing the constitutionalists as godless traitors to Islam. And beneath the surface, Atabak's sweet-laden trays arrived regularly—each hiding crisp banknotes in false bottoms—subsidizing the Sheikh's movement. At the same time, the Prince watched, navigating a tightrope between conviction and compromise. Their second meeting bore none of the tension of the first. The balance of power had settled into a fragile equilibrium. Each faction had played a card and now waited for the other to make its move. Sheikh Nouri held the strongest hand. The Shah wore the expression of a man perpetually aggrieved. The Majlis functioned like a true parliament—by fits and starts—propelled by a thicket of guilds and societies that sprang up like weeds. The further one traveled from the capital, the louder the calls for reform. In the radical northern provinces, voices openly called for the separation of mosque and state. The Great Atabak moved among them all with a sure and practiced foot. Time had softened his edges but sharpened his urgency. The Prince, meanwhile, assumed the posture of a student, studying statecraft at the feet of its most consummate master.

"We do with what we have; God provides the rest," said the Sheikh, all humility and show. Smiling faintly, he gestured toward the trays of sweets the Prince had brought. He invited him to sit. A sherbet of sour cherries appeared, served on a silver tray. "Your

Highness has grown in wisdom this past year. Your brother, alas, continues to vex us. But then, not every son can be a comfort to his father in old age." The remark was a half-offered olive branch wrapped in thorns. One of the Sheikh's sons had publicly joined the parliamentary radicals. He had, in a way, exposed his wound. The Prince let it pass.

"Sheikh, the Great Atabak sends you his deepest respect. He asked me to inform you that the Majlis has accepted Article 2, word for word, as you drafted it. They only request that you end the assemblies and allow the Majlis to resume work." At the height of his power, the Sheikh had used the parliament he loathed to institutionalize a Sharia council—his council—as a theocratic filter on all legislation. But he wasn't yet ready to retreat while ahead.

"Your Highness, be my witness," Nouri said, raising his voice with performative passion. "For a year, we've been maligned—accused of thievery, false witness, even of hiring ruffians to murder innocents. The Babis and Bahá'ís mock our faith freely. They've taken the hearts of our Muslim brothers in the Majlis. Praise God, we have a Muslim king who understands the threats facing our land. And praise God he has recalled from exile a true leader of men: His Excellency Amin Soltan, the Great Atabak."

The Prince could match each accusation with a name, a place, or a date. The Sheikh would deny every charge with his typical righteous bluster. But he had worked hand in glove with the Shah to incite riots in Tabriz, Anzali, Rasht. Just last week, one of his thugs assaulted a staffer from the French legation. Here sat a believer, yes—but also a cold strategist who could revise Machiavelli's *The Prince* with fresh chapters. "Sheikh, the Atabak you rightly praise bids you to leave the sanctuary of Shah Abbdol-Azim in peace.

You belong in Qom, tending to the souls of your flock. You have accomplished what you came here to do."

"Accomplished?" the Sheikh roared, and eyes flared. "My work has only begun. Have you read Article 1 of the Constitution? It declares our state religion as Islam—the orthodox Ja'fari doctrine of the Twelve Imams, which the Shah must profess and defend. Do you see any mention of Babis or Azalis? His Majesty has asked me to guard the faith. That is my sacred charge."

"Sheikh, Article 2 ensures Article 1. Both Sheikh Tabataba'i and Sheikh Behbehani have accepted your terms. They persuaded the Majlis to include your text exactly as written. You also gave your word to uphold the constitution."

A misstep. The mere mention of his rivals incensed Nouri. He snatched a paper from the stack beside him and brandished it like a weapon. "He dares to vouch for my behavior?" he shouted. Sayyed Tabataba'i had signed a pledge to disperse the crowd at the mosque in exchange for Article 2. His true motive had been to protect Nouri from a volatile Tehran mob. The papers had just exposed telegrams between the Sheikh and the Shah, evidence of their orchestration of the chaos in Tabriz. That had driven Nouri into sanctuary. The Sheikh's voice grew hoarse and wild. "He tells that chamber of infidels he'll drive me from the capital for pitching a tent in God's house?" His saliva flecked the letter in his trembling hand. "That dullard Behbehani dares to question my knowledge? Who are they to agree or disagree with me?" He launched into a storm of theology, hurling one reference after another. The older clerics murmured in assent while the younger watched with reverent dread. His fury silenced the mosque, and even the printing press fell quiet. "You may throw my words at me till Judgment

Day," And just as suddenly, the storm passed. He unclenched his fists. He said in a calmer, almost tender voice, "But know this: I will swear a hundred lies a day on the Qur'an if it serves the kingdom of God."

He resumed, his lecturing cadence familiar to mosque pulpits worldwide. "Each time we meet"—he smiled sweetly—"Your Highness excites your servant. Still, tell the Great Atabak that all will end well. I cannot promise what others may do, but I will do what I can to ease tensions."

Then, eyes narrowing with cunning, he asked, "I wonder how Your Highness will choose—between building God's kingdom on earth or man's palaces in heaven?"

"Your Reverence knows I am but a child when it comes to such matters," the Prince replied carefully. "I am a pious Muslim."

He had won what he came for—the Sheikh's tacit agreement to end the sit-in. Now was not the moment to push further. "It seems to me," he added with delicate irony, "that a man who takes up the task of building the kingdom of God on earth often ends up building the palace right here for himself—and calls it heaven."

The Sheikh chuckled into his beard. Then, with theatrical generosity, he raised a hand toward the Prince as though introducing a prodigy to an unseen audience. "Your Highness puts us all to shame with such wisdom—and so young an age."

"Do you pray, boy?" Professor Dal's voice pulled me from the echo of Sheikh Nouri's rage.

What is it with all the questions? I thought.

"I've forgotten the words, Arbab," I said quietly. "I prayed when my father was alive. We did it together when I was a kid. After he died, I stopped. I'm a bad Muslim."

"A bad Muslim, eh?" he mused. "You're a naughty Muslim. Do you know how to spot the worst sheep in a flock?" He asked another question, but he didn't wait for an answer.

"It's the wolf, my boy!" He chuckled at his joke, then broke into a coughing fit that left a spray of spittle on my neck. His ribs pressed hard against me—two sharp stones marking time. When he recovered, his voice came low and bitter.

"I'll show you a bad Muslim. A Muslim who feasts on people's faith to feed his glory. The sheep's clothing is no longer needed or in fashion."

He laughed again—longer this time—and the past fell silent around us momentarily. Like a break in older movie houses, he took his time. As my eyes warmed toward sleep, he took up where he had left off.

When Sarda Mirza entered the house, he knew some calamity had happened. The Prince had collapsed in the hall, soaked in blood, weeping without restraint. Nemat and Ghorban-Ali stood by, paralyzed as if caught in the wrong play.

Sardar rushed forward, cradling his brother like a wounded child. "What happened? Who is hurt?"

"They killed him," the Prince whispered.

"Who? Killed who?"

"The Great Atabak," he said. "I was with him. We had gone to read the Shah's letter before the Majlis. The Shah had finally agreed to sign the Supplementary Laws. The Atabak was radiant—he felt victorious. We walked out of Baharestan with Sayyed Behbehani. The sunlight was so bright—it blinded us. Then I heard a crack—like a wheel breaking. And Atabak ... Atabak fell." He stopped and swallowed a sob. "I wrapped him in his cloak and laid him flat in the carriage. I sent a servant for Hakim Bashi. But within half an hour—" his voice failed. "He died in our house. I've lost a father all over again."

The following day, the newspapers were ablaze with the story. A soldier had tried to stop the assassin. He was stabbed. The gunman then turned the revolver on himself—thus securing his place as the new darling of the liberal intelligentsia. In his pocket, investigators found four capsules of strychnine, a piece of silver nitrate and a scrap of paper that read:

"Abbas Agha, banker of Azerbaijan, member of the Society, National Fada'i No. 41." It suggested forty other Martyrs. The liberals feasted over the death of the premier, who only eleven years earlier had brought home the assassinated Shah in the carriage. He had served only three months as the premier of Mohammad-Ali Shah.

"Still with me, my little nest of feathers?" Professor Dal's voice brought me back.

I saw the revolution tipping hard to the left. I wanted to tell them: work it out. Find some balance. Be reasonable. Maybe I could wake up from this nightmare back in my tearoom. A shy, modern Shah could serve as ballast for a strong parliament. Why not?

"I'm awake, Arbab. How did it end?"

He chuckled. "Didn't I already tell you last night? It ends the same for you, me and all of us: we die."

"I meant the revolution."

"Ah." He paused. "The tribute to Abbas Agha gave the radicals and liberals a short-term victory. But it shattered something essential. It pushed things past a limit. That moment triggered a spiral—an escalation of violence. It drained the constitutionalists.

Worse things followed. Someone threw a bomb at the Shah. Missed him—killed his French chauffeur instead. It deepened the Shah's paranoia.

Most of life unfolds in a predictable continuum. But occasionally, it takes a rare, sharp turn—redefining a man's course. For Sardar Mirza, that course correction began with the funeral of the assassin, which he attended as a good liberal. It ended nine months later with the coup d'état.

On November 12, the Shah made a state visit to the Majlis. He swore—for the fourth time—to uphold the constitution. That same day, a group of prostitutes, encouraged by the reactionaries, marched unveiled through the streets. They shocked all of Tehran by chanting: "Oh, constitution, direct our lives, for the outmoded Islam does not answer our needs." Meanwhile, Sheikh Nouri pitched tents in Gun Square, shielded by Russian protection. He publicly denounced what he called the "takeover" of the government by Babi and Bahá'í infidels. For his second act, the Shah ordered his new premier, Nasser Molk, to attack the Majlis with cannon fire. The premier refused. In retaliation, the Shah had him imprisoned and placed chains around his neck. Immediately, four thousand armed men from various guilds and societies took positions on the rooftops of Baharestan, which housed both the Majlis and the Sepahsalar Mosque. A British attaché rushed to intervene, rescuing the chained premier from what would likely have been his execution. Nasser Molk—an Oxford classmate of Foreign Minister Sir Edward Grey—departed for London the next day. In response, the radicalized northern provinces sent telegrams, threatening to remove Mohammad Ali Shah from the throne forcibly.

Then, it was over. The Shah capitulated to every demand.

Taqizadeh addressed the assembly, declaring the curtain drawn on their tragic performance. "Let us be thankful tonight," he said. "The curtain which went up last Sunday is now coming down, and in truth, it has been a tragic and historic scene . . . but now let us take leave of this scene." Of course, it had only been a play within a larger drama.

The real performance began on June 2. Amir Bahadur Jang—the elegant, reactionary courtier—sought refuge in the Russian embassy. Nationalists had called for his exile since the coronation. For over eighteen months, each side had demanded the removal of the other's diehards. Sardar Mirza's name appeared on some of those lists. He and a handful of other Qajar princes especially irked the Shah, who saw them as turncoats—family betrayers. Amid the sniping and accusations, Russia and Britain jumped heedlessly into the fray. M. de Hartwig, the Russian minister, and Mr. Marling, the new British chargé d'affaires, clarified their intentions. Strolling arm in arm from their summer residences, they met with the foreign minister to issue a warning. The Shah, they claimed, felt unsafe and feared for his life. The two diplomats delivered an ultimatum: an armed Russian intervention, backed by Britain, would be launched against a (nonexistent) nationalist uprising. They toured the capital, visiting grandees and high officials to drive home their message: "We will not tolerate an armed insurrection against the Shah."

The next day, at eleven o'clock, Mr. Marling called on the Prince—an appointment that, by its timing, revealed the Prince's diminished stature. As they sat over tea, impatient Marling launched into a tirade against the Majlis. The guilds and societies, he claimed, had seized control. "They write incendiary articles against the Shah—in language unprintable in *The Times* of London. His Majesty's life is in danger," he said. "What business do these nationalists have interfering with His Majesty's servants, like old Amir Bahadur Jang—a man who guards his master like a loyal hound?" The Prince sat awkwardly in one of the two enormous green leather armchairs—recent acquisitions from London, and part of Sardar Mirza's campaign to modernize his brother—balancing his saucer and tea in silence. He let Marling dispense his official nonsense, which took less than ten minutes. "Your Highness has the respect of the representatives," Marling concluded. "You must make them see sense."

"Mr. Marling, my advice goes unheeded by all parties. May I ask, Your Excellency, what has provoked His Majesty's government? You assured us of your neutrality under the Anglo-Russian agreement not long ago. You said the powers would not interfere in the internal affairs of our country." The Prince looked Marling directly in the eye. "This dispute between the Shah and the Majlis is internal. The Cossack regiment remains under His Majesty's command. I am a servant of the Shah. I have yet to see the Majlis raise an army."

"Your Highness sounds nationalistic for a royalist," Marling replied. "You know well that the guilds and societies stir the people unnecessarily."

"Yes, Mr. Marling. The first time I saw them stirred was at your British legation. The last time, they defended the Majlis from cannon fire." A tense silence fell. They sipped their steaming tea until the sounds of chaos—shouting, screaming, gunshots—broke the quiet. Nemat rushed in and whispered into the Prince's ear. The Prince's face turned pale.

"My servant tells me the Shah's Cossacks just rode past my house on horseback, slashing at the crowd, creating mayhem. Is there anything you wish to tell me?" The Prince asked with a touch of bitterness. The people often accused him of being an Anglophile—a servant of the British. Maintaining his relationship with the chargé d'affaires carried real risk.

"I am, like you, in the dark," Marling replied. His red face was contrasting with the Prince's pallor.

"There's one way to find out what is happening," the Prince said. "Let's go and see." They took Marling's Rolls-Royce and drove the short distance to the winter quarters of the British Legation, where the democratic movement had begun precisely two years earlier. A few pedestrians lingered nearby, excitedly discussing the raid. Straggling Cossacks galloped past, shouting and screaming. The Prince stepped out of the car and walked to the center of the street. Raising his signature heavy cane, he bellowed for one of the Cossacks to halt. The horse reared as the rider yanked the reins hard to the left, its neck slick with sweat. The animal nearly ran over the Prince, who stood his ground and seized the bridle. The rider lifted his whip menacingly.

"Come down from that horse, you miserable foreigner," the Prince shouted. "You dare raise your hand against a prince of the realm?"

"I am no foreigner," the rider snapped, eyes blazing.

"No Persiranian tramples his people. What is your business here? Where are you headed?"

"A plot to assassinate His Majesty has been uncovered. The Shah has retired to the imperial gardens beyond the city walls. He has ordered us to protect against any threats." The Prince laughed aloud, furious with himself for being caught off guard. He released the bridle and slapped the horse's rear, allowing the rider to go. Then he turned back to Marling. "Mr. Marling," he said, "the Shah has just doubled the bet you placed against the Majlis yesterday."

"Your Highness must believe I had no foreknowledge of these actions," Marling said.

"I don't doubt it," The Prince replied. "But your new Russian friends and the Shah coordinated Bahadur Jang's asylum in the Russian legation, the Cossack attacks and the Shah's escape to the gardens. The real question is: how have our Russian friends played His Majesty's government?" The Prince was a seasoned hand at the old game of playing one power against another—a tactic the 1906 Anglo-Russian Agreement had supposedly ended. "I wonder if I might ride with you to the imperial gardens. I doubt the Shah's life is in any danger."

They arrived at the gardens late that evening. The Prince found Azudul Molk, head of the Qajar family, drafting invitations for the grandees to visit the Shah. The notables had urged the Shah to dismiss his confidant Shapshal, the Russian acolyte. Earlier that day, Shapshal had ridden beside the Shah's carriage, sword drawn with theatrical flair, as the Cossack bodyguard escorted them from the palace. Even the most reactionary aristocrats found the Russian's theatrics galling. Azudul Molk, the peacemaker, wagered all his prestige on organizing yet another assembly of the nobility. The Prince, still regarded with suspicion, busied himself with the details. He helped draft the letters, dispatched messengers and even arranged food from the palace. The Shah, meanwhile, had ordered stacks of weapons from the city's arsenals. He was consolidating power. This time, he would not blink.

The following day, the Shah received six of the realm's most esteemed nobles and notables. None of them were radicals; each had worked faithfully within the bounds of the constitution. The Shah greeted them with unusual warmth. They spoke candidly of their fears for the country's independence, warning of Russian ambitions to annex the northern provinces. They urged him to sever ties with the pernicious Shapshal, accusing the Russians of pawning the queen's jewels. (The accusation was true, though they may not have realized that Shapshal had acted on the Shah's direct orders.) The Shah listened attentively and promised to consider their recommendations. After dismissing the grandees, he withdrew to the women's quarters.

A bugle call rang out as the guests descended the staircase and moved toward the garden. In a sudden surge, the Shah's private guard emerged. They forced the nobles down the steps, shoving and jostling them. Amid the chaos, they arrested several of the more outspoken grandees. One of them, Mutamad-i-Khagan, had wandered ahead to admire the garden and managed to evade capture by ducking behind a tree. In the Prince's eyes, this calculated betrayal forever tarnished the Shah's reputation. He resolved then and there to support his nephew's removal by any means, knowing full well that his knowledge and influence could prove decisive for the opposition. His first act of resistance presented itself immediately: Mutamad-i-Khagan had to be returned to the Majlis to inform them of the treachery. The Prince disguised him in a servant's garments and sent him off discreetly.

"Am I hearing you snore?" Professor Dal asked.

"Arbab, please continue. I'm not snoring—you know I

breathe hoarsely. I can't sleep until I know how it ends. Let me use the bucket."

Relieved, I returned. He climbed back onto my spine and resumed the tale.

At Baharestan Square, a thousand Cossack troops stood in silent formation outside the Majlis building. A carriage bearing Colonel Liakhov and six other Russian officers arrived shortly after sunrise. The Shah had appointed Liakhov Governor General of Tehran.

"A Russian Governor General? Impossible!"

Sardar Mirza, trapped inside the Majlis, peered out from a window as the spectacle unfolded. The Shah added his name to the expulsion list. The early sun, ready to begin its prayers, had risen above the eastern rooftops. It caught the brass fittings on the carriage, sending flares of golden light into the square. The windows facing west burned like polished copper. The dome of Sepahsalar Mosque gleamed like a celestial body—half-shadowed, half-illuminated. The Shah's troops, commanded by Colonel Liakhov, formed a dense arc three layers deep, their ranks extending into the narrow alleys that fed into the square. Liahkov blocked all exits. To their surprise, the Cossacks allowed other parliamentarians to enter the Majlis and join their colleagues inside. No one, however, was permitted to leave. Sayyed Behbehani and Sayyed Tabataba'i had arrived earlier and were admitted. The president of the assembly and the editor of the Majlis newspaper were the last to enter. Taqizadeh, the leader of the liberal faction, arrived at 5:30 a.m. and attempted to negotiate his way in, but Colonel Liakhov rebuffed him. Liakhov emerged from the carriage first, his chin thrust forward with theatrical pride.

"It's a miracle he can walk with his head so high," someone quipped from behind the glass. The colonel approached a white, caparisoned horse held by a foot soldier. With fingers splayed, the soldier brought his hand to his ear and offered a peasant's rendition of a military salute. Liakhov mounted and began riding along the front lines, issuing sharp commands to his men. He pointed at the six cannons in the square's center, directing each to a strategic position. With evident strain, groups of soldiers pushed the cannons to new placements at six designated spots. A young nationalist with rolled-up sleeves and a soiled European shirt descended hastily from the Majlis roof and entered the chamber. "I can take him down," he said in Turkish to Sayyed Tabataba'i, gesturing toward Liakhov. "I know I can." He proposed assassinating the Russian colonel from the rooftop.

But none present had the authority—or the audacity—to order the death of a Russian officer. In light of the recent ultimatum, consequences would be immediate and catastrophic. Every political decision thus far had been shaped by the looming shadow of foreign interference. "I could shoot Shapshal instead," the young man offered. "He has no military rank. We can claim it was an accident." They all despised Shapshal, who strutted through the ranks of the Cossacks as though he were a general. "You are a brave young man," Sayyed Tabataba'i replied. "But there will be no shooting today. Not from our side."

As if to confirm his words, someone announced to general relief: "Liakhov is returning to the carriage. He's leaving the square." Sardar Mirza returned to the window to observe the spectacle. From a distance, it had the charm of a parade—bright, orderly, even beautiful, like a scene from a Napoleonic painting.

He allowed himself a flicker of hope. Then, the first cannonball struck the woodwork around his window. The glass shattered into a cascade of needles; splinters of wood flew like shrapnel. He reeled backward in a flurry of chaos. Everyone instinctively ducked. They saw Sardar Mirza turn toward them from their crouched positions, frozen in astonishment. He looked like a hedgehog—his face and torso bristling with embedded fragments. The glass and wood spared nothing above his waist: his eyelids, nose, ears, cheeks, throat and chest were covered. His friends pulled him beneath the table under the window for shelter. The splinters lodged in his shirt rose and fell with each breath. At first, his wounds oozed white. Then, tiny rivulets of blood slowly began to leak from each puncture. His entire face turned crimson. He later insisted that the last clear image his eyes registered was the cannonball itself. He swore it up and down—however improbable.

Everyone inside now understood the extent of the Shah's deception. The night before, he had sent messages of reassurance. He had consented to a mixed committee of royalists and nationalists. Three ministers had met with the assembly president and, upon dispersing at midnight, agreed to finalize the terms in the morning. After midnight, the premier sent a final note to the assembly confirming that the Shah had accepted all their demands. They had believed it—just as when the Shah capitulated six months prior. They could not have been more mistaken.

Throughout the preceding weeks, the Prince had kept his brother apprised of events inside the palace. Ever since the Shah's feigned retreat to the imperial gardens, he had written frequently, warning of duplicity. "Here is a rule of thumb," he had written after the Shah requested powers equal to the German Kaiser: "Always believe his outrageous demands; never believe his conciliatory statements."

Sardar Mirza's closest friend agreed with the Prince's sentiment. Jahāngir Khān, editor of *Trumpet of Esrafil*, the most influential paper in the capital, was thirty, handsome, and always smiling. He dressed in crisp Western suits, his collars white and his ties always freshly knotted. His newspaper had revolutionized public discourse. He abandoned the florid formalities of courtly prose. (Esrafil, the angel who sounds the Last Judgment, had never seemed more fitting a mascot.) His columns skewered the constitution's opponents and insulted the Shah with a creative venom unmatched in Persiranian print.

Malik al-Mutakallimin and Sayyed Jamal-i Isfahani—the two fiery Azali preachers—had both objected vehemently to disbanding the thousand-strong crowd of guildsmen and society members who had camped in the square for days to defend the Majlis. The four men had grown close, bound by a shared vision and increasing trust.

Despite distrusting the Shah, for who could trust the man, Taqizadeh, the young, liberal deputy from Tabriz, watching outside, and the elder Sayyed Behbehani argued persistently for moderation. The more militant societies refused to disperse. Eventually, the Majlis negotiated a compromise: the demonstrators could gather in the Sepahsalar Mosque next door, provided they came unarmed and returned home at night. Only a hundred armed watchmen remained behind each night to guard the Majlis. In hindsight, it is hard to comprehend how these representatives could have placed their trust in a Shah who, despite having sworn repeatedly to uphold the constitution, continued to conspire against it. Lying helpless beneath the table, Sardar Mirza endured eight relentless hours of bombardment and gunfire while his three loyal allies worked to remove the splinters embedded in his body. They waited patiently for lulls in the shelling to avoid vibrations that could worsen the damage. Using the sharp end of a steel pen nib, cleaned of ink, they pressed it carefully to the root of each splinter, then pulled with small tongs—ensuring no fragment was left behind. Removing the splinters from his eyelids was the most agonizing and hazardous task. Sharp shards had pierced his lids and irreparably damaged the cornea. He would be nearly blind for the rest of his life. They wrapped his eyes in a strip of sooty cloth, and he lay there, listening to the continuing cannonade and the frantic voices around him—people rushing in and out, resistance stirring on the rooftops above.

Early in the day, still groggy from the pain, he heard an excited report that fifty of the foot soldiers had dropped their rifles and joined the defenders. Sardar Mirza wondered why they had dropped their weapons instead of turning them against the enemy. Soon after, the same man returned with graver news: a group of Cossacks had tried to flee the fighting, but a Russian officer shot three of them, forcing the others back into line. His lips had swollen like balloons. His face was distended and numb. The dust on his bloodied face resembled a bowl of rice flecked with elderberries. When he raised an arm to touch his wounds, Mutakallimi, the firebrand preacher known for his heresies, gently placed it back down. The dust caked in his mouth and throat made him desperately thirsty. Half asleep, he stirred three times—each time, the room cheered the same news: one more cannon had stopped working.

By afternoon, the cannons to his right resumed their fire. "The Sepahsalar Mosque is   rubble," someone said. "All is lost. All is lost, Your Highness," Mutakallimin repeated softly in Sardar Mirza's ear. "The Shah's commitment to violence bodes ill for us. You might want to make your peace with the Almighty." The dozen men in the room braced themselves for the end. Sporadic gunfire continued outside, but the resisting forces had been either killed or captured. They waited for the final rush from the Cossacks. The group included the esteemed Sayyids, two influential Azali preachers, two defiant newspaper editors, two loyal Majlis representatives, two presidents of the assembly and a high court judge—all enemies in the Shah's eyes. They waited for the inevitable assault. Then, a discovery: a cannonball had blasted a large hole in the building's back wall. Jahāngir Khān, the spirited editor, crawled under the table to join Sardar Mirza. "Your Highness, we need to move you. Can you stand?"

With help from Jahāngir Khān and Mutakallimin, Sardar Mirza slowly rose to his feet. Blood began flowing anew as dozens of tiny wounds reopened. His chest burned where the largest splinter had lodged. But his legs still worked. He asked to hold Jahāngir Khān's hand—it felt steadier than being lifted by both armpits. They exited behind the Majlis, into a garden they all knew well. After eight hours of bombardment, it seemed impossible to step into silence. Dazed and dust-covered, they walked through the surreal beauty of the park, its air fragrant with trees and honeysuckle. They approached the gates of a magnificent residence. The quiet was eerie. An old servant, bent in permanent deference, opened the door for them. Lifting his head with effort, he quickly tried to shut it again, mistaking them for beggars in search of scraps. They pleaded for him to summon the master of the house, well aware of their pitiful appearance.

Mirza Mohsen Khān came to the door. Married to the Shah's sister, he had heard the day's cannonade and had no wish to get involved with the Shah's enemies—but these were no ordinary enemies. Sayyed Behbehani made a formal plea for asylum, invoking tradition. This allowed Mohsen Khān to declare his house a place of refuge. Recognizing the Azali preachers and Jahāngir Khān—widely believed to be a Babi convert—he refused them entry. The Sayyids, staunch opponents of the Babi sect, supported his decision. Sardar Mirza, adjusting to blindness, stood with his head tilted to hear more clearly. He pleaded with the Sayyids, reminding them of their unity in arms only minutes before. How could they now abandon the representatives of the people to the mercy of a man with blood on his hands? Did they not understand that the Shah would deliver the harshest punishment to his greatest nemesis, Malik al-Mutakallimin? But no argument moved Mohsen Khān.

Sardar Mirza refused the offer of refuge. Despite loud protests, he left with the three rejected friends. Hakim Molk, the future premier, and Momtaz Dawleh, the president of the Majlis and the Tabriz deputy, refused entry on principle. The others entered the house in silence, shame etched on their faces. "Will you refuse us even water?" Mutakallimin asked.

"I refuse you life," Mohsen Khān replied bitterly. "But I am no Yazid," referencing the tyrant who denied Imam Hussein water before slaughtering him. He shouted for a servant to bring water, then slammed the door shut. The seven men collapsed in the gray dusk beneath a large tree, some barely able to sit upright. They weighed their options. Distrustful of Britain's recent maneuvers, they chose to seek asylum with either the Ottoman or French legation. As they debated how best to reach safety—likely in pairs or small groups—the Shah's soldiers surrounded the area. A long whistle sounded. Then the soldiers stormed in, attacking with fury. One merciless soldier found Sardar Mirza, who had wandered blindly, disoriented more than attempting escape. The soldier grabbed him by the collar, hurled him to the ground, and dragged him like a sack of onions. Sardar kicked and struggled to stand, clawing at his shirt to keep from choking. After ten chaotic minutes, they chained the five remaining men together with a single iron link that clasped their necks and wrists. Half-conscious, Sardar Mirza reflected on life's absurd turns: the man dragging him might have kissed his feet only hours ago.

Then, a rifle cracked. A man groaned, "They've killed me." It was true—they had shot Haji Ibrahim Aqa, the deputy from Tabriz. Meanwhile, the two senior statesmen—Hakim Molk and Momtaz Dawleh—had hidden among the trees. Momtaz Dawleh knew the gardener, an acquaintance of his manservant. The gardener led them to a small room in the park and showed more honor than his master. At midnight, he took them to the manservant's home. The next day, they requested sanctuary at the French embassy.

The captured men were shoved into a crude cage of rusted pig-iron bars, teetering on a rickety wagon. A soldier kicked the cage door four or five times before it finally shut. They hauled them off toward the imperial gardens. Small clusters of onlookers watched in silence. "The Shah no longer bothers with appearances,"

Mutakallimin observed grimly. "It's a bad sign. He wants to make examples of us."

The Prince had arrived just in time to hear the cannonade. Each passing hour brought him closer to despair. He feared he would never see his brother again. Taqizadeh stood beside him. Though it was light enough to be seen, the crowd covered them. They turned their eyes to the front of the square, where cannon fire roared. They wandered further to see the Sepahsalar Mosque—its dust-covered dome now looked like ancient ruins. When the Cossacks finally launched their assault, the Prince knew they had to leave. He forced Taqizadeh into a carriage.

"Your Highness, it is too dangerous for you to be seen with me," Taqizadeh protested.

"I have no intention of being seen with you," the Prince replied, giving the driver an address. "We must convince Mr. Marling to let you into the British legation."

"That would mean exile," Taqizadeh said. "I cannot abandon my comrades at this turning point in our history."

The Prince turned to him, incredulous. "Sayyid," he said, using the title denoting descent from the Prophet. "This 'turning point in our history' has already passed. Do you not see? There are no more comrades. I may have lost my brother today." (He did not believe it in his heart.) "The Shah has murdered his cousin and uncle. Killing you would be halal to him—perhaps even a delight. You can still fight. But not from a grave. Let's get you to the legation." Taqizadeh dropped his head in sorrow. They arrived at the British Legation to find a cavalry of Cossacks standing guard.

"Can this be possible?" Taqizadeh asked. "The Russians

blocking entry to British soil?" Only then did it dawn on him that today was not a continuation of the past. The rules had changed.

"It's not the Russians," said the Prince. "These are Liakhov's men, under the command of the Shah. They act like Russians when dealing with us and like Persiranians when dealing with the English. They are Perussians," he added, pronouncing the word with an affected English accent. He gave Taqizadeh's knee a light slap, but neither man laughed. "You'll be safe in my house. It's two minutes from here. I'll send a message to Mr. Marling. I must return to court to learn the fate of my brother. Try to get some rest."

The Prince arrived at the imperial gardens after dusk. "Your brother lives," Azudul Molk, the head of the Qajar family, informed him. Mohsen Khān, the brother-in-law, had reported on the Azalis who had requested asylum—among them, the Prince's brother. From a second messenger sent by Mohsen Khān, they learned the chained apostates, captured by the brave soldiers of the Shah, would arrive in an hour or two. The Prince began his first round of entreaties with Azudul Molk.

"I can't predict the Shah's intentions yet," the elder statesman replied. "I will do what I can, but I must warn you—he is not forgiving anything." The vile cart creaked into the Shah's garden with the prisoners. Nothing could have prepared the Prince to see his brother and the others as they stepped onto solid ground—covered in dust, haggard and in chains. Something was wrong with his brother's face beneath the handkerchief covering his eyes. And why was his head twisting back and forth as he walked, as though he couldn't see where he was going? No force on earth could have stopped the Prince from running to embrace his brother before all the courtiers and guards—except the iron grip Azudul Molk clamped around his wrist.

"Don't make a fool of yourself, son," said Azudul Molk, "or we will lose your brother as surely as the sun will rise tomorrow." He added, "The Shah has already signed death warrants for several prisoners. Consider the two Azalis—Jahāngir Khān and Malik al-Mutakallimin—already dead. The list includes a cousin of His Majesty. And your brother as well. We must plead for him separately." The soldiers moved the prisoners to the stables, where they joined more than two dozen others—men from every walk of life—chained together like toy trains on a track.

The Prince sought an audience with the Shah to plead for his brother's life, but the monarch had retired to his private quarters. The Prince roamed the palace all night, begging anyone who would listen to intervene. Courtiers offered polite, sympathetic faces, but none gave him hope. Around midnight, he bribed a guard to let him visit his brother at the back of the stables. Inside the pitch-black stable, he heard the soft clomp of hooves and the quiet snorts of muzzles. He found the prisoners sitting along the mud-and-straw wall, lit by the bright moon. Sardar Mirza was at the end of the chain link. The pulsing sting from his wounds kept him from sleep, signaling infection. The Prince sat gingerly beside him and called his name.

"Is it you, brother?" Sardar Mirza whispered, elated. They embraced and kissed, just as they had in childhood, oblivious to the chained men around them. Despite their misery, the others teared up at the sight of the brothers' devotion. They spoke late into the night. The Prince gave Sardar Mirza more hope than he could summon for himself. Before sunrise, he slipped away to resume his diplomacy before the first call to prayer. The guards arrived to escort Sardar Mirza, Jahāngir Khān and Malik al-Mutakallimin. Two guards attended each man. They looped coarse ropes around their necks with rudimentary hanging knots. Their feet, still wet from ablutions, the prisoners were dragged roughly into a circle of dirt surrounded by beautiful trees. The ropes scraped their necks raw.

On one side of the clearing sat the Shah, grim, fists on knees. Behind him stood Shapshal, Azudul Molk, Amir Bahadur Jang and a few others. No ceremony, no speech. The Shah didn't offer any justification. Convinced of his absolute power, he sat silently as the condemned men faced him. Behind the Shah stood a bull of a man whose hairy shoulders jutted like mounds on either side of his neck. His dense, black beard reached his eyes, which were dull and black. He wore a leather apron.

"Do a merciful job," the Shah said.

The executioner—a former butcher of sheep and cattle—approached Jahāngir Khān with a slow, swaying gait. His arms hung like a gunfighter's, and he carried a slender dagger in his right hand, oddly pointing upward toward his wrist.

"Make peace with your maker, you miserable traitor," he shouted as if performing for a crowd. His voice startled birds from the trees. Silence fell.

"Long live the constitutional government," Jahāngir Khān said. He pointed to the ground and declared, "O, Land, we are killed for the sake of your preservation." The last two words came out muffled. The guards pulled the ropes in opposite directions. Jahāngir Khān's face turned a purplish red, swelling like a spoiled tin. His tongue fattened and spilled from his mouth. Blood dribbled down his chin. A sudden jerk hurled a clot of blood onto the executioner's apron. Instead of recoiling, the butcher stepped forward, met the dying man's gaze, and thrust his poignard between two ribs. With his left hand on Jahāngir's shoulder for leverage, he forced the blade toward the heart in a slow, viscous journey. He stepped back as the editor of the most celebrated paper in the history of our benighted country and exhaled a final, impossibly long breath before collapsing lifeless. "Here dies a traitor," the executioner announced, gesturing with both palms.

Mutakallimin stood just inches away, frantically murmuring Koranic verses. Sardar Mirza, blindfolded, could not see the horror—but he knew. The executioner turned to the preacher, narrowed his eyes and mimed a horn next to his temple before pointing at the next victim. "Prepare to die, you apostate vermin," he declared theatrically.

"I am at peace," Malik al-Mutakallimin said.

The guards pulled the ropes taut, flattening his dusty, bushy beard against his neck. His end was no different from his friend's.

The butcher turned to Sardar Mirza. The young man, still twisting his head left and right tried to understand what had happened. Suddenly, a cry broke the air. The Prince appeared from nowhere and threw himself into the dust at the Shah's feet.

"Your Majesty, take my life. Spare him," he sobbed.

Gasps rippled through the assembly. The Prince lost all gravitas, confidence and dignity in that humiliating prostration. Here lay a desperate man. Stripped of society's illusions, he saw what truly mattered. "His death is my death. Kill me now—or, if he dies, kill me later." His milky blue eyes stared wildly from the ground.

Azudul Molk and Amir Bahadur Jang bent down simultaneously, whispering into each of the Shah's ears. They urged moderation. Azudul Molk warned against shedding royal blood—a young uncle's. Amir Bahadur Jang argued the boy had suffered enough. Sardar Mirza, they all agreed, was a lightweight. Why lose the Prince, a promising young man? Everyone knew the Prince would be lost if his brother died. The Shah's jaw clenched. The muscles in his neck bulged. He reluctantly stayed the execution with a small, repeated motion—clenching and unclenching his fist in the executioner's direction.

The butcher, unfazed, walked away in the same calm gait. They discarded the two bodies like trash into the moat beyond the garden. For the second time, Mohammad Ali had nearly killed his young uncle. As with the first time, Sardar Mirza almost died from his wounds. He recovered after months of care, only to be exiled by the Shah. Sardar Mirza left for Paris without regret and never returned. This time, unlike after the childhood beating, he did not forget. To forget would have been an insult to his fallen friends.

Professor Dal ended the story.

"Say goodbye to Sardar Mirza, my boy. You already know how he dies: in a comfortable bed, surrounded by loved ones, in Paris. Now we must both sleep," he said. "I'm dead tired. Could you help me on my side? I don't seem to have command of my limbs."

I lifted that collection of bones. The Professor weighed next to nothing. By the time I had crossed the room with him in my arms, he had fallen into a deep, discreet sleep.

THE EIGHTH NIGHT: 1000

THE WRITER WANTS TO WIND DOWN

Much falls into place on the penultimate eighth night. My prince-ling, ever the puzzle-solver, reveals a sexual orientation that com-plicates the narrative. Mr. Ahmadinejad, President of the Islamic Republic from 2005 to 2013, once famously declared that such orientations do not exist in our country. This revelation adds a new layer to the brotherly competition, transforming it into something fiercer—especially concerning the magnetic Hamid.

My princeling's descriptions, the dual-cultural life his family led in the waning years of the Pahlavi dynasty should impress the muti-cultural crowd. It was rare, but not impossible, to step out of Papa Noel's Christmas party and onto the takieh stage, where one could mourn the martyrdom of Imam Hussein among fellow Shi-ites. I can't imagine a more vivid embodiment of multiculturalism than those two scenes placed side by side. But take my word, they didn't mix well.

The religiosity of such lamentations should not distract us

from the era's brutal and unsavory political decisions. Much hinges on the reactionary Ayatollah Nouri's Article 2—a cornerstone in the Islamic Republic's vast edifice of religious law. Our princeling will soon discover the significance of the unloved Nouri, and the lasting impact of his vision.

Did you notice how we cheated on the seventh night? We enlisted Mammad-Ali as a freelance narrator, subcontracting his voice to fill in the narrative's gaps. The historical record is woefully inadequate when it comes to the atrocities of the Iran-Iraq War. To offer some perspective: in our 2,500 years of offensive and defensive warfare, no conflict claimed as many lives in a single decade. As individuals, we don't weep for crowds. We cry for individuals. The Surgeon's account of Sardar Mirza's comrades, executed under the orders of Mohammad Ali Shah, moved me to tears. It marked the beginning of unraveling that once-pure vision of a democratic revolution. To my non-Iranian readers, I offer an apology. Reading a history book filled with double- and triple-dashed, apostrophized names demands commitment. If you have lasted through seven nights, your dedication speaks for itself. We take a more leisurely route downhill until the last uphill sprint. I call it the heartbreak hill in honor of our Boston home.

THE NARRATOR REMEMBERS THE NIGHT
OF THE CORN FLAKES

*"Some facts should be suppressed, or, at least, a just sense of propor-
tion should be observed in treating them."*

The Sign of the Four—Sir Arthur Conan Doyle

Dear Ms. Vakil,

I hope the development of Mr. Hekaiatchi meets with your
approval. I listen to his recordings repeatedly with a fascination
that borders on obsession. I am astonished by his feats of memory.
Had he possessed a more commanding voice, I dare say he might
have satisfied even his father's exacting standards of storytelling.
An innocent at heart, he occupies a precarious social position in
which the wrong marriage could push him down to the lowest
rungs of society. You can hear him express these qualms with strik-

ing clarity—when he contemplates meeting with you and reflects on his living quarters above Mammad-Ali's shop. But who am I to speak? Unmarried, I've descended my rungs two steps at a time.

Here in the heart of Puritan Massachusetts, I lead a strictly moral life: moderate drinking, a judicious number of acquaintances, mild exercise and limited use of pornography. If I were to confess any indulgence, it would be my love of film. Middle age has brought a bouquet of minor ailments, requiring a high-fiber, low-calorie diet. I carry my bowl of granola—necklaced with banana slices and topped with pink yogurt—to the apartment window and look out. I chew the tasteless granola, using the yogurt to muffle the crunching sound I loathe. In my inner eye, I picture myself: a thin, well-maintained man in his fifties, more white than black in the hair department (grateful to have any at all), barefoot, bathed in early northern light, gazing at some infinite point beyond the traffic on I-95. I believe I resemble someone in a cereal commercial.

I report these small details late in our correspondence to reassure you of my normalcy. It's a hard-to-shake habit among us Persiranians in the U.S.—pandering as a form of acclimatization. I've trained myself in the finer points of American football, though I care not a whit for the sport. It helps to say, "I'm not that kind of Persiranian, but your kind of Persiranian." Why are we so eager to please? Why do we seek the good opinion of the Western man? I want to say it's because we have good reason to be ashamed of our government's behavior. I am ashamed. But look back, and it's worse. For the past hundred years, we've practiced a servile, shameful foreign policy—right up to the final days of our last Shah. He consulted the British and American ambassadors about his bowel movements, for God's sake. It makes one want to whisper something favorable about the pirates in charge today.

Ms. Vakil, as I get closer to the history I witnessed as a child—the history I lived—my narrative starts to resemble a gossip column. Forgive the name-dropping (my mother called it "social chin-ups"). I no longer move in those circles, and no one but historians like yourself cares about these pusillanimous people long gone. I admit I've bullied you into reading about my clan by interspersing it with the more strategic material I knew would interest you. I promised to tie my final days in prison to events seventy years prior. I'm now ready to offer some details about my father's rise and fall during the amnesiac reign of the last Shah of Iran.

1953 was special. To me, it's a black hole, a singularity. As if we'd crossed a political event horizon and emerged from that year stripped of all political expectations. After the CIA-aided coup of 1953, we became a Stepford society. The Americans lost their innocence by orchestrating the return of the young Shah, Mohammad Reza, from Italy—at the expense of Mossadegh, the fiery, aristocratic, brave, canny, flawed, yet republic-driven premier (a cousin of our grandfathers). They didn't do it alone. The British, with their usual duplicity, played their part. The CIA chief, Allen Dulles, approved one million dollars to bring down the popular prime minister. Before the coup, Mossadegh asked for my father's support—cousin to cousin—on several occasions. He invoked the memory of the Prince. "Times have changed," he told my father. "Your loyalty is misplaced. His father, Reza Shah, killed your father. Beloved by your villagers in Poonak, you must see the people's misery." But my father, loyal to the monarchy, refused. He remained a steadfast royalist, even when the Shah fled to Italy. He instructed my mother—then in Paris—to send him money. After the failed coup attempt, my father welcomed the Shah and Queen Soraya back with open arms. His cousin Mossadegh never forgave him.

The coup, possibly the most damaging precedent in American foreign policy in the twentieth century, succeeded. It was a crude but lucky operation, spearheaded by Kermit Roosevelt Jr., who handed out cash to switch the national vision from republic to monarchy overnight. It gave the CIA a false sense of confidence. MI6 also fiddled with the knobs, but always gloved they left far fewer fingerprints. They believed they could predict the uncontrollable variables of other societies. Even with the catastrophic blowback (a term first coined about the Mossadegh coup), the CIA began a string of bizarre global operations. Here, you see the soft underbelly of democracy. It is, painfully, a prompt forgetfulness, and it works—for those on the inside. But what about us, the non-voting victims of twisted foreign policy, who live with its consequences fifty years later? We trade democracy for memory. Am I becoming plaintive? I don't mean to dwell on the cluelessness of American foreign policy, Ms. Vakil, but rather to underscore the political complacency of Persiran after Mossadegh. As I've said, we experienced the most pleasant and economically prosperous period in our modern history. I don't recall any discussion of civil society. Reading the spirited letters between my grandfathers, I envy their era despite its violence and primitiveness. Their debates mattered. After 1953, political talk became mere gossip, rumor and innuendo—about the Shah and his entourage. The aristocracy abandoned its ancient role of tempering royal excess.

Contrary to the theory that degeneration strikes in the third generation, I argue that, in this case, the second generation dropped the ball. For five years after the coup, my parents orbited the Pahlavi court like satellites. They accompanied the Shah and Queen Soraya on official travels. My mother and the queen, both daughters of European mothers, became fast friends. The two couples cut dashing figures on the world stage. You can Google photographs of their travels—to the U.S., Europe even the Soviet Union. I remember silver daguerreotypes on side tables and framed portraits on the walls. My parents were photographed with Hollywood stars—Audrey Hepburn and Tony Curtis—and politicians and royals—Nixon, Khrushchev, Eisenhower, Queen Juliana of the Netherlands, Gustaf VI Adolf of Sweden.

At first, the riches trickled from the limitless American spigot. By 1979, they gushed. Ms. Vakil, I am an unapologetic materialist. Ask any man who's lost it all: having is better than not having. During his years abroad, my father developed an unshakable faith in the science, philosophy and politics of Western man. He had faith, plain and unexamined, but not an intellectual cell in his body. Unversed in method, he embraced a kind of Western determinism. Trivial baubles seemed to him the magical products of a perfected system. He believed in a conspiracy that explained everything, and he welcomed it. By the time we were born, he had already begun to transition mentally to the American way of life. The first symbol of this conversion was his leather jacket, modeled on General MacArthur's. Culturally, the family had long considered itself French in aesthetics and German in engineering and expertise. Professor Dal had once encouraged their German sympathies, only to dissuade them later. But he could never pry away my father's love for Western glitter.

After 1953, my father fell for the Americans. He replaced his prized German pen, precisely calibrated to hold eighty drops of ink, with the sleek Parker 51. We swapped the Mercedes for a sky-blue Oldsmobile, the Grundig for a Westinghouse and Wagner for Gershwin. With the zeal of a hobbyist, he embraced every detail: he bought a hamburger grill (which doubled nicely for hookah coals), and built a backyard bowling lane near Gorban-Ali's quarters (it turned to splinters by winter). We chewed bubble gum and read comic books. Large-bodied Americans wandered through our house. Their wives arrived without warning, irritating my mother.

Young Americans, their braces gleaming, swam smooth, confident laps in our pool, making us look like frantic paddlers. The chattering American wives could have talked the old Prince's mother into silence—but they had access to heaven. They could enter paradise at any hour of the day with their bobbed blonde hair, pencil-sharp high heels and red polka-dot tank tops. That paradise was the American Arms Supermarket in Tehran: a land of shiny floors and gleaming metal carts wheeled through aisles lined with neat stacks of canned food. Even my mother briefly lost her bearings there. You could mail-order anything. A polite young private sat behind a large wooden counter, dutifully writing down her endless requests for cigarettes, chocolates, scotch and hula-hoops. Somewhere in the world, American taxpayers paid to locate and deliver the items. Our infatuation with the supermarket reached its height on what became known in our family as the Night of the Corn Flakes. This night marked both the zenith and the collapse of my father's short, ultimately bitter career in government. Corn

Flakes—then a generic name for all cereals—had begun appearing at our table courtesy of the American Arms Supermarket. At first, it was Kellogg's Corn Flakes, but soon came Rice Krispies, Aleph-ba (Alphabits) and, eventually, Shredded Wheat.

Once a year, my father hosted a grand dinner party for the foreign diplomatic corps: ambassadors, consuls, attachés and young career officers. The house underwent a thorough transformation. Servants scrubbed every corner. They transported enormous carpets from the bank vaults. We reopened the long-unused kitchen in the basement (close to where they later built my cell.) We borrowed cooks from friends and family. The household staff starched their white uniforms until they were stiff as calling cards. Food preparation began days in advance: soups thick with dried fruits like pomegranate and sour cherries; dolmas—sweet grape leaves, meticulously rolled and stuffed with spiced meats; skewered kebabs and meatballs arranged in perfect rows; an array of pilafs— rice golden with saffron, scented with cinnamon and dotted with apricots, lima beans, or chicken and lamb. For dessert, there was baklava doused in rosewater, grated fruits topped with crushed ice, creamy rice pudding and fresh fruit baskets served on silver and gold trays.

That year, in late July 1959, my mother left for one of her more extended sojourns in Paris. It left my clueless father in charge of planning the dinner. He added a gastronomic surprise. The who's who of Tehran's diplomatic circle arrived. The American ambassador and his wife broke protocol to attend. The Soviet ambassador came alone, his chest weighted down with medals. The virile Turkish attaché wore lemon-colored gloves. The sophisticated Indian consul stepped carefully to avoid harming microscopic life. The Spanish diplomat gleamed in a velvet dinner jacket. The guests circled one another, permanently smiling, like victims of a strange congenital illness. The domestic guest list was no less formidable: the ineffectual premier with the head of a mastiff brought his French wife. His cabinet, including three future prime ministers—each as useless as the next—buzzed around him. A diminutive court minister appeared and disappeared in the crowd like a ghost. The dashing founder of SAVAK, the newly formed intelligence service, mingled amiably—though twenty years later, the very organization he led would assassinate him. The stone-faced minister of finance, a humorless military man, came despite disliking everyone, especially my father. An industrialist said to control 83 percent of the nation's heavy industry arrived with his weighty wife. The lone representative of the bazaar, a princely rug merchant, brought Turkoman rugs as a gift. Rod-stiff khaki army uniforms drifted among the black-tie crowd. The ladies sparkled, free of any Islamic coverings. Not a single turban was in sight—how one grows nostalgic for such days.

The evening began with a cocktail party in the garden. White-gloved servants carried trays of whisky and soda. At 9:00 p.m., my father announced dinner. Giddy with drink and hunger, the guests went indoors to the round tables arranged in the salon and adjoining dining room. The most esteemed guests—the American and Soviet ambassadors, the premier, the court minister and their wives—were seated at my father's table. Before the meal began, my father, animated and cheerful, gave a short speech praising the American ambassador. With each florid adjective, the Soviet ambassador's eyelids fluttered like mosquito wings. My father concluded the speech with a flourish: "And finally, ladies and gentlemen," he declared, "in honor of this great American, we will begin our dinner with a typical American dish." Polite applause followed. The lights dimmed. Crickets chirped outside. Seconds ticked by. A gong sounded. The dining room doors flung open dramatically to reveal a line of servants holding large silver bowls filled with an assortment of Corn Flakes, high on their stretched hands. They formed like a polished dance troupe, distributing bowl after bowl. Soon, Honey Smacks, Sugar Puffs, Life and Special K piled in small mounds on plates meant for pilaf and kebabs. The ladies looked nervously left and right, their mouths downturned, as Cocoa Puffs—those bland, puffy orbs faintly cocoa-flavored—approached. Trix, in orangey orange, lemony yellow and raspberry red, looked like something meant for dessert. Dry Weetabix sponged up saliva, leaving guests speechless.

At this staggering cereal display, the American ambassador half-rose from his chair then sat in stunned silence. Two camps formed: the first, familiar with cereal protocol, nibbled without milk to avoid offending my father. The second, bewildered by the blandness, ate with solemn curiosity so as not to insult the Great American. A plump Italian man-boy with fuzzy sideburns exchanged a horrified, conspiratorial grin with the suave Spanish attaché. It would make an excellent addition to their catalog of foreign horror stories. The English consul and his wife behaved as perfect sports. The vegetarian Indian consul, oblivious, munched contentedly. They all consumed bottles of fine wine with unusual quantities of dry Rice Krispies and Shredded Wheat. No one posed the red-or-white question of wine.

While the dining room crunched and crackled, the American ambassador began a subtle diplomatic effort to inform my father of cereal etiquette and salvage the situation. "You know, sir, in our country, children indulge in a bowl of cornflakes for breakfast," he explained. "Sometimes they mix it with sugar and milk." (The "sometimes" was a diplomatic gesture of tact.)

The Soviet ambassador, unfamiliar with cereal norms, misread the comment as arrogant pride. "Yes," he thought, "and we serve caviar to our donkeys!"

"An expensive breakfast," thought my father, similarly bemused. He had paid a small fortune for the imported goods at the American Arms Supermarket.

"With what utensils does one eat this?" the court minister inquired. "A fork is out of the question, and it's too slippery for a spoon. Are fingers permitted? You know, Her Majesty the Queen of England eats chicken with her fingers." The Soviet ambassador remained silent, seething like a volcano.

"Do you eat this in the Soviet Union?" asked the premier, scrutinizing the flakes like a scientist.

"No, Your Excellency," the Soviet ambassador replied smoothly. "We experimented with the form some years ago, but our people were not impressed with its nutritional content."

"Not impressed?" the American blurted. "For Christ's sake, we're talking about cereal. What's the big deal?"

"Precisely. No big deal," the Soviet said with a smile.

The American stiffened at the jab. "We wouldn't expect to impress the Soviet people with taste alone," he said. "Please, look around the room at the variety. To Americans, diversity—the right to choose—is the spice of life." The dining room had become a theater for ideological contest.

"Spice? You call this spice?" the Soviet asked. Several guests silently agreed. "It's an illusion of choice. As far as I can see, there's no difference between this and this." He gestured at a bowl of Raisin Bran and another cereal arriving.

"This is not like the difference between a Pechenochnyi torte and a piroshki filled with onion, mushroom, meat and rice—or better still, between Chicken Kyiv and a Bellini with caviar and cream." He had the guests nearly in tears, dreaming of Russian delicacies. Then, with a grin and revolutionary flair, he added, "All our cuisine, I might add, has its origins in peasant food."

"Caviar comes from peasant food?" my father asked, catching the diplomatic blunder that others missed. "Your red caviar is served on your peasants' tables, sir? On our side of the Caspian, we produce the finest caviar in the world—fit for royalty."

"I didn't mean to insult Persiranian caviar," the Soviet said quickly. "We all know the quality of the sturgeon growing on your sweeter side of the Caspian."

The American ambassador, back on the offensive, rose with renewed vigor. "We didn't invent cereal to titillate the taste buds, Your Excellency," he said. "We created it to improve public health. Our free citizens manufacture various cereals without permission from any government bureaucracy. Yes, sir!" His voice carried the twang of a man burning his mouth on a French fry. "We trust our system. Private enterprise. Our people. That's how we award military contracts. We trust our fellow countrymen." The American gained ground, but the Soviet offered one last missile.

"Your Excellency is a fine lawyer," he said. (The American indeed had a Columbia Law degree.) "Me, I am the fat peasant son of an even fatter peasant." He laughed at his wit. "But as we Russians say: 'We too don't beat flies with our noses.' We've already surpassed you in rocket technology—directed by our Central Committee."

My father interrupted, not grasping the full intensity of the exchange, and launched into an earnest defense of all the excellent American appliances in our home. He promised to show the Soviet ambassador one of the earliest televisions in the country.

"You must not be afraid of new ideas," the American ambassador declared, grinding the Russian's rockets beneath his heel like stepping on a handful of Rice Krispies.

"We are afraid of nothing," the Russian replied.

What had all the makings of a diplomatic disaster ended with the American ambassador expressing heartfelt gratitude to my father for his unexpected assistance in the debate. Both ambassadors dutifully filed their reports to their respective governments. Within a few weeks, the American's dispatch spurred my father's rise through the ranks. I have before me now, courtesy of the Freedom of Information Act. The Russian report, by contrast, disappeared into the recesses of the Soviet collective memory—until it resurfaced eight years later and precipitated my father's fall.

Ms. Vakil, allow me to draw your attention to a far more consequential debate that occurred just days later, on July 24, 1959, at Sokolniki Park in Moscow: the now-famous Nixon–Khrushchev Kitchen Debate. This exchange elevated my father's earlier dinner-table duel from the realm of the absurd to something close to prophetic. That later debate, too, began with food and kitchens as metaphors, and, as I compare them, I find lines repeated verbatim in the two events. Few may have noticed the precedent set that night over Corn Flakes, but the American ambassador certainly did. In his report—written after the Kitchen Debate—he plants his flag like an inventor staking a patent claim. To his credit, he cites my father as his co-debater. Only weeks later, at the imperial court, the Shah played Belote with three companions: Professor Dal, my father and Mr. Hajebi. None held official positions. Mr. Hajebi—an elegant man of limited aptitude—always dressed in a deep navy blazer, a sky-blue Indian cotton shirt and a soft foulard tie constrained by a rigid collar. His French cuffs bore heavy silver links engraved with the imperial lion. He smelled faintly of lemony aftershave. He was known for a particular poker flourish: once, tossing down three kings, he declared, "With your help Sire, I complete my royal flush." Dal and Hajebi smoked, cigarettes dangling from their lips, one eye squinting against the rising smoke. The Shah smoked with an onyx holder. My father cradled his cigarette between curled fingers in a Humphrey Bogart pose.

"The American ambassador tells us you are a brilliant man," the Shah said. "We remember you from youth. We remember guts—but not brilliance. Cut."

Professor Dal cut the deck.

"I wouldn't give much weight to the ambassador's comments, Your Majesty," my father said.

"He advises us to give you a government post," said the Shah, dealing the cards.

"I'd advise against taking his advice, Your Majesty—or we'll be short a hand," said Dal. "Pass."

"Do you want a position?" the Shah asked my father.

"Pass," said Hajebi.

"I am bored, Your Majesty," my father said. These were simpler days among old friends before the ceremonial burdens of the late 1960s.

"Why didn't you say something sooner?" the Shah asked. "We could have arranged it."

"Pass," Dal said forcefully.

"Well, we can kill two birds with one stone," the Shah continued. "Satisfy the ambassador and help a friend. Not a bad bargain." He glanced at his hand. "Contra. But what shall we give you? You're not exactly an academic."

"Your Majesty owes me nothing," said my father. "Pass."

"We think we do," the Shah replied. Dal and Hajebi passed quickly. "We've given it thought—and we've got just the job for you." The cards paused. Smoke rose in four steady streams. The sounds of a party drifted into their alcove from the grand hall nearby. "You'll take the sports portfolio," said the Shah. "Re-contra."

My father looked up, delighted—he loved sports. But he caught Professor Dal's subtle shake of the head, a warning signal. Unsure of its meaning, he pressed ahead as always when faced with a challenge. "Your Majesty honors me," he said. The others smiled and raised their glasses to him.

"We're not sure it is an honor," said the Shah. "The post is steeped in politics. You'll be the first civilian to head the Federation of Sports. Your cousin here tried to warn you." They all laughed. Five years after the American-backed coup, a certain innocence still lingered among them. "So long as you don't pull a Thomas Becket on us," the Shah said, smiling warmly, almost fatherly, "we can keep playing cards."

The Shah didn't like mixing business with pleasure. He divided the world into three kinds of people: those who worked for him and owed him blind obedience, his friends and everyone else. My father had just entered no-man's-land. Ms. Vakil, have you ever seen a sailor's knot called the Zeppelin bend? It's remarkable how easily it comes undone. My father's brief government career was just such a knot—tied to the fate of a national hero, it easily unraveled. You will remember our folk hero—the wrestler. (As with the sacred names of God in Judaism, I won't utter his name.) I believe he was the most beloved Persiranian figure of the twentieth century. Even my brother and I—who could not agree on the color of a pomegranate—were united in our admiration. We could recount every detail of his matches. Like my father, he basked in his popularity, incapable of imagining anyone disliking him. The entire nation adored him—everyone except one man.

The Shah could not stomach the wrestler's fame. He was obsessed with his popularity, constantly asking whether people loved him. I remember one card game, late at night, after a few drinks, when Professor Dal, exasperated, quoted the Brothers Grimm: *Spieglein, Spieglein an der Wand, / Wer ist die Schönste im ganzen Land?* "Mirror, mirror, on the wall, who is the fairest?" He said it in German so the servants wouldn't understand. He left the answer unsaid, though it hung heavily in the air: "You, Your Majesty, are popular—but there is one more popular than you." When that unnamed wrestler took his own life, the nation mourned with unmatched intensity. The tributes were well-earned. He embodied the nation's ideals: humility, strength, honor. He was a son of the Luti tradition, a bearer of its values of moral courage and masculine integrity. Raised in the impoverished south of Tehran during the 1930s, he trained in zurkhanehs, the old-style gymnasiums where drums accompanied contests of strength and, if the mood struck, verses of the epic poet Ferdowsi. He had the stocky, muscular build of a born wrestler. His soft brown eyes carried a deep vulnerability. He once described his skin as white—"but it turns pistachio green after a twelve-minute match." His broad, sheepish smile transformed his whole face.

My father compared his celebrity to Pelé. But there was something more expansive at work. He did win medals—but he was not dominant. In one early interview, he admitted that he had spent more time on his back than his feet early in his career—"on mats so filthy a dog wouldn't lie on them," he laughed. Lutis prized modesty above all. He won two Olympic golds, two more at the World Cup, plus five additional medals. But unlike Pelé, he didn't fit the global market. He fit ours. No shopkeeper would take money from him. Outside Persiran, no one had heard of him—except other wrestlers. There was always a vulnerability in his interviews. He once envied how a gold medalist bowed an extra half-meter to receive his prize. "Second place," he said, "is as far from first as a servant is from a minister." When he did win gold, he marveled at how little it changed him. "I'm the same circus animal on the mat," he said, "only more people salaam me." He was unafraid to show his feelings. After defeating his Swedish rival Palem, he asked why Palem hadn't offered the customary congratulatory kiss. "My sweat had already dried," he said, genuinely hurt. It never occurred to him that Palem probably never even kissed his mother goodbye.

Politics complicated his life. At thirty-three, he trained for his fourth Olympics in Tokyo. Keeping with Luti tradition, he pledged allegiance to a higher authority—Mossadegh, not the Shah. They let another athlete carry the national flag. He understood. For him, wrestling was an addiction, his daily fix. He knew he had no hope against the 22-year-old Russian Medved, the most outstanding freestyle wrestler of his time. He finished fourth—no medal, just fresh scars. They forced him into a two-year break. My father convinced the SAVAK to let him wrestle again at age thirty-five at the World Championships in Ohio. When the Shah appointed my father as Minister of Sports, our unnamed wrestler had already passed the peak of his career. His suicide—at the age of thirty-seven, in Room 23 of the Atlantic Hotel in downtown Tehran—shocked the nation. Hotel staff discovered him after coming to offer assistance with a flat tire on his car. They forced open the door when he failed to respond to their repeated knocks. He had taken poison.

In a nation steeped in conspiracy theories, the blame fell swiftly on the SAVAK. The absence of foam at his mouth convinced many that the secret police had administered the poison posthumously. Others claimed they had injected air into his veins. To my father's horror and disbelief, even I—only ten years old at the time—asked him whether "they" had killed our wrestler. The next day, the daily newspaper sold 1.5 million copies—five times its usual circulation of 300,000. Photographs of the wrestler's body, taken during the autopsy, were published in every paper and magazine across the country. Someone's hands turn his head for a better shot in those images. The long, thick, zipper-like scar running down his chest from the rapid autopsy filled the public with dread. Fearing an explosive reaction from the public, my father rushed to the burial. The orderly line to view the body stretched for a mile but soon broke into chaos. Friends of the wrestler had to wrest his body away from the mob. With great difficulty, they wrapped him in a cashmere carpet and transferred him into an ambulance. The vehicle sped off, chased by hundreds of mopeds and motorcycles. By four o'clock that afternoon, they reached his birthplace and buried him. On the traditional seventh day of mourning, a million people visited his grave. My father, stricken with a convenient "diplomatic flu" case, stayed home. No official could have attended without risking consequences—from the crowd or the Shah.

All evidence points to premeditated suicide. He left behind a brief note, absolving everyone of blame. He kept diaries. One entry reveals his fixation on death and hints at domestic troubles with his young wife of two years: "Truth is always clear. Please, God bless our ending. Why did you create me?" Three days before his suicide, he wrote: "Sport is good. Winning is good. Losing is bad. Marriage resembles sport." Two days before: "She threw me out of the house. She screamed at me to get the hell out." In the margin, he scribbled: "Suicide is so difficult. You have no idea how bad I feel." He arranged his affairs meticulously. A notary friend witnessed the transfer of his home to his two sisters. Another notary signed off on his will. At thirty-seven, given his political stance, he saw no future. "After our due date," he wrote, "we get thrown into the garbage." He refused to be a soldier in life's arena if he could no longer be the general.

THE FAT STORYTELLER SQUIRTS
HIS WAY TO HAPPINESS

"Premature for whom?"

Arguably: Essays—Christopher Hitchens

Baba, tell me: Do we compare every walking woman to a pre-destined mold in our head? Or do we pick a woman as we taste, smell, touch, hear and see different women? As a child, you told me the stories of the *One Thousand and One Nights*. Before I knew the facts of life, you sketched women with delicacy and detail. I would stiffen with pleasure. You once described a princess with a "waist thin as a hair's breadth." Of another you said, "her body bent daintily with the weight of her breasts." You could make a boy's head twirl with your insinuations: "He stretched his hand toward the warm shadows of her thigh." Baba, I lived with your sentence for weeks. When you said, "They confused each other with kisses on the mattress," in some way, I understood. But, I misunderstood, "Come pierce me violently with your lances; you are indeed an experienced rider." You amused yourself by telling an eight-year-old suggestive stories.

Baba, I don't know how to tell you. I want to confess. I mentioned Zahra's visit to my room. She continued to tiptoe into my room, slipping into my bed each night as stealthy as a submarine; she claimed she slept more comfortably nestled next to me. Hours before breakfast, she left my bed so as not to raise suspicions. Her visits disrupted my sleep. Her ample backside fit perfectly below my belly. You are familiar with my accidental spills. They have gotten me into trouble many times. In my visits to the New City, before the revolution, the whores would kick me out of bed and follow me onto the veranda, shouting abuses at my manhood. In truth, I was the ideal customer to them: no trouble. The waiting customers in the courtyard below laughed.

I shock you, Baba. Me, visiting whorehouses in New City? Indeed, Uncle Saiid, your brother, God bless his soul, took me there for the first time when I turned sixteen. I hope he keeps you company. He made me laugh. I can imagine worse people you could spend eternity with than Uncle Saiid. He never mentioned my weight or joked about it. He told me to accompany him to collect his shirts from his tailor. Why we had to go so far from the bazaar to get his shirts quickly became evident.

The Hosseini brothers, one deaf and the other dumb, made shirts. They lived symbiotically. The front of their house was a legitimate tailor shop. The yard at the back had a door. It opened to New City. Each working house in the area had a yard. Metal folding chairs in the courtyard served as an informal waiting room for the paying customers. The Hosseini brothers' front shop gave a more discreet entry to New City. The chaotic front street brought face-to-face fathers and sons, uncles and nephews.

Fatmeh, their sister, conducted the more profitable business as the madam of a full-fledged whorehouse. The lucrative arrangement offered plenty of discretion. The Hosseinis' shirts covered the first-floor windows: glued-on curtains of patched blue, red checks, gauzy light yellow. After a round of unimaginative sex, the customer came away, for a handful of change, with one of the brothers' abysmal shirts. Men recognized one another's indiscretions for years by their colorful Hosseini shirts. In that whorehouse and a few others, I nearly lost my virginity. Nearly, you might ask? Baba, you know the rest. The sight of them down there sufficed for my fireworks to go off and quickly expire. In the next few years, I tried several times to test my ability to delay gratification. But I lose control when I look down at where we come from.

Now Zahra lay, uninvited, in my bed, her heart-shaped backside well ensconced under my belly. Half awake and half asleep, I must have rubbed her the wrong way. The resulting wetness woke her up. I expected her to be outraged. Instead, she cleaned me with a heart-wrenching gentleness. Baba, would you believe in my renewed excitement it recurred? Zahra smiled: she felt complimented, she said.

The next night, she took matters into her own hands—if you know what I mean—and she did the same the next night. On the third night, after I had been satisfied once, she offered me the taboo entrance. With strict integrity, she insisted on the protection of her virginity. Baba, for the first time in my life, I resided in a woman's body without immediate consequences. After our act, the longest and sweetest five minutes of my life, I told her about my troubles with women. She smiled and said, "There's nothing wrong with you down there. You need a warm-up before parking the car in the garage." She laughed a delicious laugh, like silver raining down. Baba, her laugh captured me for life.

We had a grand old time for some weeks. I began to sleep better than she did.

On a Saturday morning—the first day of the week, with a day's work ahead—we had fallen asleep after a long, frolicsome night. I woke with a start to see tiny Mammad-Ali looking at us from the head of the bed—if possible, even more cross-eyed than usual. At the sight of his daughter in bed with me, he stuttered and spat Zahra's name like a serpent spitting venom.

"Get out of bed, you daughter of a whore."

Cool as a queen, Zahra stepped out of my bed in her nightgown. She picked up her chador from the chair and covered herself with an elegant whirl of her hand. She didn't leave. She didn't scream; neither did she say a word. She stood at the head of the stairs and watched her father.

Mammad-Ali had a surprise for me. From behind him, out of nowhere, came a switch. He whipped it a few times in the air: *whit, whit*. Without warning, he began hitting my exposed legs as the nearest part of my body. The bloody mark of the stick appeared instantaneously. Recoiling in horror, I struck a womanish pose, now exposing my flank.

"Ay, ay!" I shouted. "Have you lost your senses, old man?"

"I will now demonstrate who the old man is," he said. *Whit, whit*—immediately, my thighs burned. It was clear staying exposed in bed would not do. I scrambled around the room. He shouted at me for hurting his daughter's chance of a good life. "You, sir, need a good beating. I will take care of it for you right now."

I again heard the *whoosh* and felt the sting on my skin.

"Stop beating me," I squealed, crashing into the large sacks of pistachios and rice. Pounds of rice spilled all over the floor like waves of white ants. Hundreds of pistachios danced in a corner of the room; I crunched pounds of dried chickpeas under my feet as I scrambled to avoid the bite of the stick.

"I will beat you, sir, for the sake of my daughter and for the love I had for your father. You need a beating, and I am the man to mete it out."

Whit, my skin broke into fresh welts. As I retreated, my shoulder caught the shelves full of goods. A bag of walnuts on the top shelf did a slow-motion dance as if of two minds: to spill or not to spill? We all stopped to watch as hundreds of nuts fell to the floor with the sound of a thousand horses stomping around the room. The beating resumed.

I began to beg. "Why beat me, Mammad-Ali? I love your daughter."

Mammad-Ali stopped. He looked at me incredulously. "You love my daughter? That is how you treat a woman you love. You rob her of her virtue. You should have asked me for her hand."

The thrashing began again. I felt the burn on the backs of my thighs; he continued to find targets with remarkable accuracy for a man with poor eyesight. I fell to the floor among bars of soap and a large tin of yellow cooking oil. I put my arms up to defend my face from the relentless whipping.

"For the love of God," I whimpered, "I swear by everything

you believe in I will take your daughter to the notary this hour and marry her."

He raised his hand to recommence. Zahra interrupted.

"Enough, Agha-joon," she said. "I told you he is an honorable man."

She grabbed the stick from Mammad-Ali, who yielded without protest. He smiled at me benevolently with the gaze of a loving father.

"Son, you have to forgive me. I lost two sons in the war. Zahra is all I have left. I couldn't leave her future in the dark. Now I have gained a son." Mammad-Ali's acute-angled eyes glistened with a film of tears. I sat there, stupefied. My hand, finding itself at rest in the can of cooking oil, began unconsciously rubbing the oil on my body.

Mammad-Ali approached me as I sat, legs apart, on the floor. He crawled between my legs to give me a full hug. When he failed, he opted to pat my stomach, as he had when we first bonded over the loss of his sons. I continued to rub the magic cooking elixir on my welts with great satisfaction.

"Agha-joon, go get some sweets. We can celebrate for breakfast," my practical Zahra instructed. Mammad-Ali went happily downstairs without further debate.

"How did he know?" I asked.

"I told him," Zahra said.

"You *told* him?"

"Yes," she said. "How long do you think I would have let you park in the back garage, for goodness sake?" She laughed her silvery laugh.

"Why did you let him beat me mercilessly for so long? I feel like a hundred bees have stung me."

"Oh, that. His idea. He figured when he joins your Baba, your Baba will thank him for it."

"My Baba never beat me."

"You get the point," she said.

In the evening, welts and all, I returned to see Ms. Vakil. Zahra went out with friends to shop for her wedding. Baba, I wanted to see her alone. We had developed a good relationship. No, Baba, I don't have dishonorable intentions. When my Zahra goes around the table, swinging her ampleness with the ease of an athlete, she fits the mold God created in my brain like a jeweler fits a delicate brooch into its velvet bedding.

I won't lie. I like the smooth sliding of the elevator door in Vakil Khanoum's apartment building. I love the feel of my socks on her parquet floor. I feel a hundred pounds lighter. I like the discreet lighting illuminating her paintings. I like her library. I like the cream puffs waiting for me. I don't want to disappoint her.

I sat in the living room. I waited for Vakil Khanum to come downstairs (yes, I like a house in an apartment building!) The elderly housekeeper brought tea and sweets, quieter than a house cat; I noticed her when she appeared from behind me with a full tray. She placed the tray on the glass table without a clink. Vakil Khanoum walked in with the authority of a General . She looked at me with mild amusement.

"What happened to your face?" She asked.

"I ran into a bunch of branches," I said. She didn't ask for details.

I outlined for her the story of the unnamed wrestler, warning her not to mention his identity in the narrative. "Why not?" she asked.

"I don't know," I said. "Professor Dal asked me not to mention it. He feared it could revive questions better left unanswered." My face pleaded for discretion.

"Not to worry," she said. I will respect your—or Professor Dal's—wishes. You know everybody will know anyway, don't you?"

Then she asked, "Have you gotten any further with retrieving the documents?"

I hemmed and hawed. "You know all this," she pointed to the tape recorder, "has little weight without some original documentation. Take the microphone and begin your narrative." I began the story of the wrestler and the Shah.

THE SURGEON REMEMBERS THE
WRESTLER AND THE SHAH

"All good drama has two movements, first the making of the mistake, then the discovery that it was a mistake."

The Dyer's Hand—W. H. Auden

I spent my eighth morning in this prison, without any contact from the outside. I calculated the day of the week—it was Friday. I stared at the wall the entire day, realizing that no one would care if I spent the next fifty years here. I would simply become like my cellmate. That morning, something was different. My storyteller, the man who always produced his daily oil, did not. It was Friday, and he slept well past midday. The guards, too, respected his rest day and did not intrude. He awoke and sat cross-legged like an

Indian fakir, watching me with a nasty, judgmental stare. "And who might you be?" he asked finally.

"Arbab, I am Hekaiatchi," I replied, bored with the usual routine.

"I've seen you before," he said, narrowing his eyes. "Have they planted you here to discover my wells? It's no use, you know." I ignored him. We both ignored each other.

As always, we regained our usual footing. The weak Islamic crescent moon hung above like a two-dimensional decoration, offering little light to the dark cell. Professor Dal's outline shuffled toward me with the careful steps of an old man. With great difficulty, he crawled from the end of my cot along my legs like a mountaineer scaling a smooth rock. He used the strings of my pajamas to pull himself up, and I held them tightly, trying to preserve whatever remained of my modesty. Then, he grabbed my shoulders with both hands and heaved himself into his usual position, panting as though he had just run a long race. "We come close to many endings here, my boy," he said, pausing to catch his breath. "Give me a moment." Tonight, I will not tell you the whole truth. Please understand, my boy, I don't intend to deceive you, but I cannot say with certainty that anything I share from here on actually happened. Nima, in the final year of his government career—soon to be unceremoniously toppled—was a figure I had distanced myself from. I had returned to my upstairs room in this building, where people now thought me mad. The two who still paid me any attention were Nima and Lili. This prison is no different from the self-imposed exile I chose. I could walk in the garden, but I never ventured outside. Nima and I maintained our Friday evening dinners, and Lili joined us when she was in town. She lived mainly in Paris now; the sight of the two boys—always fighting—depressed her. She could not bear their constant bickering. Soraya, the Shah's second wife, now divorced, also chose Paris as her home. The two women, still beautiful and elegant, maintained their friendship. By then, the sixties had arrived in Europe. Their pictures, taken in Paris nightclubs or on the beaches of Monte Carlo, graced the pages of Paris Match.

The Shah had remarried, and Lili could not transfer her loyalty to his new queen. Nima, on the other hand, did. He never understood the conflict. His allegiance to the Shah remained unwavering, no matter whom the Shah married. A slow, inevitable shift came over everyone's relationship with the Shah. His surge of self-confidence in the early sixties had been a boon for the country. I spent many pleasant evenings playing cards with him, far removed from politics. But when a man rises to power and develops a messianic vision, the whispers start—rumors and advice, reports of betrayal and disloyalty. Then came the foreign press, accusing the Shah of megalomania and paranoia. I will not comment on the accusation of megalomania. As for paranoia, that term refers to an irrational fear of imaginary threats. The Shah had survived numerous coups, narrowly escaping one assassin's bullets while another found their mark. Each premier he appointed during his early years plotted his downfall with the Americans, the British and the Russians. No, there was nothing imaginary about the threats he faced. He distinguished between friends outside the political sphere and those within the government. Upon gaining power, the latter often became embroiled in plots and conspiracies, where he expected blind obedience. Once in a governmental position, a friend inevitably lost his trust. Nima saw himself as a friend to the Shah, but the Shah had moved on. I foresaw Nima's dilemma: the Shah would eventually ask him to perform actions that Nima's conscience could not allow. Under Nima's leadership, Persiranian sports—especially wrestling—entered a golden era.

The national wrestling team won dozens of medals, and the Shah's love for success in sports seemed to know no bounds. For five years, all went well. But the beginning of Nima's downfall came with an innocent request from a stranger. The man, small and fit, full of enthusiasm, had arranged an introduction through the Minister of Education, to whom Nima reported. He proposed creating a Federation of Karate under the Ministry of Sports. Nima politely refused, fearing that, like professional wrestling, karate could lead to accidental deaths. He believed Persiran had not yet matured enough to distinguish between showmanship and freestyle wrestling. The man left quietly.

A few months later, we all accompanied the Shah to the Caspian for a vacation. I sat on the royal deck in the shade while Nima and the Shah sped to sea on the Riva.

"What is Riva?" I asked.

"My apologies, my not-so-fluffy bed. How could I expect you to understand our world? The Riva is a dreamboat made of beautiful mahogany. It's an expensive boat."

I said nothing. His breath now smelled foul, and his voice trembled like it might fail. He reminisced in silence before abruptly resuming his tale.

They jumped into the boat as two close friends, helping each other aboard. The Shah, muscular and broad-shouldered, and Nima, sinewy and lithe, were both tanned and handsome in their swimming trunks and dark sunglasses in the prime of their lives.

As they sped off, the Shah at the wheel, the mixture of gasoline, seawater, wood and suntan lotion filled the air—vital and expensive. I remember thinking of them as two princes of the realm. I felt optimistic about the country. It was 1965. The Khomeini altercation was behind us, Kennedy no longer lived to harass us and we controlled our oil revenue. Technocrats were returning from Europe and the U.S., full of ideas. Somewhere, far from land, the Shah eased up on the accelerator. The two men spoke beneath the humid sun. Their conversation would soon change the course of our lives. Under his tan, Nima returned looking as gray as worn asphalt. He said nothing throughout the day. We dined on the second-floor terrace of the beautiful Hotel Chalus. Who could forget those soups, served from silver tureens by waiters in immaculate tuxedos? Or the lightly burnt aroma of the succulent chicken kebabs?

"Arbab, have mercy on me. We are in prison. I haven't eaten anything worthwhile for eight days."

"I can tell," he said. "You've lost your legendary padding. I'll skip dinner for your sake." Later that evening, we walked through the hotel's orange and lemon garden, the air rich with intoxicating scents. Nima looked like a Hollywood star, dressed immaculately in light blue pants and a short-sleeved black shirt. He told me how the Shah had steered the boat from the port into the open sea. They had enjoyed the high speed, the boat cresting each wave before landing with a hard thud. After ten minutes, the Shah backed off the throttle. He let the engine grumble in neutral, then switched it off entirely. The boat bobbed up and down with the swell of the sea. The Shah brought up the visit from the man who had wanted to start a karate federation. "Why did you refuse him?" he asked.

Nima reminded the Shah of the wrestling-as-entertainment fiasco.

"Right," the Shah acknowledged. "Nevertheless, we want you to organize and encourage the new federation. We will provide the funds."

The request didn't seem outrageous. The king of the realm wanted to introduce karate to his people. What could be the harm? Nima, curious, asked the Shah about his sudden enthusiasm for the sport. The Shah's answer was simple, yet it revealed either his arrogance or naïveté about power's limits.

"You know," he said with a smile, "the university students stage demonstrations as regularly as a woman's period." He paused for effect. "Instead of sending the military, which risks higher casualties, we want to have a group of young men trained in karate at our disposal. They could help with the students."

"But, Your Majesty, shouldn't they train under the army's supervision?"

"We said," he emphasized, "we don't want them to have any links with the government. We want a group of young men who will voluntarily defend our point of view. Lord knows, none of the rest of you will."

Nima started to respond, but the Shah cut him off. "Don't argue. Do as you are told," he snapped. He fired up the engine and slammed the accelerator, nearly throwing Nima overboard. At that moment, Nima glimpsed the autocratic man the Shah would become ten years later—the stiff, overbearing figure who lectured the West with a gaze fixed on a false horizon. He practiced at shedding his softer, more vulnerable self.

Due to budgetary constraints, the Shah repeatedly delayed the launch of the Karate Federation. Nima hoped the Shah had forgotten about it and had found another way to solve the student problem. A deeper rift, intertwined with their conversation on the boat, soon appeared. It concerned a wrestler whose name I cannot mention. This incident occurred a few months before the World Wrestling Championships in Toledo, Ohio. I met the wrestler at the height of his career when he arrived at my office for a medical consultation.

"You met him?" I asked.

"I did," said Professor Dal.

"What was he like?" I asked.

Professor Dal merely laughed and continued. I examined the wrestler. He suffered from epididymal-orchitis, a bacterial infection of the scrotum. A deeply shy man, he couldn't meet my eyes as I explained the diagnosis. After much hesitation, he asked if everything would be alright when he married someday. I assured him that a few weeks of antibiotics would cure him. His troubles went beyond the infection. He had taken fourth place at the Tokyo Olympics. The mediocre result pleased the Shah. Despite the poor showing large crowds greeted him at the airport, which displeased the Shah. Even worse, the wrestler supported Mossadegh and the Persranian National Front. The Shah issued an ultimatum: his wrestling career was over unless he recanted. He refused to bow to the Shah's demand.

"The popularity of this man remains, to me, inexplicable," the Shah told me in frustration.

Surprised, I advised him, "Actors, I have heard, hate to perform opposite children and dogs. Your Majesty, leaders like you do not engage in popularity contests with children and dogs." He laughed, but I doubt he truly heard me. Nima arrived on the sports scene after the wrestler's career peaked a few years back. He had decorated himself with medals of every color. During the qualification rounds for the world championships, Nima entered the stadium amid unrelenting chants of the wrestler's name. The chants had a dangerous edge. Nima addressed the crowd with a conciliatory speech, enjoying a modicum of popularity—though certainly not on the level of the wrestler. He promised the crowd he would try to convince the unnamed wrestler to come out of retirement. The next day, Nima received a summons to the palace. He had to explain his promise. We sat at our usual card game, one of my last visits to the palace. When Nima walked in, General Aiadi sat as the fourth player, with Hajebi and me. There was no seat for Nima, so he stood. The Shah didn't look up.

"I'd appreciate your explanation of why you would countermand my orders," he said to Nima.

"Your Majesty, I promised I would try. He is thirty-five. His effect on the team would be psychological."

"Are you daft, or are you just pretending to be?" the Shah said sharply, throwing his cards down on the table in disgust. "You've put us in an impossible position, Nima. If we refuse, we look mean. If we allow him to return, we surrender to the mob. God forbid he wins a medal—the country will celebrate him for the next hundred years. Do you understand our position now?"

"Yes, Your Majesty," Nima replied, shocked by the Shah's harsh words. "Your Majesty, I think it best for me to resign."

The Shah's face changed color. He looked incredulous, then

turned to the other three men at the table as if seeking their validation of the stupidity of the man standing before him.

"And what do you think your resignation will signal to the country?" the Shah demanded. "That I'm angry at your meddling? And then what? Do I let the man wrestle after you've resigned?"

I intervened. Nima had called me in a panic right after his speech, and I had spent much of the night thinking it through. "Your Majesty, may I suggest a possible solution?" I asked.

The Shah looked at me scathingly. "Ah, to the rescue of the family? Go ahead, say your piece."

"Your Majesty should order the man to come back. Most people know of his retirement. Tomorrow, the newspapers will headline 'His Majesty Orders Wrestler Out of Retirement.'"

"And what if he refuses?" the Shah asked.

"Nima will go down today to invite him back to the team. He won't refuse Nima," I said.

The Shah picked up his cards with a slight enthusiasm. "Keep me informed of your progress, Nima. It might make me the mob's favorite," he said with a hint of sarcasm.

Nima started to take his leave, but the Shah remembered something. "Make sure he doesn't pick up a medal."

"I'm sure he won't," Nima replied.

"Not good enough," the Shah snapped. "Do whatever it takes to make sure he doesn't." Nima, looking puzzled, didn't move.

"Don't keep playing the innocent," the Shah said. "Pay the organizers to give him a difficult draw."

The card game restarted. Nima left. Nima delivered. The unnamed wrestler kissed Nima's shoulders, a sign of deep respect.

"I know nothing else, Mr. Poonaki. Your asking me to rejoin the team means a great deal to me. I will get in shape for the meet." Nima faced a delicate situation. He reasoned that no one could win a medal at thirty-five. What harm would it be if the man wrestled his toughest opponents early in the tournament draws? The wrestler would have to face them at some point—why not sooner? Back then, light corruption tainted many sports. Back-room deals ensured that the strongest opponents ended up in the finals; weaker contenders often threw matches to give a teammate a better chance with a more favorable draw. Money exchanged hands. Our hero drew the Turk and the Russian, two young and celebrated champions. No one could have foreseen the humiliation that awaited the unnamed wrestler.

In the preliminary match, the Russian easily dominated him. His teammates, watching from the side of the mat, cried openly at his humiliation. He walked off the mat, stripped the straps from his shoulders, and turned to Nima with profound disappointment. "You fed me to the wolves, Mr. Poonaki. Was it necessary? I came here to win a match from a Bulgarian or a Canadian. How can I face my countrymen? How could you?" He helped his team-mates during the rest of the competition. He stood by their corner between rounds and acted as a water boy. Nima didn't return with the team. He flew to Paris, staying for three months. When he returned, the Shah welcomed him warmly. Nima resumed play-ing cards with us once again, looking restored. Lili warned me. "Nima has changed," she told me. "He avoided everyone in Paris." I had developed health issues, losing a great deal of weight and feeling fragile—though, despite what you might have heard, I was still sane.

During a private dinner, Nima told me that the Shah had reminded him of the Karate Federation. Dejected, he said he planned to resign the next day. I had always thought it wise; I hadn't wanted him to take the job in the first place. When I saw him the following Friday, he looked more upbeat. He told me he had handed in his resignation. Unexpectedly, the Shah had shown him much kindness. He told Nima to think about it. If, after returning from the Grenoble Winter Olympics, Nima still wanted to resign, the Shah would give him the Ministry of Tourism to keep him entertained. Nima drained his wine glass in one gulp. "I have several ideas on how to boost tourism," he said. "You know, France understands tourism like no other country. After the Winter Olympics, I'll visit Paris and look up my friends in the French government." My Nima—full of simple, infectious enthusiasm. "First, I must visit Moscow for a series of four friendly wrestling meets," he added.

I wondered why Moscow. Given his pro-American stance, the Shah's relationship with the Soviets had soured. The Russians never liked Nima. I warned him to be careful. He told me the friendly meets represented a rapprochement, much encouraged by the Shah. Within days of his arrival, Nima made headlines. Upset by the atrocious refereeing by the Soviets during the first of the "friendly" meets, he pulled out all his wrestlers—a bold move, he confessed, driven more by anger than strategy. The Iranian ambassador in Moscow called Nima a fool. But it paid off. The Russians respected force—and they remembered it. The referees showed a little more fairness for the next three meets. It resulted in an even split—two meets to two. When Nima returned, the Shah laughed heartily. His pride in Nima's audacity was evident to everyone in the court. For two weeks, Nima was riding high. The rumor mill in the court buzzed with speculation that he would be named a future minister. "He may be different from the old Prince, but he has the Poonaki blood," people said.

But Nima had planted the seeds of his fall from grace in Moscow. On the last night of their stay, he and the deputy discussed his departure from sports over a scotch and soda at the hotel. The deputy asked if Nima had decided to start the Karate Federation. "He made me humiliate a man I loved," Nima responded. "Not in a thousand years would I serve this majesty." His friend quickly silenced him, pointing to the chandelier above. The Soviets bugged all hotels used for foreign visitors. Nima forgot the conversation. The Soviet military attaché passed the conversation to General Nematollah Nassiri, head of SAVAK, courtesy of Yuri Andropov, the newly appointed head of the KGB. Nima had always resisted SAVAK's interference in sports and had never cultivated a relationship with General Nassiri. The general shared the tape with the Shah. The ax fell swiftly. The next day, without warning, the newspapers reported Nima's dismissal for malfeasance involving government funds. Lili contributed her own money, and I sold many works of art to help replace the missing funds from the Ministry of Education. The scandal raged for months, severely depleting our wealth. Nima couldn't understand his harsh treatment. The Shah frequently dismissed people but rarely with malice. Nima contacted old friends and well-connected people, but few spoke to him. Those who did couldn't explain the anger directed at him. His treatment of the wrestler had shaken him. The loss of the Shah's trust broke him. Years later, on his deathbed, the court minister reminded Nima of his misstep in the Moscow hotel. The Shah had declared, "So be it; he will not serve this majesty for a thousand years."

"If he loved anyone outside his family," the dying minister said, "you were it. As his oldest friend, you broke his heart." Nima understood. There were no excuses. He had failed the high standards of friendship—twice in months. He had been disloyal to his King and betrayed a man of impeccable integrity. Professor Dal fell silent for a while. Used to his ruminations, I remained still. He quoted a poem I had often heard my Baba repeat:

> *When the unjust judge*
> *Without justice,*
> *Horrible, horrible things are done.*
> *But more horrible things are done*
> *When justice judges*
> *The unjust judge.*

The sun had cleared the window ledge. Professor Dal fell silent. I drifted to sleep, not noticing when he returned to bed.

THE NINTH NIGHT: 1001

THE WRITER REFERS YOU TO THE EPILOGUE

Thank you, reader. My guidance has come to an end. We have journeyed far together, and our puzzle pieces are falling into place. I now hold the final piece, the centerpiece—the jewel at the heart of this mystery. Yet, overshadowing everything is the dark specter of death. Much like our universe, history seems drawn to tales of death and destruction, as though compelled to record the darker chapters of existence.

In the midst of all the death, you read of a comic moment involving Corn Flakes that gave way to something more historically significant: the exchange between Nixon and Khrushchev during the Kitchen Debate. The absurdity of their high-stakes confrontation only amplifies its comedic value. I must admit that I fabricated the Fat Storyteller's naughty encounter with Zahra. After all, who would be able to provide me with such intimate details? Remember the poetic license I asked for? But the Surgeon's account of *The Wrestler and the Shah*—this, I swear, with my hand on my heart, satisfies historical truth.

I find myself reconsidering the title chapter. *The Shah and the Wrestler* feels more fitting, but I choose to honor the Wrestler, the man with the greater soul. I can name him: Takhti, a figure who holds a sacred place in the Iranian imagination. He embodies the qualities we often find lacking in ourselves: forthrightness, incorruptibility, purity and strength. And no, as the ultimate writer, I refuse to entertain the notion of his murder. Such speculation plays into a national trait—our obsession with conspiracy theories. We invented conspiracies long before they became fashionable or ubiquitous. They were our pastime, filtering our hard-earned cynicism through layers of nonsense.

As the pages grow thinner in your right hand, the mystery of who-wrote-it edges closer to its resolution. One of S.S. Van Dine's rules for writing detective stories states that the writer must direct the reader's indignation toward a single, irredeemable villain. I ask you: who is the most black-hearted of them all? If you haven't yet unraveled the truth, I will reveal everything in the Epilogue

THE NARRATOR COMES CLEAN

In the groves of their academy, at the end of every vista, you see nothing but their gallows. Reflections on the Revolution in France

—Edmund Bure

Dear Ms. Vakil,

Qui vivra verra—he who lives shall see. How deeply you sadden me. You tell me that the living version of my storyteller passed away at the age of 46 from a heart attack—penniless, divorced and forced out of his second tearoom by his wife and best friend. It adds an unexpected poignancy to my story. Now, I understand how I came into possession of all the documents. Ms. Vakil, I remain deeply grateful for your support and for introducing me to Mr. Hekaiatchi, who, as you can see, merged quite naturally with my storyteller. You have, I might add, inherited these papers in a strangely circuitous way. I have received every scanned item from "our suitcase." I will send you dozens of emails with individual attachments. You would have contacted me had you known they were in my possession these past twenty years.

I understand your fear, Ms. Vakil. Without the originals, these attachments are indeed worthless. But do not despair. I have arranged for the suitcase to come under your control by placing it with the Boston Public Library—not with the arrogant Widener at Harvard. I have named you its executor. After a lengthy correspondence that spanned nearly two years, you may wonder, "Why the lack of trust?" I trust you entirely; I have taken measures to ensure the original papers never fall into the hands of the hyenas back home. I want the record to remain clear between "our" revolution and "their" revolution. Their revolution, as they claim, happened by happenstance. They point to the Imam's cassette tapes distribution in mosques as evidence of superior organization. Please. Half the people who walked the streets then didn't know of a religious figure among them. The truth, Ms. Vakil, is that the revolution fell into their laps. With little sacrifice, they rode the ultimate wave better than any surfer. They still look surprised.

Someone once asked the Chinese Premier, Chou En-lai, to comment on the effects of the French Revolution. "Too early to tell," he responded. More than a hundred years have passed since our Constitutional Revolution, and we can now comment. The religious constitution beat the civil constitution with a half-Nelson. A series of cynical acts completely crushed any democratic instinct within the Iranian psyche. It resulted in a country bankrupt by any measure. I imagine that, in 1979, the herd of religious ignoramuses experienced heady emotions—everything seemed full of possibility. As Khomeini descended from the Air France plane, the clerics high-fived and pumped fists—or their clerical equivalents—in Qom. For a century, they had dreamed of building the kingdom of God on Earth.

Thirty years have passed since then. But do we need another upheaval? It could get worse. Sometimes, I wish I could blink, and presto, they vanish from the face of the Earth. Let heaven have them. Let non-criminals—despite all their flaws—manage our complex, challenging, and wonderful world. Our revolution, the earlier constitutional one, sprang from a humanist tradition. I want to make bold claims; I consider it the purest revolution. Even when it failed, it never descended into the inhuman aftermath of the French Revolution. It simply petered out after victory. I claim it represented us as a people to a tee. Ms. Vakil, I want to put the facts into perspective. Or, more precisely, I want to put the Prince's perspective into perspective.

After the bombardment of the parliament, Mohammad Ali Shah began his despotic rule. The Russians appeared invincible with their proxy, Colonel Liakhov, at the head of the Cossack Brigade. The constitutional forces were in disarray—killed, exiled or hiding. The reactionary forces controlled all institutions; the capital belonged to them. For the next eighteen months, the Great Powers tried to force the Shah to reconstitute the Majlis. The Shah proclaimed that the Majlis contradicted Islamic precepts. Sheikh Nouri backed the Shah. The resistance, initially defensive, began in Tabriz. The Shah ordered a siege of Tabriz, but the Tabrizis knew him too well. The Shah, never a quick learner, did not know the Tabrizis. He threw everything at them: the army and the infamous brigand Rahim Khan with his 500 mercenaries. He allowed them to loot and rape the citizens of Tabriz.

The people set up barricades to resist the reactionary forces. An illiterate man named Sattar Khan emerged as a leader of the constitutionalists. A former bandit and a former cellmate of Rahim Khan, he organized a ragtag army of four thousand revolutionary troops, some from Transcaucasia. After ten months of street fighting, they captured two of the city's twelve districts. Sattar Khan expelled the bandits and then the religious Islamiyah Society, which was even more dangerous than the brigands. The barricaded city quickly recovered and resumed its business. Frustrated, the Shah appointed the old premier, the reactionary Ain Dawleh, as governor. He stationed troops outside the city. By February, the reactionaries had encircled the city, and the siege of Tabriz began, meant to starve the population. Toward the end of April, Russian troops—no doubt with an eye on our northern territories—crossed the border and occupied Tabriz. They ended the siege and disarmed the revolutionaries. Several other cities followed Tabriz's lead. They mounted similar resistance to the Shah's autocratic rule and set up their constitutional governments. Isfahan was the first, and other cities soon followed.

In May, a revolutionary army from Rasht moved toward Qazvin, ninety miles north of Tehran. The radicals refused to follow the liberal lead, no doubt because they remembered the outcome of the "compromise" reached before the bombardment of the Majlis. The rebel armies from the north and south joined forces, closing in on Tehran in a pincer movement right under the noses of the Great Powers. By early summer, the foreign press predicted the fall of Tehran. Fall it did. The Shah's forces surrendered, and the Shah escaped to the Russian mission in Zargang. Russian troops descended on Tehran to restore "peace." The end of the Qajar dynasty now lay in sight.

I now come to the end, several ends. We have walked through the terrain of my life together—you and I, Ms. Vakil. Let me take your lovely hand. May I show you around this large house like an eager real estate agent? I have spared you the stretches of normal boyhood. I sense you prefer a sweeping canvas. But no incident, for me, shines brighter than the hunting trip.

The silvery river rose from deep within the violet mountains like a thread of saliva. The black pebbles beside the river—disk-like, smooth, and hard—crunched awkwardly under the mules' hooves. Four sheared sheep walked along with us, the trip's provisions. The guide, a broad-shouldered man with a thick mustache and a rifle across his back, smiled permanently. Behind him, Tari sat astride a mule, also broad-shouldered, relaxed, and confident. He spoke excitedly to the guide. Our father, Nima Poonaki, with one night's white stubble, wore an American military combat uniform. He talked to a peasant walking gingerly between the mule and the rock face. I rode behind them, delicately ugly, lips cracked into scabs, out of rhythm with the mule. I maintained a "we shall overcome" gaze. Hamid rode half a mule's length behind me like a shield against the precipice. We arrived at the campsite around 2:30 pm, through a narrow passage halfway up a mountain. From a distance, the tarpaulin tents, ready for our arrival, resembled green mold on a stale piece of bread; coming closer, they fluttered like flags before the battle. The guides had set up the camp on a flat patch of ground surrounded by dry mountains of various metallic colors. It felt as if we were camping inside a volcano. The tall mountains gave the sun only a few hours to cross the sky.

The sky had already turned into a deeper cobalt blue when we arrived. The shadows grew longer, jagged like the peaks that surrounded us. Hunting on the south side of the Alborz chain was difficult. We pursued wild ram, antelope and stag, aiming for the longest antlers. We all wanted to set records. No sooner had we arrived at the campsite than one of the guides spotted a brown bear. It stood on a small rock plateau half a mile down a gorge. The guides whispered "Khers, khers"—"bear"—around the camp. The dry wind carried our scent for miles; with a slight shift, we could waste days of careful tracking. We took turns looking through my father's binoculars. The bear paced and circled, oblivious to our presence. His snout, dirty white from dust, burrowed furiously into his front left paw. A splinter must have dug deep between his footpads. He twisted his powerful back to delve deeper. The pain from the splinter explained his disregard for our smell. My father claimed the shot first, but then my brother begged for a chance to take it. Reluctantly but proudly, my father consented. We circled, positioning ourselves about two hundred yards away from the bear, keeping the wind at our backs. The bear grew increasingly agitated, stood on its hind legs, then dropped softly back onto its front paws, bucking up and down with each movement, sending dust into the air.

Tari lay flat on his stomach, placing the rifle on a flat stone. As always, on moments like these, Hamid abandoned me and lay beside Tari. They were brothers in sport and hunting. I stood off to the side, feeling resentment. I hated Tari most during these moments. Hamid whispered advice to him like a caddy guiding a golf pro. The rest of us fell silent. We could hear the wind soughing through the air, the distant growl of the bear—a baritone rumble. It circled itself tighter and tighter.

The first bullet struck the bear below the chin, right through the upper chest. It was a large-caliber rifle with enough power to stop the animal in its tracks. The bullet hit with force. It threw the bear back against the rock behind it. The second bullet pierced the heart. The bear collapsed instantly, dead before it hit the ground. Tari's shot was impeccable—one of the best anyone could recall. The two guides jumped and sprinted up the slope toward the fallen animal. One of them signaled its death by swiping his hand across his throat in the universal sign of finality. By the time we reached the bear, the guides had already begun their work. They cut the bear open, starting low, between the legs, and slicing up toward the solar plexus. The bear's snout, damp and dusty, lay against the ground. With swift, jerking movements, the guides worked to expose the animal's teeth. The taller guide, with his hands deep inside the bear's body, pulled out the liver, still warm. It glistened. He held it out to us, but only Tari accepted. That prompted Hamid to take a piece. The guide cut two pieces, and they chewed them slowly. The stockier guide began eating the kidney. The rest of us watched silently as my father smiled with pride, shaking his head in mock disgust; a peacock pleased with the display.

The guides blindfolded a mule and lashed the bear's carcass to it before bringing it back to camp, where they immediately began to skin it. Streams of white fat ran through the gelatinous pink flesh, and the hand-like bones of the bear were eerily reminiscent of a human hand. As evening fell, we gathered around the fire, wrapped in thick pustins—Afghan sheepskin coats that still smelled faintly of living sheep. The temperature dropped rapidly, from a high of 100 degrees to below freezing within hours. Spirits were high. We ate tough kebabs, drank scorching tea and smoked soft opium beneath a sky so clear it felt like we could reach out and touch the stars. I think of that night as my second birthday. I don't claim any premonitions, but the clarity of that evening—the violence of the bear's death, the mixture of people from all walks of life celebrating the kill with ancient stories—has stayed with me. Over time, it has taken on a marble sculpture's polished, static quality, frozen in vivid detail.

Tari went to bed around eleven. Hamid bid us goodnight and retired to his tent; he had gained middle-class status. The mountain people treated him with respect. My father saw Hamid as the son of a village headman. I turned on my flashlight. The servants had prepared my bedding in the tent and folded the corner of the rough brown blanket in a neat triangle. Like a dog-eared page in a book, it reminded me where I was. Every minor detail took on symbolic significance. I slept like a child.

The next day, we woke at 4:30 am. As was his habit, my father set off with a guide and a mule toward the western part of the mountains. He preferred hunting alone. With the other guide at the front, we made our way south. The servants stayed behind at camp, waiting for our return later in the afternoon. We rode all morning through dangerous paths littered with sliding stones. We spotted some game—a herd of rams across the mountains, far off in the distance. The guide pointed them out with his naked eye while we scanned the area through binoculars. I felt like a blind man struggling to make out the animals. Then, a barely perceptible movement in the distance revealed the herds, like bacteria stirred under a microscope. By 2:00 pm, disappointed, we headed back. Hamid and the guide rode ahead, conversing animatedly. Tari rode in the middle and I followed behind more cautiously. If the guide had noticed Tari napping, he would have warned him about the danger of the slippery path. The path wasn't particularly narrow, but it was covered with thin, flat stones that had become slick from the sun. At first, I laughed when I saw Tari's mule slip ahead of me. Then Tari slipped too—and then he was gone. He disappeared from my view, sliding down the mountainside.

Hamid and the guide had gone a hundred yards further down the path. I jumped off my mule and looked down the mountainside but couldn't see anything. I shouted. My voice didn't carry in the wind. I sat down and began to slip and slide toward where Tari had vanished. I saw his hands gripping a jagged rock. He had slid down a chute or animal path and caught himself on a small promontory, slowing his fall. His body dangled, his legs swinging in the air. He tried to pull himself up, but I could see his fingers struggling to hold on. I slid down closer to him. I heard him swear, his voice calm despite the peril.

"Easy, damn it, you're sending stones down on me," he muttered. Hamid and the guide saw us for the first time. From their vantage point, lower down the path, they could see Tari dangling. How had they not noticed a whole mule sliding into the gorge? I'll never understand.

"Can you hold on?" I shouted, trying to offer reassurance.

Tari's head was just visible above the edge. Below him was a 100-foot drop, with rocks scattered everywhere. I secured my foot in a dried-up root. It looked like an old suitcase handle. I stretched toward him and grabbed his wrist while he clung to the rocks with his other hand. My body scraped against the rough ground, my cheek grinding into the rocks. The guide and Hamid were scrambling up the path, racing to help.

"Pull so I can get my left elbow up," Tari said, straining.

I didn't pull—I held on to the weight of his body. His wrist scraped against the sharp rocks.

"Tell me you remember stabbing me with the fork," I said, my voice steady.

Tari's voice strained in reply, but there was no fear in it. "What?"

I repeated the question, one word at a time.

"Yes, yes, I remember sticking the fork into your throat. I lied about my amnesia," Tari said, his voice softer now.

"Don't patronize me. You aren't in a position to do that," I said, more firmly.

"What did you expect me to say?" Tari asked, his words strained from the effort. "I've told you a thousand times, I don't remember."

"I expect you to tell me what we had for lunch," I said.

Hamid and the guide had reached the top of the path. "Hold on, I'm here," Hamid shouted, trying to encourage me.

Tari hissed through his teeth. "How can I tell you what I ate years ago?"

"It's what will save your life. It will make it clear between us," I said, the sharp edge of the rocks cutting into my wrists as his weight continued to pull me downward.

"I don't remember, damn you," Tari said, the healthy fear creeping into his voice.

"They're getting closer. I won't wait long," I said. "It's between us, I promise." The guide and Hamid slid toward us, calling out, their voices lost to the wind. I could feel Tari's palm slick with sweat as it slid from mine.

"Ratatouille!" Tari shouted. I started pulling him up. Hamid reached down, his hands sliding into place beside me. I looked at him, surprised by the look on Tari's face—a strange, shocked expression. Hamid's good luck charm, which I gave him that night, hung out of his shirt. Then, unexpectedly, my hand slipped. I could feel the sweat from our palms mingling, and just like that, Tari fell. It was a quiet fall—a soft thud, like the back of a fork hitting a ratatouille dish.

We rushed down the path to where he lay among the rocks. But there were no miracles, Ms. Vakil. Tari was gone. His body shook violently from the shock, then stilled. We stared at each other for a long, silent moment. Under that godless sky, I had killed my brother. His death didn't bring freedom or remorse—it was simply a natural end to a long-simmering tension. Tari's memory of the fork incident was irrelevant. The guide's face was pale, his lips gray from fear. He imagined what my father would do. Hamid sat beside me, his hand pressed over his face as though trying to wash away his grief. The memory of our conversation is unclear to me, but it went something like this:

"I let him go," I said.

"You let him go," Hamid replied.

"His hand slipped."

"His hand slipped."

Neither of us spoke of the puzzle piece, the pendant. It matters little now; the mechanics of the slippage did not create guilt. A jury would find me guilty of delay—of those few moments of interrogation. No one heard it. Let me give you one final glimpse of the camp: the tents, the campfire, the bear and now Tari. I can still see the tears rolling down my father's unshaven face. I see Tari's body, wrapped in a white sheet, draped over the blindfolded mule, swinging rhythmically, head and feet moving in unison, as precise as a pendulum. I take my bow before the distorted faces of the spectators.

The next time I saw Hamid was four years later when he came to my house to arrest me. Ms. Vakil, I choke up even now. How can I choke up with so much hate? Can one love someone they dislike? Or dislike someone they love? I will let my fat avatar close the house for one last time. He is no longer a mere fictional figure, is he? In the flesh, he seems the least likely man to have done history a favor. But he did. And then he died at the age of 46, leaving no secrets behind to take to the grave. Let him and his ancestors rest in peace.

THE FAT STORYTELLER SINGS

"Everything that goes into my mouth seems to make me fat, everything that comes out of my mouth embarrasses me."

Gabriel Garcia Marquez

Baba, I am to be married. Are you happy for me? I have not been as honest as I should have been about my fiancée. I want you to forget all the gossip. She will be Mrs. Hekaiatchi. Bless this wedding, Baba. "What will I do for money?" you ask. I have enough stashed away. My work with Vakil Khanum has been lucrative, and I completed it without getting into trouble. As you'll see, we won't emigrate to Turkey. I disappointed you when I signed over the teahouse. I had no choice. They kept me for nine nights in the worst prison. I wasted away in that madhouse.

I have saved some money and Mammad-Ali, my soon-to-be

father-in-law, has savings to help us start a small teahouse nearby. Baba, I promise you, Zahra and I will work hard to make it successful. It won't have the beautiful pool, the fountain in the center, the fenestrations in the upper walls, the intricate woodwork or the gold-encrusted cushions, but a small teahouse is a beginning. Do you remember Alireza, my small, snot-nosed friend? When you saw him, you would offer him a handkerchief. He'd wipe his nose with his sleeve and give that funny, shy, bewildered smile at the offer. He never quite understood the connection. He was the son of Tavakol Agha, the locksmith whose shop was across from Mammad-Ali's. We could hear his machine grinding away day and night to feed his family.

Last month, Tavakol Agha died of a heart attack while hammering a sheet of metal. Forty-eight years old. I ask you, Baba, how could someone so young die from a heart attack while working so vigorously? God, in His mercy, gives no warning.

Alireza wants nothing to do with shaping keys anymore. He worked alongside his father all his life, but now he's grown into a good-looking man and wants to be a television actor. His workshop, which we saw a week ago, looks like a hole in the wall is covered in grease and oil. It has a high ceiling with windows so opaque you'd think the skin of a melted candle covered every inch. It lets in a soft, diffuse light that reminds me of your teahouse and how light came through the fenestrations above. It needs a good cleaning, but it has potential. One day, I can get a permit to read a few poems by Ferdowsi for these ignoramuses. But for now, we want to focus on the teahouse. We'll offer a few dishes cooked by Zahra. She can cook a crow and make it taste finger-licking good.

"You could do better," you buzz in my ears. No, Baba, I could do a lot worse. You don't understand the times. The effects of the war have given rise to the sisters of Zainab. They uphold Islamic regulations. What hole did they crawl out of? I've never heard of a more foul-mouthed group of women. They remind young girls of their religious duties. The roving bullies in the streets make up rules on the spot. We all act crazy. I've grown, Baba. I need to navigate these stormy waters. One day, you wake up to find a friend has turned into an enemy. The next day, that same enemy reverts to a friend. Now, I have Hamid the Jackal for a friend. Under his plush wings, I will prosper. Please, Baba, don't prejudge my choices. I was terrified of seeing him in the street for a long time. I was too afraid to step outside while I lived in the room above Mammad-Ali's shop for months. You called me a coward. Well, I stepped out to meet Vakil Khanum and everything changed. I'm about to become a businessman and start a family. I know Hamid put me in the madhouse—but he also got me out. He got what he wanted. Neither of us holds a grudge.

I'll tell you about my visitor on the ninth day. You'll understand. On that morning, as I slept the carefree sleep of the innocent, I heard the usual clanging of the door as they came to take poor, wasted Professor Dal away for his ablutions or makeup or whatever they did to him every morning. He never told me what they wanted from him during the day. Why all the strange markings? Why did he defecate and vomit without shame? Why did he think he produced the bulk of this country's oil? I reckon daylight shut down his brain. When the sun rose, he went mad. His eyes looked dead to the world. To sleep better, I faced the wall. I ignored the guards as they dragged him away. Another late night with Professor Dal on my back had taken its toll. I needed sleep. Baba, you can get used to anything. I woke up around noon and ate the grub, bad as it was. I relieved myself at three, in the privacy of my cell—with great satisfaction, I might add. I waited for dinner. Then, the Professor crawled on top of me to tell me stories well into the night. A few walks in the garden might have improved my stay, but a man could do worse. A man gets used to a life without struggle.

I felt the guards' presence next to my bunk. Before I could turn around, one grabbed my ear and pulled it to the point of tearing it off my head. "Ay, ay, ay," I howled as I followed the hand to wherever it led me. It led me down the corridor in the basement. The laughter of the two guards echoed as they escorted me. I received my ration of kicks to my backside. It hurt. I'd lost some padding after my nine days. I stepped outside for the first time in over a week, disoriented, stumbling behind the hand dragging me by my ear. I entered a windowless room. It looked blindingly bright. Baba, it looked like the hospital room you took me to when I was eight, where Mother died. Fluorescent lights shone on the spotless metal sinks along one side of the room, similar to the chemistry lab in my high school. A neat row of shiny, metallic surgery tools sat on a blue towel. I also saw a few pieces of electronic equipment, like radios with oversized dials. White tiles covered the floor, with a drain in the middle. Several people were assembled in the room, waiting for me. Believe it or not, Baba, I recognized Hamid right away. He joked and laughed among them, and his audience respected him. Hamid winked at me, smiled and motioned for the guard to release my earlobe. Two other Islamic brothers, fierce-looking men, stopped laughing.

Baba, I can't exaggerate the effect these two had on me when

I met their eyes. Do you remember when I embarrassed you during a visit to the zoo? I howled to go home. I was six. The yellow eyes of the lions in the cage terrified me. I sensed their complete indifference to my existence. I understood myself to be a piece of raw meat. Baba, these men had the same gaze—but much worse. They weren't indifferent to my being; they required my absence. I lowered my eyes immediately. Another heavyset man (I never use the word fat to describe anyone) sat on a stool in the corner. He had a hose in his hand. His head down, he twirled its brass nozzle. A servant type, he never lifted his head. Hamid came over and put his arm around my shoulder. "Salman, my brother," he said. "Do you know where you are?"

"Mr. Poonaki's house," I said without hesitation.

One of the men whistled. "Impressive," said Hamid. "You've spoken to the mad Professor? You know, he never talks to us." He looked at his partner accusingly. "What has he told you?" The other man moved toward me. What did he mean by "us"? I feared for the Professor's safety.

"You put me inside a cell with a raving lunatic," I said. "All I hear from him every night are screams and shouts while he sleeps. His nightmares haven't let me get a wink of sleep in the past week." I couldn't have been convincing, as both men started toward me.

"Easy, boys," Hamid said. "Let's not forget why I'm here. Give us a second. I'm sure I can convince Mr. Hekaiatchi here to cooperate." The two men shrugged. "We'll be outside if you need us, Hamid Agha, Mr. Hamid." The heavyset servant opened the door. They left the room. The servant closed the door and returned to his stool, twirling the brass nozzle.

"Salman Jan, Salman dear," Hamid said with infinite patience. "Do you know where you are?"

"A mental hospital?" I replied, my voice full of hesitation.

"Do you know what's on offer in this room?" I didn't answer. I looked around. "Let me give you a tour." He threw a friendly arm over my shoulder and moved me around the room. "See this here? It looks like a radio, right?" I nodded in agreement. "Well, it isn't a radio. It gives you a high-voltage shock that makes you forget who you are. But that's not the worst of it. When they connect it to your balls, you'll agree to anything. Now, I've never tried it myself, but the two gorillas you met tell me your balls get so shocked"—he grinned—"they suck themselves right up inside your body. They go so far up that they have to punch your bladder hard to get them to pop back out again. Then they zap those fragile, wrinkly little sacks again: punch, zap, punch, zap, repeatedly." He walked me a few feet farther, his arm still on my shoulders, and pointed at the tools. "Brother, see these shining tools? The Americans designed each one to hurt something inside or outside your body. The one there peels the nails off your hands. The larger one de-nails your toes. The cute little hammer breaks the fragile bones in your foot, one at a time." He said all this without drama. I cried in fitful sobs. The fellow on the stool wore a shit-eating grin and exposed the most distorted set of teeth I had ever seen.

Hamid, ever the attentive guide, still had his heavy hand on my shoulder as he pointed to various heavy-duty hooks screwed into the ceiling. "You see those, Salman?" he asked, gesturing as if to show me a grand mosque. "They tie your hands behind your back with chain link, then hang you on those hooks. By the way," he added, sizing me up, "you look good. Have you lost some weight? But I should warn you, even if you were as thin as I am"—he motioned to his lean frame with both hands—"dangling from those hooks will dislocate your shoulders in under a minute. The pain, they say, makes you pass out for a few seconds, then you come to, only to black out again. And so it goes." He watched me sob with a look of concern. "But the worst of it all," he continued, waving his hand like a museum guide, "is for me to leave you alone with those two animals for an hour." He gestured to the door. "I can make all this go away with just one signature."

Confused, I looked at him. "What signature?" I asked.

"I need you to sign the teahouse over to me," he replied.

"My teahouse?" I asked, still not understanding. "But you already own it."

Hamid flushed red with surprise. "You know that, and I know that, but a complication has come up. Do you remember the local mullah, Haj Rajab?" I nodded. "Well, he showed me a forged letter from your father. In it, your father promised to transfer the teahouse to the local Islamic foundation if you die. Lucky for you, I brought you here. You'd be dead by now," he said with a twisted laugh. "Haj Rajab claims you're missing and dead." He laughed indignantly as if to suggest, "Who could question my motives?"

"Two things need to happen," Hamid said, waving two fingers in front of my face like twitching donkey ears. "First, you need to sign these papers today." He pulled out a stack of rolled papers from his inside jacket pocket. "Second, I'll fetch you tomorrow morning, and we'll visit Haj Agha at the revolutionary court. I'll swear on the holy book that you transferred the property to me. Your presence will be proof enough that you're still alive."

"Swear on the Koran?" I asked, feigning innocence. "I'd be doomed to eternal damnation! I can't do that."

Hamid looked at me incredulously. "You want me to leave you with those animals?" he asked, pretending to move toward the door. Baba, you'd be proud of me. I stopped crying and spoke to him as a man.

"If they kill me, you won't have a teahouse," I said. "Hamid Agha," I continued, "why don't I sign the document outside these walls with witnesses?"

He looked at me in surprise before laughing. "You're learning, my brother," he said. "I'll pick you up tomorrow morning. If you do this, I'll help you in other ways." Baba, I, of course, wanted nothing more than to get away from that insane asylum-turned-torture chamber as quickly as possible. The following day, everything went smoothly. The rest, you know. I ended up, scared out of my wits, living above Mammad-Ali's store. Darling Baba, please understand. I've appreciated your constant buzzing in my ear these past months. It reminds me of your care and love for me. I've been through so much and disappointed you many times, but losing your teahouse tops it all. You've stayed angry, judgmental, demanding and caring. Now, I need your blessing. I see a new beginning for Zahra and me.

I will take the suitcase full of papers to the Spanish embassy this afternoon. The Spanish consul will take the case under a diplomatic seal. They will transfer it to the public library in Boston. Boston is a city in the United States, Baba. The same town where Mr. Verdi lives. Can you believe it? The papers could cause quite a stir: the mullahs would have moved heaven and Earth to find the people spreading rumors about Sheikh Nouri. Tonight, Vakil

Khanum will pay us well for the papers. Zahra and I deserve it. But that's not all. We made much more money when we got our hands on the documents. I must tell you about our daring operation. Baba, you will be proud. Remember when I went to see Vakil Khanum? She told me the famous Professor Dal's oral stories didn't amount to much without the documents. Don't misunderstand, Baba. I narrated the reminiscences well and she liked them, but she needed papers to prove the stories about the twin princes. Imagine, Baba, if every time you told the story of Rostam and Sohrab in your teahouse, someone drinking their tea demanded proof. "Show me Sohrab's birth certificate," they might say. Or imagine someone calling out, "I don't believe you, Hekaiatchi, unless you show me the marriage certificate of Rostam and Tahmineh." Or someone puffing on their hookah shouting, "Hey, Hekaiatchi, show me a photograph of the spot where Arash's arrow fell to delineate our border."

You must appreciate the times, Baba. It's not like you used to say—that the telling of the story is in the telling of the story. The world has changed, and telling a story now needs documentation to back it up. Good old Professor Dal told me that Verdi Agha hid a whole suitcase of papers in the house gazebos before his arrest ten years ago. When I returned from Vakil Khanum's apartment, Zahra couldn't stop talking about how we might access the suitcase. She is something else, isn't she? Quiet as a mouse, shy as a rabbit, but perseveres. "Which of the three houses?" she asked, even before we had settled into the taxi. "What floor? Were there guards around the gazebos? How many people worked in the insane asylum? Did they all go to sleep at night? How many guards at night?" I couldn't answer her questions. I had only been in the main house once and quickly left. I wanted nothing more to do with it.

From my room upstairs at Mammad-Ali's store, I could see what was happening at the teahouse—my outings to see Vakil Khanum had made me bolder. Whenever I saw Hamid leave the teahouse, I showed my face around the neighborhood shops. People remembered me and greeted me with sympathy. They welcomed me back into the fold. I started to come out during the day without worrying about Hamid's whereabouts. One day, I accidentally bumped into him as he hurried into the bazaar. He didn't react strangely. "Where have you been? See me. I'm in a hurry now," he said. I realized he assumed I was around. I no longer felt important or dangerous to him. A weight lifted from my chest. It felt good to reconnect with the people I grew up with.

One day, Zahra, unwilling to let go of any opportunity to build our teahouse, brought Alireza to lunch. Alireza and I hung out like we did when we were kids. He wasn't the brightest, but he was a good man. He dropped out of school in the ninth grade, just like I did. We went our separate ways, but at first, I felt a surge of jealousy. His looks made me self-conscious. I thought Zahra must have invited him to make me jealous. Alireza ate Zahra's pilaf eagerly, tearing into the bread and rice. He cleaned his plate with a gusto, suggesting he hadn't had a good home-cooked meal. After lunch, Zahra got up, swinging her beautiful backside to fetch tea. Poor Alireza watched her, clearly starstruck, as she worked with the samovar. My blood boiled like the water in the samovar. I could almost hear it whistle in my nose. Zahra told Alireza that her cousin had lost the key to an abandoned house in Ferdowsi Square. Could he help? Alireza twirled his mustache confidently, promising no door could resist him for more than five minutes. I swear he winked. I fought the impulse to throw him out, but Zahra told him her cousin worked long hours and that I would meet him at 10:00 pm to get a key made. Baba, I didn't realize until later that Zahra had arranged to enter one of the gazebo houses through the back door of the alley.

At about 10:15 pm, Zahra and I arrived in the dim alley. Alireza sat beside his cart in the dark, surrounded by hundreds of keys on large steel rings. He had filled the cart with tools, rags, sandpaper, files and a small cutting wheel. It looked like an innocent enough scene—an artisan helping a couple return to their home. It wasn't until later that I realized Zahra's cleverness. She had orchestrated this whole thing. Alireza made the key for her without raising suspicion. Baba, I tell you, she would beat any man with her cleverness. Zahra tried the key in the door. It slid effortlessly into the brass keyhole and turned smoothly, causing the door to open as if it were Ali Baba's cave. She quickly shut it again, a satisfied grin on her face. She thanked Alireza with another promise of lunch, and we walked in the opposite direction down the alley. Once Alireza was out of sight, Zahra and I retraced our steps. She looked around to ensure no one was watching, slipped the key back in, opened the door, grabbed my coat and pulled us inside the dark house. She giggled, and I whispered, "Have you gone crazy?" But soon enough, I couldn't help myself and joined in her laughter. She pulled a flashlight from her bag—she had thought of everything. The Poonakis had boarded up the buildings years ago, leaving no light to escape through the front windows. The guards at the front house, where I spent ten days, had no visibility inside. I'd caught a glimpse of part of this building from my cell in the basement. Zahra and I moved through the house quietly, inspecting everything.

The air inside smelled of mold. The plaster walls, swollen with water damage, were bloated and cracked. Scattered large wooden crates lay across the floors in every room. Created with two-by-fours, they had been made ready for shipment overseas. Now, they lay abandoned, nearly impenetrable. We didn't have the tools to break open the thick wooden planks crisscrossing the sides of the crates. We could hear the creaks of the stairs above us, but I didn't dare climb them, afraid they might collapse under my weight. Despite the danger, there was a childish thrill in what we were doing. We had stumbled into the forgotten possessions of a wealthy family. Everyone assumed the three abandoned houses were empty. We didn't find any of the papers mentioned by Professor Dal. The crates were full of furniture but no documents. We needed help to open the crates. Then, I thought of Hamid.

Zahra and I discussed it, hesitantly at first; she distrusted Hamid. I agreed, but I argued that we had no choice. We couldn't just break into the boxes ourselves. Hamid had enough influence to get us inside. Zahra considered it for a night before agreeing to accompany me to the teahouse to see him. I was on edge—Zahra's fearlessness was a comfort, though I wasn't sure my nerves could hold. We arrived before the teahouse, and memories flooded my mind, shaking my resolve. Not much had changed inside, but the clientele seemed wealthier. We didn't enter the teahouse itself but knocked on his office door. Hamid was alone, seated where my father used to sit. None of his usual sycophants were present. He looked surprised to see me with a woman but greeted us politely. He didn't pay much attention to Zahra; her squint made people uncomfortable, but I had grown used to it. After a brief and awkward silence, he asked how I had been. I nodded toward Zahra and said, "Thanks to God, all is well." I reminded him of his offer back in the "resting home." Hamid seemed to appreciate my tact. "How can I help?" he asked. I told him about some valuable objects hidden in an abandoned house I knew of, without giving him the location. He was interested but wanted to know what was in it for him. I suggested we share the proceeds from selling the furniture we found.

He smiled. "I always take 80 percent of the cut, but before you argue, let me clarify," he said, raising three fingers. "You won't pay for a single coin's worth of expenses. I'll cover all the labor, all the equipment, and all the transportation costs." He lowered one finger and added, "All you need to do is sit back and collect your 20 percent."

Zahra, ever bold, added, "Hamid Agha, we're about to get married. Why not give us thirty percent to help us start our life?"

Hamid laughed. "A shirzan, a lioness, I like her," he said, his mood lightening. "I'll give you twenty-five percent as a wedding gift."

"Agreed," Zahra and I said in unison. I had him swear on the Koran to uphold his side of the bargain. He did. I gave him the location of the house. He was incredulous.

"You mean those buildings aren't empty?" he asked. "I've been by there for years. They're planning to demolish them soon." He chuckled. "This is going to be easy." Hamid wasted no time. The next day, he arrived with three trucks and five workers armed with crowbars, all in broad daylight. Imagine how easy it must be for some people. We didn't even need to enter through the back alley.

The trucks rolled in behind the grand building and backed up to the three gazebo-like houses. A team of Afghani workers—Hamid's cost-effective solution—jumped out, ready to work. Some of the guards from the lunatic asylum even came to help. They dismantled the boarded-up buildings. It allowed light to flood inside. A sense of excitement swept over me. It reminded me of when you bought me that red tricycle, Baba. The moment of anticipation, the thrill before the discovery—I could never forget it.

The workers began prying open boxes of exquisite, well-preserved furniture inside the gazebos. There were dining tables large enough to seat forty people, delicate side tables with brass legs shaped like animal claws, statues of turbaned slaves holding trays of food and water, writing desks with soft green leather so smooth it blended seamlessly into the wood, and giant beds that seemed custom-made for royalty. We found leather suitcases packed with women's clothes, kitchen tools, brass pots and pans, and other delicate items, all wrapped in foul-smelling naphthalene. Some boxes held silver hairbrushes, while others contained large mirrors with round golden frames resembling the sun. There were items I'd never seen before, including a card dealer shoe, which Hamid explained. We opened more boxes. They revealed more treasures. But despite all this wealth, I didn't find any papers. We found boxes of leather-bound books, each one tightly bound with plastic. I flipped through them, hoping for loose papers, but none fell out. By afternoon, I had searched two large boxes in the upstairs room of the middle house—the one that likely belonged to the Prince's first wife, the daughter of the Shah. The boxes contained dozens of silver frames with photographs of the Poonaki family. I unwrapped each frame carefully, looking at the images of their lives—joyful, tragic, glorious and ruined. The photographs chronicled three generations.

I saw the young princes, their heads shaved, wearing uniforms with wide white collars. I saw them among a group of children, standing with their father, Nasser al-Din Shah. There were pictures of the princes as they grew, one attending the Dar al-Funun Technical School in Tehran. I saw photos of Sardar Mirza, the older prince, who had left for Paris, and Saleh Mirza, the more serious of the two, holding a cane and exuding authority. The more recent photographs had Nima and Lili, as well as the twins at different ages. They looked beautiful and rich; the boys did scowl at each other. Their wedding pictures revealed a lavish lifestyle, with presidents, queens and movie stars in the background.

At the bottom of the boxes, I found photos of the second pair of twins, but I couldn't see Verdi's face. As usual, he faced the camera with his left side turned, concealing the scar from the bite. The photos showed the Poonakis standing apart, their expressions turned down. One photo stood out—a picture of the twins with a peasant boy, their arms around each other's necks, smiling without care. Hamid came over, looked at the picture, and laughed. "That's me," he said. "Spoiled rich kids. I'll be richer than all of them one day." Before I could respond, he got up and left. Hamid had just revealed his true self, and I felt a chill. The realization hit me— there were no coincidences. Hamid ran the operation for Mad House from day one. How had I not seen it before? His influence, his control over everything, had been there all along. He directed the compound.

At five in the afternoon, I stepped out to a payphone and called Vakil Khanum to relay the bad news. We couldn't find the papers. She asked if we'd missed a safe. I explained how the workers had easily stripped everything, tearing down walls and would sell the tiles. The buildings were now fully exposed. I told her about the photographs, but she wasn't impressed. They weren't the kind of documentation she had hoped for. Still, could you bring me the photos? When I returned downstairs, I found Zahra and Hamid discussing how much the furniture would get. "I should have driven a harder bargain with Hamid," Zahra whispered, clearly scheming. I went upstairs to retrieve the photographs, but the workers had already taken them down. Panicked, I rushed down the stairs, taking them two at a time. One of the lower steps buckled under my weight, sending me tumbling forward like a character from a cartoon. I crashed a few steps into the foyer. Hamid rushed to help me up. He didn't laugh, and his genuine concern was unexpectedly touching, even in my pain.

"I need the photographs," I said, still dazed.

"Not part of the deal," he replied, all business. "Those frames will fetch a good price." Zahra nodded in agreement with him. I might have gotten angry if the circumstances allowed for it, but I focused on what mattered.

"I don't care about the frames," I said firmly. "You can keep those. I want the photographs." Hamid reluctantly agreed. He ordered two sturdy Afghan workers to unload the boxes of frames from the trucks.

"We clear out in the next hour," he said. "You get the photos; we'll take the frames to sell to the silversmith." I sat down on the bottom step as the workers brought in two boxes, each packed with around 150 frames of all kinds: round, square, rectangular, small, medium, large, silver, onyx and gold. Zahra sat beside me as we began sorting and extracting the photographs, starting with the small, round ones at the top. The intricate frames initially made it difficult, but soon, we got the hang of it.

And then, Baba, I had a moment that felt as magical as Ali Baba's "Open Sesame." When I unhooked the back of the first large frame, instead of finding filler paper holding the photo in place, I discovered the first handwritten document by the Prince. The elegant nastaliq script filled the paper, continuing sideways in the margins at the angle customary for that era. I opened the next frame, and again, original documents—historical treasures—were tucked behind the photograph. I ran outside, grabbed an old suitcase filled with clothes and emptied it on the floor. In the next hour, I filled that suitcase with priceless historical documents. I saved a suitcase full of my country's history, Baba. I'm sure this will be the best thing I ever did. Aren't you proud of me now? To his credit, Hamid honored our deal. In the following weeks, he paid us a sum I had never imagined saving. Whether it was precisely twenty-five percent of the loot, I didn't know, but it was enough to get us started with a small teahouse we rented from Alireza. Alireza never became a TV actor. Instead, he worked for us as a waiter, occasionally creating tense moments when he ogled Zahra's backside.

I went straight to the Spanish embassy. I didn't want the documents to stay in Mammad-Ali's store for another minute. I then did what my conscience had been telling me to do—I changed the address Ms. Vakil had given me to the one I had for Mr. Verdi. I had promised the Professor I would deliver the papers to the last surviving Poonaki. I dressed in women's clothes for the last time, knowing the Islamic government monitors the entrances to foreign embassies. Without a word, the embassy doorman took the suitcase from under my chador. You see, Baba, I've gained a measure of courage. Then, as cool as a cucumber (though I sweated plenty), I went to Ms. Vakil's apartment as darkness fell. I told her about my adventure but didn't admit to finding the papers or changing the address. I gave her the photos. Baba, I hoped her contact at the Spanish embassy wouldn't call her. But if they did, I wasn't afraid of her anger. I had fulfilled my promise. Mr. Verdi would probably never know who sent him the papers. Zahra's reaction when I returned empty-handed wasn't pleasant—but at least we had made a pretty penny.

In Ms. Vakil's house, I picked up the microphone for the last time to complete the story. Imagine, Baba, my scribblings and tapes will one day accompany those documents. Baba, you know a good story when you hear one. Who else could I share this magnificent story with if not you? One day, I will tell it to my grandchildren, though it's too dangerous to speak of now. As for me, Baba, you can rest. You need not hover over me or buzz advice in my ears. I have taken all your counsel to heart because you are wise. Now, go and rest where your fathers rest. Your son has a good start, a good wife, a generous father-in-law, a small fortune, the respect of the neighbors, and a corrupt government. What more could a man want? After I'm dead, someone will read what I've written about kings, princes and mullahs.

THE SURGEON ENDS ALL STORIES,
INCLUDING HIS OWN

"Either he is dead, or my watch has stopped."

Groucho Marx

On the ninth morning, after making a deal with Hamid to sign over my teahouse, I returned to my cell feeling great. The thought of leaving the next day had me practically whistling with joy. But then I heard Professor Dal whistling from his bunk. His whistle, though, was far from reassuring. A strange, gurgling sound came from deep in his chest, followed by labored breathing that ended in a weak whistle, almost like a comedian pretending to snore. I touched him on the shoulder to make sure he wasn't choking. He jumped up suddenly, like a jack-in-the-box.

"Right, ho. Time to go," he said, his voice thick with effort.

"Today's my turn to go," I replied. "You can rest."

"Rest?" he asked incredulously. "How can I rest? I need to produce the oil, or this country's going down the drain." He chuckled at his pun. "You get it, don't you? Down the drain? By the way, who are you? My new cellmate?"

I didn't answer. Even the most clueless people can learn something.

Then, in the middle of the room, he stood up naked. He looked more pathetic than when I had first seen him. He seemed like nothing but a skeleton. His large teeth stuck out from a mouth that had receded terribly. He would have fit right in with an anatomy textbook. His eye sockets were deep and hollow, and his blue eyes bulged like a fish in a bowl. His body had no muscle or fat; his pelvis was oddly shaped, like kidney pans. He grunted, making exaggerated facial gestures, trying to get his bowels and bladder to move. He threw his head back as though trying to push oil through every opening. But nothing came out. His eyes widened in surprise. He looked even more like a skeleton. He hunched down again and grunted as if trying to defecate. Again, nothing. Finally, he let out a high-pitched fart, longer than expected, and it ended with a pathetic, out-of-tune rumble, like a balloon losing air. Tears ran down his wrinkled face. He pointed to them. "All I can produce now is through my tears. This country is fucked. What will they do without my oil? I don't know who you are, young man, but you are one of the luckiest men alive."

"How so?" I asked.

He tapped his index finger to his nose. "Because, young man, you know we've run out. No one else knows," he said. "You've got a short time to make money from this information." Then he went back to bed, falling into an unhealthy, whistling sleep.

I spent the afternoon dreaming about what it would be like to leave this place. I imagined the different kinds of food I'd eat, visiting the public bath, sleeping in a clean bed. But then reality hit me. I had no money and no place to stay. I couldn't bring myself to visit the places I used to go in the bazaar. What was I going to do? In that space between fantasy and reality, I drifted off to sleep. The Professor's voice roused me from my doze in the dark.

"Boy, are you there?" he asked.

"I am, Arbab."

"I can't control my legs," he said. "Can you come and help me get to you? We've got some unfinished business."

I shuffled over to his bed and lifted him like a child, one hand supporting his head, the other under his knees. He weighed next to nothing. I sat on my bed, leaned against the wall, and cradled him as I had lifted him. I curled my legs up and held him more comfortably. His head lolled against my neck. I felt a deep pity for this man. He had loved one woman completely, selflessly. Just sharing space with her had been enough for him. Yet this man, who had let his youthful Nazi sympathies outweigh all his good deeds in the operating room, saw his ten years in this prison as his rightful punishment.

"I don't know what you're thinking about," he barked in my ear, his breath turning into something more menacing, "but I don't like it. Feel sorry for the dogs of the world, not for humans."

"I'm not feeling sorry at all. I'm overjoyed," I said. "They will let me out tomorrow."

"I bet I'll leave this place before you ever do." He laughed.

"They promised me," I replied.

"What deal did you make?" he asked.

"Nothing."

"Liar."

"I'm signing over the teahouse," I said.

"Good boy, nothing of substance. Your soul is intact," he said.

"It's everything I own, everything my father and grandfather left me. What am I going to do tomorrow, out on the streets?" I asked.

"Go find another tearoom. Live your life without fear of others. Haven't you learned anything from what I've told you? I've told you stories about the most powerful people—kings, grandees, opportunists, religious zealots and even the wisest men—all eating dirt and consumed by it. I must tell you more endings; I've exhausted all my beginnings."

The saddest time came a few years before I ended up in prison. I lived in my apartment, quietly, forgotten. Once full of life and laughter for seventy years, this house had begun to die the slow death of all neglected homes. Tari's death had destroyed any semblance of family life. Shortly after the funeral, Lili left for Paris, vowing never to return. Verdi returned to his boarding school in England to finish his secondary education. I lived in the house with Nima. He spent his days drinking, alone and desolate. We lived in separate wings. The old servants had found jobs with the nouveau riche, but a couple stayed on. They moved through the house like ghosts, bringing me my meals. I had become like the mad aunt in the attic of a novel. Nima and I rarely spoke, not out of anger or spite but because we had both lost interest in life. I would watch from my window, two floors up from where I am now, as Nima wandered in the overgrown garden. It was strange how a home could turn into a prison by someone's declaration.

One warm May night, I woke to a frantic knock from the servant who cared for me. "Agha, Agha, Sir! Please come quickly. Agha, Sir, looks in a bad way!" I took my time getting down to the first floor. I already knew what I would find. In the petit salon, where we once celebrated birthdays and family gatherings, I found Nima's head bent lifeless over the beautiful leather-topped desk, surrounded by a pool of vomit. He had drunk weed killer. It had burned through his esophagus and stomach lining, causing a pain-fully drawn-out death. Yet, not a sound had escaped to alert anyone to the agony he had endured. His bloated, greenish face bore no resemblance to the handsome young man he once was. The weight he had put on had obscured any trace of his former athletic build. He was just a middle-aged man now, his body and mind decaying while I grew old in my room. We had all seen Nima's kindness and natural charm in every interaction. *Tout le monde l'aimait, mais personne ne se souciait de lui,* Lili had said. "Everyone loved him, but no one worried about him. Not even us."

Looking at photos of old men compared to their childhood pictures doesn't affect me much. I see two entirely different people: a child and an old man. But seeing the heartbreaking transfor-mation from youth to middle age is something else. You witness promise corrupted, the youth trapped inside a decaying shell. Nima's photographs looked like distorted perversions of what he once was. When did Nima lose his youthful, willowy look? When did the weight come on? It appeared on his shoulders like heavy, sloping cushions over baggy shirts. The added pounds kept his face tight and shiny, like he had undergone multiple facelifts. In his youth, his eyes were like black pools of sensitivity. Now they were hidden behind puffy slits, giving him a mean appearance, though he was never mean. He had been the kindest, most generous man I had ever known. The puffiness came from drinking, and the drinking was his way of coping with depression. We knew so little about depression back then. Lili would have said, "He has nothing to be depressed about."

I had wept for him long before his death. When I found him he had already been gone for years. The slow disintegration of everything he had once believed in, the moral decay he had suffered and the humiliations he endured were almost too much to bear. Lili's unforgiving glare when he told her of Tari's death was more than he could handle. All mothers blame their husbands for the death of their children, tracing every tiny detail back to when the father might have pushed the child to take risks. Nima had pushed Tari, but he had always been cautious with Verdi. When a child dies, someone must be blamed.

Nima didn't leave a note. I called in a favor from an old medical student, now a well-known doctor, who diagnosed a heart attack as the cause of death. It was unnecessary subterfuge, for the daily newspaper only ran a brief two-line notice and the court remained silent. I called Lili in Paris to inform her. "Please take care of him, as you always have," she said. "I'll let Verdi know at his boarding school. He now carries our family's name." Her voice was abrupt, devoid of warmth. I remembered how kind she had been to young Nima when his father died in Switzerland. Now, a brief phone call to her son would be enough to announce his father's death.

I never spoke to Lili again. She died in a skiing accident in Chamonix, caught in a freak avalanche. The French press made more of her death than our press had of Nima's suicide. *Paris Match* paraded old photos of her with the Shah from the 1950s and 60s. A part of Lili would always belong to the French. With both parents dead, Verdi decided to forgo university and took charge of his modest inheritance with great determination. He could have had a successful career, but the religious Alaric soon disrupted our lives. I move quickly through the deaths of the Poonaki family, my comfortable floating coffin, for I've already foretold these deaths through the stories I've shared with you. But the death of the Prince carried far more weight for us—the Poonakis and the country. It was 1938, dear boy. Imagine a cell like this one, perhaps larger or smaller. I never saw it. A telegram arrived from The Prince's secretary:

RETURN IMMEDIATELY STOP THE PRINCE ARRESTED BY REZA SHAH STOP SERIOUS SITUATION STOP THE CROWN PRINCE CANNOT HELP.

It wasn't the first time the Prince had been imprisoned. Reza Shah, the founder of the Pahlavi dynasty, had long held a particular affection for the Prince, who had been kind to him during his early Cossack days. However, now Reza Shah had arrested him to display his authority. There were no hard feelings between them, but Reza Shah had changed. By then, he had already murdered four of his closest allies—men who had helped him rise to and maintain power. The secretary's concern was justified, for this arrest seemed tied to Reza Shah's increasing paranoia about nonexistent political rivals. The Crown Prince had attempted to mediate, but now he sent a message acknowledging his own helplessness. At fifty-three, the Prince sat in prison, feeling at least twenty years older. He had endured too much chaos, greed and disillusionment. He had witnessed the exile of two Shahs—his detested nephew and his innocent grandnephew—and had seen the Qajar dynasty pass with little regret. He had supported the rise of the new Pahlavi dynasty, but as a conservative at heart, he could not bear to oversee the abolition of 2,500 years of monarchy.

"Would Your Highness like some tea?" Nemat, his servant, would ask through the small opening in the door.

"No, thank you. Go to the house and fetch me a blanket. It's getting cold. Winter is upon us earlier than I expected."

"Yes, Your Highness. I'll be back by lunchtime."

Already October? Just three days earlier, the head of the Tehran police had driven by the garden and knocked at the door. They sat down to tea. The officer explained his orders, speaking with evident embarrassment. "Not my first time," the Prince said, fully aware of the recent arrests and the reported deaths. Few had left the prison alive in recent months. Sitting alone in his cell, The Prince missed his garden. He imagined the leaves on the ground, sticking to the soles of people's shoes. As children, he and his brother had played in the garden, removing their shoes to peel the leaves off one another's soles. They would press the prettiest ones between the pages of their Larousse dictionary. The Prince never recovered from the death of his brother the year before. It was an open wound that could only be healed by their reunion. He sighed often, lost in his longing to join his brother. With war looming in Europe, the Prince disagreed with Reza Shah's increasing ties to Germany. He saw no future in opposing Russia and England. But he kept his counsel to himself, knowing that Reza Shah would see any advice as a challenge to his authority. The Prince had withdrawn, retreating to his country house in Poonak to care for his fruit trees. He opened a book to read Oscar Wilde's *The Ballad of Reading Gaol*. Prince Firouz had translated this very book in the same cell before they strangled him in prison on Reza Shah's orders. Reza Shah's killing of Firouz had completed the elimination of the four men who had helped him seize the throne. The Prince pondered a line from Wilde's poem: "And all but lust is turned to dust in humanity's machine." He closed the book. The word lust captured a passion for life, a desire to matter. Had he mattered? Had he helped make change happen, or had he simply been a cog in the machine, ground to dust like the rest?

Sheikh Nouri had described him as a man driven by anger twenty-eight years before. The Prince had visited the Sheikh in this very prison. On their third and final visit, they met during the summer. Their first meeting had been a careful exchange, each assessing the other in a world both understood. In their second meeting, they had unknowingly found themselves in the eye of a storm. The Sheikh, confident of his power, had continued his uncompromising sit-in at the grand mosque, weaving plots within plots. As the civil war ended, they had played all their cards. Beneath the surface of all the celebrations, the factions had shifted to serve the new stakeholders. The victorious armies from the northern and southern provinces had little understanding of the capital's life, let alone the inner workings of a court in disarray. The swift fall of Mohammad Ali Shah shocked both Russia and Britain. Mohammad Ali Mirza, a demoted king, kept his life.

Meanwhile, the democrats, whispering of a republic, had made both the Russian czar and colonial Britain uncomfortable. The court and its reactionaries, now in disarray, included a few reasonable men who still supported the monarchy. After a year of humiliation, the Prince found himself at the center of these conflicting factions, courted by all sides. He laughed softly. "Suddenly, the English came to my house like old friends, and the Russians sidled up to me at court without shame. Those proud Bahktiari peasants needed lessons in etiquette. And the armies from the provinces—victorious but clueless—ran through the streets, making everyone's lives miserable. They needed food." He quoted with relish: "One day you sit on a saddle; the next day you carry the saddle on your back." The Prince took great pleasure in negotiating for Mohammad Ali Mirza's exile. He never referred to him as "Shah." "The ex-Shah stayed in the Russian embassy," he said. " I am generous but enjoyed driving a hard bargain with him. We got back the crown jewels. I imagine the Russians wanted us to pay his debts with them. Don't misunderstand, though. He received a generous pension. As usual, he broke his word and tried to reclaim the throne. He forfeited his pension. He was so convinced of his divine right to rule that he would accuse the Almighty of breaking His promise. I split hairs over every demand he made. We questioned his representatives until we nearly came to blows." Years later, the Prince's eyes sparkled when discussing his revenge. He had reduced the ex-Shah's pension as much as he could. "I did it all for my brother, you know," he said. "But you know what? I also did it for myself. I could never forgive him for the bastinado in Tabriz." Then he slapped me on the back with a hearty laugh.

The Prince took no pleasure in seeing Sheikh Nouri in prison.

He volunteered, but not out of cruelty. He thought that informing a man of his death sentence should be done as humanely as possible. A nine-judge panel had found Nouri guilty of causing the deaths of four people. Though the concept of a "friend of the court" was foreign, the twenty-five-year-old Prince had performed his duty. He met with members of the committee and repeatedly told them of the Sheikh's danger to the country's stability and his tendency to break his word. Nouri had caused harm and death to many innocent people. By the time of the Shah's abdication, Sheikh Nouri had few friends left. The clergy disliked him for his high-handedness; even one of his sons agreed with the execution order. The Prince believed Sheikh Nouri was a far more dangerous man than the ex-Shah. The ex-Shah was unintelligent and lacked vision; he desired to rule in the autocratic style of his ancestors. He had overreached and the forces of change had overwhelmed him. The Sheikh, on the other hand, was no reactionary. He had played the most revolutionary hand of anyone and for the highest stakes. He had desired a fundamentalist society, but he had lost for a time.

The Prince, mindful of protocol, sent word ahead of his intention to visit the Sheikh. He entered the prison with a severe face. The Sheikh, thinner than before, looked like an ordinary merchant without his turban. The Prince used to say, "Don't remove a man's headgear if you prefer to keep a high opinion of him."

"Welcome to my humble abode, Prince. Why the glum face?" Sheikh Nouri asked. "Who died?" The Prince said nothing.

"Ah, I see," the Sheikh said. "By what method?"

"Public hanging," the Prince replied.

"Public. Do you think I will serve as an example? My friends tell me you did your utmost to make it possible."

"For all it's worth," the Prince said, "I didn't want it to be public."

"Do you find me as dangerous as that? Are you prepared to go down as the man who executed the first mujahid in our country's history? I have that privilege, you know. Are you ready to open your family, your descendants, to the charge of mullahcide?"

"Sheikh, I don't know about the privilege, but you've caused much unnecessary harm to this country. I don't deny my role in your sentence. The committee was unanimous. Your colleagues in Atabat, living in Iraq, consented." He didn't mention that the Sheikh's son had agreed with the execution; he saw it as unnecessary cruelty.

"You give me too much credit," the Sheikh said. "My colleagues give me too little. If those colleagues had given me what was due, I might not have been as obtrusive. Your Highness, from boyhood, no one could compete with my religious learning. Yet the Almighty saw fit to make me a jealous one. This jealousy," he waved his hand vaguely, "when it rages in me, it takes control. Every time I read or heard the praises of Sheikh Behbehani or Tabataba'i, it left me in a rage. What can I say, but God willed it so." He smiled gently at his confession.

"Sheikh, are you saying all those sit-ins, all the beatings your people meted out and all the pain inflicted on the constitutionalists all arose from your jealousy of your two colleagues?"

"Don't be so dense, man," the Sheikh snapped. "God placed this one crack in me so that when the time came, I would have the grit, the long-term courage, to carry out His work."

"And what work would that be?" The Prince asked.

"Go read your constitution," the Sheikh said. "I have planted the seed of heaven within your godless document. Could I have stayed the course if this imperfect, unreasonable emotion didn't overtake me? And look at you, despite your outward logic, you run on," he hesitated, searching for the word, "I would say, anger. Yes, you don't have an ounce of jealousy. Your engine runs on the fuel of anger."

The vein in the Prince's neck pulsed. "That seed of heaven you claim to have planted has been uprooted. No one pays it heed. Do you see any laws going to the ulama for approval? Your colleagues in parliament killed it. If I have any, my descendants will be proud of the document my brother and I helped write. I will do my best to warn them against your dangerous thinking."

"You and I do anger well with each other, don't we?" the Sheikh asked sweetly. "Don't be angry with a man you will kill shortly."

"Please forgive my outburst," the Prince said. "You and I think as differently as a table and a chair."

"True," the Sheikh said. "Remember, Your Highness, the seed of a tree takes years to take root. Time is on my side." He gave a dry laugh. "Well, not quite on my side. Will I see you tomorrow?"

"Yes," the Prince replied.

"If Your Highness would bid me goodbye now, I must write letters. I will not send you in peace nor forgive you. I prefer us to remain enemies. You will be in my thoughts and letters."

"The quality of our enemies judges us, Your Grace," the Prince said. He remembered the unease he felt leaving the prison. The Sheikh's threats were real. Years later, he would sit in jail, deeply worried for his son and niece, even though the danger of a religious surge had ebbed. He worried more about his son's careless, open-hearted generosity than some long-ignored article in the constitution.

The next day, the population witnessed the first hanging of a religious grandee. The first time always brings discomfort to those involved. Everyone hoped that Sheikh Nouri's hanging would set an example for the other clerics. A large crowd gathered at Toupkouneh Square. The Sheikh faced his death bravely. People said he even kissed the rope, but the Prince told me nothing like that happened. The Sheikh said, "On the Day of Judgment, these men"—he pointed directly at the Prince—"will answer to me for this." He pointed to the rope. "I was never a reactionary, nor did I embrace the constitutionalism of Sayyed Behbahani and Sayyed Tabataba'i," he said. "It was merely that they wished to better me, and I them."

The Prince could never get over the Sheikh's statement. Throughout our lives together, he would shake his head and say, "Beneath a noble deed flows a sea of misguided intentions."

Sheikh Nouri may have heard his eldest son at the foot of the gallows urging the national volunteers to bring this sad business to a speedy end. He recited these words: "If we were a heavy burden, we are gone; if we were unkind, we are gone." The crowd, clearly against him, cheered. "Do your work," he told his executioners. When the rope tightened, his turban fell from his head. The photo of him swaying is indistinguishable from any other robber or murderer. The Prince did away with the custom of leaving the body to rot as a warning to the wise. He ordered the body brought down within minutes. The family, grateful for the favor, removed it for cleaning and anointing. A group of seminary students watched the Prince with unadulterated hate.

In prison now, he recognized the irony. No one remembered their private feud centered on principle on his side, driven by vanity on the Sheikh's side. Would vanity defeat principle in the end? The Prince did not trust his ability to foresee the future. A chilly draft brought the Prince out of his reverie. Where was Nemat with the blanket? He should have opted for the tea instead. He heard the clanging of locks and keys. "Thank God you are back," he said. Then: "Who are you?" He peered at a large man standing in the half-open door. The man, respectful, stayed in the corner, his hands clasped before his crotch, eyes downcast. "Your Highness, my name is Ahmad the Six-Fingered," he said. The Prince involuntarily looked down at Ahmad's hands. Ahmad, not self-conscious, raised both enormous hands to show the extra digit hanging loosely next to each of his pinkies. "They don't do much, Your Highness. They get in the way of work," Ahmad said. The sound of the muezzin calling the midday prayer echoed into the cell.

"Do I have time to pray?" the Prince asked. Ahmad was well-known in the prison as the executioner of several other grandees, which left no doubt about his mission.

"You do, Your Highness," Ahmad replied, touched.

The Prince stood up. Ahmad held the ewer so he could wash his hands. The Prince completed his ablutions, unfolded his silk rug, and handed Ahmad some money. He placed the prayer stone at the head of the rug, where he put his head and kneeled before God. He heard Nemat's voice greeting the guard outside. The guard stopped him from entering the building. Nemat began questioning the guard, trying to understand the difficulty of delivering a warm blanket to his master. The Prince kneeled and mouthed the last words of the midday prayer. Nemat began to scream and cry. "What are you doing to my master? You are killing him. Don't kill him, please. Are you not humans? Master, are you there? Master?" The Prince felt the useless sixth fingers fall on his clavicles. The grip around his neck tightened so fast that it may have made him think of how women deal with chickens. I imagine his last thoughts: "Where can I find my brother?"

"I received the official telegram the same day as the one from The Prince's secretary," the Professor said, now a whisper. His breath barely touched my neck. "It said:

THE PRINCE DIED OF NATURAL CAUSES, A HEART ATTACK, STOP NO NEED TO INTERRUPT STUDIES STOP FULL STATE FUNERAL STOP REZA SHAH PRAISES HIS SERVICE TO THE NATION STOP.

Professor Dal brought me out of my teary state. "My boy," he said, his voice hoarse. He nuzzled closer to my ear, and I felt his eyelashes brushing my cheeks. "You have listened. Understanding the dust side of the equation will take you a lifetime. You will leave this prison in a few hours to live your life. If you keep stories like the ones I told you, you will keep the Prince, the Poonakis, and me alive. Before I could get angry with him—for he had again insulted my father and grandfather, though he captured their philosophy so well in his last words—his eyelashes stopped brushing my neck. His head fell most distinctly upon his chest, leaning against mine. It fell so heavily that I thought I heard his neck crack. I lifted him into the middle of the cell. The red rays of the early sun had cleared the top of the cell's half window. In the middle, I stood a 300-pound piece of lard, my shirt off in the heat, my prisoner trousers revealing my thick calves. The skeleton of an old man with long white hair encircling his bald head shone in the redness of sunlight, cradled in my arms like a newborn feeding on my droopy breasts. I wanted to shit, piss and vomit all at the same time in his honor. Instead, I shed silent tears. They ran down my cheeks unchecked.

CAN A NARRATOR DIE?

'When my head is off, set it on this plate and have it press down firm upon the powder to stop the bleeding. After that open the book. The least of the secrets being this: when my head is off, you turn three pages of the book, then read three lines upon the left hand page, my severed head will speak and answer any manner of question.'

One Thousand Nights and One Night

Dear Ms. Vakil,

With sadness, I write these final words, marking the end of our correspondence. As promised, I have delivered all the historical documents, and now I pen these last pages, which contain nothing of historical significance. Whether you choose to read them is entirely up to you. What happened to a man who, throughout countless pages, has detailed every aspect of his family's history and the most intimate parts of his life but has never revealed the core of the pain he endured during the 200 hours of incarceration I suffered in my own home at the age of twenty-two? Life, as it often does, passes by without leaving much to mark one day from the next. Most weeks blur into one another without distinction, and I liken it to a stylus smoothly gliding across the grooves of an old vinyl record. It produces beautiful, even great music. Then, suddenly, a child, with playful disregard, lifts the record arm and repeatedly scratches the vinyl back and forth. No matter how fine the music once was, those scratches ruin it forever. For those of us who've experienced it, these sharp moments, the peaks, over-shadow everything else. We live the rest of our lives hearing only fragments of what was once whole. I've recounted these scratches on my brother's, my parents', my grandparents', and my vinyl. We have had our share, you'd agree.

I must face those nine nights. Unlike my maternal grandfather, I do not possess the mental mechanism to lock such memories away, to exile them into some deep crevice and cordon them off. I relive it all again as a form of retribution for the one indulgent moment that ended my brother's life on the rocks of the Alborz mountains. You be the judge.

Unsurprisingly, my favorite constitutional protection in my adopted United States is the Eighth Amendment—the notion that punishment should fit the crime. With few exceptions, ordinary citizens are exempt from torture, no matter their alleged crimes. I reflect on that now as I relive what happened to me. Imagine, if you will, the first night. The servants' room in the basement bore no resemblance to Professor Dal's quarters, which he occupied for ten long years. I met him during my miserable evenings when they tormented us both. The room was ordinary, with a door and an old-fashioned keyhole locked from the outside. Upgrades to proper cells with thick, secure doors would come later. I could see the third pavilion-like house from the half-window in my room. In my cell, a familiar room without furniture, they left a few remnants of my childhood: a broken balsa wood airplane and a soccer ball. It all disappeared by the morning. The first night passed uneventfully, save for a tiny detail. It suggested deliberation on their part: they provided me with prison garb—striped pajamas and plastic sandals.

I felt a vain aversion to those sandals; It epitomized my captors. They held the keys to power—and my cell. A polite voice came from the door, asking me to leave my clothes outside to be collected when they served dinner. Dinner, I thought? Was my jailer a disgruntled butler? These seemingly trivial details underscore the calculation behind it all. Remember, chaos had ruled in the early months of the revolution. Like all revolutions, the new regime dealt with emergencies with entrepreneurial efficiency. What was happening in my house felt like a preemptive, well-thought-out operation. Yet, on that first night, none of this registered. I must describe my state of mind. What do we truly mean by the word "privileged"? When steeped in privilege for generations, it seeps into the core of your being. You may call it arrogance, but it's an undeniable trait, etched into you over time. This arrogance, this unshakable sense of entitlement, fueled my resistance when the torturers tried to force me to sign away my possessions. It wasn't bravery. No, it was simply an ingrained sense of entitlement. They needed more than a few quick bursts of applied stress to break this deeply embedded sense of privilege. I resisted, but I was no match for them. Within days, these experts sculpted a new person out of me. That person, the one they created, has remained with me for the rest of my life. Ah, but I circle to avoid the heart of it.

The next day, two young men escorted me from my cell. I had no idea what awaited me. They led me to a familiar room in the basement. It had once been old Nemat's—he had the seniority to claim the largest room. The room had no windows, and the concrete walls amplified sound, ensuring no one outside would hear a thing. Two bureaucratic men sat behind a small table; their mustaches distinct. They were like Dupont and Dupond from the *Tintin* comics, the mustaches crucial for identification. They sat me in front of them and questioned me. They asked about my background and family. They aimed to link us to the Shah's regime as closely as possible, not a difficult task, as you can imagine.

After a few hours of often repeated questions, they left the room. I sat with Hamid, who sat in the corner silently. They returned with a pile of papers. "Please sign these," one of the men said. "They're in triplicate, so don't miss any." They assured me they'd allow me to return to my room if I signed. I asked if I could read the documents, and they replied indifferently. I read through them: powers of attorney, giving control of my affairs to unknown religious foundations in Qom. They stipulated transferring all my property to causes I'd never heard of, but the phrase "without undue pressure from anyone" caught my eye. I refused to sign. My refusal didn't surprise them. The man tied me to the chair with rope—one length for each arm and leg—and I noticed the design of the chair accommodated the restraints. The man across from me began rolling up his sleeves, preparing for what would come next. With deliberate movements, he cracked his knuckles and stretched his neck. He slapped me—a lazy, meaty slap. The shock of it was jarring. I'd never been hit in the face before. At first, I thought, "It hurts, but it's not a big deal." But before I could process the thought, his other hand struck me, and then again, over and over. I started to black out. Through the haze, the other, younger man asked, "Are you tired, Habib Jan?

"I can use some help," Habib said. As I grew more familiar with their method, I understood the message. They could switch places indefinitely, but I couldn't endure that long. They swapped positions. One of them had to steady the chair from behind. The younger man mimicked the other's movements to the smallest detail, rolling his sleeves up on his much thicker, hairier arms. His first slap overwhelmed my senses. The second slap landed from the left. What were the odds of two ambidextrous torturers? I begged them to stop, as I couldn't imagine enduring many more hits. But he didn't stop. I soon realized this was also part of their routine. Once the cycle began, they wouldn't listen to my pleas. They focused solely on completing tasks like bodybuilders in a gym pushing each other to continue.

If you're a fan of Bond films, you might remember *Diamonds Are Forever*, with the two thugs, Mr. Kidd and Mr. Wint. My torturers looked more handsome, but the dynamic felt eerily similar. How long it went on, I cannot say. They never once asked me about signing the documents again. They just kept striking my face until I could no longer feel it. They slapped, me, not with enough force to throw me on the floor. but methodically.. My teeth loosened and bled continuously, to the point where I nearly choked on my blood.

If I started to choke, they'd stop, gently lower my head, and let the blood flow. One would even rub my head softly, like a mother comforting a sick child. When my neck felt like it might snap from being thrown side to side, they stopped and discussed soccer scores as if nothing extraordinary was happening. They seemed to know the limits of the human body. At some point in the afternoon, I blacked out. They tipped the chair backward—it was probably designed for that purpose—and I lay with my feet facing upward. Then, they began beating my soles with a doubled-up cable. I heard myself begging for forgiveness, though I couldn't explain for what. I told them it wasn't my fault, though I didn't know what I was denying. I promised to do anything they asked, even agreeing to sign the documents. I called out to Hamid to intervene, begging him for mercy. Anything to stop the pain, anything to get a moment of rest, a chance to remember who I was.

The two youths came in around late afternoon, got under my armpits, and dragged me back through the corridor to my cell. I saw Professor Dal dragged past me. I wasn't hallucinating that first day. I don't know how long I lay there before I became aware of someone rubbing ointment into the soles of my feet. I could barely speak, my swollen jaw so large, I could not see past it. Then, someone fed me broth through my clenched teeth. I opened my eyes, half-conscious, to see Hamid caring for me. A wave of self-pity washed over me. My head was resting on his lap, and I clung to his thighs, pleading for him not to leave me alone. He complied, crawling into the bunk beside me and holding me tightly in his arms. He spoke to me softly, told me he loved me, kissed my ears repeatedly and promised to do everything he could to save me. We talked in whispers, like old lovers. Despite the pain in my face and feet, I fell asleep in his arms.

The second day, I woke groggy and alone. My face weighed a ton. I thought I had slept with thick shoes until I saw my bare feet. I swung them around and tried to place them on the floor, but my body instinctively recoiled from the pain that awaited me. The same two youths came in, supporting me as I hung between them. I tried to keep my feet off the floor, but they helped me as we walked to the same room as before. The two men sat behind the desk, as they had the previous day, and asked about my health, glancing at Hamid. They repeated the questions from the day before, writing down my answers with the same careful attention. After a while, they left. Hamid stayed seated, unmoving. The lipless one came back with the sheaf of papers, fanning them in front of me as he had before. "I don't believe you need to reread them, do you?" he said. A choreographed routine with a tiny difference: Hamid sat across the room, now in a different role. His presence comforted me. I silently hoped for his intervention. But I refused to sign the papers. They exchanged a brief, understanding glance. They showed no emotion as they instructed me to strip. "Everything, please," the lipless one said. I took off my prison pajamas. They tied my hands with rope, wrapping it tightly and neatly. Then they asked me to stand on the chair. I did so with difficulty. They assisted me, and the older man followed me up. He grabbed my arms and pushed them upward. That's when I noticed the heavy meat hook hanging from the ceiling. He placed the rope around my hand and hooked it. Before I could comprehend the situation, the man stepped off the chair, supporting my weight, while the other one pulled the chair out from under my feet.

My mind focused on survival, and my body instinctively reacted to the relief of having my soles dangled in the air, my toes brushing the floor. But then the realization hit: my body weight pulled on my shoulders, and the pressure increased. The bureaucrats prepared something. Seconds stretched into eternity. I heard the distinct sound of a high-velocity object whistling through the air. A stiff, rubbery, thick whip lashed across my midsection, and then it wrapped around me. The searing burn of it continued even after it unwrapped from my body. I looked down, expecting to see blood, but I saw only a darkening gray hue spreading across my torso. As I glanced up, the older man's left hand moved again with the same slow, deliberate motion. He delivered two quick strokes, each unfolding the horrors of what I was about to endure. In those two strokes, my mind understood something terrible: no matter how quickly I signed the documents, they would not stop. I would have to endure the pain. My brain processed it all in an instant, and I screamed. They waited until I regained consciousness. How they knew when I can't say. I knew better than to betray that I was awake by opening my eyes. They switched places, whipping me from head to toe. I watched gray ridges form across my body like thin wires had been routed under my skin. The lacerations didn't bleed. I could feel my shoulders popping out of their sockets, one at a time. I blacked out from the pain.

This, Ms. Vakil, marked the beginning of my first tentative exploration into yoga, though I had no name for it then. When extreme pain overwhelms the body, the "I" in the mind splits. One part desperately searches for relief, while another observes the suffering "I," trying to find a way to lessen the pain. On that day, my second "I" tried to distract the first by retreating into a memory of calmer times. I focused on the nights I'd spent gazing at the stars with my grandfather at our country house. The continuity and calmness of life, the oneness of it all, gave me a sense of peace. At some point, they cut me down from the hook. I lay flat on my back, my body heavy and aching. The younger one grabbed my hand, twisted it painfully, and placed his shoe on my shoulder. I screamed. In a quiet, confident voice, he assured me he wouldn't hurt me further that day. And, unbelievably, I believed him. He twisted my shoulder back into place with a sharp motion, then did the same with the other.

I awoke in my cell to find Hamid at my side, rubbing ointment into my wounds. "Tomorrow," he said, "you must sign. You can't resist them. These two are the best of the SAVAK, the Shah's secret police. The Americans trained them for years."

"Help me," I pleaded. "Tell them to stop. I am not guilty of anything."

"I can't help you until you sign," he said. "Once you do, I'll see how I can get you out. I'll arrange for you to leave the country—Europe, America. You can't stay here anymore." He fed me more broth, as he had the night before. I fell asleep on his lap, listening to the soft glow of his cigarette as it burned brightly the outer edges of the paper in the dark. I heard the door open, and the next thing I knew, I was seated in front of the desk with the fanned-out document before me. A pen floated in the air right in front of my eyes. I shook my head in disbelief. The pen fell with a loud thud onto the papers. I was confused—why had they not allowed me to sign? My hands and feet were bound, but when? I tried to think. Yesterday? No, the day before.

I felt the thick leather belt secured around my head, anchoring me to the chair. They upended the chair again, my feet in the air, my back pressed to the floor. Then, the memory of the beating on my soles resurfaced. Was it two days ago? My brain, independent of my will, screamed. After a few moments, I stopped because no one was beating my feet. I heard the men discussing the day's schedule. It struck me that the older bureaucrat seemed to disagree with the plan. My heart pounded against the constriction of my pajama top, my eyes darting nervously from side to side. Despite immobilizing my head, I could see an ordinary tin ewer used to water our garden. I remembered a summer morning when Nadali, our old gardener, carried two large ewers. One at a time, he dipped them into the swimming pool. As the last gurgle of water signaled that each was full, he lifted the heavy vessels to water the plants with a shower-like spout.

The younger man dragged the large ewer toward me. Hamid handed him a hose connected to a brass faucet mounted on the wall in the corner of the room. I remembered grazing my shin on that faucet years ago while running from my brother in the sanctuary of Nemat's room. The hose began to fill the ewer. I heard the tinny echo of water hitting the bottom, then a change in pitch as the vessel filled. It warned me of some impending cruelty. The younger man pinched my nostrils, pinning them tight with his thumb and forefinger. I opened my mouth, and he stuffed a towel-like material in it. He shoved it deeper, causing me to gag. Then he inserted cotton wool into each of my nostrils, pushing more into my nasal passages with his pinky until tears welled up from the pain. The sensation was like what a doctor might do after a nose job, packing the nose while the patient was under anesthesia. I could still breathe through the sides of my mouth because the towel-like material was porous. But with each breath, panic set in. I couldn't get enough air. Habib, the older man, brought a chair and positioned it so that my head, still on the floor, was aligned with the middle of the chair's front legs. He sat, and I saw his legs and crotch above me. He lifted the ewer and placed it between his legs, balancing the bottom on the chair. Slowly, he poured a few drops of water onto my face, adjusted the chair, and poured a few more. The process continued. He glanced up at his friend, inviting him to pay attention. Water poured endlessly over my face.

Ms. Vakil, you likely know how news outlets have covered waterboarding in recent years. It's not a new method. It's been practiced from the Spanish Inquisition to today, and in the early twentieth century, they knew it as "water curing." It may sound like a relaxing spa treatment, like one might receive in Baden-Baden: "A day of water curing will cleanse the liver wonderfully, and it will do the patient good," they might say. But when they used it on me, it was anything but. The younger man pinched my cheeks between ewer refills to give me a moment to breathe. But let me say this clearly, Ms. Vakil: Anyone who defends waterboarding as a form of aggressive interrogation should try it for a full day. Many have died under less skilled hands than my torturers'. No one can describe the sensation. The water continuously pours over the towel and cotton, clogging the material and stopping all airflow. It is suffocating. It's like drowning—running out of oxygen, desperately trying to reach the surface, but you never get there. It's like a nightmare you can't escape unless you black out. But even when you black out, it's not relief. It's a terrible way to die slowly, only to wake up to it again, and again, and again. The panic, the primal terror of imminent death, is what gets you. Then, when you black out, you come to, and it starts all over again. There's no escape. In these moments, the strategy I once used—retreating into a separate "I" to observe the pain—didn't work. It wasn't just physical pain. It was panic and fear for my life. Pain, when pushed to such extremes, becomes something else. Under this kind of torture, they assault the most basic human instinct: survival. That day, I passed out from suffocation nearly a dozen times. The Islamic Republic no longer uses this method, but it remains an effective tool. Water curing leaves no marks, which is an advantage for governments that prefer to avoid evidence. For countries like the United States, this makes it harder to prove, while for benighted countries like ours, physical damage is much more effective for control.

Back in my cell, I recovered quickly from the physical effects, though I reeled from the beatings of the previous days. Hamid spent the night with me again. The next day, they repeated the process: dragged, seated, questioned, and offered the pen. I refused to sign. Stripped, bound and upended, I waited for the next round—whether it would be the traditional beatings or something more abstract like water curing. I could see the two men's trousers as they stood with their backs to me, busy at the table. I heard metal clanking. Hamid sat on his haunches against the wall, watching me. "What are they doing?" I asked, my voice hoarse. A vision of my childhood came to me. I remember my mother took me to a doctor as a boy. She stood beside me as I lay on the examination table. I could see down my body where my navel and penis aligned. I saw the back of the doctor's white coat between my knees. I heard the quiet roar of a flame as he prepared something. I saw him lift his hand, and to my delight, a jet of liquid shot into the air. I laughed, and my mother laughed with me. But then the doctor turned and held up a metal syringe, the needle protruding threateningly between his fingers. My brain immediately processed the thumb positioned to push the needle into me. I snapped back to the present as I heard the breathing of a gas flame in the room. I saw the gleaming piece of metal in the younger man's hand. Before I could comprehend what it was, he used it to burn across my right toenail. The searing pain shot through my leg and body, snapping me back to full consciousness. He held my ankle as support and twisted a pair of heavy pliers back and forth until my toenail ripped off. The effort was evident on his face, though the nail came off easily, like pulling apart a stick of gum, with a satisfying sound.

Ms. Vakil, I've been told I'm lucky—denailing dates back centuries. European Christians used to insert a sharp wedge of wood between the nail and flesh, hammering it in until the nail separated. They took their time with me, wanting me to remain conscious. Afterward, they asked Hamid, pale as the walls behind him, to hose me down and give me as much water as needed. They weren't trying to dehydrate me. I needed to develop more complex strategies to cope with this stage. I tried to focus on memories of pleasant evenings, but all I could hear were my screams. It felt as though a series of "I"s formed within me: one "I" struggled, another "I" observed from a distance. Would you laugh if I told you that the third "I" imagined resting my head on my fourth-grade teacher, Mrs. Doustan's chest, as I watched horrors perpetrated on one of me?

"Why didn't you sign?" Hamid asked me later. "I thought we had agreed." I couldn't answer him. I couldn't even talk. "I was going to sign," I wanted to say, but my head shook in refusal. "Why don't they offer me the choice of signing while I'm wide awake? Why don't they ask me to sign every five minutes like in the movies?" But I couldn't form the words. And deep down, I already knew the answer: If I refused to cooperate, I would face another day of torture.

Hamid brought Mercurochrome, a topical antiseptic, to prevent infection. He applied it lightly with a brush, but I could feel every hair. Finally, he poured the yellow-orange liquid directly over my toes. That night, my body went into shock. As I trembled, the bed shook violently. Hamid brought in two more blankets, tied a cloth around my head to stop my teeth from chattering, and held me close, sitting on the bed. I leaned against him, going in and out of consciousness—or sleep—throughout the night. At five o'clock on the morning of the fifth day, I woke to the door closing as Hamid left my cell. The noise of hammers and saws started up.

My new injuries made the slapping from the first day seem harmless. I woke feeling like I had just come out of anesthesia after a major surgery. There was no question of moving, yet my mind was strangely clear. The question that plagued me was: What was Hamid's role in all of this? He had told me he worked for some of the most influential figures in the newly formed Islamic Republic. He even hinted that he had access to the imam himself. I laughed weakly. Through clenched teeth, I said, "I haven't seen the twelfth imam's return. Which one of the twelve are you talking about?" He didn't take the bait. When he heard about my imminent arrest, he wanted to take control of the operation, claiming it was for my benefit. But I couldn't help but ask myself the obvious question: if Hamid had access, how could he have stood by while they tortured me endlessly for days? His relationship with my two torturers seemed odd. On the surface, he appeared to be helping me, bringing me water, and cooling me down when they ordered him to. But I started to wonder if he was the one giving the orders.

As dawn broke through the narrow window of my cell, I noticed that the two men looked to him before starting their work each day. They sought his approval before they moved. It became clear: Hamid had been playing me all along. I had been the patsy. The rule is simple—if you don't know who the patsy is, you are it. How could I have been so naïve? How else did he come into my room each night? My weakened state had clouded my judgment. My desperate need for some psychological comfort each night had made me blind to the strange dynamics at play. This realization only deepened my pain. The injustice of it all suffocated me as if they had stripped away my existence with no appeal. It was as though the screen in my mind was shutting down, reducing everything to a tiny point of light, ready to go out. Time seemed to slow down as I sank further into the dark abyss of my thoughts. As the first light of day touched my cell, self-righteous anger surged. Anger, I knew, keeps people alive. It doesn't heal, but it preserves. It brought my ego back to life. I would fight to the death. I will show them. Anger, however righteous, brought more pain. When they entered the room, I begged them to drag me backward instead of forward. The thought of having my broken feet dragged across the floor was unbearable. Clotted blood, hardened and dry, held together with the sticky remnants of Mercurochrome covered each toe. It was a grotesque sight, and I feared that if they dragged me too hard, my skin would tear open, starting the blood flowing once more.

As they dragged me through the corridors, I saw workers building smaller, more secure cells in the basement. The lipless man fanned out a set of documents before me, his eyes gleaming with pride like a poker player at a felt-covered table. It was a sleight-of-hand move, and I saw through it for a moment. My indignation swelled, and it didn't go unnoticed. Both men saw the change in my demeanor. "My apologies, Habib," the younger one muttered to his partner. "It won't happen again." It was clear that the young torturer had made a mistake, letting his pride show. The performance continued. They tied me to the chair, and as usual, I stared at Hamid, hoping to convey my moral outrage. What did he see? A broken, half-conscious man with eyes that seemed to struggle to stay open, saliva running down his chin as he tried, in vain, to show defiance. It didn't matter. They sat me in the all-purpose chair and began their work. They tied my hands above my head to a ring in the ceiling. They secured my lags, each limb hanging uncomfortably from the sides rather than the front, in a painful and degrading position. The electric current came from a bulb overhead, connected to a simple box with a black knob. Two thick wires emerged from the box—one with a blunt end and the other with an alligator clip. And then, to my horror, the lipless man stuffed a wetted steel wool scrubber into my anus and attached the wire to my genitals. The cables, like twisted braids of wire, dug into my skin. I could feel the sharpness of the electricity coursing through me.

Habib, the broken-nosed senior torturer, took over. He showed his partner a kind of compassion, perhaps a silent acknowledgment of the earlier mistake. He wiped the sweat from my body, careful to keep my resistance high so that the shocks wouldn't kill me. The torture lasted for hours. I hardly remember the details—just the smell of burned flesh and the unbearable pain. They focused on my extremities—my nipples, genitals, testicles, legs, and arms—delivering shocks to the most sensitive areas of my body. I counted over a hundred spots on my skin—deep bruises the color of ripe blueberries. The pain was unrelenting. Suddenly, everything changed. I sat before them again, and Hamid watched from the corner. They offered me a pen and a document to sign. I was confused. Why had they deviated from their usual routine? Why give me a second chance in one day? My mind, foggy and disoriented, couldn't piece it together.

I had lost twenty-four hours, and time had folded in on itself in the gap. I couldn't remember what had happened between then and now. I couldn't even recall sleeping, blacking out, or how I had changed clothes. It was as if the hours had evaporated entirely. I had a strange, tingling sensation throughout my body, but I was free from the intense pain as if my body had gone into a numb state. Despite the confusion, my anger at Hamid's betrayal remained fresh. I refused to sign. I had no memory of what had happened, but I knew the essence of my anger hadn't changed. I had resoled to die. The torturers didn't respond as I expected. There was a sense of grudging respect from them, though it didn't alter their approach. They continued with their methodical routine.

They tied me to the chair again, arms splayed out, prepared for what would come next. I understood their intentions immediately when I saw the pliers. It wasn't the tool you'd expect in a hardware store. The pliers were surgical, designed to remove something delicate, like a fingernail. The torturer—now back in charge—set up with an unsettling calmness, placing a bucket beneath my hands. He pulled up a chair and sat before me, cigarette dangling from his lips, one eye squinting to avoid the smoke. Then, he took the pliers and moved to my right index finger. Every fiber of my being screamed to resist, but I couldn't. He held my finger flat and pulled the nail slowly, expertly. It was agonizing. I won't linger on the details of what came next, Ms. Vakil. It's too painful to recount. The pliers twisted and pulled, tearing the nail from its root. The sound was sickening, like peeling two strips of Scotch tape. Blood spilled onto the table, soaking the desk and collecting in the bucket below. It was all so methodical, so organized. He finished wiping the blood off with a surgical wipe, pressing down hard with alcohol. The pain was unbearable, and I blacked out. I drifted into a surreal dream-like state, floating between different realities, memories of my childhood merging with the present.

I woke, feverish and sweating. Hamid sat next to me. He tried to comfort me with a wet cloth on my brow, but I flung it away in anger. The pain shot through me in waves. He tried to calm me down. "What's wrong with you?" he hissed. "Today was unnecessary. You agreed to sign. Why do you keep resisting?"

"You're one of them," I sobbed. "You've sold me out."

He paused, his voice calm. "Of course I am. I've always been one of them."

His words stung, but he added, "I've been one of them all my life. But here I am, ready to protect you."

"God, I hate to think what I would go through if you weren't protecting me," I croaked. "I don't need it anymore. I'll sign tomorrow." He stayed quiet for a long time, then leaned closer. He spoke in a low voice, not a whisper, but with an air of finality. "This isn't about your houses or your money. Your life is in danger. The old man has condemned the Poonaki family. Your grandfather signed the order for the execution of a Sheikh. This happened seventy years ago, and the old man has never forgotten it. He wants to reshape the country in his image, and he will not allow any descendants of the Poonakis to survive him."

I struggled to comprehend the words, but I understood enough. "I convinced them to keep you in this house so I could stay in charge. If you sign tomorrow, I'll go to Jamaran and see if I can get you out of the country."

"Are you telling me that whether I sign or not, they will kill me?" I asked.

"Not these two. But yes, unless I work something out. If you don't sign, those two will break you down, no matter how long it takes," he replied.

"Do they work for you?" I asked.

"I inherited them," he answered. I couldn't stay awake any longer. As I drifted into unconsciousness or sleep, I dreamt of him licking my neck, ears, and each one of my mutilated fingers.

On the eighth day, I signed the documents. My grip on the pen was awkward. I cried from pain and anger as I signed. The two men sat quietly, savoring their victory. Without a word, Hamid left immediately. The two youths had used a stretcher to carry me for the last two days. Workers had taken the door off its hinges and were now installing a metal one. I slept through the noise. My fever reached its peak at dusk. On the morning of the ninth day, I woke to find the two torturers sitting silently in two folding chairs. They watched me sleep. As soon as I woke, my heart raced. Terrified, I burst into tears. "I signed, I signed," I repeated. My body shook with fever and convulsions. Was I dreaming of the signing ceremony? They calmed me, telling me they wanted to talk. The older man, Habib, spoke with an apologetic tone. "Mr. Poonaki, please don't confuse us with the new breed of interrogators under the new regime. My friend and I worked in the old regime for years. If I told you how lucky you are to have had us interrogate you, I know you would be outraged. But we are your first, aren't we?" he asked. I lay there, paralyzed, and nodded. He continued.

"Let me tell you, Mr. Poonaki," he said, as if pitching a business idea, "I have worked in this line of work for over twenty years, my friend here for five years. We trained in various programs in the United States and Russia. We took courses in psychology and medicine at Tehran University. I know it's hard for you to believe, but we follow something like the Hippocratic rule. Well, not exactly," he added, grimly smiling. "My partner and I swore to interrogate in a way that doesn't cause long-term physical injury to the prisoner, no matter what his heinous crimes. It's not the right time, but your injuries will heal enough within a month for you to resume normal activities. Within a year, you won't feel any pain. You'll have some evidence of your wounds—tattoo-like spots on your extremities. Unfortunately, your nails won't grow back, but humans don't need nails for most things. We take pride in our profession, Mr. Poonaki. We don't use interrogation techniques to maim or destroy citizens."

I spat blood into a small plastic container next to my bed. "By interrogation techniques, you mean torture?" I asked.

The two men exchanged looks, as if dealing with a naïve child. "Mr. Poonaki," said Habib, "I hope you understand. We don't apologize. We don't judge the guilt or innocence of prisoners. Our goal is to minimize the overall discomfort for each person." He emphasized this by chopping one hand into the palm of the other. "You're an educated man. We see ourselves as scientists. Our decision to give you the choice of signing the documents once a day comes from a great deal of work and study. We, and other colleagues, have analyzed reams of data." He nodded, affirming his point. "It's true. You might need to invest a day or two upfront to make your point, but I assure you, this method is more humane. It reduces the average torture time and tightens the standard deviation by reducing the few outliers who resist, even though you lose on the quicker, cowardly types. You might ask, why put the cowardly type through a full day when they're ready to spill the beans immediately?" He found the cowardly types disgusting. "The latest studies show that a full day of interrogation encourages even the cowardly types to cooperate more freely and for a longer period, rather than skipping straight to it."

I lay there, stunned by the conversation. My mind struggled to process it. "What do you want from me?" I managed to ask, terrified beyond measure. After a brief pause, Habib glanced at his partner, and the younger one took over the explanation. "Mr. Poonaki, please understand that your interrogation has been special. Indeed, you are special. You lasted more than a week. You don't hold the record, but we have a unique opportunity to learn from you." I doubled over from cramps, which they mistakenly interpreted as resistance.

"I know, I know," the younger man said, helplessly raising his hands. "We could have waited a few more days, but we have a busy schedule. The times, you know." He shrugged again as if he had no control over it. My stomach growled, and I felt my body wracked with more pain—blood-soaked diarrhea and urination, which didn't seem to embarrass them. "We know you may not want to cooperate with us," the younger man continued, "but I want to persuade you through argument." He smiled. "Your feedback will help us reduce interrogation time. We rarely speak to a prisoner." I lay there in shock, trying to comprehend. They wanted data—feedback on their methods. It reminded me of the death camps and Dr. Mengele. I groaned from the muscle cramps and the burn marks covering my body. Could I refuse? Probably not, I answered myself. I nodded, and their excitement was palpable. They couldn't contain themselves.

"Did we make a mistake with the water cure?" they asked. I nodded.

"I told you," the older man said to the younger one. "You had time to recover, didn't you?" I nodded again.

"What about the electric shocks?"

"I don't remember," I replied.

"You dialed it too high," the younger one told Habib.

"Same result—more time to recover," Habib lamented, slapping his forehead in frustration. They asked about every detail. How did I feel each night? When did I pass out? How would I rate the pain on a scale of one to ten? When should they use the water cure? They answered in unison: use it with the cowards. It's most effective after a full day of interrogation. They continued asking questions, mostly to confirm their suspicions but occasionally seeking clarification.

"Did you swallow too much water during the cure?"

"Yes," I answered.

One of them remarked, "You know, the Orientals used to jump on the stomach of the victim to expel the water." He smiled at the 'Oriental' method's stupidity. "It's out of the question if you're concerned with long-term effects," he added. They discussed the finer points of the electric shock treatment. If it had caused memory loss, they would need to reduce the voltage, but how could they maintain the right pain level? Seeing that I was exhausted, they thanked me profusely and assured me my answers would help lessen the pain of others. As they left, they left me with one unsettling thought. "Mr. Poonaki," Habib said, "you should appreciate professionals. The new generation replacing us—they're brutish peasants. Don't resist them like you resisted us. We use patience as a technique. They don't know the difference between inflicting pain and causing damage. We've seen them in action. Many prisoners die in their hands. Few survive more than three days, and if they do, they live the rest of their lives in wheelchairs." I groaned in response. Habib approached to touch my brow, but I winced from his touch.

Ms. Vakil, I think I hurt his feelings.

"You'll be good as new in a few weeks," he added in a doctor-like tone. "Make sure you drink the broth," he instructed as he knocked on the metal door. It opened, and the other man—whose name I never learned—entered, bringing the broth and placing it on my bunk. They left, leaving me drenched in sweat and struggling for breath. The sound of keys clanking on metal doors woke me in the evening. I heard the door open and close in the basement as they finished preparing it to become a prison. Hamid arrived and greeted me in a formal tone. "Mr. Poonaki, the Imam's office, in its infinite mercy and compassion, has agreed to set you free," he said. "This gentleman"—he gestured to someone in the corridor—"will take care of everything." I lifted my head, expectant, but the man couldn't enter because Hamid blocked the entrance. I watched Hamid's face, which seemed tired and beaten. In a whisper, he said, "I loved you both. If you ever see him, tell him that." Hamid left, and his companion, a hulking man, greeted me jovially.

"Friend, it looks like they've hurt you here," he said. "Your pain is over now, I promise you. I'll stop all the pain." He approached me, hands open, like a magician revealing his empty palms. In his hand, he held the leather strap once around my wrists, stretched out like an offering. In my feverish state, tears in my eyes, I swear I saw a sixth finger dangling from each of his hands.

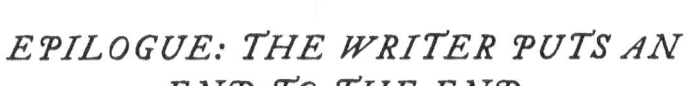

EPILOGUE: THE WRITER PUTS AN END TO THE END

"The past is never dead. It's not even past."

William Faulkner

Many of you suspected my involvement in this work, perhaps seeing me as a guide, a Virgil leading Dante through the Nine Circles of Hell. I used the virtual youth serum available to authors: with a few sentences, I shed thirty years and thirty pounds to introduce the lovely, creamy Ms. Vakil as she navigates through the historical manuscripts of a fictional writer. At seventy-five, I had spent most of my life not as a historian but as a human rights lawyer in Tehran's Palestine Square. With the help of six dedicated female volunteers, I risked everything to document human rights violations during the Shah's regime and the kleptocratic, mullah-

cracy rule we now call the Islamic Republic. Over the years, countless courageous students passed through our midst—some I still
hear from, while others lost to the ever-brutal regime. For many
years, I frequently visited the United States to visit my daughter
and grandchildren, always returning to the polluted air of Tehran
with more hope than the system deserved. My age, along with the
backlash from the Green Revolution, ended my career three years
ago. I live five thousand miles away in Boston, in an apartment
much like the princeling once occupied. He and I share a love of
the movies.

I wrote under a pseudonym. Although we worked together
during difficult times, I am not the Nobel Prize-winning Shirin
Ebadi. We labored tirelessly to document the barbaric, pitiless
tormentors of innocent individuals. When she won the Nobel
Prize in 2003, I smiled through gritted teeth: don't we all love to
indulge our egos and bask in the high of such recognition? I have
come to accept her symbolic role among us, though not without
a twinge of envy. Unlike Mrs. Ebadi, I never pursued a career in
the justice department. After studying law at Tehran University,
I set up a small practice focused on family law. I continued until
the 1979 revolution. When I could no longer practice, I focused
on human rights work. For many years, I dreamed of bringing the
Constitutional Revolution to life—it was the crowning moment of
our modern history. I longed to write a detailed history set amidst
the intrigues of prewar and wartime Europe: La Belle Époque in
France, the prerevolutionary Russian Empire, the sadomasochistic
Weimar Republic, the abject poverty of the war years in Europe, the
cynical politics of the English and the self-righteous volunteerism
of the Americans—all imposing their rules on our impoverished

country. We, more than most, understood the rules of the game. We had centuries of practice. The government played its cards well but had little hope of winning.

All the research and gathering resulted in dozens of notebooks. In a rare moment of clarity, knowing my time was short, I decided to cross the murky line between fact and fiction. The idea of telling my story over nine nights came to me early. I had always admired *The Book of the Thousand and One Nights*. When I was no more than four or five years old, my large-breasted dayeh, while feeding my younger sister, created a sense of tension by holding the scimitar over Scheherazade's head night after night. After each visit, she would playfully squirt a quick stream of milk at me from her engorged breasts, and I would try to come up with a story of my own. But I always fell asleep before I could finish.

I based Dal, an anagram of Professor Adl, the famous surgeon and the Shah's Belot partner, on a real historical figure. Like all fictional types, Dal quickly grew beyond my control. His presence created difficulties, as he coexisted with real historical figures, making chronology a nightmare. Sometimes, luck helped. I hadn't planned on sending young Dal to a gymnasium in Berlin, but I had to hurry. The older Wassmuss, the Lawrence of Persia, was about to meet his maker in Berlin in 1931, and the young man wasn't yet ready for university. So, I sent him to Berlinisches Gymnasium. The introduction of Harold Nicolson in Tehran was a natural fit, but placing him in Berlin as an attaché was pure serendipity. This encounter in Berlin allowed me to plausibly incorporate his rescue of Professor Dal at the war's end. However, I had to ensure Nicolson's retirement party at the Buccaneer's Club on December

16, 1929, went as arranged by history. He left Berlin shortly after meeting the budding professor.

I don't allow my characters to change history. The strange escape behind the Sephsalar Mosque happened, as reported. Mohammad-Ali Shah did execute the escapees. The British bombardment of the Tangestani tribe in Khuzestan is a minor footnote in history books, though I can't fathom why. The British always emphasize their diplomatic approaches, conveniently leaving out events that don't fit their narrative. The current mullahcracy has undoubtedly destroyed our country's economy and wasted at least two generations of its citizens. I've taken great care to avoid an anti-Islamic stance to avoid accusations like those leveled at that poor Indian writer. Years of detailed work, evidence gathering, and personal witness to horrible deeds define our thoroughly corrupt regime. It is a final amen to all that.

Mr. Poonaki existed. I visited him during one of my humanitarian trips to provide books, underwear and toiletries to political prisoners. He was a handsome young man, disfigured on his right cheek, as though someone had pressed a finger into it and twisted it, leaving a permanent scar. In his early twenties, he had gray hair and deep-set eyes, with natural bags underneath. He resembled El Greco's suffering John the Baptist. When I first saw him, his pupils darted back and forth. He barely understood his arrest. Most prisoners of the revolution spent too much time searching for a cause behind their fate. Like many crime victims—and make no mistake, this government is the major criminal organization in the country—Mr. Poonaki got shuffled in the randomness that followed the chaos. I offered him books and cigarettes. He lit one immediately, crossing his left arm over his chest, resting the elbow of his cigarette-holding hand on his palm. He threw his head back in a feminine gesture and took a long drag. He asked me if I had a religious instruction book. His question struck me as odd. He spoke Farsi with a barely detectable French lilt. I asked him what religious instruction he needed. He whispered that he needed to learn how to pray. Most modern, well-to-do young men of prerevolutionary times never learned to pray five times daily. It seemed a wise survival tactic. He knew what was to come. He had likely prayed by mimicking the actions of others while mouthing nonsense, like my granddaughter pretending to play the violin in the school orchestra. He feared being caught not knowing the basics of his religious duties.

The second time I visited him, he looked beaten but less scared. I offered to contact his family. He told me he had none. His name was familiar to me. I conducted a light investigation, interviewing several friends and acquaintances. It turned out that Mr. Poonaki had lost both his parents. They had no siblings. He had lost a twin brother in a skiing accident when he was sixteen. The *Kayhan* newspaper reported the heartbreaking effort to rescue his brother from an avalanche. They found the frozen body. He died during the helicopter transfer to the hospital.

The last time I visited Mr. Poonaki at Evin, I couldn't recognize him. His hands had swollen to grotesque proportions. They had wrenched off three of his fingernails with pliers. By then, I had seen enough prisoners to recognize the signs of brutal treatment. In the early days, foreign governments and humanitarian organizations were slow to address the mistreatment of political prisoners. Once again, he had fallen in a time when physical evidence didn't matter to the Republic. I asked him, probably without thinking, how he was doing. He whispered that they had beaten him with cables for a solid day. The word "solid" in his description disturbed me. It stayed with me, this* implication of continuous, unrelenting violence. "Solid," he repeated, as though it was a weight he couldn't shake. "I don't know why. They ask nothing of me. They tell me I deserve it, that the Imam wishes it." He looked puzzled. "Which imam?" he asked. Before Khomeini, Shiites revered the Twelve Imams, following the Prophet's lineage. By taking the title of Imam, Khomeini had set himself among these revered figures. Mr. Poonaki was confused and clearly in agony, but I could no longer detect the fear from the previous visits. Survival had granted him a strange sense of dignity, even pride.

"They don't let me sleep," he said, his voice flat. "They told me why I am here." He paused, eyes distant. "They accuse my family of being responsible for the death of some Ayatollah named Nouri. Who was he?" He shrugged, palms open in a gesture of confusion. "My father was a doctor. Did this man die under his care?" He seemed like a bystander to his own *suffering.

"How do you cope?" I asked, searching for any sign of hope or resilience.

A fleeting, painful smile appeared on his face. "In my mind," he said softly, "I live entirely in my ancestral home. I never leave. I remember every detail. I look at my cell and see our childhood room—my brother's and mine—two of everything: two closets, two soccer balls, two model airplanes. You know, we didn't appreciate each other like we should have before he died. We fought all the time. I'm a rational man. I know the mind plays tricks, but I still feel his presence. I loved my life—I lived quietly, working at the Carpet Museum. Now the pain makes his presence stronger."

Meanwhile, the killings and torture of the mujahideen faction—the actual threat to the Islamic government—continued. My visits to Evin grew less frequent as the government's brutal crackdown expanded. The honeymoon period for the Islamic Republic ended in bloodshed when a bomb killed seventy-two members of parliament, triggering a wave of violence that led to more executions, often conducted in the dead of night. They executed communists summarily without any external witnesses. The numbers are unclear, but the survivors' testimonies have since corroborated the government's ruthless actions. I asked about Mr. Poonaki's whereabouts a few times. "He's in solitary confinement and cannot receive visitors," they told me. Days turned into weeks. I focused on other prisoners, but gnawing guilt kept questioning me: "Could I have done more for him?" I assumed, with a heavy heart, that he had been swept into the tide of executions that had claimed so many lives.

Then, one warm Friday afternoon in April, as I walked out of Evin, I noticed a strange figure trailing me—a fat man, to be precise. His large, beetle-like brow jutted out oddly, almost comically. He would follow me for a few steps, then stop, change his course, and waddle ahead. I picked up the pace to put distance between us. After a few more turns, I paused around a corner and waited. When he passed by me, he seemed to realize he had lost me. Seeing me behind him, he did a double-take, his face flushing with anxiety. Wiping his brow with a soiled handkerchief, he stammered, "Please forgive me, Vakil Khanum. We can't be seen together in public. I have crucial information about someone you are interested in." He raised his eyebrows, attempting to convey that we shared some unspoken understanding. I was perplexed but agreed to meet him the next day in my office.

A series of bizarre meetings followed. He never volunteered a name. My friends dubbed him "Hekaiatchi," meaning "the storyteller," for his tendency to tell outlandish lies. For a few kernels of truth, I would have dismissed him outright. He came to my office accompanied by his large, lazy wife, who seemed to only half-listen to his ramblings, correcting him whenever he misspoke. If she didn't speak, it meant she had fallen asleep, snoring like a hippopotamus.

It soon became clear that the Hekaiatchis were motivated by money. "I was Mr. Poonaki's cellmate," the man claimed, shaking his head slowly, his double chin wobbling. "They killed him. I can tell you for sure."

"You saw it?" I asked, skeptical.

"Well, not with my own eyes, but they came for him one day. He was in bad shape. After that, I never saw him again." He glanced slyly at his wife.

"Don't tell her anything more until I hear the jingle of her coins," she interrupted, crude and transactional.

I asked them to leave, thinking it a hoax, but he dropped a bombshell. "They killed him because his grandfather hung Ayatollah Nouri." It shocked me.

"They killed him because his grandfather killed someone a hundred years ago?" I asked. Yet the young Poonaki had asked me the same question during my last visit.

"Not someone," Hekaiatchi said. "The Imam considers Nouri

his spiritual guide. The Imam witnessed the hanging when he was six years old. He swore to take vengeance on all the descendants of his killer." He discussed a suitcase of documents Mr. Poonaki had referred to one night in their shared cell. Hekaiatchi claimed he had it in his possession after his release. "I'd say Mr. Poonaki was a little funny," he said.

"You mean humorous or in the head?" I asked.

"You know what I mean, ma'am?" he said. He then made a ring of his thumb and forefinger while he slid his other index finger back and forth through the ring with an accompanying breathy whistle.

"That's enough," I said. I handed the wife cab money. I ordered them to go home. I said if I found corroborating evidence, I'd be willing to pay them more. I asked how to get in touch with them.

"We'll come back Wednesday afternoon," the wife said before the man could answer. "You needn't worry about contacting us."

In a few days, I had verified the story. Indeed, Mr. Poonaki's grandfather was one of the ten men who sat in judgment of Sheikh Nouri. The story of the young Khomeini's presence at the hanging sounded apocryphal, though his father had undoubtedly witnessed it. The country knows Khomeini adhered to the Sheikh's vision of an Islamic state. I paid the couple more money and sat them down for another interview. "Please tell me about why they arrested you," I said. "What did you do to end up in Evin?" All the lies resumed. He claimed he hadn't been a good Muslim; they caught him with a pudgy hand in the till. He claimed his father owned a small teahouse. The local mullah declared it a den of sin. With waves of tears, he included gobs of irrelevant details—small asides grew into torturous excursions into all the unfair episodes of his life.

After an afternoon of shenanigans, I decided to stop any further involvement with this useless windbag.

"You must stop lying," I said. "The only way you could have ended up in Evin would have been to be a political agitator, an enemy of the state or a taghouti" (an idol worshipper, a label applied to the last regime's affluent families). "I don't see you belonging to any of these groups."

"Tell her," his wife said.

"Tell me what?"

"There is another way for me to end up at Evin," he said with a strange, oily coyness, arching his eyebrows for effect.

"I will not play twenty questions," I said.

"I work there," he said triumphantly. "I am one of the guards."

After much deliberation with friends, I organized another interview. "One of the guards?" We thought the story had legs. It excited us. I offered him double the money I had paid during the previous interview—if he came without his wife. He looked uncomfortable, so I made the deal sweeter: I'd pay him in dollars.

"Two sadis," the woman interrupted, waving two ringed, fat fingers at me. She required two one-hundred-dollar bills. She understood the money exchangers on Ferdowsi Avenue didn't accept smaller bills. I insisted on seeing the suitcase's contents. They finally agreed. I suspected that, alone, he'd talk more freely. As a guard, he could give me information about other prisoners and their fates. The interview started badly. Hekaiatchi brought a suitcase full of papers about Mr. Poonaki. It contained a bureaucratic history of the poor man: birth certificates, a high school diploma and some letters from his father—mostly father-to-son homilies. He had gone to Beaux-Arts of Paris and studied art history. Hekaiatchi's possession of the pitiful suitcase showed the authorities had no interest in the poor young man. I questioned Hekaiatchi about his guard duties, schedule, and detailed responsibilities. He sank quickly into layers of lies. At some point, I remember shouting at him aggressively. All the women in the outside office stopped typing. It had the required effect: he broke down crying. "I am the apash," he told me.

Incredulous, I said, "Your job is to water the garden?"

He stopped crying as if shutting off a faucet. He pulled out his still-soiled handkerchief. He dried his broad, flat face. He looked at me under his beetle brow as if talking to a naive child. "I hose down the room," he said with exaggerated patience. Seeing my childlike incomprehension, he amplified. "I attend the torture room, ma'am," he said. "When they finish, I wash down the blood." He went on. "I saw Poonaki die in front of my eyes. I saw many die in front of my eyes." He broke down again. I detected sincerity—a catharsis from witnessing horrible deeds inflicted on humans. He recovered. He said they had tortured Poonaki whenever they were not too busy with the hard-core enemies of the state. I asked him how it had ended. He mimed a knot in front of his throat, sticking his tongue out to the side. My heart went out to this pathetic man. A nobody looks for a custodial job. They hire him to wash and clean a torture chamber. He stands in a corner of the room. He watches the horrors perpetrated on other humans.

I handed him the two hundred dollar bills as promised. One of the typists took a picture of him and me with our strained, awkward smiles. I pledged more Ben Franklins if he came back. He said he would. He never did.

Orders by the leader to kill an innocent descendant of one

of the signatories of Sheikh Nouri's hanging sound medieval. The Shamsi calendar converts 2025 to 1404. Our dates support our ignorance.

ACKNOWLEDGMENTS

All the credit goes to Maryann Karinch and Judith Bailey, my Armin Lear Publisher and editor. They did not waver. They backed me, and here they publish a second novel. We call this doubling down. No doubt they took a chance on me, whose bet has yet to cover us in glory.

Thanks to my brother and wife, who read the manuscript patiently. They read well. Babak Veyssy and Soad Kousheshi corrected my French and taught me the rules of the Belot game. Alex Benet, my talented cousin, designed the genealogy map.

I write for my two daughters Leila and Homa that maybe one day one of their children picks one of my books and says, "is this fellow related to us?"

ABOUT THE AUTHOR

Born in Iran, the author earned an MFA from the University of New Hampshire. He has published short stories in *The Kenyon* and *Massachusetts Review*. The novel *1001: A Dream of Nine Nights* was a critical success, earning reviews such as this:

> It is rare—truly rare—to find the perfect blend of brilliant writing and great story telling. These books are the ones that settle into our souls, the characters become a part of our extended family, their travails and adventures influence us in unspoken ways, and they make us just a little better as people. Marquez, Allende, Khaled Hossein, Harper Lee ... to this list I add Yahya Gharagozlou.

He currently resides in Wellesley, Massachusetts.

www.ingramcontent.com/pod-product-compliance
Lightning Source LLC
Chambersburg PA
CBHW031025030726
47497CB00004B/1002